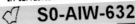

Dear Reader,

No doubt you are on the verge of your annual summer vacation. Don't forget to pack the essentials – suntan lotion, sunglasses and the two latest sizzling novels from *Scarlet*!

Cody Aguillar, in the exciting sequel to Tina Leonard's novel *It Takes Two*, never does anything he doesn't want to do! Lavender-haired Stormy Nixon is also used to getting her own way, so when the two meet in *Desperado*, something's gotta give! Also this month, you are invited, by Clare Benedict, to *Sophie's Wedding*. Three women gather for their best friend's wedding, and while Alison wonders if she'll ever find true happiness, Francine must decide between an old love and a new opportunity, and Carol asks herself if her own marriage is worth saving.

Next month sees the start of our exciting *Scarlet* hardback series. Watch out for our very special launch title and let me know what you think! Also, don't forget to complete our questionnaire this month – you could win a sassy *Scarlet* T-shirt!

Till next month,

Sally Cooper

SALLY COOPER,
Editor-in-Chief – *Scarlet*

PS: To reserve your copy of *Dark Desire*, our first *Scarlet* hardback, send us your details NOW!

CLARE BENEDICT

SOPHIE'S WEDDING

SCARLET

Enquiries to:
Robinson Publishing Ltd
7 Kensington Church Court
London W8 4SP

First published in the UK by Scarlet, 1998

A copy of the British Library Cataloguing in
Publication data is available from the British Library

ISBN 1-85487-882-4

Printed and bound in the EC

10 9 8 7 6 5 4 3 2 1

PROLOGUE

Ten years ago – midsummer – a northern university

'Keep still for a minute!'

Sophie tried to frame her three friends in her camera's viewfinder. Alison, Carol and Francine carried on talking and laughing as if they hadn't heard her. Perhaps they hadn't. She didn't like to think that they were simply ignoring her.

She wanted a perfect shot – to be a reminder of a perfect day. They had all worked so hard for this moment. There had been three years of lectures and examinations, reading and studying into the small hours, not to mention a few desperate nights when they hadn't got to bed at all. And now they had their reward.

Today, the sun shone in the clear blue sky and a gentle breeze rippled through the leaves of the graceful old trees. And just a short while ago the new graduates had come streaming out of the dignified Victorian building to gather on the manicured lawns. Clutching rolled-up degree certificates in one hand and a glass of sherry in the other, they mingled with their parents and their former lecturers.

After today, most of them might never see each other again. Friendships made at university often became merely happy memories for so many people. But Sophie

1

had no intention of losing touch with the three other girls who had come to mean so much to her. As she focused her camera her gaze was full of admiration. They looked so impressive in the academic caps and gowns that they had hired for this once-in-a-lifetime day – no wonder they were excited.

'*Alison – Carol – Francine!*' Sophie tried again to get their attention. 'Look at the camera and smile – *pull-lease!*'

'Oh – sorry – wait a minute . . .' Carol glanced at her and grinned. 'I'll have to fix my hair!'

Sophie sighed and lowered her camera. Carol's cap had tipped forward drunkenly over her brow. Her abundant, shoulder-length brown hair had come loose from whatever arrangement she had started out with. Now, it blew in fly-away wisps across her pretty face.

To look at her, nobody would ever guess that Carol is by far the cleverest of the four of us, Sophie thought. She looks like a harum-scarum schoolgirl rather than the only one in the whole year to get a first class degree.

'Let me.' Alison, trying to recapture some of her usual cool competence, came to Carol's rescue. 'Wait a minute – hold these, will you?'

She handed Carol her degree certificate and her glass – a mistake, for now Carol had to juggle with two certificates and two glasses, as well as submitting herself to Alison's ministrations.

The glasses tilted dangerously, slopping the pale gold liquid on to the lawn, and they started to giggle again. The third member of the trio, Francine, sighed exaggeratedly. 'For goodness' sake, you two, stop behaving like children!'

Francine looked perfect, of course. She always did. Nearly as tall as Alison and just as slim and shapely, she possessed worldly sophistication in contrast to Alison's understated, blonde elegance. Francine's cap was set at just the right angle on the short, sleek, dark hair and she had managed to make her academic gown look like a fashion statement.

She was frowning slightly as she sipped her sherry. Sophie thought she looked preoccupied. But finally the other two were still.

'We're ready now, Sophie,' Alison called. 'Look, I'm the tallest, so I'll stand in the middle and slightly behind, with Carol on my right and Francine on my left. Is that OK?'

'Oh – perfect – just perfect – wait a minute – can you move in a bit closer? And why don't you raise your glasses?'

'Wait!' Carol shrieked. 'If I hold my glass up with my left hand, you'll see my engagement ring!'

Behind Carol's back Alison smiled patiently and Francine cast her eyes heavenwards in mock despair.

'OK,' Sophie said. 'Ready, now? Smile – that's it!'

The camera shutter clicked. Carol, Alison and Francine began to move away.

'No – wait – I'll take another one, just to make sure. I think Carol's hand was shaking . . .'

Carol and Alison grinned and took up the pose again but there was no mistaking Francine's frown. Sophie hesitated and looked up from the camera but, before she could say anything, Francine caught her anxious glance and her brow cleared. She raised her glass to Sophie in ironic acknowledgement before pinning on a radiant smile.

Sophie took the picture then all their heads turned at the sound of a familiar voice. Alan Kennedy strolled towards them, smiling broadly.

'There you are, Carol,' he said. 'I've been looking for you. Your parents and mine have got together and there's talk of a slap-up meal – in fact my dad's already booked a table at the best restaurant in town.'

3

'Oh, Alan, really?' Carol looked dismayed and Alan put his arm round her shoulder.

'Don't worry, love. They're all getting along fine together.'

Carol sighed. 'And they don't mind that we want to get married, soon?'

'They've taken it very well, especially your mum – she seems to have taken quite a shine to me.'

'Oh, I knew that *my* mum and dad would be OK,' Carol said. 'I'm sure they still think that education is wasted on a woman. They've probably been hoping and praying that I'd find myself a good husband while I was at university – and their prayers have been answered! But your parents . . .'

'I know; Dad gave me a lecture about not tying myself down to someone totally "unsuitable" while I still had my way to make. But that was before they met you.'

'And then they were instantly overcome by my beauty!' Carol's spirits began to rise again and she showed signs of giving way to mirth. Alan smiled patiently.

'No, not that –'

'They think I'm ugly?'

'Try to be serious for a moment, Carol. Actually, my parents seem to be impressed by the fact that such a brainy, prize-winning young woman from such a re-spectable family would even look at me twice. Dad said you'd be an asset to my career – the power behind the throne and all that.'

'I've always wanted to be an asset!'

'Oh, shut up!' Alan bent his head and silenced her with a kiss.

Francine raised her eyebrows but Sophie and Alison watched the scene indulgently. Carol and Alan had been an item ever since they'd met at a disco in their first year.

'It was like the scene in the movie *West Side Story*,' Carol had later told Sophie. 'Our eyes met across a

4

crowded dance floor and that was it!'

Carol was small, rounded and pretty and frighteningly intelligent, but she had a zest for life which had attracted Alan immediately. He was a few years older than she was. He had worked in industry for a while before deciding that he would get further faster if he obtained a degree in business administration, the same subject that Carol was studying. Carol had very soon persuaded him that it was possible to work hard and also to enjoy life.

'Come on, love, we shouldn't keep them waiting.'

'No, of course not.' She looked round at her friends uncertainly. 'We-ell, I suppose it's time to say goodbye.'

Alison, usually so calm and unruffled, looked as though she was finding it difficult to speak. 'Yes, well, it's not for ever, is it? I mean we'll keep in touch, won't we?'

'Of course we will. Sophie will make sure of that,' Francine said. 'Now why don't we break this up before we all start to blub?'

Francine's dry, humorous tone brought Carol's smile back and Alan began to lead her away.

'Wait a moment!' Sophie exclaimed. 'I'll just take a picture of the two of you before you go. You look so good together in your caps and gowns!'

And they did, Sophie thought as she lined the shot up. Alan was not much taller than Carol but he had a good physique and his reddish brown hair and green eyes were very attractive.

Sophie hesitated. Carol was smiling her usual generous smile but Alan's impatience was showing. She was reluctant to record his displeasure for posterity.

'Hurry up!' Carol pleaded.

'I – oh – all right –'

Suddenly Francine stepped forward and said, 'OK, you two, ready steady, smile! That's it – take your shot, Sophie.'

5

And she did.

As Alan and Carol walked away and merged into the crowd, Sophie turned to Francine and said, 'Thanks, Francine. I – I didn't like to say anything, you know . . .'

'Well, you should have done. Alan Kennedy can be an old-fashioned male chauvinist pig when he wants to be.'

'Oh, no,' Sophie breathed, 'he treats Carol very well.'

'Sophie! If you could hear yourself! Are we supposed to be grateful that one of the lords of creation treats a mere woman well!'

'No . . . you know what I mean,' Sophie murmured uncomfortably. She really didn't want Francine riding her feminist hobby-horse, not today. After all, it wasn't as if she didn't agree with most of the things Francine believed in. What suited Carol wouldn't necessarily suit her, but she believed in live and let live – everybody was different.

Francine must have seen her worried frown because she was smiling as she continued more reasonably, 'Look, I accept the fact that he loves her but he's not half as bright as she is. In fact I have a nasty suspicion that he'll feed off her brains to advance his own career. He'll dominate her completely if she's not careful.'

'Oh, surely not,' Alison interjected. 'I mean, Carol's far too intelligent to let that happen.'

'Intelligence has nothing to do with it,' Francine countered. 'The poor fool loves him so much that she'll probably let him walk all over her.'

Sophie was shocked at Francine's vehemence. 'I thought you liked Alan. I know I do.'

'And so do I,' Alison added. 'Alan Kennedy is hardworking and reliable. Unlike some of the prize specimens we've met here in the last three years, he's good oldfashioned husband material.'

Francine snorted derisively and Sophie quickly put in,

6

'Oh, I know that's not what you want, Francine – at least not right away – but Carol *wants* to get married.'

'God knows why,' Francine sighed. 'I mean, with a brain like hers, she doesn't need a man to support her.'

'It's not a matter of supporting her,' Alison said. 'You know very well that Carol intends to find a job and go on working until –'

'Until Alan's career has taken off and he's earning enough for them to start a family! Great! What about having a career of her own?'

'Look, Francine,' Alison's tone was chilly, 'we all know how you feel about a woman's place in the world today, but you'll have to accept that not everyone has the same goals as you do.'

'Of course I accept that. It's just that Carol is our friend and I hate to see her wasting her life.'

'Well, then, you'll also have to accept that whatever you or I or Sophie thinks is of supreme unimportance to Carol now. She's in love with Alan, he's in love with her and how they conduct their lives from now on is none of our business.'

Alison's tone made it clear that it was pointless for Francine to say any more and the two girls looked at each other levelly.

Sophie glanced from one to the other uneasily. 'We're not quarrelling, are we? I mean, after today, it might be ages before we see each other again and . . . and . . .' She trailed off uncertainly and her friends looked contrite.

'No, we're not quarrelling,' Francine said. 'You know me. I just can't help saying what I think and I know I go over the top sometimes. In fact I'll have to learn to control myself once I start work at the television studios. I'll have to learn to be more diplomatic.'

'You certainly will,' Alison said with some asperity. But she was smiling.

Francine grinned. 'And what's got into you today,

anyway, Alison? You've never said much one way or the other about the joys of matrimony, and yet now you seem to approve of the fact that Carol is rushing headlong towards her doom.'

'Perhaps it's because I'm doomed, too.'

'*What?*' For once Francine didn't seem to know how to respond beyond that one startled word.

It was Sophie who pulled herself together first and faltered, 'Alison – you – does that mean . . . ? But you aren't, I mean you haven't got –'

'A boyfriend? But I have. Well, a fiancé, actually.'

Alison laughed when both Sophie and Francine immediately looked at her left hand. She raised it slowly and began to tug at the fine gold chain that she wore around her neck. 'If it's a ring you're looking for, I've been wearing it on this chain.'

Both her friends stared in awed fascination at the engagement ring that she revealed.

Finally, Francine exclaimed, 'It's magnificent! I've never seen such a large diamond. Something like that would almost be worth compromising my principles for! Is it real?'

Alison laughed, not at all offended. 'Yes, it's real.'

'But why haven't you been wearing it?' Sophie asked. 'I mean properly – on your finger?'

'Well, Francine's right, it is a large diamond. I thought it might look a bit ostentatious next to – I mean . . .'

'Next to Carol's little diamond chips!' Francine blurted out.

Alison looked uncomfortable and Sophie squeezed her arm. 'You did the right thing. That was kind of you.'

'Obviously this mystery man isn't a student. He couldn't be.'

'What do you mean, Francine?' Sophie was puzzled.

'Sophie, dear,' Francine grinned, 'no student could afford an engagement ring like that. Unless he has a very

8

rich daddy, that is, and if there are any like that in this worthy provincial establishment, they've been keeping an extremely low profile. So I've deduced that Alison's fiancé is not a student – in fact he must be loaded.'

'Stop it, Francine.' Alison suddenly sounded uneasy.

'What is it? What have I said that isn't the truth?'

'It's not that – it's just that – here he is. Francine, Sophie, I'd like you to meet Paul Cavendish.'

Sophie stared up at the aristocratic-looking man who had suddenly emerged from the surrounding crowd. He was tall and rangy with a tan that hinted at hours spent in the open air. His suit was expensive and yet he looked ill at ease in it; as though he were unused to the constraints of collar and tie.

His hair was as fair as Alison's with the added attraction of genuine sun-bleached streaks and his blue eyes were surrounded by fine lines. Sophie realized with a shock that Paul Cavendish was at least ten years older than her friend – and probably more.

'I'm happy to meet you at last,' he said. 'I've heard so much about you.'

'Well, we haven't heard anything about you.'

'*Francine* – shut up!' Sophie hissed, and Alison's flush became deeper, but her fiancé smiled.

'No, I won't shut up. Alison, why have you been keeping this gorgeous man a secret?'

Sophie groaned but Paul Cavendish's grin became wider. 'It was a joint decision to keep quiet about our engagement.'

'Why?' Sophie couldn't help asking. And immediately felt herself flushing. Had she overstepped the bounds of good manners?

But Paul regarded her kindly. 'Alison thought that you might not approve and I suppose I agreed with her.'

'Why should we not approve?' But Sophie thought she knew what his answer would be – and she was right.

'Well, I have to admit it – I'm quite a bit older than Alison . . .'

'How much older?'

'Francine!'

'No, it's OK, Sophie, I'm thirty-eight.'

'And Alison's just twenty-one – yes, quite a difference.'

'Francine, *please* –'

'No, don't worry, Sophie.' This time it was Alison who spoke. 'Francine's reaction is just what I expected it would be and I had enough to worry about with my final exams without inviting any further hassle from her.'

'So the engagement's fairly recent, then?' Francine was quite unabashed. 'I mean if it was your finals you were worrying about, Paul must have proposed to you within the last year at least?'

'Yes, it's recent –'

'But we've known each other since Alison joined the University Camera Club last year,' Paul said.

'Camera Club! *National Geographic!* That's it!'

Francine looked triumphant but Sophie was totally confused. Even more so when she realized that Alison and Paul seemed to know exactly what she was talking about.

'We all laughed at you,' Francine continued. 'We couldn't understand why you wanted to mix with all those sad nerds who inhabit darkrooms –'

'Oh, Francine . . .' Sophie's protest was hardly audible this time. After all, no one else seemed to care.

In fact Alison was smiling broadly. 'Paul came along to give a lecture –'

'And that explains why you suddenly started bringing home dog-eared copies of the *National Geographic* and the like, instead of more interesting magazines.'

'Please explain.'

They all turned to look at Sophie and Alison smiled fondly. 'Paul is a photographer.'

'A very famous photographer,' added Francine.

'Should I have heard of him?' Sophie asked.

'Depends what kind of magazine you read. You see Paul is a combination of photographer and explorer. A kind of Action Man. He travels to far distant places, climbs mountains, treks through deserts and jungles, even plumbs the oceans for pictures – all to present to the armchair travellers who prefer to get their thrills second-hand. Am I right?'

'More or less,' Paul answered and he seemed totally unoffended by Francine's flippant tone.

'So you were impressed by Paul's talk at the Camera Club, Alison?'

'Very impressed – and also by the slides and prints he brought along to illustrate his points.'

'But how did you actually meet?' Sophie asked.

'Alison asked some very intelligent questions and afterwards we got talking. I asked her if she'd like to have a drink with me –'

'– and it went on from there,' Alison said. She looked as though she wanted to bring an end to the conversation, Sophie thought.

'Well, you never said a word to us!' Francine sounded offended.

'No . . . well . . . I was a little unsure about how you would take it. After all, Paul is older than I am; I was afraid you would think he was just a –'

'Father figure.' Francine finished the sentence for her.

'That's right,' Paul said. 'To be honest, I was worried about that, too. Alison lost her parents during her first year here and she has no other family. Don't think I wasn't aware of that from the start –'

'Paul – I think your mother is trying to attract your attention.'

Alison was pointing towards the long tables set out under the trees. A tall, elegant older woman was waving

11

the red-bound programme in their direction. 'Oh, yes, I was supposed to come over here and get you,' Paul said. 'I suppose we'd better go.'

'Not before I've taken a photograph of you both together,' Sophie said. 'Oh! That is if you don't mind being snapped by a rank amateur!'

'Not at all. Shoot away!' Paul placed an arm around Alison's shoulder and their smiles were natural, their pose relaxed.

After Sophie had taken her shot and they had said a last goodbye, they strolled away though the crowd to where Mrs Cavendish waited for them.

'Don't they look terrific together!' Sophie said when they were out of earshot.

'Great – a handsome couple.'

'So why do you sound just a little cynical?'

'Do I?' Francine asked. 'I didn't mean too. 'Paul Cavendish is tall and good-looking and obviously not short of cash . . .'

'But?'

'Oh nothing really. It's just in spite of her denials, Alison could have been looking for someone to replace the father she adored. I mean, losing her parents the way she did – a car crash while they were on holiday – waving them off and never seeing them again. OK,' Francine suddenly grimaced comically, 'I can see the way you're looking at me – I'll shut up! Sophie, has anyone ever told you that you're hopelessly romantic?'

'No, and I don't think I am.'

'So, surrounded by all this abundance of young, healthy male animals, some of them intelligent, why have you been living like a nun? Unless you've been waiting for what our mothers might call "Mr Right"?'

'Can you believe that I just didn't fancy any of them?'

Francine regarded her speculatively. 'Yeah, I can accept that. You're just more choosy than I am!'

Sophie tried not to think of all the 'healthy male animals' that had passed through Francine's life during the last three years. None of them had lasted very long and the relationships all seemed to have ended when Francine chose. And with no regrets.

'So if you're not a romantic, what are you saving yourself for?' Sophie asked Francine with a sudden flash of insight.

Her friend's eyes widened. 'Very clever – but I'm not going to answer you. All I can say is that I'm shaken to the core that two of my dearest friends seem to be so happy to rush into matrimony! And, now, I really must go and find my parents. There's someone here that I don't want them to bump in to.'

'Would you like to explain that statement?'

'Not really. Go on – take one last shot of me – *on my own!*' she emphasized. 'Will this do?' Francine drew herself up into an impressive pose. Then, almost as soon as she'd heard the click of the camera shutter, she grinned, waved and was gone.

Sophie stared after her. Chattering groups formed, broke apart and then regrouped around her but she stood alone. She was aware that the crowd seemed to have thinned a little.

'Sophie?'

She looked around. Her mother was regarding her patiently.

'Oh, Mum, sorry –'

Guilt surged through her. How long was it since she had thrust her own degree certificate into her mother's hands and rushed off with her camera in order to find her friends? However long it had been, her mother didn't seem to mind.

'Shall we go over and collect our drinks?'

'Oh, of course. Haven't you had one yet?'

'No, I preferred to wait for you, dear.'

'Oh, Mum, I'm sorry, but I wanted to take everyone's photograph – and I wanted you to meet them – but they've gone – and now –'

'That's all right, dear. I'd appreciate some time alone with you. I've been wanting to tell you how proud of you I am. And also how proud your father would have been today.'

'Oh, Mum –' Sophie began to move towards the refreshment table.

'Just moment. Give me the camera, will you? I want to take your photograph.'

'All right – if you have to.' Sophie's tone was diffident but her smile was genuine.

Laura Blake was glad to be able to hide her own expression as she bent her head to look into the view-finder. Not wanting to push herself forward and perhaps embarrass her daughter, she had watched from a short distance as Sophie had taken the photographs of Alison, Carol and Francine and the two prospective bride-grooms.

She had heard much about the three girls and she had been glad that her daughter had found such a lively and seemingly decent bunch of friends. She supposed it was understandable that today they were excited and full of plans for the future, That wonderful, terrifying future that was already rushing towards them. They just couldn't wait to set out headlong to meet it.

And yet . . . surely they could have paused just long enough to ask Sophie to have her photograph taken with them? Seemingly it hadn't occurred to any one of them.

Laura adjusted the camera and studied her daughter. She saw herself when young. Although today her waif-like child actually looked impressive in her academic cap and gown.

She acknowledged to herself that her daughter was nowhere near as pretty or attractive as her three friends.

14

Sophie had mid-brown hair, mid-brown eyes and un-distinguished features. And yet the hair was soft and shining and the eyes large and lambent. In Sophie's case they really were the mirror of her soul.

Laura had heard Francine's confident young voice breaking through the surrounding chatter. She had heard the crack about 'Mr Right'. Well, Laura hoped that one day 'Mr Right' would indeed come along – and that Sophie would be as lucky as she, herself, had been.

She suppressed a small sigh and when she looked up all traces of her frown had vanished. 'You look terrific,' Laura Blake assured her daughter. 'Hold that pose – smile – that's it.'

CHAPTER 1

Ten years later – a Monday in April – London

The sun was bright but there was still a cold wind winnowing up the narrow alleys from the river. Francine climbed out of her producer's car and watched as the worried young woman hurried towards them along the narrow Docklands street. The studio's set-builders had installed gas lamps and constructed stagey shop-fronts to make the street look Victorian.

The cobbles were authentic and, in spite of her Sloaney clothes, the publicity aide looked far from elegant as her high-heeled shoes slipped and slithered dangerously on the wet stones. Wet because the scene they had been filming that morning had required gallons of artificial rain to be sprayed on the actors – not the main players, of course, only some minor characters and the extras.

Those extras, dressed like the London poor of yester-year, were still damp. Their clothes steamed visibly in the spring sunshine as they queued at the mobile refreshment van. The smell of fried food was pervasive and Francine wrinkled her nose in disgust.

But everyone looked pleased enough as they collected free plates of food and plastic mugs of tea or coffee. Francine noticed that actors and technicians mingled democratically at the long trestle tables. But of Matt McConnell, the man she had come to interview, there was no sign.

The publicity aide – she had introduced herself earlier that day as 'Araminta-but-everyone-calls-me-Minty' – hugged her clipboard to her body like a shield. She looked anywhere except at the waiting television crew.

Rob Baines, Francine's producer, had also got out of the car, and he came round to join her. She turned to him and smiled. 'How much do you bet that the outstandingly egotistical Mr McConnell has changed his mind about seeing us and that we've trailed all the way down to Hollywood-on-Thames for nothing?' she asked.

'He wouldn't do that,' Rob replied. 'Matt McConnell wants publicity both for himself and for the film he's making. In fact he needs us more than we need him.'

'Does he?'

'Sure he does. You know very well, he hasn't made a decent film since *The Next President* in 1994, when he was nominated for the Oscar – that's four years ago. Mr McConnell is in danger of becoming one of yesterday's stars. If he has any sense, he'll co-operate.'

'I hope you're right, Rob. I'm not in the mood to nurse along oversized egos.'

Rob gave her a sideways glance. 'Anything bothering you, Francine?'

'Why do you ask?'

'Well, you don't seem to be as together as you usually are – dare I say it, not quite so professional?'

'*You* can say it – but nobody else can.' She smiled at him companionably. 'And I'm sorry, Rob. It's because I've just moved house, I guess, and also I haven't made up my mind whether I should sign my life away to the BBC for another three years.

'But you're right, I shouldn't let my private worries

show – not when I'm working. I promise I'll pull myself together.'

'You'd better, because from the expression on Minty's face – ridiculous name – I think we're just about to be granted an audience with the once great and still beautiful Matt McConnell.'

' "Beautiful", Rob? Do you fancy him?'

Rob grinned. 'No, he's too muscular for my ascetic taste, but, even if I did, the emphatically heterosexual Mr McConnell wouldn't fancy me.'

'*There* you are, Miss Rowe!' the publicity aide breathed, as though she hadn't been aware that they had been waiting around on the same spot for the past two hours. 'Mr McConnell will see you now,' she said. Minty's pale blue eyes behind her fashionably large-framed spectacles were huge, and her awed, breathy tone seemed to convey that Francine was almost unbelievably privileged.

'Good.' Francine smiled at the girl. It was her policy, whenever possible, to stay on friendly terms with lesser mortals who, after all, were only doing their job. She didn't want to get a reputation, like some other successful women in television, for being an awkward, high-handed bitch.

Rob turned to give the thumbs up to Norm, the cameraman, and Geoff, the sound man, who had been sitting patiently in their Range Rover. Then he turned his clipboard round to reveal a small mirror secured there. 'OK, Francine, do you want to adjust your make-up?'

It didn't take her long to smooth her dark cap of hair. A quick renewal of her lipstick, which was exactly the same scarlet as her trouser suit, and she was ready.

Minty stood and waited like an obedient child. 'So where is he?' Francine asked her. Behind her Norm and Geoff were unloading their equipment and she didn't want them to have to carry it for miles along the water-front if Matt McConnell had decided to decamp to his luxurious hotel for lunch.

'Oh, Mr McConnell has agreed to see you on the set. He thought it would make some interesting shots for your cameraman.'

And some nice publicity shots for him, Francine thought, but she didn't say anything.

'We've got a caravan set up in one of the warehouses. Mr McConnell is resting – but he's willing to give you ten minutes.' Minty's young face took on a worried expression.

'Ten minutes!' Francine exclaimed, and Minty looked as if she might burst into tears.

'That's wonderful,' Rob interjected hastily. 'Now, lead the way, Minty, we don't want to keep Mr McConnell waiting, do we?'

The unhappy girl led the way back along the cobbled street followed by Francine and Rob with Norm and Geoff bringing up the rear. On the way Rob did his best to calm Francine down. 'So we've only got ten minutes – you're good enough to make every minute tell.'

'But Rob, this isn't just for the news; we're supposed to be contributing to the weekly film magazine pro-gramme, too. They'll want at least twenty minutes –'

'Don't worry. Norm and Geoff can take shots of the set – you can interview some of the minor players – the extras, the crew, the caterers even. You must see that there's enough here to make a good little feature.'

Francine looked around at the cameras, the lights, the actors and the technicians – all the paraphernalia of film-making – and her brow cleared. 'Of course there is, Rob, and I'm sorry – again.'

There was more than one caravan inside the echoing, old warehouse but Minty made her way to the biggest and the most luxurious-looking. Francine and her crew waited at a respectful distance while the girl climbed the short flight of temporary wooden steps and knocked reverentially at the door. It opened immediately and Matt McConnell appeared. He directed a radiant smile towards Francine.

'Francine!' he exclaimed, 'Great to see you! And I'm always happy to oblige the BBC!'

What a ham, Francine thought to herself, greeting me as if we were old buddies when he probably hadn't even heard of me until poor Minty set up the interview.

She was aware of Rob shuffling uneasily beside her and she hoped that she hadn't let her sour thoughts tweak her professional smile out of place. At least the guy's prepared to be pleasant, she told herself, even if it's only going to be for ten minutes.

She appraised him as he came down the steps and walked towards them. There was no denying that, in his late thirties, the American film actor was still outstandingly good-looking. He had classically hewn features, dark blond hair, blue eyes and a body so well muscled that it could look a little incongruous in formal clothes; especially the formal clothes of an aristocratic Victorian gentleman.

He'd look better in jeans and an open-necked shirt, Francine found herself thinking. Or, better still, wearing nothing at all. She smiled self-mockingly at where her thoughts were taking her.

Francine introduced Matt McConnell to Rob and after a perfunctory handshake and a brief smile the actor got down to business.

'You won't be shooting the interview in here, of course —'

'Of course not —' Rob seemed affronted that anyone would think he would settle for such a boring background as a warehouse.

But Matt McConnell hurried on, 'I thought the film

21

set outside here would make the perfect backdrop. Olde worlde shops – gas lights – very atmospheric. It's all ready for the next scene, as a matter of fact.'

'That's great, Mr McConnell,' Norm, who never wasted words if he didn't have to, stepped forward. 'And, as it's all set up, I'll be able to use the existing lighting – that way we'll get the effect you want, right?'

The movie star shot an appreciative glance at the cameraman. 'Right – that's terrific – I think you've got a good team here, Francine. What's your camera-man's name?'

She told him.

'Norm,' he said. 'Just remember that this is my best profile, will you?'

He turned his head to demonstrate and then stood still obediently while Geoff hid a small microphone at the opening of his Victorian waistcoat. Francine pinned her own mike just inside her jacket.

The row of 'Victorian' shops looked almost real, she thought. Except that all but one were merely façades. However the door of a Gentleman's Outfitters was constructed to open. Obviously this doorway was needed for some part of the film's action.

Matt McConnell suggested that the interview should begin with him looking as if he were coming out of the shop and feigning surprise and pleasure at finding Francine standing there.

'I'll say something like, "Hi, there – what a nice surprise!"' he suggested.

She thought the idea a bit cutesy but she didn't mind going along with it and Rob had no objections. After all, the film was fantasy. *Time Will Tell* was the story of a mysterious American, played by Matt McConnell, who appeared in Victorian London to track down and appre-hend a maniacal killer.

Of course he would turn out to be from the 'future'

22

and, equally predictably, he would fall in love with a girl from the 'past'. That much of the storyline had been made public – in fact the film company couldn't keep it secret because *Time Will Tell* had been adapted from a best-selling novel.

As soon as Norm and Geoff had set up their equipment, Rob directed an establishing shot of Matt McConnell coming out of the shop doorway, greeting Francine and beginning to talk to her. Then Norm moved in close so that the camera was just behind Francine's shoulder and there it stayed, focused on Matt McConnell's strong-jawed face while she got down to the business of interviewing him.

It wasn't difficult. As Rob had predicted, the film actor was eager to co-operate; Francine began to feel that she was almost sleepwalking through the whole experience. She had done so many of these kind of interviews before; it was too easy.

She elicited the information that Matt McConnell was pleased to be in England, that in his opinion the special effects guys over here were the best in the world, that the storyline was exciting and, yes, if you twisted his arm, he would admit to hoping that the film would lead to a sequel – at least one sequel and maybe more.

He arranged his perfect features into what passed for an expression of genuine regret when Francine forced him to admit that the young English actress who was playing the lead in the film would probably not appear in the following films.

'I think each film should have a new female lead – a new love interest for the hero,' he said. 'What better than an attractive young French star if the next story takes place in Paris . . . an Italian actress for Rome . . . that would add a bit more spice, don't you think?'

Francine wondered, but didn't ask him, if he intended to spin the sequels out until he had been right round the world's capital cities 'adding a bit of spice'. She also stopped herself from telling him that one of the reasons she had never liked James Bond was his chronic inability to form a permanent relationship.

But she couldn't help saying, 'Oh, I don't know, television's Superman married Lois Lane and it didn't seem to affect the viewing figures.'

She caught Rob's indrawn breath and she didn't have to turn to look at him to realize that she had sounded waspish. But luckily Matt McConnell had chosen to take it as a joke.

'Well, I don't claim to be Superman,' he said disarmingly. 'But remember, Superman has been around for a very long time – perhaps I'm too young to settle down yet.'

Oh, yes, Francine thought, very good, and she found herself liking the guy in spite of his obvious self-regard. He wanted to succeed, get to the very top of his profession, and he was prepared to work at it, even if it meant being charming to an asp-tongued female television reporter.

The interview ended with smiles all round. Rob persuaded the actor to walk away from them along the Victorian street rather than vanish into the shop again. And then Matt McConnell waved goodbye and went to talk to the film's director.

'You were great,' Rob told her. 'Now just hold it there while Norm focuses on you and you can repeat some of those questions straight to camera.'

Francine obliged. These shots, called 'cut-ins', would be edited into the film when they got back to the studio. This way it would look as though she and Matt McConnell were having a normal, two-way conversation. But while she repeated her questions to camera, she had the sensation, again, that it was all too easy.

After the cut-ins she was happy to wander round the

Docklands set interviewing anyone that Minty set up for them. It wasn't long before she had enough material. Norm and Geoff said they'd like to stay on for a short while to film some actuality – interesting sights and sounds which might be of use to add to their feature.

'The editing suite's booked for four-thirty,' Rob reminded them, and then he and Francine left to head back to Television Centre. 'I could drop you off at your apartment if you like,' he told her. 'It's not too far from here, is it?'

'But my car's at Television Centre.'

'Haven't you heard of taxis? Seriously, you could go home and try to rest for a couple of hours before it's time to start editing the film.'

'Do I look as though I need a rest?'

'No – it's just –'

Francine knew she must have sounded sharp and she regretted it. 'I'm sorry, Rob. Oh, lord, how many times is that? I seem to have been apologizing to you all day!'

'Francine, you don't have to say sorry to me. We've worked together for a long time. Long enough for me to know that something's wrong –'

'No – nothing's wrong –'

'Well, then, something isn't right.' Rob grinned and glanced sideways. Francine couldn't help smiling at the fine distinction.

'Listen, Rob, what I hinted at earlier is true. Moving house has been hectic. After, all, I was in that flat in Fulham for years – ever since I first came to work for the BBC, in fact. I just didn't realize that I'd accumulated so much junk.

'I should never have decided to move without taking time off. But, you know me, I always think I can handle everything. The result is that I've been in the new apartment for three weeks, just about, and I'm still surrounded by overflowing packing cases.'

25

'So do you want to go home now and do a little unpacking? I could help you.'

'God, no!' She saw Rob's raised eyebrows and hurried on, 'I'm not spurning your offer of help, it's just that I'd rather keep my mind on my work during the day. Once I leave the place in the morning I have to forget about everything there until I get back at night. I'm no good at mixing two areas of my life. That's the way I am. Single-minded.'

'OK, Francine. But I'll treat you to the best lunch the staff restaurant can come up with as soon as we get back.'

He seemed to be happy to let things drop. Earlier, Francine had admitted to him that the decision whether or not to renew her contract was also weighing on her mind. She was glad that he didn't bring it up now. She knew that he wouldn't like some of what she might say.

The new deal that was being offered to Francine involved Rob too. Their executive producer Peter Curtis had come up with an idea for a new series for her and he wanted Rob to produce it.

Rob knew that she was undecided, but he thought it was because she didn't know whether to sign another three-year contract or go totally freelance – less security but more money. He didn't realize that it was the whole concept of the new series that was bothering her.

If I tell him, he won't really understand, she thought. He seems to be happy doing this kind of work – he'll wonder why on earth I want to rock the boat.

Francine knew she had been lucky to have been assigned a producer like Rob Baines. As well as working well together, they had become friends over the years but he had never overstepped the mark, never tried to become too familiar.

She had decided long ago that he probably knew the old story of how she had got into television in the first place. Malicious gossip had a habit of circulating for a while, going under cover and then reviving.

There had been one or two snide hints in newspaper features about her now and then. How she owed her first job in regional television to the fact that she was sleeping with the right person while she was still at university. But, by the time she had moved to London, even though the person in question had come, too, no one could deny that, however she'd got the job in the first place, she had real talent.

But of late she was beginning to feel increasingly that any talent she might have was being wasted, frittered away on trivia. That feeling she had had earlier that she could have conducted the interview with Matt McConnell in her sleep. And it wasn't the first time that it had happened.

Sometimes she was shocked to discover that, when they returned to the studios to edit the film, she hadn't the faintest recollection of the questions she had asked. And yet, there was Rob saying that the piece was great, that she was marvellous, and there was the film to prove that she had done another professional job.

She could hardly remember the feeling of excitement she used to have before she started work. The tidal wave of adrenalin that used to surge through her once the interview began, and the sense of triumph she allowed herself when she knew that it had been a job well done.

She hadn't started off interviewing celebrities. In regional television there had been human interest stories concerning ordinary people, local sports stars, visiting politicians. But, once she got to London she had been steered, without realizing it at first, towards the 'show-biz' end of television.

And she knew she was good at it. She didn't crawl like some interviewers when they were faced with a famous person. It just wasn't in her nature to be overawed or intimidated by anyone. Francine treated mega-stars and even royalty as though they were ordinary people. She asked them the questions that other ordinary people wanted to hear the answers to.

Sometimes her sharp brain steered her into dangerous waters, but she'd never seriously offended any of the people she'd interviewed. Perhaps she should have done . . .

What's the matter with me? she wondered. For weeks now I've simply been going through the motions. It's not that I want to leave television – I still think it's one of the most exciting areas to work in. But somehow the challenge has gone. Perhaps it's time I moved on. But if I don't take up Peter's option, where will I go?

She glanced at Rob. He was concentrating on negotiating the London traffic and a slight frown marred his handsome features. Very handsome features. He was good-looking enough to be in front of the cameras himself, she had once told him.

'Don't patronize me, madam,' he had responded. But she knew that he was secretly flattered.

Of course a lot of the newer, younger staff wondered about her and Rob. He so tall and handsome, she, who had once been voted the most beautiful woman in television. And they chose to work together as often as they could. She supposed it would be easy for people to imagine that they were a couple. But that was only until they discovered that Rob was gay.

A very few insiders knew the truth about her, she guessed. Or people with long memories. Every now and then a clever, young female journalist would sharpen her claws, dip her pen in vitriol, and enjoy speculating in her newspaper column who the man behind Francine Rowe might be. But that was only if there was a temporary scarcity of other targets. Nobody really cared.

No, Francine mused, we seem to have got away with it for a very long time.

In the staff restaurant there was the usual sprinkling of famous faces, but they were outnumbered, as ever, by the many, many more people who worked behind the scenes. Programme staff, technicians, scene-shifters, make-up, wardrobe, secretarial, security staff; so many skills, so many different kinds of talent. The television centre was like a small city – and everyone had to eat.

'Hi, Francine, how did it go?'

Francine looked up from her brazil nut salad to see the producer of the film magazine programme standing over them.

'Fine, Tristram, just fine. You'll get your twenty minutes of videotape,' she said.

'Good. And, by the way, a young woman calling herself Minty just called my office on behalf of Matt McConnell.'

'Oh?'

She was uneasy – if anyone called the office after she'd interviewed them, it could mean a complaint. Or worse than that, they wanted to view the tape before it was transmitted – and there wasn't always time for that.

Rob's mind was working the same way. 'Problem?' he asked.

'Don't worry,' Tristram said. 'No problems. Matt McConnell just wanted to know when we were going to use the interview so that he could watch it – and probably record it. I told him the times to have his tape ready.

'Oh, and, Francine, he'd also asked Minty to say how much he'd enjoyed being interviewed by you. He says if he can come up with anything else during the filming that would make a good story, he wants only Francine Rowe!'

'I'm overwhelmed!'

Tristram's sudden smile made him look years younger. 'Do you remember that prize-winning leek grower you interviewed who played non-stop Beatles albums to his young plants?' he asked.

'How could I forget him?'

'Am I missing something?' Rob interjected.

'Once the poor guy had been interviewed by the fair Francine, he couldn't stop phoning the studios,' Tristram explained. 'He wanted her to come and interview him again about his prize marrow –'

Francine choked over her coffee. 'Don't, Tristram –'

'– or anything else in his garden. He even suggested that she should come and sing to his tomatoes –'

'You're exaggerating – he wasn't as bad as that!'

'Oh, no? You should have heard what the girls on PBX had to say about him!'

'I see,' Rob said. 'This was when the two of you were working in regional television. Leeds, wasn't it?'

'Yeah – before fame and fortune called Francine to London.'

'You too, Tristram, you too.'

Francine smiled as her old colleague took his leave and threaded his way through the tables to collect his own lunch.

'Can I get you anything else?' Rob asked her. 'They've got some wicked pastries.'

'All those calories!'

'Go on – indulge yourself for once. I'm going to.'

'OK – and some coffee too, please.'

While they demolished their pastries and sipped their coffee, the editor of the morning news programme approached the table, smiling politely but eyebrows raised.

'Don't worry,' Rob saved him the bother of asking his question, 'I'll cull three minutes of Francine's interview for you and put it on your desk before I leave the building tonight.'

'Thanks. Great.'

The man walked off and Rob looked at his watch. 'Right now I have a script to look over but, if your desk is clear, why don't you find a quiet corner to put your feet up for a while?'

'No, Rob. I think I'd better go and have a word with Peter.'

'Oh?'

'Yeah. See you later.'

She left the restaurant and took the lift down several floors. As she hurried along the curving corridor, she felt guilty for not being more explicit with Rob. But she couldn't have been. She didn't know herself what she was going to say to their executive producer.

Peter Curtis was expecting her. He came into the outer office when his secretary announced her and led her into the inner sanctum himself. He was of medium height, with a good physique, and although his light brown hair was beginning to go grey, it only made him looked more distinguished. He was also very astute. Which was why he'd risen so far in the corporation.

'Well, Francine?' he asked when they were both seated.

'Peter, I just don't know.'

'I can't understand your hesitation. It's a great idea and you're just the girl to handle it.'

'But, Peter, the title of the series is so corny – *VIPs*!'

'It might be corny but it's exactly right. The VIP lounge in an airport – not always the same airport – we plan to go to America, Europe, Asia, even. And you interviewing the people who are important enough to be waiting there –'

'Wonderful,' Francine couldn't keep the sarcasm from showing. 'Rich businessmen, minor royalty –'

'Yes, yes, Francine, but there'll also be pop stars,

31

sportsmen, movie people – and don't forget, we'll know in advance who'll be there because we'll be liaising with their PR people.'

'So it's free publicity again –'

'Don't be so cynical. Free publicity for them, maybe, but it's also good entertainment for the rest of us. Interesting people – different lifestyles. And, you know, journeys are always intriguing.'

'I know. I'm sorry, it's just that –'

'Is it your contract that's bothering you?'

'Maybe.'

'Look – I'll agree to whatever you want – you can sign another short-term contract or go totally freelance – as long as you sign up for a whole series of *VIPs*, that is.'

'So you'd still own me.'

'No. That kind of deal would mean that you could do other things. I would see that the relevant clause was inserted. But your first loyalty would be to me, naturally.'

'Naturally.'

Peter Curtis suddenly smiled at her. 'Don't forget, I know you, Francine. I know what you're capable of and I know that you can make a good programme great. You've always had the ability to add that extra zest. I don't know how you do it, but I spotted it from the start.'

'Yes, I know, and I'm grateful.'

'So will you promise to think about it very carefully? You owe me that much.'

Francine sighed. 'I suppose I do.'

CHAPTER 2

Tuesday morning – the West Country

Carol Kennedy frowned as the aroma of burnt toast rose up and mingled with the lingering odours of last night's Chinese takeaways. She switched off the toaster, fished out the blackened bread with a kitchen knife and dropped it, still smouldering, on to a plate. She couldn't be bothered to do another slice – and it didn't look too bad, she thought, just crisp around the edges.

She pushed aside some of the clutter on the kitchen table to make room for her plate and her mug of instant coffee and sat down. She looked miserably at the one slice that she allowed herself and then defeated the whole plan by spreading it thickly with butter and honey. Then she poured milk into her coffee and added two spoons of sugar. I may be a pound or two overweight, she reasoned, but breakfast isn't the right time to cut down on calories. I need energy to kick-start my brain into action and get me through another hectic day.

Suppressing all thoughts of the cream cakes that she and Stacey usually had for elevenses, she bit into the toast. She also managed to dismiss the inconvenient fact that the pub lunches she had started sharing with her boss, Luke Travers, were usually garnished with French fries so delicious that she couldn't resist them.

One slice of toast and honey was no big deal, she thought, and besides, she needed the comfort of it right now. It was part of being able to indulge herself, here in the cluttered little kitchen, in the peace and quiet of the early morning before Alan came down and the day began in earnest.

She reached over to the television perched on the counter-top and switched it on. She had just heard Alan go into the shower and after that he would be using the hairdryer, so, if she kept the volume low, she would get away with it.

Get away with it! she thought, and was angry with herself for how duplicitous she had become. But, at some time over the years, she had learned that it was better to avoid arguing with Alan over some of his edicts. Edicts that came straight from his parents' book of rules on how the right sort of people conducted themselves. Some of their ideas were ridiculous.

For example, what on earth was so wrong with watching television in the morning? Alan said that kind of thing was only for the simple-minded but it wasn't as though she was going to sit around all day in her robe watching one programme after another while the house went to hell. She was only catching up with the news before she went to work, for goodness' sake, and if it was entertaining as well as informative, what on earth was so wrong with that!

Carol suddenly giggled and spluttered sticky toast crumbs over the table. She looked around her kitchen in mock despair. The house had already gone to hell – ages ago. She might be the brightest employee that Luke Travers had ever had – God's gift to Travers' Transport, he'd told her – but housewife of the year she certainly wasn't.

Carol glanced round as raindrops began to spatter against the window and frowned. She hoped it was only an April shower and that the rain had not set in for the day. One of her windscreen wipers was sticking, the one on the driver's side, and she didn't relish getting out every now and then to adjust it. She had been meaning to have it fixed but kept putting it off. Her little Fiesta hatchback was due for a service soon so she'd thought she'd leave it until then.

As the sky clouded over, the kitchen grew dark and she stared out at the sky, searching hopefully for a patch of blue beyond the black clouds. Then a changing pattern on the television screen caught her eye.

The newsreader had disappeared, to be replaced by a Victorian street. Carol watched as the camera zoomed in on a little row of shops. The doorway of one of them was opening and a tall Victorian gentleman lowered his head as he stepped out. She recognized Matt McConnell, the American film star and grinned. What she was seeing must be a scene from the movie he was making over here.

But wait a minute . . . he was talking to someone . . . a woman dressed in a fashionable and very un-Victorian red trouser suit . . .

Francine! Her old friend was interviewing Matt McConnell!

Carol forgot about the rain and the state of her car for a moment and settled back to watch. Francine seemed to be asking all the right questions because Matt McConnell was smiling. And he became ever more expansive and enthusiastic about his work and his future plans. Every now and then the camera cut to Francine's animated face.

She was still beautiful, Carol acknowledged. Nearly black hair framing fine-boned features, fair skin, cat-slanted, tawny-brown eyes – and she was so well groomed! The scarlet lipstick matched the red of her jacket exactly and the gold stud earrings were just big enough to glint through the smooth fall of hair. Hair

35

which was so neatly cut that it was almost geometric.

Carol twisted one of her own escaping locks round her fingers and sighed. She never seemed to have time for appointments at the hairdresser's. By the time she got back from work the beauty parlour in the village was closed and she hated giving up Saturday mornings. That was when she tried to catch up with the housework.

But she guessed that Francine's bandbox appearance owed nothing to the hairdressers and make-up girls at Television Centre. Francine had always made the most of herself, even when she was a student. Whereas, let's face it, I was always a mess and probably always will be, she accepted sadly.

And the years have been kind to Francine, Carol realized. Somehow that depressed her. Paradoxically, when they had been at university, Francine had always looked a little older than her years. Even when they had all met up in Freshers' Week, Francine hadn't looked a bit like a new student, someone straight from school, like Alison, Sophie and Carol herself.

The four of them had teamed up pretty quickly. At first, the other three had all been under the impression that Francine was one of the second-or third-year students who were acting as guides and counsellors. She seemed so confident, so sure of herself.

Looking back, Carol realized that Francine had only looked older because she acted older. Even although she depended on her full grant, and money was tight, she never allowed herself to descend into slobbiness. That didn't mean that she didn't wear jeans and oversized sweatshirts like the rest of them – it was just that she always managed, somehow, to look well-groomed and even fashionable.

And now, when life had recently tipped them all into their thirties, it was Francine who looked younger than the rest of them. Carol brooded about the last time they had all been together. Was it two years ago? Yes, it must have been. The occasion had been Paul's funeral . . .

Poor Alison, there had hardly been any sign of the radiantly attractive girl she had once been. But, then, to lose your husband so tragically when you were still so young – and to be left with the responsibility for a young son and a collection of ghastly in-laws. No wonder she had looked so tired and lacklustre.

Sophie, like Carol, had shown the small but unmistakable signs of the passing years. But Francine, dramatic in black and more elegant than any other woman at the funeral, even Paul's painfully aristocratic mother and sister, seemed, incredibly, not to have aged at all.

'She's got a portrait in her attic,' Alan had murmured to Carol as they followed the coffin to the graveside.

'Who?'

'Francine.'

Alison had frowned. 'What are you talking about?'

'You know, *The Picture of Dorian Gray*, the story by Oscar Wilde.'

'Oh, yes . . . didn't he make a bargain with the devil?'

'Something like that. Anyway, Dorian Gray never appeared to grow older, he always looked young and handsome; but his portrait grew more and more hideous.'

The trees in the country churchyard shook raindrops down over the mourners and Carol shivered. 'Well, I don't believe Francine has a portrait like that,' she whispered to Alan. 'She's just – oh, she's just Francine!'

And, truly, there was nobody quite like her, Carol mused now, as she watched Matt McConnell walk away down the Victorian street on the television screen. By the time she had finished her coffee the news item was over and the weather report had begun.

'Showery with bright patches,' the weatherman informed the viewers.

Well, all I want is to be able to find a bright patch big enough to get me all the way to Avonmouth without having to get out of the car to adjust the windscreen wiper, Carol mused.

She was just about to stand up and clear her mug and her plate into the sink when Alan came into the kitchen. She reached out to switch off the television, flushing miserably.

Alan made no comment. 'Where's my grapefruit?' he asked.

'What?' She stared at him, round-eyed.

'You offered to prepare a grapefruit.'

'Oh, Alan, I was going to, I thought there'd be plenty of time . . . but . . .'

'You had better things to do.' He glanced at the television set sarcastically.

'Sit down. I'll do it now.'

Carol was angry with herself, not just for forgetting to prepare Alan's breakfast as promised, but because she had given him cause to criticize her. He seemed to do that so often lately.

She dumped her dishes in the sink, ignoring last night's plates and the congealed residue of food. She turned to take one of the grapefruit from the large bowl on the table to find that Alan had already taken one.

'No – let me –'

He ignored her and reached into the drawer for a sharp knife. He shook his head. 'For goodness' sake, Carol, this drawer is dangerous. Won't you ever learn to put things neatly into the proper compartments? I could have cut myself.'

'Sorry. Look, I'll do that. Why don't you sit down? I think I heard the paper arrive, I'll get it for you.'

By the time she returned with the morning newspaper, Alan had cut the grapefruit in half and was just about to start easing the flesh away from the sides.

'Alan, give the knife to me, I insist. You might get juice on your suit.'

Her husband allowed himself to be pushed towards the table; he took his seat and started to read the paper. They didn't speak to each other as Carol finished preparing the grapefruit, covered half of it with a clean saucer and shoved it into the fridge. He might eat that tomorrow, she thought. She dropped a teabag into a mug, noting that there were only a couple left, and switched on the kettle. 'This won't take long. Do you want a slice of toast?'

'Yes, please – if you can manage not to turn it into a burnt offering.'

For a moment she was furious, and then she saw that he was smiling. It was a tired smile and it was definitely strained around the edges, but it was a smile, nevertheless.

'OK.' She grinned in response. 'Honey or marmalade?'

'Marmalade. If you remembered to get some.'

'Oh! Alan, I didn't – I'm sorry . . .'

'Honey, then.'

Alan turned back to the table; the smile had gone. The moment of closeness had gone. Carol was devastated – that wasn't too strong a word. For a second or two, just then, when he had smiled at her, she had glimpsed the old Alan – the Alan she had loved so passionately.

But then, a split-second later, it seemed, the man she had married had once more become the stranger that he had metamorphosed into over the past ten years. When had the process begun? And why? How could two intelligent people who had loved each other so much have become these two sad strangers?

The rain had stopped by the time Carol eased her car into the stream of traffic heading towards Avonmouth, and for that she was grateful. The M5 was always busy. She wouldn't have dared pull over on to the hard shoulder to get out and fix her windscreen wiper. No, if it had still been raining she would have to have taken an alternative route along minor roads, and that would have taken forever.

When Alan's firm had transferred him from Teesside, they had chosen a house in a new development on the fringes of a tiny village in north Somerset. Property in the West Country was more expensive than in the northeast of England and the financial inducements the developer had offered, such as a low interest rate for the first two years, had been tempting.

Anything nearer to Bristol was out of their price range. But, perhaps we should have made the effort, Carol thought, not for the first time. We must be spending more on travelling and running two cars than we would paying a higher mortgage. She usually left for work well before eight in the morning. Alan didn't have to leave so early, otherwise they might have shared a car. They were heading roughly in the same direction.

But then, Alan didn't seem to finish work at a regular time any more. Carol never knew when he was going to be home and it made preparing the evening meal difficult. It never seemed to occur to him that, if he was going to be delayed, all he had to do was pick up the phone.

'Hi, Carol, come on in, you're just in time for a cuppa,' Stacey called out to her as she walked past the secretary's office just before eight-thirty.

Carol paused in the doorway. The kettle had just boiled and the tiny room appeared to be full of steam. Stacey grinned as she took two mugs from the top drawer of a filing cabinet and plonked them on her desk. A jar of instant coffee, a box of teabags and a bag of sugar followed.

'Tea or coffee?'

40

'Coffee.'

'Yeah – me too.' Stacey spooned the coffee granules into the mugs. 'Heavy night last night,' she said. 'Tried the new wine bar on White Ladies' Road – they were giving out free drinks to all the ladies with an "escort". Don't know what kind of plonk it was, but by the end of the night I wasn't acting much like a lady. Good job I had my escort to see me safely home!' A rueful smile played about her lips as she poured the hot water, carefully, on to the coffee granules. 'Well, at least my hands aren't shaking – look.' She laughed a little shame-facedly.

Carol tried not to show that she was troubled. Stacey was only nineteen but she was confident and worldly-wise in a way Carol had never been. Nevertheless, the idea of her drinking too much and being at the mercy of some predatory youth worried her. The world had moved on, she knew, things had changed – but not that much.

She realized the girl was grinning at her. 'Why are you looking at me like that, Stacey? I haven't said anything.'

'You don't have to. I can see what you're thinking. And don't worry, the escort was my brother Mick, and he gave me an earful. Even if I hadn't already decided that I didn't like the way it made me feel, I would never drink that much again.'

'Oh . . . good . . . but I wasn't going to sermonize, you know.'

'I know. You're OK, Carol.'

'Thanks, I like you too.'

Stacey looked embarrassed. 'Well – er – the milk's in the fridge – I'll go and get it – just put this lot away for me, will you? I don't want any of those villains to know where I hide my own supply!'

By 'those villains' she meant the drivers and porters. Luke had provided a drinks machine for them in the rest

41

room next to the small kitchen but they were always grumbling about it.

Stacey eased past her and Carol watched as she walked away down the narrow corridor of the portable cabin which was the temporary headquarters of Travers' Transport. Luke was in the process of extending and modernizing the original office block and meanwhile he had hired a couple of self-contained modular buildings to accommodate the 'brain-centre' of his growing transport empire.

The girl was tall and shapely. Carol had never seen her dressed in anything except a crisp white blouse and navy tailored skirt. She was the image of an efficient and orderly receptionist/secretary – except for the diamond chip nose stud and the hair. Stacey's short hair framed her attractive, young face in ragged spikes and Carol had giving up guessing what its natural colour might be. For a week or two now, it had been a rich burgundy.

'Morning, gorgeous!' Carol heard the greeting from one of the men as Stacey opened the door leading into the rest-room and the kitchen beyond. After a moment or two of the usual good-natured banter Stacey came back with a small jug of milk.

'The sooner I get that lot sorted out with today's assignments, the better,' she said. 'Honestly, Carol, I don't know why I put up with them.'

'You like them really.'

'Yeah, I suppose I do – they're not bad if you know how to talk to them. And having five older brothers of my own helps in that direction.'

'I'm sure it must.'

'Now, don't just stand there, pull that spare chair up to my desk. Let's enjoy the last few moments of peace before the phone starts ringing – or Mr Masterful walks through the door.'

Carol smiled as she dragged a chair up and sat down.

'I've been meaning to ask you, why have you started calling him that?'

'Mr Masterful? Well, it suits him, doesn't it?'

'Suits him? I'm not sure what you mean. At first I imagined that you were just being flippant.'

'Flippant? *Moi!*'

'But lately I've begun to wonder whether I've been missing something – some in-joke?'

'Well, I suppose you could put it like that.'

'Explain.'

'Carol! Haven't you haven't you ever noticed the way he looks?'

'Looks?'

'You *must* have noticed! I mean when he calls you into his office you're only sitting at the other side of his desk, for heaven's sake. That's what? About three feet away from him. Not to mention the working lunches you've started having.'

'They *are* working lunches. I mean, we talk about work, about the survey I'm doing –'

'Stop!' Stacey held up one hand, palm out. 'I believe you. My brother Davey works behind the bar there, remember? All I'm saying is that you must be blind not to have noticed what a knockout Mr Travers is.'

'Well, I suppose . . .'

'Don't tell me that staring into your computer screen all day has damaged your eyesight!'

'Well, no, at least I don't think so . . .'

'So, unless all those graphs and spreadsheets have scrambled your brain, you must be aware that he's absolutely scrumptious.'

'Yes, of course I've noticed that he's good-looking, if that's what you mean. But it still doesn't explain why you call him Mr Masterful.'

'Blame my mother.'

'I beg your pardon? Have I missed something?'

'No, it's all the paperback romances she reads. The cupboards in our house are stuffed full of them. Any spare minute the poor woman has and she's away in a wonderful world of beautiful, feisty heroines and handsome, masterful men!'

'Oh, I see . . . or at least I think I do.'

'Yeah, well, remember the brochure we had done recently? All those maps and graphs and the beautiful colour photographs?' Stacey opened a drawer in her desk and fished out the brochure in question.

'Yes, very good,' Carol said. 'The photographs show the transport fleet off to its best advantage. I remember thinking how stunning the articulated vehicles look – especially the long, cool refrigerated number.'

'Very funny. But it's the photograph on page two that I'm talking about.' She flipped the brochure open and turned it to face Carol. 'Look, this one – Mr Travers himself, staring straight into the camera and looking – well – masterful.'

'So that's when you started calling him that? When you saw his picture in the brochure?'

'Well, to be honest, it wasn't until I'd taken it home to show my mum. I wanted to show her the picture of me sitting at my desk, looking efficient, but it was ages before I could get her past page two. "Stacey," she said, "your boss looks exactly like that gorgeous man on the cover of the book I'm reading! Look!"'

'And did he?' Carol asked.

'The spitting image – except that Mr Travers had more clothes on!'

'So you think he looks like a character in a romantic novel?'

'Yeah. But why are you so surprised? Don't you agree?'

'I suppose so . . . I mean I've never thought about him in that way before . . .'

44

Stacey gave her a hard look. 'How long have you been working here now?'

'You know the answer: nearly a year.'

'And you've never really thought about how gorgeous your boss is? Well, all I can say is that your husband must be a real hunk. Lucky you.'

The phone rang and Stacey put down her mug and switched into her working mode straight away. She gave a distracted smile as Carol mouthed, 'See you later,' picked up her mug of coffee and went to her own office.

It had taken her a while to get used to the way Stacey talked to her. The girl was friendly and open and she expected Carol to be the same. But she had never overstepped the line and become too familiar and, once the business of the day started, she became totally professional. Carol knew that Luke was lucky to have her.

Carol's office wasn't much bigger than Stacey's. She put down her coffee, well away from the keyboard, before switching on her computer. Then she sat down and stared at the screen as it blinked into life.

She was reluctant to admit it to herself, but she was vaguely troubled by the conversation they had just had. If you could call it a conversation, that was. She couldn't believe that the girl was being devious and yet why had she suddenly decided to find out if Carol thought Luke was good-looking?

She flushed as she remembered the reference to their working lunches. Her response hadn't been the total truth. Yes, she and Luke did talk about work and her current project as they enjoyed the fare at the White Swan, but they could just as easily have done that over sandwiches in the office.

Had she been too keen to accept his first offer of lunch, and should she have refused any subsequent offers? In truth, she'd had no idea that one of Stacey's brothers worked there. She flushed. Had Davey noticed anything? No, there was nothing *to* notice, was there?

Sighing, she tapped the keyboard to summon up the file she was working on. She didn't notice, at first, that Stacey had popped her head around the door. The girl coughed gently and Carol looked up.

'Stacey?'

'I didn't bug you off just now, did I?'

'No, of course not.' But she *was* rattled. She hoped it didn't show.

'Good. I know I go on a bit sometimes. It's just the sheer joy of having another woman to talk to. Mum and I are outnumbered at home – even the cat's an old tom – and, here at work I was the only female employee until you came along.'

'It's OK, Stacey. Don't worry.'

'Right. Then give me your suit jacket.'

'My jacket? Why?' Carol frowned. If Stacey wanted to borrow it she could, but the sleeves would be too short and the dark grey wasn't really a wonderful fashion match with the girl's navy skirt.

Stacey grinned. 'You've got a stain of some sort down the front. I noticed it as soon as you came in but we got distracted.'

'Alan's grapefruit!'

'I beg your pardon?'

'My husband's grapefruit – I didn't want him to splash his suit so –'

'You splashed your own instead. Very noble of you. Now take it off and I'll clean it.'

Carol handed over her jacket obediently and tried to settle down to work. She began to scan through information on her computer screen – daily drivers' sheets, daily traffic sheets, vehicle capacity, average tonnes per load, number of drops. Her project was to pull together all the data she needed in an endeavour to come up with a

46

system that would make Travers' Transport more efficient – more effective.

Luke's grandfather had started with a single truck but had flourished sufficiently for Luke's father to retire early to a beautiful villa in Spain. Now Luke, the third generation, was poised to expand in a big way. He was hardworking and ambitious. The first in his family to have had a good education, he knew the value of proper research and preparation. And that was why Carol was here.

'Good morning, Carol.'

As always it took her a second or two to pull her eyes away from the screen and adjust to her surroundings. Luke was standing in the doorway.

His large frame filled the doorway, she thought, and felt herself flushing as her mind filled with images of the kind of masterful heroes to be found on the covers of romance novels.

She'd read more than a few of them herself – she knew how the next bit would read . . .

Luke's expensively tailored suit flattered his lean, muscular body . . . a lock of well-groomed, dark blond hair fell forward over his brow . . . Carol looked up into his piercing blue eyes . . . suddenly he smiled and . . .

Oh, no! A movement right in front of her eyes drew her attention back to her computer screen. A dialog box had appeared to ask her if she was sure she wanted to delete the file. Hastily she cancelled the command that she must have made unconsciously while she was staring up at Luke instead of concentrating on her work.

'Anything the matter, Carol?'

Luke looked concerned. He was coming into her office. She wished he wouldn't.

'No, no, it's OK, really.'

'Then why no "Good morning"?'

'I'm sorry, Luke. I was miles away.'

47

'I could see that. You were looking at me but you weren't really seeing me.'

If only that were true, Carol thought. Perhaps I was seeing him properly for the first time. Drat Stacey for starting me thinking like this . . .

Luke smiled. 'But don't worry. I know that once you get into all those facts and figures you're living in a different world from the rest of us.'

Carol didn't answer and, after a moment's hesitation, he backed out of her office. Suddenly he seemed unsure of himself. 'If there was any problem, you would tell me, wouldn't you?'

'Yes.'

'Promise?'

'I promise.'

'Good. You know, I really don't want to lose you, you're far too valuable.'

She managed a nod and a brief smile and Luke, still looking perplexed, headed down the corridor to his office.

Carol took a deep breath and tried to drag her bemused mind back to her work. But his words lingered. He had asked her to promise to tell him if there was any problem and she'd agreed. Great. Any other problem and she would be able to keep that promise.

But not this one.

For the problem was Luke himself.

CHAPTER 3

Tuesday afternoon – Norfolk

Alison knelt down in the wet grass by Paul's grave. She took a small trowel from a plastic carrier bag and began to attack the newly sprouting weeds. It had rained all morning and the rich smell of damp earth and sodden vegetation rose up to surround her. The weeds came away easily.

Paul, she thought, Paul, I'm too young to be a widow! Will I ever get used to this?

She sat back on her heels, closed her eyes and dropped her head back on her shoulders. She could hear the breeze rustling through the leaves of the nearby trees and feel the pale warmth of the April sun on her face. She tried to summon up the feelings of peace that this place should bring her but, as usual, nothing could quell the inner rage she still felt at her loss.

It was a lovely spring day and, now that the rain had stopped, the sun was shining; but the wind was cool. Here in Norfolk, you could very rarely escape the wind, even on the hottest day in summer. Alison sighed, opened her eyes and leaned forward to finish her task.

'Ouch!'

The thorny branch of the rose bush she had planted last year caught the back of her hand. She dropped the

49

trowel and raised her hand to examine it. A drop of blood, jewel-bright, oozed to the surface.

'You should wear gloves, dear.'

She twisted round and looked up to see the vicar's elderly sister coming along the path towards her.

'Oh, Miss Robertson.'

'Does it hurt?'

'No, just a scratch.'

'Here.' The old lady took a clean handkerchief from her coat pocket. 'Now, let me tidy up for you.'

'Please don't. The grass is soaking – don't kneel down.'

'I couldn't even if I wanted to.' Miss Robertson smiled. 'Or if I did, you'd have to haul me up again when I'd done. Arthritis, you know.'

Before Alison could stop her, she stooped awkwardly and bundled the uprooted weeds and the trowel into the carrier bag. 'There, now,' she said.

Alison stood up and took the bag. 'Thank you.'

'Oh, my dear Mrs Cavendish, look at the grass stains on your slacks.'

'It doesn't matter, it's just an old pair.'

'Hmm.'

Miss Robertson was looking at her critically. Alison felt herself flushing. She knew what she must look like. Baggy grey corduroy slacks, the knees worn thin and now stained bright green; an old, washed-up Fair Isle sweater of Paul's which was unravelling at the cuffs and elbows. It was hardly an outfit for the 'lady of the manor', as some of the older villagers called her.

'Would you like to come to the vicarage for a cup of tea, my dear? That's what I was coming to ask you when I heard you call out.'

'That's kind of you, but I'm on my way to school to meet Matthew.'

Miss Robertson looked at her wristwatch. 'They won't

50

be getting out for half an hour yet. You have time for a cup of tea. Unless you have some shopping to do in the village?'

'No – I've no shopping to do.'

'Well, then?'

'All right, it's very kind of you . . .'

Miss Robertson was too well-mannered not to have offered an escape route. Alison could easily have taken it and pretended that she had to call in to the village shop, but she couldn't lie to the vicar's kindly sister. So she found herself walking with her through the quiet churchyard towards the gate that opened into the vicarage garden.

The path was still wet and the breeze rippled the surface of the puddles. The older graves, long untended, were covered with bedraggled grasses and last year's fallen leaves. Alison shivered as they walked into the shadow thrown by the church tower. The church was larger than you would expect. In fact it almost seemed to be too big for the tiny village that it served. But then perhaps there had been a bigger congregation in the area when it was first built.

Paul's family had worshipped here for centuries. Generations of Cavendishes had been baptised, married and buried here. She and Paul had been married here . . . Matthew had been baptised here, and here, long before his time, Paul had been buried . . .

'You're too intelligent not to have guessed that I haven't just invited you here for social chit-chat.'

Light filtered in through the creamy lace curtains as Miss Robertson poured the tea into apple-green ridged cups. The kind of teacups that were used year in and year out at functions in church halls the length and breadth of England.

Alison was taken aback by her words and didn't know

51

quite what to say so she raised her eyebrows politely and looked expectant.

'I don't like to pry,' the vicar's sister said.

But you're going to anyway. Alison hid her wry smile as she sipped her tea.

'But people in the village have been wondering whether you've come to any decision about the orchard?' The polite words formed a question.

Alison adopted delaying tactics. 'It hasn't been a proper orchard within living memory. In fact if it wasn't for the fact that it was named as such on an old map, no one would be able to tell that it ever *was* an orchard.'

'I know that, Mrs Cavendish, but village people are traditional and your late husband's family has owned Westbrook Hall and a large part of the surrounding land for a very long time.'

'Forgive me for saying so, Miss Robertson, but that's history. The Cavendishes might once have been a rich and powerful family, but that kind of power has gone out of fashion and there's not much of the estate left now.'

'And there'll be even less if you sell off the orchard.'

Alison was startled that Miss Robertson should speak so plainly and she glanced at her sharply.

'I'm sorry if I sound rude,' the vicar's sister said, 'and you can tell me if it's none of my business –'

And a lot of good that would do, Alison thought.

'– but I'm only preparing you for the unpleasantness you might have to face if you do decide to sell the land to that property developer Mr Leighton.'

'My goodness, this is a small village.'

Miss Robertson was not a bit abashed. 'If you mean by that that everybody's business is known and discussed, you're absolutely right. That's the way it's always been in small communities like this. The world may get older and more complicated, but human nature doesn't change.'

Alison sipped her tea deliberately. She took her time before she asked, 'Is the village very much opposed to the housing development, then?'

'Opinion is divided. Some people never want things to change. Some are more realistic.'

'And you?'

'I'm a realist, my dear. I don't see how you can possibly hang on to Westbrook Hall if you don't sell the land.'

'Oh.'

Alison stared down despondently at the faded Oriental carpet. So it was common knowledge that the Cavendish family was on the brink of penury, then? Like many old families, the changing patterns of society in the twentieth century had not been kind to them.

Things had been reaching crisis point even when Paul was a boy, but he had managed to keep his family home going once he started work as a photographer. And once he became sought after and could demand huge fees, the position had eased.

But, when he had died, killed accidentally on a photographic expedition to the Himalayas, not even the insurance settlement had been enough to stave off disaster. If Alison was going to save any part of the inheritance for Paul's son, something would have to go.

'And he seems to be quite sound, doesn't he?' Miss Robertson was smiling at her.

'I beg your pardon? Who is quite sound?'

'Mr Leighton. There was an article about him in the business section of my brother's newspaper. A profile, I think they call it. When I realized who it was, I read every word. What an interesting life – he's to be admired. But, more importantly, I think you'll be able to trust him.'

'Do you?'

'And he's so good-looking, isn't he?'

Alison was astonished. 'I suppose he is. But, Miss Robertson, what on earth has good looks got to do with it?'

'Oh, nothing at all, of course. I'm being feather-brained, as my brother would tell me.'

'Feather-brained? You?'

Miss Robertson laughed. 'Oh, yes, my dear Mrs Cavendish, just because I'm a respectable old spinster, it doesn't mean that I can't be as susceptible to a handsome man as the next woman!'

'No, I suppose not.'

Alison didn't know what else to say. She had just discovered that taking tea with the vicar's sister could be a very disconcerting occasion.

'Mrs Cavendish,' Miss Robertson seemed to be concerned by her long silence, 'when I saw you going into the churchyard, I thought you looked very despondent. I just thought that I should tell you that, if ever you feel you need a bolt-hole, or someone to talk things over with, you can come here and talk to me.'

'To you?'

'You look shocked. Am I being presumptuous?' The old lady's parchment skin had flushed to the delicate pink of hedge roses. Her faded blue eyes were anxious. 'Have I offended you.'

'No – of course not – it's just – I mean I'm a little surprised.'

'I suppose I'm being an interfering old busybody. My brother's always telling me not to meddle – but it's very hard not to want to do something when I see that people are unhappy –'

'Oh, please –'

'No, dear. I know how difficult it's been for you since your husband died.'

'Miss Robertson –'

'No, my dear, let me have my say. You have no parents

of your own to help you and you've had to cope with that imperious mother-in-law of yours who doesn't seem to have noticed how the strain is affecting you –'

'Stop!' The word came out like a sob.

'Oh, Mrs Cavendish, forgive me, I've gone too far!'

Miss Robertson looked so dismayed that Alison took control of her emotions. 'It's OK – don't worry.'

'I've been tactless.'

'Please – it's all right.'

'That's kind of you to say so, but there's something else –' She held up her hand as if to stop Alison's protest. 'You know, I really would welcome your company. You'd be doing me a favour if you dropped in to see me now and then.'

'Really?' Alison was surprised.

'Oh, yes. You probably know that I came here to help my young brother with the boys when their mother died?'

'Yes. I was told you gave up your job. Teaching, wasn't it? And you came to take charge of the vicarage.'

'It was my duty to help but I did so willingly. The two boys were so loving, so sweet, it was just like having my own family. But I never imagined that I would be staying here so long.'

'Why not?'

'My brother is a vicar, my dear. I thought every single unmarried or widowed woman in the parish would set her cap at him. I was sure that it wouldn't be too long before Ian married again. In fact I hoped that he would. It took me a long time to realize that the job of looking after the boys was mine for as long as I wanted it.'

'But why – I mean why do you think he hasn't married again?'

Miss Robertson sighed. 'I think Ian was so much in love with Margaret that he had the crazy idea he would be betraying her if he found someone else.'

'I can understand that.'

'Can you? I'm sorry to hear it.'

'Why do you say that?'

'Because you're a young, beautiful and loving woman. I don't think Paul would have wanted you to remain alone for the rest of your life.'

Alison rose swiftly. 'I must be going. It's time to collect Matthew from school.'

'You're angry with me and I don't blame you.' Miss Robertson got to her feet more slowly and took Alison's cup away from her. She put it down on an occasional table. Alison didn't know what to say to her and Miss Robertson continued, 'Mrs Cavendish, please come and see me again – and bring Matthew. Now that my nephews have grown up and left the nest, I miss young people's company.'

Alison wasn't angry so much as disturbed by what Miss Robertson had said. Also she was embarrassed. She hurried through the narrow hallway. A soft sound of distress made her turn back as she opened the front door.

The old lady looked so anxious that she found herself saying. 'I'm not angry – really. And I will call again – and I'd like to bring Matthew.'

'Oh, I'm so pleased.'

'And, Miss Robertson –'

'Yes?'

'If I decide to sell the orchard to Greg Leighton, you'll be the first person outside the family to know.'

'Mum, may I go to Oliver's after tea?'

Alison and Matthew were alone in the kitchen of the old house. They sat and faced each other across the scrubbed pine table. A soothing warmth radiated across the stone-flagged floor from the tiled recess where the Aga burned night and day. This was a comforting place to be and Alison cherished the times she spent alone here with her small son.

'Mum?'

'Oh, Oliver's. I suppose so. But are you sure his mother won't mind?'

'No, everybody goes there. She makes chocolate cake.'

'I see. Mrs Morton has stolen your affections with her superior chocolate cake!'

'Mum!' For a moment Matthew looked anxious but then he saw Alison's smile and he grinned. 'You make nice chocolate cake, too, but everybody can go there to play and they make a noise and . . . and . . .'

'And you can't have such good fun here because of your grandmother,' Alison finished for him, and Oliver looked serious again.

'But it's OK when Gran goes off to Aunt Daffy's, isn't it, Mum? I mean, you always let me have my friends home then, don't you?'

'Aunt Daphne,' Alison corrected him automatically, but she smiled nevertheless.

She was filled with love and gratitude by her son's loyalty. Even at the tender age of eight, Matthew knew that his mother had a difficult time coping with his grandmother and he didn't want to make life more difficult for her.

'OK, Matthew. Finish your meal and I'll walk with you to Oliver's house.'

'Thanks, Mum. Ruth will bring me home again.'

Ruth Morton was Oliver's older sister. She was a cheerful teenager who didn't mind helping her own mother with her young brother and sister. Sometimes, when Ruth walked back with Matthew, she would stay and chat to Alison. Perhaps she was grateful for a small break from her own happy but crowded home.

A few weeks ago she had offered to sit with Matthew and old Mrs Cavendish if Alison wanted to have a night out.

A night out? Alison had been startled. She'd considered the idea and dismissed it immediately. The very thought of it was ridiculous. She had nowhere to go and, more important, no one to go with. No, she didn't think that she would be taking Ruth up on her offer in the foreseeable future . . .

When she got back from the village, her mother-in-law was watching television in the first-floor sitting-room. Small and beautifully proportioned, the room was nevertheless north-facing and difficult to keep warm. Alison knelt to make up the fire and Lilian Cavendish acknowledged her presence with a petulant sniff.

'Where have you been, Alison?' Her old, thin, aristocratic voice was querulous.

'Just down to the village. Matthew has gone to play with his friend, Oliver Morton.'

'Again? Do you think that's wise?'

'I'm not sure what you mean.'

'Really, Alison. You know exactly what I mean. Matthew spends too much time with the village children.'

'The children he plays with are his friends. It really doesn't matter where they live. You've told me yourself that Paul had friends in the village.'

Perhaps her mother-in-law sensed Alison's underlying edge of steel and her tone became conciliatory. 'Yes, my dear, Paul was always very democratic, just as his father was. But remember, when he was only a little older than Matthew he went away to school. The right kind of school.'

'And Matthew won't be going to his father's old school because I simply can't afford it.'

'Oh, Alison . . .'

Her mother-in-law's voice quavered and Alison felt a twinge of remorse – and then angry with herself for feeling it. She had been brutally frank but she had spoken nothing but the truth.

'Look, I know you speak like this out of concern for your grandson,' she began.

'Paul's only child –'

'But he really won't come to any harm, you know. The local school is very good – and, no, I refuse to worry about the kind of people he'll meet there. Now can I bring you a tray?'

Mrs Cavendish senior was silent for so long that Alison thought she might have gone too far this time. Because she had loved Paul so much, she always tried to imagine how difficult it must be for his mother – not only to have lost her beloved son, but to be left in near penury with a daughter-in-law she had never really approved of.

Poor old thing, Alison often thought. But now she knew that her reserves of sympathy were just about used up. Am I at the end of my tether? Do I really look so miserable that the vicar's sister has to come running after me in the churchyard to offer tea and sympathy?

'Alison! Look!' Her mother-in-law's voice broke into her wistful reverie.

She looked down to find that the old lady had leaned forward in her chair to gaze at the television set. 'That's your friend, isn't it? What's her name? Francine!'

Alison looked at the screen and smiled. It was indeed Francine. She looked as if she were thoroughly enjoying herself talking to – who was it? Oh, yes, Matt McConnell, the American movie star.

'What programme is this?' Alison asked.

'Oh, it's not a programme – it's a trailer – is that what you call it? A trailer for some film magazine programme on later this week. She's so clever, isn't she, your friend?'

'Yes.' Alison smiled, glad that Lilian Cavendish had dropped the subject of Matthew's schooling.

'And Daphne says that she remarkably well-mannered and polite, too – for that type of person, I mean.'

Alison knew very well what her mother-in-law meant

by 'that type of person'; she meant someone who didn't come out of 'the top drawer' – another of her ridiculously outdated phrases. However, she was too weary to challenge her. She didn't want another demonstration of her snobbish values.

How on earth could this woman have given birth to Paul? she wondered for the umpteenth time. Paul's older sister Daphne was exactly like her mother but Paul must have had the good fortune to take after his kindly and intelligent father. Charles Cavendish had died only one year before Alison had met Paul but he lived on in his son's memory. How she wished she could have known him.

'Oh, by the way, Alison, your friend phoned when you were out earlier.' The early evening news had begun on the television and Lilian Cavendish turned away from the set, bored.

'Francine phoned?'

'I beg your pardon?'

Her mother-in-law frowned and Alison resisted the temptation to shake her.

'You said that Francine phoned earlier.'

'No, I didn't. I said that – your – friend – phoned.' Lilian Cavendish enunciated each word slowly as if she were talking to an idiot and Alison felt her jaw clenching.

'So, which friend do you mean?'

'The other one – oh, you know – they were all here on the day of Paul's funeral.'

Alison saw the familiar haunted look suddenly appear in her mother-in-law's eyes and she spoke as gently as she could. 'Do you mean Carol – Carol Kennedy?'

'Is that the untidy, plump young woman? No, I don't mean her. It was the other one – the ordinary-looking one – Sophie. That's right, Sophie – such a pretty name for a plain little mouse.'

Alison took a deep breath and let it out slowly. Why

did Mrs Cavendish take such pleasure in belittling her friends? She had described Carol as plump and untidy when she could have remembered her as lively and having a brilliant brain. Sophie was a plain little mouse instead of a decent, kindly and loyal friend. And, even Francine, who had obviously won her admiration, was not exactly the right kind of person!

'Sophie. Did she leave any message?'

'No and she didn't leave a message the other time either.'

'Other time?'

'Yes, she called once before – or maybe twice. Daphne was here, she answered – I forget to tell you.'

'I see.' Alison controlled a surge of anger. She could never decide whether her mother-in-law was genuinely becoming increasingly forgetful because of her advancing years or whether there was another agenda.

'But don't worry. I think she said she'd call again. Or did she want you to call her? I can't remember.'

'Then I'll phone her as soon as brought up your tray. Or would you like to come down to the kitchen for your meal?'

'The kitchen?' Her mother-in-law's lips formed a moue of distaste.

'Yes, the kitchen. It's much warmer in there.'

'Oh, I'm sure it is, dear, but I don't think so.'

A surge of rebellion almost overwhelmed Alison. She wondered what kind of logic could make it alright for Paul's mother to avoid ever entering her own kitchen whilst her daughter-in-law was expected, not only to do the major part of the work, but also to wait on her hand and foot.

After all, she isn't seriously ill, Alison thought. She's simply old and weary. As weary as I am coping with the grief and the problems caused by Paul's untimely death. And Paul's sister, Daphne, is no help at all. Oh, she calls over constantly to see her mother, I'll give her that, but the pair of them just sit and wind each other up. They go on and on about the problems but they've never come up with one practical solution. I don't know how much more of this I can stand!

'Is something the matter, Alison?'

'Matter?'

'You've gone quite pink. I do hope you're not coming down with anything.'

'That would be very inconvenient, wouldn't it?'

'I don't know what you mean.' The older woman looked startled.

'Don't you?' Alison faced her grimly and her mother-in-law flushed.

'If you mean who would run the house, you mustn't worry, dear.'

'Really?'

'Of course not. We'd simply ask Mrs Simpson to come in for a few more hours. I'm sure she needs the money.'

'Ye-es,' Alison sighed. 'And we haven't got it. No, don't worry, I'm not ill. Now, I'll go and get your tray.'

Alison had reached the door when Mrs Cavendish suddenly called out, 'Oh, I almost forgot, there was another phone call for you. Mr Leighton – he wants you to call back as soon as possible.'

Alison gripped the door handle. 'As soon as possible?'

'Yes, but I'm afraid you'll have to wait until tomorrow now.'

'And why's that?'

'Well, Mr Leighton said that he'd be leaving his London office early. He wanted you to call before four o'clock. I'm so sorry it slipped my mind, dear.'

Alison stepped out of the room and closed the door behind her with exaggerated calm. As she went down the back stairs, once only used by servants, she found that she was shaking with rage.

Slipped her mind, indeed! Alison believed nothing of the sort. Paul's mother was 'forgetful' because her sense of priorities was different from Alison's. They were different from those of most normal, kindly people, come to that. Anything that didn't concern Lilian Cavendish just wasn't important enough to remember!

But this last 'slip of the memory' was deliberate, Alison was sure of it. Lilian knew very well that Greg Leighton wanted to buy part of the property, the old orchard, and she was opposing the sale every inch of the way.

It wasn't that she minded losing the orchard, it was the idea of having houses built there. The distance between the Hall and the village couldn't be far enough as far as she was concerned. She wanted to keep the sense of being isolated from 'ordinary' people.

Alison warmed up the soup that she had made earlier and was still fuming as she set the tray. Fortunately her mother-in-law was on her best behaviour when she gave her her meal, and even asked whether they should make the effort to watch Francine's film interview together.

'Perhaps,' Alison muttered and she returned as quickly as she could to her refuge – the kitchen. She made herself a cup of tea and sank thankfully into the old armchair by the Aga.

Is this what my life has become? she mused. Just getting through every day as best I can? When Paul was alive his mother wouldn't have dreamed of behaving like this. We would all have eaten together in the dining-room and, although she obviously didn't approve, she never said a word when Paul insisted on helping me in the kitchen.

Whenever he was away on an assignment, Alison remembered, Paul had always insisted that Mrs Simpson should work extra hours. He knew what his mother was like. Thank goodness for Matthew, Alison thought.

And, of course, Matthew was the reason why every effort she had to make was worthwhile.

His father had died, so tragically before he should have done, so it was up to her to try and salvage something for his son. Paul had never been concerned about money or privilege, but Alison knew how much Westbrook Hall had meant to him. Paul's sense of family and continuity had been very strong. She knew how much he would have wanted Matthew to be able to go on living there.

She was roused by the sound of the doorbell. She smiled and got up to leave the kitchen. And then she paused. Why would Ruth Morton bring Matthew back to the grand entrance at the front of the house when she had long ago got into the habit of coming to the back door?

She shivered as she crossed the lofty, oak-panelled entrance hall. The house was cold, cold and – dare she even think it? – damp. If she sold the orchard she could use some of the money to carry out much needed renovations and repairs. Yes, she would call Greg Leighton first thing in the morning; she would tell him that she was ready to discuss his offer.

But, as it turned out, she didn't have to wait that long. When she opened the door, he was standing there.

And he was angry.

CHAPTER 4

'Don't you believe in returning telephone calls, Mrs Cavendish?'

Greg Leighton was wearing a dark business suit. He had loosened his silk tie and undone the top couple of buttons of his blue shirt. The result was casual but his tone was controlled and formal. He was attempting to conceal his anger with a perfunctory smile – and only just succeeding. Alison had to drop her eyes to conceal her amused reaction.

She was tall but he was almost a head taller, she found herself staring at the dark brown hair revealed in the open V at his neck. Vigorous, curling hair . . . she wondered how much of the broad expanse of his chest it covered . . .

'Mrs Cavendish?'

'Oh – yes?'

She felt the slow burn of embarrassment creep up her neck and begin to spread out across her face. She was reluctant to meet his eyes, nevertheless she raised her head. She prayed that he had not been aware of where she had been looking – and what she had been thinking . . .

But his dark eyes revealed no knowledge of her intimate imaginings, instead they snapped with impatience. 'I phoned you today – I left a message for you to call me.'

'Yes, I know, and I'm sorry –'

'You *were* intending to call me, I take it?'

'Of course. Why on earth wouldn't I?'

'Because I've phoned you at least half a dozen times in the past fortnight and you've simply ignored me.'

'Oh, no –'

'When I first approached you about selling part of the estate to me, you promised that you would think about it –'

'Yes, I know – and I have –'

'Well, then, if you've decided against it without even letting me show you the plans, I wish you'd had the good manners to tell me so instead of wasting my time like this.'

Alison glared at him. She had no doubt that he had called her – why should he lie? And she knew very well that her mother-in-law would have 'forgotten' to pass the messages on. It would be interesting to find out why she had finally bothered to do so today. Probably she thought that she might not be able to get away with her delaying tactics much longer.

But that was another problem. Right now, Greg Leighton's hectoring tone had stung her into anger.

'And, of course, your time is so valuable that your needs take precedence over everyone else's,' she said. Her words were reasonable but the underlying tone was glacial.

'I – what do you mean?'

Perhaps he hadn't expected her to react that way and he was momentarily thrown off course. The course of righteous indignation, Alison thought with wry humour. Oh, he might be big and important and good-looking; but sometimes grown men, even intelligent, successful men, could behave just like small boys.

'I mean that I know very well that you're clever and prosperous,' she continued, 'the kind of man who is

66

profiled in the upmarket newspapers. And no doubt you expect us lesser mortals to jump to attention whenever you issue commands –'

'I don't issue commands – you make me sound like some kind of – of despot!'

'Very well – what do you do? Give orders? Whenever you give orders, then.'

'Mrs Cavendish –'

'But just because every minute of your day is taken up with making more and more money –'

'It's not! Mrs Cavendish – what's the matter?'

'The matter?'

'You – you're crying –'

'I'm not!'

'You are –'

'Don't shout at me!'

'I'm not shouting – look – come here –'

But it was Greg Leighton who came to her. Dropping the briefcase that Alison hadn't noticed that he was carrying until that moment, he stepped out of the fading sunshine of the April evening into the cool, echoing hall.

She backed away from him and at the same moment the idiotic thought that she shouldn't have kept a guest standing on the doorstep floated up into her conscious mind. 'Yes, that's right, how rude of me . . .'

'Mrs Cavendish –'

'Do come in . . .'

'Hush – please –'

The next moment he had taken hold of her shoulders. The gesture was both reassuring and restraining. She tried briefly to move away, but he pulled her towards him and, as his arms enfolded her, she stopped resisting. She dropped her head on to his chest and gave way to a storm of grief.

Ever since Paul's death, she had felt like a punchbag in a gym, unable to avoid the blows rained on her. Blows so relentless, so severe, that she felt as though she had finally had all the stuffing knocked out of her. Mindlessly, she sagged against this man – this stranger – gratefully accepting his support.

He didn't say anything. He neither soothed nor patted, he simply held her until her sobs subsided. But, even after the sobbing had ceased, she was strangely unwilling to move out of the circle of his arms.

'Mum – where are you?' Her son's voice echoed through the house behind her.

Alison stepped backwards and lifted her head languorously. The look she saw in his eyes almost started her off crying again. 'Please don't,' she whispered.

'Don't what?'

'Look at me like that – as if you cared what happens – I'm not used to it.'

She was horrified to see the concern replaced by self-loathing. 'What is it?' she asked.

'I shouldn't have come here and spoken to you the way I did.'

'Why not?'

'I should have realized what you must have been through – I've been totally insensitive –'

'No – it's all right – really –'

'Mum! Here you are!'

Matthew emerged from a doorway at the back of the hall and came running towards her. A pretty, fair-haired teenage girl was not far behind him.

As Alison turned to greet her son she heard Greg Leighton murmur, 'I'd better go.'

'No, wait –' she called. 'I really do want to talk to you about the sale of the land – can you come tomorrow?'

'No, I have to go away on business – I'll be away for about a week – that's why I was hoping to start negotiations today.'

'Oh, I see.' Alison looked at him helplessly.

'Mum?' Matthew tugged at her sleeve.

'Yes? Oh, sorry, Matthew. This is Mr Leighton. Mr Leighton, this is my son, Matthew and our friend, Ruth Morton.'

Greg Leighton smiled at both of them and Ruth stared up at him with wide-eyed appreciation.

'Thanks for bringing Matthew home, Ruth,' Alison said.

'Oh, that's all right, Mrs Cavendish.' Ruth seemed to have difficulty in tearing her eyes away from their visitor but eventually she managed it. 'Listen – I've got an idea!' she exclaimed.

'What's that?' Alison smiled at her.

'Well, I wasn't being nosy but I couldn't help overhearing that you and Mr Leighton want to talk business. So why don't I get Matthew his supper and get him ready for bed and you could talk right now?'

'Yeah!' Matthew said and Alison felt the slightest twinge of jealousy.

'Oh, I don't know, Ruth, I know Matthew would like that, but Mrs Cavendish will need her supper, too.'

'The old lady? Sorry! I mean your mother-in-law? That's no problem; I'm used to helping my mum with our gran. Now you just leave everything to me and go into the study or somewhere. I'll bring you a cup of tea – or anything you like.'

'I've got an even better idea.' Greg Leighton had been listening, thoughtfully, but now he smiled.

'And what's that?' Alison asked. She had a faint suspicion that she wasn't going to like what he said next. She was right.

'I think we should take your young friend up on her offer but instead of going into the study I'll take you out for a meal. Would that be all right, Ruth?'

'Sure – so long as I can phone my mum and tell her what's happening.'

'Tell her I'll make sure that you get home safe,' Greg said.

'Wait a minute –' Things had moved too fast for Alison. 'I thought the whole idea was to talk business?'

'Oh, it is. Haven't you read in those newspaper profiles that men like me get their victims wined and dined and then cheat them out of millions?'

Matthew looked up with owl-like eyes. First at Greg Leighton's face, then at his mother's and then back again. 'You're kidding,' he said. 'You wouldn't cheat my mother.'

'Too right. I just want to take her out and try to get her to relax a little. Do you think that's a good idea?'

'Yep.' Matthew turned to pull at Ruth's hand. 'Come on, Ruth, we'll have supper in the kitchen.'

'Matthew!' Alison called after him in a sudden panic.

'Yes, Mum?'

'Don't you mind?'

'Mind what?'

'That I'm going out?'

'No. Why should I?'

Alison was at a loss. She didn't want her son to be clingy, but she supposed she wanted him to miss her just a little bit. Then, suddenly, it was all right again when Matthew let go of Ruth's hand and came racing back across the hall. She scooped him up into a fierce bear-hug.

As she put him down again he whispered, 'Don't worry, I'll be all right. But Ruth says you'd better go and have a shower and get changed. You can't go out like that.'

'It seems everything has been decided for me.' She shrugged as she turned to face the tall man waiting by the door. 'Would you mind if I just go up and put some other clothes on?'

'I wouldn't mind at all. I'd be delighted.' He grinned

and Alison suddenly realized what a sight she must have looked in her grass-stained slacks and Paul's old sweater.

'Would you like to wait in the study? I could get you a drink or something.'

'No, that's all right.' Greg picked up his briefcase and closed the door. 'I'll find my way through to the kitchen, if you don't mind. I'd rather chat to Matthew and Ruth than sit in solitary splendour.'

'OK – Oh, lord –' Alison broke off.

'What is it? Is there some problem?'

'No problem – it's just that I completely forgot to collect my mother-in-law's tea tray and take her a cup of tea –'

'Don't worry about it. You just go and get ready and I'll ask Ruth to see to things.'

'But Mrs Cavendish won't be expecting –'

'It doesn't matter – I'm sure Ruth will explain things perfectly. Now go and get ready – *please*.'

'Yes, sir!' Alison couldn't help saying as she sped up the stairs.

In her wonder and confusion at the strange turn of events she didn't remember about the other phone call she was supposed to make.

Carol looked glumly at the mess in her kitchen. When she had left that morning, Alan had been drinking his coffee and reading the newspaper.

'Bye,' she'd called, and had received a grunt in reply.

Carol sighed. Alan had stacked his dirty dishes on the bench top along with all the others, making no attempt to wash any of them. Once, she would have smiled indulgently and set to and cleaned up, but she didn't feel at all like smiling now. When had she lost her sense of humour? She couldn't remember.

She had already dumped her briefcase in the hallway and now she tried to find room for the couple of bags of shopping on the table. They perched there precariously, nudging aside the sugar bowl, the salt and pepper, the sauce bottles and the empty marmalade jar.

Carol took off her jacket and began to unpack the bags. With any luck she could store the groceries and clear up the kitchen before Alan came home. She might even manage to have his meal ready and waiting for him.

She was dog-tired. The work she was doing for Travers' Transport was interesting but it was demanding. Most days it left her drained and ready to go home and put her feet up and relax. Instead she had had to struggle round the supermarket to catch up with her shopping and face the usual drive home.

However, the dinner she planned required no great culinary skills. Sophie had taught her how to make a keen spaghetti bolognese while they were students together. Alan had liked it then and, even now, it was a way of cheering him up.

Cheering him up? Carol thought half-mutinously. *Why should it be up to me to cheer him up – what about me? Does he ever stop to wonder if I'm happy?*

She took a litre and a half bottle of red wine out of one of the bags and opened it. It was cheap wine – you could tell that even before you looked at the label because it had a screw cap instead of a cork. But she intended to use some of it in the bolognese sauce and their budget just didn't run to pouring expensive wines into the cooking pot.

With a nod to her absent husband and his strange rules, she refrained from putting on the television and set to work. It didn't take too long to clear the kitchen and wash the dishes but, by the time she started slicing the onions and crushing the garlic, she was ready to pour herself a glass of wine.

When the kitchen was gleaming and full of the smells of winey, garlicky sauce, Carol, glass in hand, wandered through into the living-room and groaned anew. How could she have forgotten the mess in here? She glanced at her watch. Half-past seven. Alan had been working late recently on his new project but he was usually home by now.

I might just have time she thought, if I stuff all the papers under the cushions and dust only the bits that you can see. Swiftly, she gathered up newspapers, magazines and unanswered correspondence – some of it not even opened – and hid everything from sight, then she flicked around with a duster.

When she had finished she turned off the overhead light and in the glow of the smaller lamps the room looked quite presentable. And I won't have to vacuum the floor, she thought; the light's dim enough to hide the fluff and the crumbs on the carpet. With a sigh of contentment, Carol sank down on to the sofa with her glass of wine. She kicked off her shoes and lifted her feet up.

She drew her brows together as she wondered if there was anything else she ought to have done. She ticked it all off in her mind. She had set the kitchen table with a clean checked cloth – the only one that didn't need either washing or ironing – and set up the cheeseboard and a bowl of fruit. The bolognese sauce was cooking gently and she had left a large pan of water to come to the boil slowly. The pasta was ready on the bench to be dropped into the pan the moment Alan walked through the door.

I think I've covered everything. Carol's frown eased away. Now, if I can just have five minutes to unwind before he arrives I might be able to meet the poor man with a smile. Not that he deserves it!

The glass of wine had helped the process of relaxation. Normally, Carol didn't drink very much. Every now and then, they would treat themselves to a bottle of wine to

73

have with their meal but she couldn't ever remember a time when she had drunk alone.

Pity Alan wasn't home yet to share this moment of peace with her . . . She'd been looking forward to seeing her husband tonight. She needed to see him. She felt herself flushing as she acknowledged that his favourite meal and the large bottle of wine were intended to achieve more than simply cheering him up.

How long was it since they'd made love? Carol was dismayed to realize that she couldn't remember. No wonder I've suddenly started seeing Luke Travers as some kind of romantic hero, she mused.

Angry with herself, she tried to push all thoughts of Luke aside. But they wouldn't go away. Wearily, she sank back against the cushions, closed her eyes and, with an almost guilty pleasure, let her mind replay what had happened earlier that day . . .

'I'm off home now. Will you man the telephone until I get back?'

Carol blinked and glanced up from her computer screen. Stacey stood in the doorway.

'Don't I always?' Carol asked.

'You're a pal!'

Stacey waved and Carol heard her high heels tap their way along the corridor to the exit from the temporary building.

Luke had promised that the new office block would have altogether more luxurious facilities. Until then, Stacey chose not to eat sandwiches in 'the shack' as she called it. Her new acquisition, a second-hand white Vauxhall Nova, meant that she could travel the short distance home to her mother's cooking.

Carol and Stacey had to take separate lunch hours otherwise Stacey had assured her that she could have come too. The limited accommodation in the portable office block meant that Luke couldn't really take on more help, although the volume of business demanded that he should.

Luke . . . Carol thought.

As soon as Stacey came back he would stop work and take the very few steps it needed to bring him to Carol's office.

'Lunch, Carol?' was all he usually said, and she would save the file she was working on, close it and switch off the computer. Then she would go with him to the little pub that served the most delicious lunches.

There was absolutely nothing questionable about those lunches together, she assured herself. As she had told Stacey earlier, Luke really did talk business and there had never, ever been anything remotely personal about their relationship.

So why did she suddenly feel that she ought to find some excuse – some reason why she should not go with him to the White Swan today? Was it because of Stacey's teasing about him being a 'knockout'?

Carol knew how attractive he was. It would have been hard not to notice from the start his tall frame and his chiselled features and the way a thick, shining strand of dark blond hair always flopped forward across his brow . . .

Stop it! Carol screamed inwardly. *What on earth is the matter with me? Luke Travers is my boss and I am a respectable married woman. I'm married to Alan Kennedy who is good-looking, clever and . . .*

And what?

Carol's thought processes derailed abruptly. Could she also say that Alan was loving, caring, kind? Perhaps he had been once but, now, she couldn't honestly remember a single day that he hadn't criticized her, whether by silent disapproval or by outright carping.

And usually he was right to complain, she thought.

Let's face it, she was not the sort of wife he wanted. To her horror she felt a dangerous pricking at the back of her eyes and she rubbed at them to try and stem the flow of tears.

'What's the matter, Carol? Eye-strain?' Luke was standing in the doorway. She hadn't heard him approach.

Hastily she opened her top drawer and took out a tissue. She dabbed at her eyes and took her time before she answered him. 'Yes, that's right.'

'I've told you, you should take the recommended breaks while you're working with the computer. I don't want you suing me in future years.'

'I do take breaks – and I won't be suing you. It's just that this particular piece of work is complicated and – and I probably got carried away . . .'

'OK. Now let me carry you off to the Swan for your lunch. Stacey's back – I've just heard her parking with the usual panache.'

'Oh, no, she hasn't bumped your Rover again, has she?'

'No, I think it was your Fiesta.'

'No!' Carol rose to her feet in panic. With all the bills they had to struggle to pay, damage to her precious little car would be the last straw.

'Carol,' Luke looked sheepish, 'I was joking. I looked out and saw her coming. Now get your jacket on and let's go.'

'No.' Carol let out a sigh and sat down again.

'Look, I'm sorry, it was a rotten joke but it wasn't that serious. Don't be angry with me.'

'I'm not angry. I just can't let you go on buying me lunch like this.'

'Why not? Seeing as I can't provide proper facilities at the moment, surely I owe you a lunch now and then?'

'But it's more than now and then, isn't it? It's become

almost every day.'

'You're right. You'll bankrupt Travers' Transport if you go on eating french fries the way you do. So I suggest that today, you buy my lunch. How's that?'

'Oh, Luke . . .' Carol began to laugh weakly.

'That's better.'

'What's the joke?' Stacey had appeared behind Luke and she questioned them, her face bright with interest.

'No joke,' Carol answered. 'In fact I don't know why I'm laughing; he was being rude about the amount of french fries I consume.'

'Mr Travers, you're no gentleman,' Stacey bantered.

'You don't know how right you are,' said Carol.

'Explain.'

'Well, the remark about my appetite was nothing compared to what he was implying about your driving.'

'Mr Travers!' Stacey exclaimed in mock indignation.

They all laughed and, by the time Carol had put on her jacket and they had left the office, she had almost forgotten that she had decided that she really shouldn't go to lunch with Luke Travers again . . .

Carol awoke with a sense of panic. She knew time had passed and yet she hadn't been aware of falling asleep. As she forced herself into full awareness she glanced at her watch.

Nine o'clock!

She leapt up from the sofa and her wine glass tumbled off the sofa on to the floor. She caught her breath as she noticed the stains on the sofa and the carpet. It must have fallen out of my hand when I dropped off to sleep, she thought in dismay.

She stared down gloomily. The sofa was old, it had come with them when they moved here, and the cover would slip off and wash. But the carpet had been new. Would she be able to remove the dark red stain from

77

their cream-coloured carpet easily? she wondered. But she didn't wonder about it too long because something else was demanding her attention.

Burning! She could smell burning!

She rushed through into the kitchen. An acrid smell caught at the back of her throat and she coughed and spluttered as she seized the pan and lifted it off the cooker. The bolognese sauce that she had prepared so lovingly was a sticky, blackened mess. It was past saving.

She dumped the pan in the sink. The hot metal hissed in the water and the kitchen filled with steam.

'No,' Carol sobbed. 'Oh, no . . .'

At that moment Alan walked into the kitchen. He stopped and stared at her, saying nothing.

'Alan!' she screamed. 'You're late! Where were you?'

'I had to work late.'

'You could have phoned me –'

'Why? You knew I was working late – I told you.'

'When? When did you tell me?'

As she heard herself shrieking at him, part of her knew that this was all wrong. She had planned such a lovely homecoming for him – the house looking tidy for once and his favourite meal cooking – why, oh, why had she fallen asleep . . .?

'I told you last week when I explained my new project to you. I *thought* you weren't listening.'

'I was – I was – it's very interesting!'

Alan smiled faintly. 'Interesting or not – you didn't pay enough attention to remember my new work schedule.'

He walked over to the sink and peered into the pan. 'This, I take it, is my supper.'

Carol hurried over to the cooker and was relieved to find that at least the water in the large pan had not quite boiled dry.

'Well, it was – I fell asleep but it's not too late. Look, I can still cook the pasta – and if I open a tin of chopped tomatoes and grate some cheese –'

'Forget it. I'm tired and I'm not very hungry, anyway.' Alan poured himself a glass of wine. 'I'll just take this through to the sitting-room and relax for a while.'

Carol's face was grim as she watched him walk out of the room. It was too much to hope that he wouldn't notice the wine stains on the carpet. The carpet that his parents had helped them pay for.

Wearily, she turned back to the sink and filled the burnt pan with water. Her head was aching and she was hungry. She boiled the kettle and made herself a mug of hot chocolate. Then, grabbing a whole new packet of custard cream biscuits, she went straight upstairs to bed.

CHAPTER 5

Tuesday evening – London

'Goodnight, Miss Rowe.'

The security guard smiled at Francine as she walked through the deserted foyer of Television Centre. She returned his smile tiredly, pushed through the glass doors and then headed out across the car park towards her latest reward to herself, her new silver Puma sports coupé.

Francine worked hard and she had no one to spend her considerable earnings on except herself. She was neither mean nor greedy and she would have helped her parents in any way she could – she knew they were struggling to make ends meet on her father's meagre pension. But they wouldn't let her. They wouldn't even speak to her, as a matter of fact. She had given up hoping that they would ever change their minds and welcome her home again.

So, why shouldn't she have the best car she could afford, the kind of clothes that went with her lifestyle and a luxury riverside apartment? She knew that her parents would never believe that she had bought all these things herself – they would think that her 'fancy man', as her father put it, had provided them for her.

Her father was wrong. Everything she owned had been paid for with her own money. Over the years she'd

worked and saved and made one or two sound invest-
ments. Financially, she was completely independent.

But what of her emotions? Francine wondered as she
pulled out into the steady flow of traffic. Am I as
emotionally independent as I've always imagined I
am? Her self-sufficient way of life had always been a
source of satisfaction to her. Now and then over the years
she would think about her friends from university and,
perhaps a little smugly, compare their lives with her own.

But it gave her no satisfaction to see that Carol, just as
she, Francine, had predicted, was becoming a domestic
drudge, totally committed to putting Alan and his career
first in spite of the fact that she probably had the better
brain.

And Alison . . . she, too, had married for love, only to
have her happy life snatched away from her by that tragic
accident. Now the poor girl was stuck with bringing up
her son alone in a draughty mansion with very little
money and no help from her late husband's snobbish
mother and sister.

Sophie had a limited form of independence, of course.
But what a boring life she must have. Living alone with
her widowed mother in that ghastly northern industrial
town. No men friends that Francine had ever heard
about to liven up her nights and spending her days
teaching lumpish teenagers.

Francine often thought that of the four of them she was
the lucky one. And yet why call it luck? She had worked
damned hard for what she had. So, it was difficult for her
to admit that her treasured privacy sometimes felt like
loneliness.

Most of the time her own company was enough for
her, she supposed. But she despised herself for her
pathetic elation when occasionally her lover said he
could stay the night instead of hurrying home to his wife.

She was beginning to hate the fact that she never knew

for certain when she would see him. Whether he would manage to find time to call at her apartment after work, or whether she was destined to spend another evening alone in her 'ivory tower', as he had humorously named her new home. Her impregnable, fairytale apartment high above the capital city.

But girls in fairytales usually had a prince somewhere, didn't they? A handsome prince who came along and rescued them. Do I need to be rescued? Francine mused ruefully . . .

The streets were wet from the recent shower and reflected lights from shops and fast food outlets glimmered on the roads and pavements. It was long past the rush hour, but the roads were still busy as late workers hurried home and pleasure-seekers headed for the West End in buses and taxis.

Damn it . . . Francine realized that, tired as she was, she had automatically turned towards her old apartment in Fulham. Another five minutes and she would have been there.

It had been on her mind lately that she really ought to call by and see if there were any messages for her. She had changed her phone number when she moved and, wishing to stay ex-directory, she'd decided it would be unwise to give the new number even to the young couple who had bought her apartment from her. So she had promised them that she would keep in touch. If there was anything urgent to deal with, they were to contact her secretary at Television Centre.

I could call in now, I suppose. She smiled, finding herself tempted to see what they had done with the place. She knew they had planned to redecorate. No, she decided, it might be inconvenient. They haven't been married very long and they probably look forward to uninterrupted evenings together. I'll phone them as I said I would.

And, besides, I should get home . . . he might be waiting for me . . .

After finding a suitable side street, Francine pulled in and turned round. Soon she was heading back along a route that would skirt around London's West End before finally crossing the River Thames via London Bridge.

Her journey home now took half an hour or more, depending on the traffic, but the extra twenty minutes' driving time was more than compensated for by the sheer luxury of her new apartment and the most dramatically beautiful vista in London.

And another bonus was the car parking. All her years in Fulham, Francine had resented having to pay for a resident's permit in order to park in her own street. She couldn't even be sure of finding a place near her own front door. But, now, secure parking came as part of the deal.

The lift from the underground garage was warm and well-lit. Francine was alone and she allowed herself to relax and close her eyes as she was carried up to her apartment. She stepped into the foyer, closed the door behind her and shrugged off her jacket. She pushed aside a packing case to gain entry to the cloakroom and sighed at the sight of even more packing cases stacked up against one wall. Then she forced herself to dismiss them from her mind and closed the door.

There were no lights on in the living-room but she knew he was there. The door was ajar and she could hear speech coming from the television set. She smiled. Whenever he arrived anywhere, even at her villa in Spain, the first thing he did was switch on the television and surf through the channels. It seemed that he could never leave work completely behind him. She entered the room quietly.

He wasn't actually watching television. She saw his silhouetted shape standing at the floor-to-ceiling win-

dow. He had taken off his jacket and he was standing at
ease as he looked out at the stunning view of Tower
Bridge.

Lights sparkled in the windows of the buildings on the
far side of the river. The buildings themselves rose up
against the city skyline as though they were part of a
massive a film set. The sight never failed to captivate
Francine. She gave a small sigh of satisfaction.

'Hi, Francine.' He'd become aware of her presence but
he didn't turn around.

She watched as he raised a tumbler to his lips and she
experienced a small surge of hope. 'Are you staying
tonight?'

'No, what makes you ask that?'

'You're drinking.'

'Just this one.'

'I see.'

Disappointment knifed through her but, as usual, she
decided to make the most of whatever time they had
together. She slipped off her shoes and went up behind
him. She put both her arms around him and rested her
head on his back. She could feel the warmth of his body
through the fine lawn fabric of his shirt. 'Shall I make us
a meal?'

'No.'

'It wouldn't take me long to whip up an omelette – and
I've plenty of salad in the fridge.'

'Nancy will have supper waiting. Besides, I haven't
much time.'

'So why bother to come?'

She moved away from him but he turned quickly and
caught hold of her shoulder. 'Don't sulk. You know why
I've come.'

Francine looked up into his face but, with the window
behind him, it was hard to read his expression. He
slipped an arm around her and pulled her close.

'Wait –' She brought one hand up between them and pushed against his chest. 'I wanted to talk to you – about the new programme – I've an idea of my own – something different –'

He groaned. 'Not tonight, Francine. I don't want to talk about work tonight.'

'But it's important to me –'

'Francine, work is always important to you. I knew right from the beginning of our relationship how ambitious you were. But I didn't care if you came to me for the wrong reason –'

'What do you mean?'

'Come on, Francine. You were a young, intelligent and very beautiful woman. I'm twenty years older than you are –'

'But you were attractive – still are –'

'And I was also well established in local television – where you wanted to be –'

'We've discussed this many times,' she interrupted him. 'You know it wasn't just because I wanted you to help me get a job that I allowed you to seduce me.'

'Did I seduce you, Francine? Did I really? Or was it the other way around? That night, just before your graduation ceremony, when you turned up at the studios and told me that you wanted some advice, that you trusted me to guide you . . .'

'That was genuine – I did trust you – I did want you to guide me.'

'But you knew I was interested in you, didn't you? Ever since I first met you while I was making that programme about the university? I wanted to continue our acquaintance – not just because of your undoubted potential as a broadcaster.'

'Of course I knew there was something between us,' she replied. 'I couldn't help being aware of the chemistry – I felt it too –'

'So you "allowed me to seduce you" – right there on the studio floor. And the fact remains that, besotted as I was, I did help you get started. I've helped you and guided you ever since. And whatever you say your true feelings were and are about me, mine have never changed.

'I still desire you – still want you and, right now, I refuse to discuss your damned career.'

Francine didn't know when he'd got rid of his drink but now she was aware that he had started to unbutton her blouse.

'No, wait –'

But he slipped one hand behind her head, cradling it while he brought his mouth down on hers demandingly. She could taste the whisky on his lips and on his tongue as he prised her lips apart and began to probe deeply and possessively.

She tried to hang on to all the things she had wanted to say to him tonight – all the things that had to be said – but her body betrayed her. She felt her nipples harden and strain against the lace of her bra as her lover's hand found her breasts and began to caress them.

When he took his mouth away from hers, she snatched a breath and groaned, 'No, please wait –'

'I won't wait – not a minute longer.' He took hold of her hair and dragged her head back and away from him so that he could lay a trial of kisses down the curve of her neck.

When he pushed aside her bra and found her breasts with his lips and tongue, Francine felt the old, familiar throbbing begin, deep inside her. He removed her blouse and began to unhook and unzip her skirt. Impatiently, she helped him remove her clothes and his own until they were touching skin to skin.

'Peter,' she breathed, 'Oh, Peter . . .'

They sank down on to the softly carpeted floor.

* * *

Their meal was halfway over and Alison was alone at the table in the restaurant area of The Plough. The place was cosy rather than stylish but she was glad that she had taken the trouble to dress up a little. The simple high-necked sleeveless black dress that she was wearing now was infinitely more suitable for an evening out with an up-and-coming property developer than the old slacks and sweater she had been wearing earlier.

She had been dismayed to find that the dress hung on her a little more loosely than it used to, but it was full-skirted so it didn't look too bad after she had fastened the broad belt one notch tighter. She had dried her blonde hair so that it fell softly round her face and wore her mother's pearls. She hadn't wanted to wear any of the jewellery that Paul had given her. Somehow that wouldn't have seemed right . . .

Greg Leighton was smiling as he walked back to the table. 'It's OK, we don't have to hurry over our dessert. I phoned the Hall and Ruth is quite happy to stay the night. I also phoned her mother, who gave permission and insisted on sending Ruth's father along with Ruth's night things and a dozen fresh eggs for tomorrow's breakfast.'

'Oh,' Alison said weakly. 'And now, I suppose the whole village will find out that I've been out to dinner with you.'

Greg took his place at the table. 'Well, they already know that, don't they? I mean if we'd wanted to be discreet we'd hardly have come to the Plough, would we?'

'I suppose not.'

'This is a small village,' he continued, 'and just about everybody who comes here to drink or dine here must know who you are. And the staff here certainly know me.'

'Why's that?'

'Because I take a room at the Plough whenever I have

to stay here on business. As a matter of fact I've booked in tonight.'

Alison shot him a startled glance and he replied before she had time to define her alarm.

'It's all right. I've asked for my usual single room. I have no intention of luring you upstairs and seducing you into selling your land at on outrageously advantageous price.'

'So why are you staying?' Alison covered her faint embarrassment with what she hoped was a bright social smile.

'So that I can enjoy the rest of this wine and maybe order a brandy with the coffee and not have to worry about driving back to my apartment in London.'

As he spoke he picked up the bottle of red wine and examined the label. 'You know,' he grinned at her, 'until quite recently I hadn't a clue about fine wines. But I'm enjoying the learning process – and I'd say that this isn't bad for a village hostelry, wouldn't you?'

'Not bad at all. But no more, please – oh –'

She'd made a move to cover her glass with her hand but was too late. He'd already topped it up and poured the remainder of the bottle into his own.

He smiled. 'Don't worry, I'll walk you safely home. It wouldn't do to get the lady of the manor drunk and let her fall into the hedgerow.'

'Oh, please,' Alison murmured, 'don't call me that.' But she laughed softly all the same.

'That would be quite some scandal, wouldn't it? The younger Mrs Cavedish discovered snoring drunkenly in a ditch. It would keep the village gossips going for years.'

'And it would confirm Mrs Cavendish senior's view that her son had married beneath him,' she added, drily.

Greg shot her a quizzical look but didn't take the conversation any further. 'Shall we order the dessert now?' he asked.

'I don't think I could manage any, really.'

'Nonsense, of course you could and, just to make it easier for you, I'll choose. Trust me?'

'Yes, although I don't know why I should.'

While Greg studied the menu Alison glanced around the comfortable dining room, her gaze lingering on the oak beams, the white, rough plastered walls and the open fireplace where a real fire burned. There hadn't been many customers in the restaurant the evening and, by now, only two other tables were occupied.

One by a couple whose children were at the village school. She had seen them delivering and collecting their two little daughters at the school gates and, also, on open evenings. They had recognized Alison straight away; the young woman's face had registered surprise and then delight.

The other couple looked like tourists. They were old enough to be retired and they were relaxed and happy. Alison had experienced the usual sharp pangs of regret that she had to endure whenever she saw older couples enjoying each other's company. She and Paul should have had those golden years to look forward to.

Molly Harding, the wife of the landlord, arrived at the table with their desserts.

'Oh, Greg, no!' Alison said.

'What's the matter? Don't you like apple pie?'

'Yes, I do – but there's so much – and all that cream . . .'

Mrs Harding arranged her comfortable features into a smile. 'Mrs Cavendish, if you don't mind my saying so, that's exactly why Greg ordered it. He thinks you need – oh, dear . . .'

'Mr Leighton thinks I need what exactly?' Alison asked.

Molly blushed and looked uncomfortable. Alison had noticed, of course, that she had called him by his first name. Now a further depth of intimacy was revealed in the nervous look she slanted at Greg and in his reassuring smile.

'Er – I think Molly meant that –'

'It's all right.' Mrs Harding had recovered her composure. 'I'm not afraid to tell Mrs Cavendish what's obvious.'

'And what's that?' Alison knew that she sounded ridiculously high and mighty but she had been stung to think that these people had been discussing her.

'Mrs Cavendish, dear, the truth is I've seen more flesh on a scarecrow. Everybody's noticed –'

'Everybody?'

'Well, folk in the village. We've all noticed how you've just been wasting away and it's time something was done about it.'

'Oh.'

Alison was at a loss for a suitable rejoinder. She hated being the subject of any kind of gossip but Molly Harding looked genuinely concerned. Eventually she said, 'I see – so I suppose that explains the leek and potato soup, the mountains of bread rolls, the roast chicken with all the trimmings and now this ridiculously large portion of apple pie smothered in cream –'

'*Home-made* apple pie,' Molly interjected.

'Very well, *home-made* apple pie, if it makes any difference.'

'Of course it does!' George exclaimed, 'That's why I come here – for home comforts.'

Once more Alison couldn't help noticing the easy smiles Greg and Molly Harding exchanged. She must be years older than he is, she found herself thinking. Definitely attractive but in a full-blown, mature and well-rounded way. Is that the kind of woman he likes? Plump and cuddly? Is that why he's gone out of his way to feed me up tonight . . .?

What am I thinking? The words screamed through her

brain. Greg Leighton is only interested in my property, not my body. And if he is having an affair with Molly Harding it's certainly not any of my business.

But what did he mean by home comforts . . . ?

'Mrs Cavendish,' Molly had stopped smiling. 'I didn't mean to upset you. Especially as Greg told me that he wanted you to relax and enjoy yourself –'

'Did he?'

'Yes, I did,' Greg put in. 'And I've no ulterior motive other than to make up for shouting at you earlier.'

'Shouting at me?'

'When I came up to the Hall. I'm ashamed of myself. I was impatient and overbearing just because you haven't answered a few phone calls.'

'You had every right to be annoyed. It's only good manners to return calls.'

'But I suspect that you weren't told about them. Right?'

'Right.'

'Well, whatever the reason, I sensed at once that your life has been difficult lately. And that's probably an understatement. I wanted this evening to get to know you – become friends even – before I start harassing you about the sale of your land.'

'Look, I'll leave you now,' Molly began to back away, 'but I would appreciate it if you would both eat up your apple pie before it gets cold.'

'We will, Molly, I promise you,' Greg assured her. 'And would you bring us some coffee when you see that we're ready?'

When she had gone Alison began to eat her dessert; it was delicious. Greg smiled at her.

'You'd better clear that plate or I'll be in deep trouble,' he said.

'I'll do my best. I wouldn't want to put you in Molly's bad books.'

He must have read the half-formed suspicious in her eyes. He shook his head and laughed softly. 'There's nothing between Molly and me, you know.'

Alison knew that she was blushing. 'I didn't think there was.'

'Oh, yes, you did, and I'd like to make it clear, right away, that I'm very fond of Molly Harding but I'm also fond of her husband. And, incidentally, anyone who's seen Alf would be very foolish to embark on an affair with the love of his life!'

Alison grinned as she brought Alf Harding to mind. The landlord of The Plough was an ex-wrestler, was built like a tank and had never had any trouble controlling either the village lads or troublesome louts down from the city for a night's drinking in the country.

'I see what you mean.' she said.

'So when I said I like my home comforts I simply meant the clean, comfortable rooms and the good food – especially the good food. I don't like pretentious eating places. If I look at a menu and find something I haven't heard of or I can't pronounce, I won't eat it. But here at The Plough, the food is not only delicious, it's also uncomplicated and wholesome.'

'Just like your mother used to make, I suppose?'

The question had been light-hearted and she was unprepared for his reaction. Greg's smile vanished – or rather it twisted itself into something altogether more cynical. 'Hardly.'

'Oh, dear, have I put my foot in it? Your mother wasn't a very good cook?'

'I have no idea. She was never in the house long enough to prepare even the simplest meal.'

'Did she have a busy social life?'

The look he gave her was so strange – for a moment she could have sworn that his dark eyes were illumined by a flash of pain – that Alison felt acutely uncomfortable. As if she had inadvertently exposed something that had been well hidden.

'Well, you could call it that.'

Greg had spoken without rancour but Alison knew that she should let the subject drop. She began to wonder about him and, for the first time, try to see past the smooth, good looks, the expensive clothes.

He was confident, his manners were impeccable, his voice was that of a gentleman – or was it? She found herself comparing Greg with her sister-in-law Daphne's husband, Nigel Remington. Nigel's braying tones declared him to be upper-class, public school, whereas a better description of the pleasing way Greg Leighton spoke would be 'classless'.

Suddenly she remembered the newspaper profile that Miss Robertson had mentioned. What had the vicar's sister said? *What an interesting life . . . He's to be admired . . .*

Interesting? Could that mean hard? And why should he be admired? Because he'd achieved success against difficult odds? Alison thought of the mother who was never in the house long enough to prepare a meal and stopped short of speculating exactly what it was that kept her so busy . . .

'Mrs Cavendish, would you like your coffee now?'

Alison looked up and smiled at Molly Harding. 'Yes, please – and that apple pie was wonderful.'

'Glad you liked it.'

Molly served the coffee and Greg ordered brandy in spite of Alison's protestations. Then, at last, he turned the conversation round to his plans for the housing development. He described his ideas with enthusiasm and assured her that planning permission would be no problem.

'I've made preliminary enquiries,' he said, 'and I've been more or less assured that, as long as I abide by the rule book, there'll be no objections. The land falls within a government-approved development zone.'

'Oh . . . good . . .'

'What's the matter?'

'N-nothing. It's just that . . .' To her dismay Alison was unable to stop a deep-seated yawn.

'Great,' Greg said, 'what a social success I am. First I bawl you out in your own home and then I bring you here and bore you to death!'

'No . . . no, I've enjoyed listening to you and I'm not at all bored, but it's late and . . .'

'You're dead beat. Mrs Cavendish –'

'Alison.'

'Alison, I think it's time I took you home.'

When they stepped out into the village street they were met by a blast of cold air which was all the keener in contrast to the cosy fug they had left behind them. Alison shivered and, crossing her arms over her body, she ran her hands up and down her bare arms.

'My God,' Greg exclaimed. 'You can't walk home like that!'

'It's my own fault – you brought us here in your car – I never thought to bring a coat.'

He took hold of her hand and pulled her towards the car park behind the pub.

'No,' she said, 'you can't drive, not after all that wine and the brandy, too.'

'I'm not going to.' He opened the boot of his car.

'Then what –?'

'Here, put this on.'

He handed her a jacket. In the darkness she couldn't make out the details but, slipping into it obediently, she felt it to be warm and quilted.

'It may be a little large for you.'

'Just a little.'

Alison held her arms towards the light spilling out

from the windows of the restaurant. They both laughed when they saw the ends of the sleeves drooping over her hands as if she were a cartoon character.

'Come here.'

'Mm?' Alison looked up uncertainly as Greg moved in close to her.

'Take this.' He dropped a scarf around her neck. 'Tuck it in. I don't want you catching cold.' Then he took her hand and drew her arm through his own. 'Now, let's get you home.'

Once they had left the village, the road was dark and shadowy. There was a moon but its light was intermittent as the ever-present wind chased clouds across the sky.

'Wonderful, isn't it?' Greg said suddenly.

'What's wonderful?'

'To be able to look up at the sky and see the moon and the stars. If you live in a big city the night sky is always spoiled by the orange glow of the street lights. And it's so wonderfully quiet here –'

'No, not quiet,' Alison said, 'the countryside is never quiet, listen . . .' They stopped walking. 'What can you hear?'

'The wind,' he said. 'I can hear the wind in the trees. And there's something rustling quite nearby – there in the ditch. What can it be?'

'Some small nocturnal animal setting out on its regular patrol,' she told him. 'Or it could be spiders hunting through dead leaves . . .'

'Ugh!' He mock-shivered. 'It's quite spooky, isn't it?'

'Oh, it can be much worse than this. One night when Paul and I were walking home from the pub, we got as far as the churchyard when there was an unearthly scream – bloodcurdling – I was scared out of my wits!'

'For heaven's sake, what was it?'

'A vixen, calling out to its mate, apparently. But by the

time Paul had explained it to me, I'd taken to my heels and was halfway home. Poor Paul had to come running after me.

'When we reached the Hall he couldn't tell me properly for laughing and we collapsed in a fit of giggles. His mother was appalled – she thought we were drunk!'

'And were you?'

'Not really – it was just – just – oh, you know . . . when you're in love . . .'

For a moment the clouds cleared and the moon shone down brightly. Alison raised her head and looked up at Greg, her face animated and her eyes shining with the memory. She saw that he was staring at her intently, frowning a little. His eyes . . . what was that expression in his eyes?

Alison looked away, strangely moved. She had remembered a happy time of her life and she had been able to share it with this man who was hardly more than a stranger. And the memory, vivid as it had been, had not left her feeling bereft. For the first time, she was comfortable with her past happiness.

The clouds scudded across the moon again and they walked on in companionable silence. The Hall was in darkness and, once Alison had opened the door, they stood in the doorway and whispered like teenagers returning from a date.

'So is it all right if we meet soon and talk about my plans in more detail?' he asked.

'Of course – and, thank you for a lovely evening. But you didn't have to take me out for a meal, you know.'

'I wanted to.'

'Well, then, goodnight.'

'Goodnight, Alison.' He turned to go but she reached a hand out to stop him.

'Wait,' she called softly.

'What is it?'

'Your jacket.' She slipped it off and handed it to him.

He stood there, seemingly reluctant to leave her. 'I'll be away on business for a while but I'll call you as soon as I get back to London. We'll arrange a meeting.'

'Fine . . . goodnight . . .'

He walked away down the drive and Alison watched until his tall figure merged into the shadows. It was only after she had closed the door that she realized that she was still wearing his scarf around her neck.

She raised both hands and pushed the fine woollen fabric up to her face and breathed in. She inhaled the fresh, lemony tang of his aftershave and a disturbing and half-forgotten warmth began to course through her veins.

No, she cried silently, *no . . . it's too soon . . . I'm not ready for this . . .*

CHAPTER 6

Wednesday morning – Lancashire

'I wish you'd eat a proper breakfast, dear.'

Sophie glanced up at her mother. 'I can't. You know I've tried, but coffee and toast is all I can manage – it's been the same since I was a teenager. That's when you started nagging me about it.' She smiled. 'And it doesn't look as if you're ever going to stop.'

Laura Blake slid a fried egg on to her own plate of crisply grilled bacon and sat down. 'You know me. I never give up if I think the cause is worthy enough. Breakfast is –'

'– the most important meal of the day,' Sophie finished her sentence for her. 'I know that, Mum. I even tell the kids at school that. But it's no good if I just can't manage to eat it.'

Her mother shook her head and then, thankfully, picked up her knife and fork. The two of them got on very well. If Laura nagged now and then, Sophie could handle it without losing her patience. And Laura could take Sophie's occasional exasperated responses without being offended.

The atmosphere in the neat breakfast room was warm and friendly in contrast to the threatening skies outside. Typical April weather, Sophie mused. She only hoped

98

that the persistent showers would have cleared up by the Spring Bank Holiday.

'Alistair will expect more than coffee and toast, I expect. A man that size needs feeding properly,' Laura smiled complacently.

Sophie sighed. Didn't she ever give up? 'And he shall be,' she said as equably as she could, 'or if he's not satisfied with the meals I make for him, he'll cook them himself.'

'You don't mean that, do you?' Laura's face registered mild disapproval. 'I mean you're not going to go on teaching after the end of the summer term, are you? He'll expect you to be a proper wife to him.'

Sophie stared at her mother in mild despair. She loved her dearly and she would be eternally grateful for the warm and loving home that she'd provided for her. Her father had died while she was still at school and her mother had been determined that their only daughter should fulfil all the hopes and dreams they'd had for her. She had gone without much in order to see Sophie through school and university.

When Sophie had started teaching and life had become easier for them, Laura had been keen to run the home they shared and keep things stress-free. Sophie knew that she had been indulged, loved, pampered and looked after sometimes to the point of suffocation. But she'd never taken advantage of her situation and was determined that she would repay the debt. If the time ever came when she needed it, Sophie would care for her mother for the rest of her life.

But that didn't mean that she agreed with all Laura's opinions. Especially not her views on a wife's place in the scheme of things.

'I'm only giving up work temporarily, I thought you understood that. Once we're settled in Scotland, I'll probably look for a school nearby. Unless . . .'

'Unless you start a family.'

Laura looked so contented, so euphoric at the prospect of grandchildren that Sophie was forced to hide her own misgivings. 'That's right, Mum,' she said.

Her mother must have caught the slight edge to her voice and she asked, 'Alistair does want children, doesn't he?'

'Yes, but remember, we're not exactly young.'

'Nonsense, you're just past thirty and Alistair is only – only –'

'Coming up to forty.' Sophie sighed. 'He may decide that, after all, he doesn't want his well-ordered life disrupted by children.'

'Oh, Sophie, you can't really think that? I mean, you have discussed it with him, haven't you?

'Yes of course we've discussed it. And I'm sure you'll probably have at least two grandchildren to spoil. Now how about a fill-up of coffee – and, as a special treat – if you've finished that disgusting plateful of calories, you can make me another slice of toast.'

As Laura set about putting slices of bread in the toaster and warming up more milk for the coffee, Sophie determinedly banished some of the darker thoughts that had been haunting her. There was no need to burden her mother with feelings so unformed that she couldn't even name them.

Before she left the house she slipped her engagement ring on to the gold chain she wore around her neck and buttoned up her blouse so that it was well-hidden. Her mother thought that this was a sensible precaution, bearing in mind the part of the inner city the school was situated in. Only recently a young woman teacher had been mugged and robbed in the school car park.

Later that day, during the lunch hour, Sophie and her friend Maggie Lomax sat with their coffee and sandwiches in the empty assembly hall. The hall was set up with rows and row of individual desks which had already been tidied up and supplied with fresh paper for the afternoon examination session.

'Poor little blighters,' Maggie said as she surveyed the temporarily quiet hall. 'Why do we subject them to this regular torture?'

'You know why,' Sophie replied. 'So they can get qualifications.'

'Why? What are they going to do with their precious bits of paper – their certificates? Will it get them a job?'

'Stop it, Maggie. You know you and I will never agree about this so let's just enjoy the peace and quiet for as long as we can. Do you want one of these cheese sandwiches? As usual, my mother's made too many.'

'Pass it over – thanks.' Maggie laughed. 'What on earth will Laura do after you're married? She'll be utterly lost. If she's anything like my mother was when the last of us left home, it'll take her months if not years to adjust her shopping habits. My poor dad piled on the weight until he insisted on taking over the weekly shop!'

Maggie had puffed out her cheeks and patted her stomach to illustrate her father's weight gain and Sophie grinned. 'Well, at first, Mum will carry on as before.'

'What do you mean?'

'She'll have the entire holiday week we're away on honeymoon to shop and bake and fill the freezer and then she'll have the rest of the summer term to feed me up before she sends me off to Scotland to join my new husband.'

'Oh, yes, I forgot that you were going to go back to Mother for a while.'

'It's the best thing to do. Alistair has to take up his new post straight after the honeymoon, so he'll have to go on his own.'

'And you're quite happy to allow that gorgeous hunk of a medic loose on the female population of Glasgow?'

'I've no choice – and, anyway, he'll be living with his parents while he hunts us out a place to live.'

'Och aye! The formidable Professor and Mrs McGregor! And Alistair's three big bonny sisters live within walking distance, don't they? No doubt they'll be keeping an eye on him for you!'

'Maggie – that's the worst Scottish accent I've ever heard.'

'I know – but I don't mind making a fool of myself if it'll cheer you up a little.'

'I wasn't aware that I needed cheering up.'

'Now don't go all schoolmistressy on me – I'm older than you are. Yes, Sophie. I do think you need cheering up. Ever since you and Alistair set the date you've been walking around like someone condemned to death rather than a young woman engaged to be married.'

'Have I? Just nerves, probably.'

'Hey, kiddo – it's me, your best buddy you're talking too. Quit stalling and tell me what's buggin' yer, baby!'

'Maggie, if that's supposed to be American it's even worse than the Scottish accent.' Sophie began to laugh weakly and then suddenly the laugh turned into a sob. To her dismay, she began to cry.

'Sophie . . . don't cry . . . please . . . here,' Maggie fished a small pack of Kleenex from her bag, 'take these and for goodness' sake talk to me!'

Her friend waited patiently for the sobs to subside. Eventually Sophie dabbed her eyes with a couple of tissues and looked up and grinned. 'Why won't you believe it's wedding nerves? I'm sure most people get them – even you.'

'Of course I did. But I know you well enough to see that you're not just feeling panicky – you've been acting as if you're carrying the worries of the whole world on your tiny shoulders.'

'You're exaggerating, as usual. But, OK, I have been

worried – about – well a few things, actually.'

'What to unburden yourself? I'm old enough to be your mother, after all.'

'Oh, yeah? Child bride, were you?'

'We-ell, big sister, then. Now come on, tell.'

'Maggie, there's not time –'

'Now you've got me really worried. It can't be as bad as that!'

'No – seriously – the afternoon session will be starting in a few minutes.'

Maggie glanced up at the wall clock and sighed. 'You're right. We don't want to start a serious discussion now. Are you seeing Alistair tonight?'

'No – he's on late duty. Why?'

'Well then, how about coming over to my place? Ken's taking our three girl monsters to the swimming club. We can have a good natter while I catch up with the ironing.'

'I'm not sure . . .'

'Well, I am. In fact I won't take no for an answer!'

'OK. My mother's going to her flower arranging class so I'll drop her off and come straight along. What on earth was that!'

They both rose from their seats at what sounded like a shrill howl of pain.

'I don't know – it was in the corridor – quick!'

They hurried towards the double doors which provided the main entrance to the assembly hall. Sophie reached them first and pulled one side open. 'Julie! What happened?'

Fifteen-year-old Julie Hunter blinked up at her from the floor. Her wire-framed spectacles hung lopsidedly from one ear and she was half-lying with one thin leg twisted under her skinny body. Her school bag had burst open, scattering pens, pencils, rulers and rubbers on the floor. Her usually pale face was paper-white. She stared up at them myopically. 'I – I – tripped –'

'Cheryl, what happened to Julie?' Maggie had arrived in the doorway and she was looking suspiciously at the other girl who was standing just a few steps away.

'I dunno. I just got here.'

Cheryl Jackson glared at them insolently. She was tall and solidly built, but that didn't stop her wearing the shortest, tightest skirt she could get away with and still call school uniform. Her blouse strained over her mature breasts. Her mouth stayed open and her heavy jaw moved constantly as she chewed gum.

Fleetingly, Sophie contemplated telling her to get rid of it. But what was the point? They were allowed to bring gum into exams and it was almost time for the exam to start. Other pupils were already walking down the corridor towards them. They began to gather round, curious to know what was going on.

'Julie?' Maggie had turned her attention to the girl who was now rubbing her spectacles on a corner of her school blouse.

'Yes, Mrs Lomax?'

'What happened here? I want the truth.'

Julie shot a panic-stricken glance at Sophie, who knelt down swiftly and began to gather up the contents of the girl's school bag. 'It's all right, Julie,' she murmured. 'I think I know why you fell.'

'Do you?' The girl's eyes widened in terror as she glanced sideways at Cheryl. Sophie's suspicions were confirmed.

'Yes, you tripped over your own shoelace. Right?' She pulled Julie's leg out from under her body gently. 'Look, it's half undone. Sophie leaned forward, obscuring the view from everyone as she made a pretence of tying up the shoelace. 'There you are. Now let me help you get up.'

She took hold of the girl's arms and noticed that she was shaking. 'Are you OK?'

'Yes, Miss Blake, I think so.'

'Good. Now go and take your place in the hall.'

She kept her arms around Julie's shoulders as she led her in. Cheryl made a sound like a sarcastic grunt and Sophie turned her head towards Maggie. 'Mrs Lomax, would you make the others line up and walk in *slowly*?' She knew that Maggie had caught on when she nodded almost imperceptibly. 'We don't want any more accidents, do we?'

Maggie had got the message and by the time she allowed the rest of the pupils to file into the hall, Julie had settled at a desk in the front row. Sophie knew that it would be pointless to question her any further. She was fairly sure that Cheryl Jackson had chosen Julie as her latest victim. But the poor child would never admit to being bullied. And in any case, Sophie wanted her to settle down and concentrate on her exam paper. But she would have a word with Maggie and they would keep an eye on the situation.

By the time Sophie set out to take her mother to her evening class, she was already regretting her promise to go to Maggie's. She had hardly admitted her misgivings to herself, let alone confide in somebody else. She considered phoning and giving some excuse but she knew that her friend wouldn't be taken in. And Maggie could be persistent; at best she would only be postponing things.

Laura had kept up a gentle flow of conversation from the moment she'd settled herself in the car. It seemed that Sophie was only required to nod and agree. So as she drove back into town towards the City College, where the evening classes were held, she let her mind wander. How much should she confide in Maggie?

They stopped at some traffic lights and she became aware of her mother's voice again. '– Everyone has been so enthusiastic – so full of ideas. Some of them have even

105

offered to come and help – and Vic Watkins says that he'll do anything he can. Sophie – have you heard one word that I've said?'

'Mm?'

'I knew you weren't listening. Never mind, I'm getting used to it. I know you've got a lot on your mind.'

'Do you?' Sophie was startled.

'Of course, the wedding, leaving your job, house-hunting. It's natural that you should be distracted.'

'Yes . . . I suppose so.' Sophie gripped the steering wheel and glanced sideways at her mother. For a moment she had imagined that Laura had sensed her worries – her misgivings – but perhaps not. Her mother's litany of things to worry about had been merely superficial.

The lights changed and Sophie was grateful to be able to look straight ahead once more. 'I'm sorry, Mum,' she said, 'what were you saying?'

'I was talking about the flower arrangements for the church and for the reception. Everyone at my class has been quite taken with the idea of helping me. They've made some really imaginative suggestions.'

'Mum – are you sure you want to take this on yourself? I mean the flowers *and* the catering? I can afford to have it done properly, you know.'

As soon as the words were out of her mouth she realized her mistake. Laura bridled. 'Don't you think I'll do a proper job, Sophie?'

'Of course I do. I meant professionally. I can afford to pay professional florists and caterers. I don't want you wearing yourself out. The mother of the bride is sup-posed to look radiant on her daughter's wedding day.'

'But I love doing things like this. You know I do. Even if I were the mother of a royal princess I wouldn't dream of letting anyone else take over.'

'Oh, Mum –'

'What's the matter? Why are you laughing?'

'I was just trying to imagine me as a princess and you handing round the home-baked sausage rolls dressed in a pinny and a tiara.'

A short while later Sophie was ensconced in a deeply comfortable armchair in Maggie's homely sitting-room. Maggie had finished the ironing before she arrived – or so she claimed. Sophie was inclined to believe that the family's clothes had been abandoned in favour of a good natter.

'Here you are.' Her friend handed her a mug of coffee. 'It's only instant, I'm afraid.'

'That's OK. I'm not a coffee snob.'

Maggie kicked off her shoes and settled her comfortable frame on the chair opposite. A coal-effect gas fire burned in the hearth between them and the overhead lights had been switched off leaving only a couple of lamps to illuminate the room.

She's done this deliberately, Sophie thought. The place is cosy and womblike. She wants me to relax and bare my soul!

'So what were you saying? Something about flowers and sausage rolls and Laura wanting to do everything herself. Are you worried she can't cope?'

'No – of course she'll cope. It's just – oh, I suppose it is just wedding nerves after all. You know from the moment we set the date everything went wrong – or at least didn't go quite how I imagined it should.'

'Explain.'

'Well, you know we decided to get married in rather a hurry?'

'Yeah – you had me wondering if you and the clever doctor hadn't been as clever as you should be!'

'Shut up, Maggie. You know very well it was because the chance of a senior post in Glasgow came up unexpectedly, and Alistair applied for it and got it.'

'I know – I was only teasing.'

'Well, Alistair asked me to marry him –'

'Wait a moment – you mean that the subject hadn't even been mentioned until then?'

Sophie frowned and sipped her coffee. 'Actually, no. I – I was . . .' she stared into the flames of the fire. What had she just been about to admit? That she had been surprised when Alistair suddenly proposed marriage? That, nevertheless, the feeling of joy had been overwhelming? That she hadn't really known until that moment that the relationship had any future?

'Well, whatever you were,' Maggie prompted, quietly, 'you said yes.'

'Yes.' Sophie sighed.

'And? – Sophie, this is like pulling teeth!'

'Sorry. And he wanted us to be married before he took up his new post so that we could move to Scotland together.'

'But you nobly said that you couldn't let the school down and you would have to work out the summer term. You must be crazy!'

'You know you would have done the same.'

'Well, maybe.'

'So we arranged to be married in the Spring Bank Holiday so that we could have at least one week's honeymoon.'

'That doesn't seem so bad. So what went wrong?'

'It seems that everybody gets married on that particular Saturday! We were lucky to get the church – and as for getting a hotel or restaurant for the reception, that was out of the question. They'd been booked up for months – some of them for nearly a year!'

'So your mother booked the church hall and decided to do the catering herself. What's wrong with that?'

'There's nothing wrong with my mother's catering, but have you seen the church hall?'

'You know I have. My monsters go to youth club there – oh, goodness, Sophie, I see what you mean!'

They stared at each other for a moment and then, in spite of themselves, they began to laugh. 'It's a dump!' Maggie exclaimed.

'Thanks for being so reassuring – that's just what I needed to hear.' Sophie's laughter had a hysterical edge to it and Maggie looked concerned.

'Look – we'll clean it up. I'll suggest that the Youth Club do it as a project – Ken will lead the team –'

Sophie shook her head, wearily. 'It's not that's it's dirty, Maggie – it isn't. It's just the – oh, you know what I mean – the whole ambience – the look of the place. Brown and cream walls, noticeboards full of tattered posters, patched lino and trestle tables – that might be OK for parish bun fights but, Maggie, this is my *wedding!*'

'Oh, Sophie –' Maggie's eyes widened with understanding, 'of course it is. And weddings should be special, gorgeous, romantic – even for sensible schoolteachers and clever hardworking doctors. By the way, what does Alistair think about it? Have you mentioned it to him?'

'I have and he simply couldn't understand what was bothering me. I got the impression that he thought I was being foolish.'

'Men!'

'Am I being foolish?'

'Of course you're not. And I'll think of something – I promise you.'

'Will you?'

Maggie came over and sat on the arm of Sophie's chair. She put an arm round her shoulders and hugged her. 'Of course I will.'

'But what can you do?'

'We-ell – for a start I'll find out where we can hire

some quality table linen to cover the trestle tables – I mean real classy stuff – and I'll get the noticeboards taken down – see my mind's gone into overdrive already!'

Sophie smiled up at her. She knew she could trust Maggie to do everything she said she would and probably more. She was glad that she had confided in her but she knew that no matter what efforts were made to pretty the place up, it would still fall short of her dreams.

'But you haven't told me everything, have you, love? I know you better than to think you'd have a fit of gloom just about the venue for your wedding reception – important as it is.'

'We-ell . . .'

Sophie hesitated and Maggie stood up and collected their coffee mugs. 'Want some more coffee?'

'Yes, please – although it will probably keep me awake tonight.'

Sophie followed her friend out into the hall and along the passage into the kitchen. Maggie stopped at the open doorway of the small dining-room and switched on the light. She stood aside to let Sophie look in. A sewing machine was on the table along with paper patterns, pins, scissors and swathes of palest pink, silky fabric. At one end of the table there was a pile of handmade silk rosebuds.

'Oh, Maggie, all this work! You should have let me hire dresses for the girls along with my own.'

'Not on your life – I'm loving it! Unless anyone else is crazy enough to ask my daughters to be bridesmaids, this is the only chance I'll get.'

'But all this for one occasion.'

'They can keep the dresses for school plays – fancy dress parties. And some days I'll just insist that the three little monsters wear them to remind me that they're real live girls.'

Back in the sitting-room with fresh mugs of coffee,

110

they sat in comfortable silence for a while before Maggie said, 'So what else is bothering you?'

'Nothing.'

'You're lying.'

'OK, nothing important. As I said, it's just an accumulation of things. I feel a bit of a fraud sitting here taking up your valuable ironing time.'

'That's OK, I've done it.'

'Oh, yes? I saw the laundry basket in the kitchen and it was full of very unironed-looking clothes.'

'Well – I did the important bits – Ken's shirts and the monsters sports kits. But you don't have to feel guilty – it's marvellous just to have a gossip now and again and let the housework go to hell.'

'I wish you could persuade my mother of that! And talking of the blessed Laura, it's almost time to go and collect her.'

Maggie let her go, although very reluctantly. Soon Sophie was sitting in her car outside the City College waiting for her mother. Raindrops chased each other down the windscreen and Sophie peered across the car park towards the large, brightly lit building. It was sixties style, the large windows giving plain views of the activities inside each layer of classrooms.

Then, one by one the lights went out and huddled figures hurried out of the main entrance and dodged across the puddles towards their cars. A group of cheerful women shouted their protest at the weather as they ran for the bus stop just outside the gates. And still there was no sign of Laura.

Sophie wasn't worried. Her mother was usually one of the last to leave. As well as helping the instructor clear up after the class, there were so many people she just had to have one last word to, including the principal college caretaker, Vic Watkins. At last, Laura appeared in the well-lit entrance foyer and, true to form, she stopped to talk

111

to him. Sophie wondered whether it had ever occurred to her mother that the man was probably smitten.

It wasn't until all the other cars were gone that Laura finally said goodbye to Vic and came hurrying through the rain. Sophie leaned over and pushed open the door on the passenger side.

'Sorry, dear, have you been waiting long?'

'No – just a few minutes,' Sophie lied.

'Did you and Maggie have a good gossip?'

'Mm . . . she showed me the girls' bridesmaid's dresses . . . they're going to be beautiful. Maggie's three monsters might steal the show.'

'Never. It will be your day, Sophie. Oh, darling, you're going to be such a beautiful bride!'

Sophie felt vaguely uneasy at deflecting her mother's curiosity towards the bridesmaid's dresses. Laura would have been hurt if she thought her daughter was worried about something and couldn't confide in her.

But then, she hadn't really confided in Maggie, had she? Not about everything that was bothering her. How could she tell Maggie, who had been her friend for many years now, that she wouldn't think her wedding day complete unless her other friends were there?

Carol, Alison . . . she'd been to their weddings. To Matthew's christening and to Paul's funeral . . . She had visited them whenever she could . . .

And Francine . . . Sophie had followed her career with interest and admiration. Francine, free from both marriage and motherhood, had been able to meet her a little more often. Sophie would go up to London for a day, now and then. A couple of times, years ago it seemed now, she had stayed in Francine's flat in Fulham overnight. They would talk about old times and about how their lives were shaping up . . .

But, now, when she had so much to tell them, they were strangely unavailable . . .

She'd tried contacting every one of them and had no luck. Each time she phoned Alison she'd had the bad luck to get Paul's mother or sister. They'd promised to pass on the message but, so far, Alison had not returned her calls . . .

Francine seemed to have moved without telling Sophie and the young couple who'd bought the flat wouldn't pass on her new number, which was ex-directory. They advised her to try Television Centre but she'd been reluctant to phone Francine at work about something so personal . . .

And, as for Carol, the first few times she tried, the phone just rang and rang and the last time there'd been a Telecom message saying that the number was unavailable . .

She knew very well that she could simply write to them – send them each a wedding invitation and enclose a letter telling them all about Alistair and their plans for the future. Anyone sensible would do that. Was it so foolish, then, to want to tell them in a more personal way? To have a long, wonderful chat over the phone as they used to have and say, 'Guess what . . . I've met this man – a doctor actually – and . . .'

And during the course of the conversation, surely at least one of her old friends would know her well enough to sense that something was wrong . . .

CHAPTER 7

Wednesday night – the West Country

This was the second night after the fiasco of the burnt dinner that Carol was sleeping alone. What was it that her mother used to say? 'Never let the sun go down on a quarrel?'

In the early days of their marriage Carol had tried to live by that rule. If she and Alan had a disagreement she had made sure that they patched things up before bed-time. And the making up had usually been delicious. Alan used to make a joke about it. He used to say they should quarrel more often!

But it was a long time since she had been able to make him respond with anything approaching humour. And, inevitably, Carol had begun to resent the fact that it was always up to her; that Alan never made the effort to put things right. But even so, she loved him so much that she still went on trying to smooth things over. Even if it meant apologizing when she didn't really think that whatever started the argument had been her fault.

Eventually – she couldn't remember when – she had become so worn down by their constant bickering that she had allowed her growing resentment to push her into deciding that she simply couldn't do it any more. If he wanted to end the day in a state of barely controlled anger, then let him. And just lately that seemed to be every day that God sent.

Even in bed, where they used to be able to forget everything except the joy of being together, there was no relenting. They would lie back-to-back in angry silence, each one trying not to move in case it would bring them into contact with the other. Infuriatingly, Alan seemed to be able to sleep whatever had been said and Carol would stay awake for hours trying to figure out what had gone wrong.

She still didn't know what had prompted her to make such a special effort on Tuesday night. She groaned and turned over in the bed, racked by anger mixed with humiliation. She was furious with herself for falling asleep and spoiling the meal she had prepared for him. And she felt humiliated because, as far as Alan was concerned, she'd made a mess of things again.

And yet she never fouled things up at work. At Travers' Transport she was methodical and efficient, just as she had been at any job she had ever had. Luke had said he was lucky to have her.

Luke . . . an uncomfortable sensation of guilt nudged at her awareness. She had been thinking about Luke when she had fallen asleep on the sofa . . . disturbing thoughts but oh, so exciting . . .

Carol pulled one of the pillows towards her and hugged it close to her body. She closed her eyes and tried to dispel the nagging sense of shame. She knew she had intended that the evening with Alan should end in lovemaking. But why? Was it because she loved and desired him or was it because she was growing more and more aware of Luke's sexual appeal and wanted to sublimate her guilty feelings by making love with her husband?

Well, it hadn't worked. The only comfort she'd had that night was a mug of hot chocolate and a packet of sweet biscuits. Alan hadn't even come to share their bed. He had slept in the spare room. Furthermore, he'd been gone before she had gone down for breakfast this morning.

And tonight he'd come home from work long after Carol had come up to bed. She'd heard him moving around downstairs. But she had no idea whether he'd warmed up the soup and eaten the salad she'd left for him before he'd come upstairs and headed for the spare room again.

So what was she going to do? Storm into the spare bedroom and tell him how unhappy she was and demand to know why he was behaving like this? Or creep in softly and slide into the bed beside him . . . her hands moving over his body . . . arousing him in the way she knew she still could? While she was still trying to decide if either of these tactics would work, exhaustion overcame her and she fell asleep.

Just over two hundred miles away, Alison had also had difficulty in getting to sleep for the second night in a row.

On Tuesday, after Greg had brought her home, she knew how hopeless it was going to be. She considered taking two of the sleeping pills that she'd had ever since Paul had died. At that time, even although the doctor had assured her that they weren't addictive, she'd stopped taking them after only a few nights. She had wanted to be fully alert in case her son or Paul's mother had needed her during the long, miserable hours of loss and desolation.

So, last night, after tossing and turning for what seemed hours, she gave in and took a couple. The pills had worked, but they had not been proof against the flood of feeling that invaded her body as soon as she had awoken this morning. She'd spent the whole day trying to deny those feelings and subjugate them in a frenzy of work both physical and mental.

She had phoned the family solicitor and told him to be ready for whatever she might decide about the sale of the land. And then she had gone round the house and listed in great detail the maintenance work that would have to be done if Matthew was going to inherit a sound property.

But now, when her son and his grandmother were sleeping and the old house was creaking and groaning in the wind as old houses do, she could deny her inner turmoil no longer. She stretched her long, slim limbs out across the cool sheets and tried to ease the tension that was building up inside her. She tried closing her eyes and breathing in deeply.

Relax . . . she told herself, *relax* . . . But her muscles remained taut and her breathing ragged.

Irritated with herself, she pushed aside the bedclothes and got up. She padded across the floor towards the window. She leaned her head against the cool glass and looked down. Her bedroom overlooked the walled garden at the side of the house.

The rain that had been threatening all day now seemed to have set in for the night and the garden below her was a rain-drenched blur. She could just make out the untidy shapes of the neglected shrubs and the tangled stems of the unpruned rose bushes dipping and waving in the wind. The garden had been neglected – like so much of the estate. If she sold the old orchard to Greg Leighton she would be able to care for Matthew's inheritance so much better.

Greg . . .

Alison moved back and eased the bottom half of the old sash window upwards. The cool air hit her body and she welcomed it. She sank to her knees and, resting both arms along the sill, she breathed in the welcome smell of damp earth and newly growing vegetation.

She rested her cheek on the back of one hand and

117

instantly became aware of the feel of her own skin. It seemed that every sense was heightened, every pore open to sensation. She could feel her long hair resting on her shoulders and her back, the cool wood that her arms were resting on and the very fibres of her cotton nightdress as it clung to her body.

The long nightdress was sleeveless and trimmed with broderie anglais. Paul used to say that, even although it had been designed to look virginal, it was nevertheless the sexiest garment he had ever had the privilege to remove.

Paul . . .

With an agonized sigh, Alison removed her arms from the windowsill and wrapped them around her body and began to rock backwards and forwards in her misery.

Paul . . . I miss you . . . I need you . . . oh, my darling, please forgive me . . .

She wasn't sure what it was she was asking him to forgive; she only knew that she had reached some kind of turning point in her life and she was completely unprepared for it.

Eventually, exhausted by guilt and confusion, she rose and stumbled back to bed. When sleep eventually overcame her, nothing had been resolved except her acceptance of the fact that she knew she was alive again. And new life could be painful.

This city never slept, never rested, never even paused to take breath. Francine stood at her window and gazed out over the Thames, the moving lights that were the cars passing over Tower Bridge, and the buildings with lighted windows on the other side of the river.

When she had first moved to London she had hardly been able to sleep for the excitement of it all. Peter had come before her and he had arranged for her to buy the flat in Fulham. He hadn't wanted her to share with any other girls, for obvious reasons, and she had found it heavy going to make the repayments on the mortgage. But she wouldn't accept any financial help from him.

Tonight she had long ago given up any attempt at sleeping. Bringing her workbooks into the living room, she'd made herself a nest of cushions on the floor and spread her notes out on a low coffee table. She adjusted the table lamp and started to make painstaking and detailed notes. If she was going to convince Peter to let her do this, she knew that she would have to be well prepared. If he could shoot her idea down, he would.

Eventually she paused and dropped the pen. She stretched and relaxed her fingers. They felt cramped. She lifted her arms above her head and yawned. She felt physically tired but even if she went to bed she knew that she wouldn't be able to sleep. Her mind was racing. Ideas were coming fast and furious and she wanted to set them down straight away. She would work as long as she had to.

But before taking up her pen again, she reached out and picked up the novel that she had recently finished reading, *Still Breathing*. She turned it over so that she could see the photograph of the author on the back cover.

Marcus Holbrook stared back at her. His uncompromising gaze was unnerving and Francine unconsciously raised her other hand and pulled her robe closed across her breast. She knew him to be in his early forties and yet his hair was either very blond or white. More likely white, she guessed, to judge by the dark eyebrows. His face was long and craggy; the tilt of his head emphasized the watchfulness of his expression.

She found herself wondering what he would look like if he smiled. Did he ever smile? She shook her head slightly. Judging from the strength and savagery of his writing, she doubted it. And yet . . . along with the savagery there was compassion and, if you truly under-

119

stood his message, there was a deeply ironic humour. Yes . . . he would be able to smile . . . and it would be a smile worth seeing.

She had to meet him – talk to him – interview him. She had read every book he had written and his latest was the best yet. She knew that she had to find out how this man – a man who lived in almost medieval isolation in a remote cottage for most of the year – could so accurately record and analyse what it was like to be alive in the world today.

The novel opened with a busy scene in a hospital as medical staff worked on a man on life support. He'd been in a road accident. Unknown to everyone, he was aware of what was taking place. The entire story went on in his head while all around him various characters came and went. The unnamed man could hear them but he couldn't communicate with them. As he reacted to their presence and thought about them – his father, his wife, his daughters, his work colleagues and his friends – the whole story of his life was revealed.

Now, the accident had given him the chance to analyse what had gone wrong, build on everything that had been good – if he was given the chance. Francine shivered when she remembered the powerful scene towards the end of the book when the medical team and his family discussed how much longer they should keep him on life support . . . the moment when his youngest daughter cried out, 'But he's still breathing!'

She laid the book down and picked up the mug of coffee that she'd made for herself before she started working. She took a sip and realized it had gone cold. How long had she been sitting here? She stared at the pages of notes she had made and then glanced at her watch. She smiled. It was a very long time since she had been so absorbed by preparing programme notes that she had let a couple of hours slip by without noticing.

On the contrary, most days recently she'd had to force herself to get through each job that was lined up for her. She was far too professional not to do her very best once she started working, but there were days when she felt that she would scream with boredom.

Would Peter back a programme like the one she had in mind? she wondered. If she went freelance and promised to do the *VIPs* series, would he provide the finance for her to strike out into something different? Probably not. She sighed. She knew that Peter, as executive producer, was happy with things just the way they were.

Peter probably saw her going on forever interviewing glamorous and glitzy people in her own idiosyncratic way. It was the very fact that Francine didn't fawn, wasn't over-impressed and sometimes asked questions that took the wind out of their sails that made her such a successful interviewer of the rich and famous. He wouldn't want to risk her successful reputation by allowing her do something so different – a serious arts programme.

And yet he should understand why she wanted more. When he had first helped her take her first steps in broadcasting he had told her that she was capable of doing anything she wanted to. He was much older than she was, of course, nearer to retirement. Had he become complacent?

Francine frowned. She remembered when he had first come up to London. He had urged her to apply for a transfer and, contrary to what some people thought, she had managed that without his help. He hadn't used any influence to get her a job. There might have been talk and that would have been too dangerous. Peter's children were still living at home and he didn't want to break up his marriage.

It had been sheer coincidence that Tristram had changed jobs at around the same time and she knew that some people, including Tristram's wife, had been convinced that it was Tristram that she was following to London. Peter had been amused and even pleased. At the time Francine suspected that he'd relayed the gossip to his own wife as a useful red herring.

Many times, over the years, Francine had wondered whether Nancy Curtis suspected that her husband had been engaged in a long-term relationship with another woman.

Does she know and does she care? Francine often asked herself. She had long ago given up any hope that Peter was going to leave Nancy. To be fair, he had never even suggested that he would . . .

Francine gathered up her notes and the book and stacked them neatly on a low coffee table. She would find some way to do it. The interview with Marcus Holbrook would just be the first in a series of programmes devoted to music, art and literature, and if Peter wouldn't go along with her plans she would have to find the funding herself.

Perhaps she could form a small production company of her own? She had plenty of contacts and she wasn't short of money. Perhaps it was time to risk some of it on herself and her own ambitions.

It was nearly four o'clock before she got to bed but Francine wasn't worried. She had a free day ahead of her and she could please herself what she did with it. Once she would have been upset that she couldn't spend her free time with Peter. She would have moped around all day thinking about what they could have been doing together. What they would never do.

They could never go window-shopping, never walk by the river, never go for a drink or have a meal in public. They couldn't go to the cinema, the theatre, a concert; they couldn't be seen in public as a couple.

When had she stopped grieving over this state of

122

affairs? Francine wondered. And why? Was it because she had accepted the situation? Or was it because, deep down, she had stopped caring?

As she drifted off to sleep, cocooned in her luxurious bedroom from the sights and sounds of the awakening city, Francine tried to push away a growing awareness that there was something lacking. A dangerous void where her emotions used to be. What was that quotation she remembered from her schooldays? *Natura vacuum abhoret* . . . Nature abhors a vacuum . . .

She stirred uneasily. She had the craziest feeling that against her will something powerful was rushing towards her in order to fill that vacuum. She tried to shut her mind to the disturbing picture that kept intruding there of a pair of dark, compelling eyes . . . a sardonic smile . . .

Thursday morning – the West Country

The only proof that Alan was still living in the same house was the fact that he'd eaten the soup and the salad she'd left him the night before and dumped his soiled shirts and underwear in the laundry basket.

Carol hadn't slept well and she'd got up and showered a little earlier than usual so she had time to load the washing machine and start it before she sat down to eat her breakfast. But she only nibbled at her toast half-heartedly and, eventually, pushed it aside.

The postman came up the path just as she shut the front door. She hitched the strap of her bag over her shoulder, smiled tiredly, and held out her hand for the bundle of letters. She frowned at the two official-looking envelopes – the ones with little cellophane windows in – and pushed them through the letterbox before shoving the three brightly coloured postcards into her bag. The postman watched her and grinned before setting off again.

She was a little later than usual and traffic on the motorway was heavy, but the traffic reports on the local radio station indicated no problems ahead. Furthermore, the sun was shining and there would be no need to put her dodgy windscreen wiper to the test. Just as well, Carol thought. *I don't want any aggravation. No snags, no foul-ups, no hassle of any kind. My life is a big enough mess already.*

Once at work, she acknowledged Stacey's cheery greeting with a tight-lipped smile and went straight to her own office. When the computer screen blinked into life she could almost feel the physical world retreating. She opened up the file she had been working on and immersed herself, gratefully, in the technical data that was so important to the firm's future.

Luke's future . . . the thought popped up from no-where and she cursed as she realized that she had entered a whole row of figures in the wrong column. *No!* she fumed silently. *Not my work – I've never let my personal problems interfere with my work before!*

It didn't take long to correct her mistake and, then, summoning up almost superhuman powers of concentration, Carol worked on all morning. She hardly noticed the unavoidable noise that carried from the other rooms in the temporary building and only looked up briefly to thank Stacey when she appeared with a mug of coffee.

Not much later, it seemed, Stacey was back. 'That coffee's gone cold.'

She heard the accusing voice and looked up to find the girl standing over her accusingly. 'Mm?' Carol frowned. 'It can't have done.'

'Why not? It's been standing there for over an hour.'

'It can't have been.'

'For an intelligent woman you haven't got a very big vocabulary. Look – I brought this in to you over an hour ago – and that lovely cream cake too. What's the matter

124

with you, Carol? Are you sickening for something?'

'No – I'm fine – it's just I didn't notice the time passing, really I didn't.'

Stacey came round behind her. She reached over to the keyboard and swiftly and expertly she saved the file and closed it.

'Stacey!'

'It's all right. I know what I'm doing. I may not have a clue what all that stuff that keeps you occupied means but I'm not computer illiterate. Your precious files are quite safe in there and you are going to have a break.'

'Am I?'

'Yes. I'll make you another coffee – in fact I'll have one myself and I'll stay here with you to make sure you relax for at least ten minutes.'

'OK, you win.'

Carol sat back in her chair and closed her eyes. The work had been going well and she really had lost all sense of time and even place for a while. But her young friend was right; it was wrong to work on for hours without taking a break.

She stared for a moment at the blank computer screen and then her gaze travelled around her cramped little office. Luke was forever apologizing about the temporary building and its lack of facilities but, in fact, Carol was happy here. The confined space was cosy, reassuring somehow. It was her own little space – a place where she could lose herself in her work and forget about her troubles.

Suddenly she thought of Sophie. Her old friend from university used to tease her gently about her ability to absorb herself in her studies. She remembered one evening when Sophie had come into Carol's room and gently closed the book she was reading. She had looked up at Sophie in surprise.

'*Do you realize that Alan has been waiting in the kitchen*

for an hour and if you don't take him away soon we'll have no food left?'

'*Alan?*' Carol had asked.

'*Yes, Alan. Your boyfriend, remember? You told the poor guy that you only had a couple of pages to finish reading. That was an hour ago and by the looks of it you've nearly finished the book! It's a good job that he loves you . . .*'

A sob caught in Carol's throat as she remembered the scene. And then she found herself remembering Sophie and all the times they had talked quietly together in the student flat that the four of them had shared. Sophie had always been ready to listen to any one of them if they had problems of any kind. Problems with men, with money, difficulty with their studies . . .

Did Sophie never have problems of her own? Carol found herself wondering. It's funny, I can't remember her ever asking any of us for advice. But then she never needed any; she was always so calm and unruffled . . .

Carol realized that she desperately wanted to talk to Sophie, right now. I'll phone her tonight, she thought. Oh, I won't spill it all out – worry her with all my troubles – at least not straight away. It will just be reassuring to hear her voice at the other end of the phone . . .

By the time Stacey came back with two mugs of coffee, Carol had remembered the postcards and fished them out of her bag. She spread them out on top of the papers on her desk.

'They look nice,' Stacey said. 'Are they from friends on holiday?'

'They're from my parents.'

'What – all of them?'

'Yes, they're doing one of those tours – you know the kind of thing. Coachloads of respectable retired people whizzing around Europe following an itinerary that would knock the younger generation for six. All three cards arrived this morning – look they've been to Italy.' Carol pushed the cards across the desk.

Stacey scanned the brightly coloured photographic views of Venice, Florence and Rome. 'If this is a tour, why did they all arrive together?'

'Who knows? Could be the vagaries of the postal delivery service. If you look at the date stamps they're all different and they were all posted more than a week ago.'

'So when are they coming back?'

'Oh – I – think – any minute now.'

Carol hid her discomfiture by picking up her mug of coffee and beginning to drink it. She was too embarrassed to admit to Stacey that she hadn't given her parents and their holiday a thought for days. Surely that was an indication of what a mess her life was? But she had an uneasy feeling that they should have been back in their bungalow in the Lake District by now. So why hadn't they phoned her? She would have to call them tonight.

She grimaced as she tasted the coffee. 'This is very sweet.'

'Two spoons of sugar; thought you needed it. And why don't you eat up that cream cake?'

'I couldn't – all those calories.'

'Have you had any breakfast?'

'Well – no, not really.'

'I thought you hadn't. You have that lean and hungry look.'

'Oh, Stacey, hardly.'

'Well, perhaps not lean, but definitely hungry. Go on – eat it up.'

'I'll halve it with you.'

'OK.'

By the time she'd eaten her half of the choux bun,

127

Carol realized that Stacey – who was more than ten years her junior – had chivvied her back into a more equable frame of mind. When she was allowed to get back to work she was actually smiling. Therefore she was totally astounded when Luke came in a little later and said, 'I'm giving you the afternoon off.'

'What? I mean, why?'

'Perhaps you've been overdoing it.'

'What makes you – Stacey!'

'That's right. She told me that you seemed to be under some kind of strain this morning. She doesn't know why and can only guess that you've been working too hard and that you need a break away from all these facts and figures.'

'She's wrong. I love my work.'

'I know you do, and for that I'll be eternally grateful. But I'd never forgive myself if you had some kind of breakdown –'

'Surely I don't look as bad as that!'

'You don't look bad at all – you never do. Even when you're tired, as you obviously are right now, you must know that you look sensational.'

'Sensational?' Carol stared up at him. 'You're teasing.'

'No, I'm not. I would never be so unkind.'

'But – I mean –' Carol looked down at her crumpled blouse and unconsciously caught at a wayward strand of hair. She looked up at Luke to find that he was regarding her intently.

'You really don't know, do you?' he asked. His voice was strangely subdued.

'Know what?'

'About the effect you have on men.'

'Effect – me – men?' Carol stared at him helplessly. Her eyes widened with shock when she saw the way he was looking at her.

'Carol, I'm not going to embarrass you or me by

spelling it out. Let's just say there's a certain kind of appeal – sex appeal if you like – that has nothing to do with conventional beauty –'

'Oh.' Carol felt as though she had been winded. She sat very still for a moment and then her old sense of humour suddenly re-emerged from where it had been hiding for years in time to save her. She looked up and managed a ragged smile. 'So you think I'm ugly?'

'What?' Luke looked startled and then he grinned. 'I didn't say that.'

'I know what you said, and – and –'

'And what?'

'I wish you hadn't.' Her smile faded and she looked down at her desk.

There was a small silence and then Luke said. 'I'm not going to apologize, but I will promise to try not to embarrass you again. Now, switch that darn thing off. I mean it. No more work for you today.'

CHAPTER 8

At about the same time that Carol had been sitting alone in her kitchen, nibbling her toast without enthusiasm, Francine opened her eyes and glanced towards the glowing figures of her clock radio.

She was surprised to see that it was only eight o'clock. She'd only had about four hours' sleep and yet she felt completely rested. She should have been feeling shattered but she pushed the duvet aside, got up and headed for the kitchen.

Perhaps her sense of wellbeing was due to the fact that she didn't have to hurry off anywhere today. She made a cup of coffee, collected her diary and the notes she'd been working on the night before and went back to bed.

For a while she sat propped up amongst the pillows and savoured her coffee, hot, black and fragrant, while she switched between stations and listened to news bulletins on the radio. This was force of habit. Working in the media as she did, she had to get her daily fix of national and world events.

Eventually, she put down her cup and switched the radio off. She opened her diary and looked at it thoughtfully. She reached for the phone and dialled a familiar number.

'Rob Baines here.'

'Rob, it's me, Francine.'

'Is something the matter?'

'No why should there be?'

'It's not like you to be awake so early on your day off.'

'No, I'm fine. Rob, I've been looking at my diary –'

'Wait a moment, I'll get mine.'

Francine reflected how lucky she was to have been working with someone who was so 'together'. He never panicked, never wasted time on unnecessary questions. He just got on with it.

'OK,' his calm voice responded a few moments later. 'Now what are we looking at?'

'Tomorrow, actually.'

'Tomorrow we're not very busy. You and I are supposed to be going over the research for the programme about supermodels and trying to decide whether we've covered every aspect. Then there's nothing until Monday.'

'Yes, I thought so. Rob, is it vital for me to be there tomorrow? I mean, can you handle that on your own?'

'Am I hearing this right?'

'Why so surprised?'

'Because you always like to be in on every stage of the planning. In the past you've insisted that you have the final say on even the smallest details. I can't believe that you're willing to leave it to me.'

'You're the only other person I would leave it to. Rob, we've been working together for so long now – you know my style – you know my preferences – I trust your judgement completely.'

'OK, Francine, there's no need to be so effusive. I get the message: you want a day off!'

Rob sounded amused, but he also sounded flattered and this made Francine feel guilty. It was true that her producer knew her well enough to be able to make the right decisions but, clever though he was, he had never

131

been intuitive enough to take those little leaps of imagination that made a good feature great. But this time she really didn't care.

'Yes, I would like a day off,' she said.

'Are you sure you're OK? You know I've been worried about you lately?'

'I know. And as I hinted to you the other day, I may have been overdoing it – you know – moving house – trying to make big decisions about my future – quite apart from all the packing cases still littering up the place . . .'

'Say no more. I'm really glad you've decided to relax a little. Look – you've got four days, why don't you just slob around – forget about the unpacking? There can't be anything in those boxes that you really need or you'd have missed it by now.'

'You're right.'

'So stay in bed – read romances – eat chocolates – and don't answer the phone.'

'Thanks for the suggestions. But, Rob . . .'

'Yes?'

'Would you tell Marsha for me?'

'Marsha Parry, your super-efficient PA? Of course I will, but I expect she'll grumble.'

'Why? Because I'm taking some time off?'

'No, of course not. But like all good PAs, she'll probably think that you ought to have told her first.'

'I'll rely on you to charm her for me, then,' She heard Rob laughing as she murmured, 'See you on Monday,' and replaced the receiver.

She smiled as she headed for the shower. The needle-sharp spray was invigorating and it was as if her doubts were being washed away. She knew that Peter might oppose her plan – she accepted that she might have to take this step without him. And she wasn't sure what that would do to their relationship. However, now that she had made her decision she felt a lot better.

Dressed in black slacks and a bright red roll-top cotton sweater, she sat down for breakfast. Over orange juice, muesli and another cup of black coffee, Francine studied a road map. Her work took her to all parts of the British Isles and she always had the most up-to-date road information.

Pushing her plates aside, she spread the map out on the table and traced her route with a finger. The journey would be easy. Or at least the first part of it would be. She would drive north up the M1, M18 and then the A1(M) until she picked up the A64 which circled York.

That should take about three and a half hours, she thought as she slipped on the jacket that matched her trousers. She decided that she would probably stop off in York, have some lunch and think about what she was going to do next.

For, in truth, although she knew what she wanted to do, she wasn't quite sure how she was going to achieve it. But as she washed her breakfast dishes then, swiftly and efficiently, packed everything she would need for the next day or two, one thing was clear. She knew that had no intention of taking up any of Rob's suggestions – except the one about not answering the phone. She wouldn't be doing that because she wouldn't be here.

While Francine was heading northwards out of London, Alison sat in the kitchen of Westbrook Hall. She wasn't alone. Daphne had arrived shortly after Alison had returned from walking Matthew to school and announced that she could stay for lunch.

Wonderful, Alison thought. She never asks if it's convenient, never offers to actually make the meal – and, come to that, she never even thanks me. She sat at the scrubbed wooden table and placed both hands round her mug of coffee as she watched Daphne.

133

Her sister-in-law was tall and bony. She was enough like her late brother to be considered handsome, but whereas he had been rangy, she was gauche. Her movements were jerky and graceless as she set a tray with a pot of tea, milk, sugar and biscuits for her mother. Only one cup, Alison thought. Oh, dear, that means Daphne's coming down here again and I can guess why.

'I won't be long,' her unwelcome visitor said as she paused in the doorway. 'Make another pot for me, will you?'

Alison sighed at the prospect of another discussion with Daphne about the proposed sale of the orchard. Daphne hadn't lived in the Hall since her marriage but, for family reasons, she was actively involved in its future.

Westbrook Hall had passed to Paul when his father had died with the proviso that Lilian Cavendish should be allowed to live there for the rest of her life or until she remarried, which was unlikely at her age. Paul's will had been similar. The house now belonged to his son; as he was still a child, Alison was his legal guardian and the same proviso had been made except that, in this case, she would not have to vacate the Hall on remarriage if her son was still a minor.

Paul had not expected to die before his mother. No mention of her had been made in his will and Daphne was very conscious of the fact that her mother's comfort and security depended on Alison's goodwill. However, her husband, Nigel, had been made a co-executor and he – and therefore Daphne – was in a position to oppose any plan Alison might have for the property if he thought the plans were financially risky.

Had Nigel come up with some new objection? Alison wondered. Was she going to have to explain everything all over again?

She rose wearily and topped up the kettle. When the

water boiled, she scalded a small teapot before adding the tea leaves. Daphne was fussy and would probably have been horrified if she had known that, when she was alone, Alison used teabags.

'Aren't you joining me?' Daphne asked when she returned.

'No, I'm drinking coffee.'

Her sister-in-law glanced over the table at Alison's pottery mug and sniffed. 'Instant coffee. Ugh! How could you?'

'How can you possibly tell?'

'It never looks right. Besides, you left the jar on the bench.' Daphne smiled fleetingly.

That's her attempt at humour, Alison thought, and she waited resignedly for the onslaught to come. For onslaught there would be, she was sure of it. Why else would Daphne want to sit in the kitchen with her? She had never, ever chosen to spend time with Alison just for a friendly chat. No, whenever she had sought her out in the past it was because she had something – usually unpleasant – to say; some forceful opinion to deliver.

'I'm surprised at you, Alison. If you had to have dinner with that man, did you have to go to The Plough?'

Well, at least she hasn't wasted any time with pleasantries, Alison thought. But she asked, 'What's wrong with The Plough?'

'My dear, you shouldn't have to ask. It's the village pub. Hardly the place for you, as Mrs Cavendish, to dine.'

'Why ever not? Paul used to take me there.'

Daphne shrugged dismissively. '*Noblesse oblige.*'

Alison regarded the older woman's haughty features angrily. 'What are you talking about, Daphne?'

'Don't pretend to be uneducated, Alison. You know very well what it means.'

'Maybe so. But I'm not sure what it has to do with

your late brother and his wife enjoying a drink or a meal in the village pub.'

Daphne put down her teacup and sat back in her chair. She sighed and cast her eyes up to heaven. Then she leaned forward again and spoke very slowly as if she were explaining something to a child. 'Privilege entails responsibility. Noble people must behave nobly.'

'Oh, come on, Daphne. The Cavendishes might be an old family but they're hardly noble!'

'And that, of course explains the difference between us – you and the family, I mean. You simply don't understand that although we may not have a title, we've lived on this land for many, many generations. That gives us a rather special place in the scheme of things. Paul, as –'

'Lord of the manor,' Alison spluttered.

'Don't be childish, Alison. Paul, as the representative of this family, liked to do his duty by mingling with –'

'The common folk!'

'With the people who have lived on our lands for centuries –'

'Your land?'

'Well,' Daphne's eyes closed briefly in acknowledgement, 'of land that used to be ours. Paul was conscious of his place in society.'

'Oh, come off it, Daphne!' Alison could control her anger no longer. 'I'm sure that nothing like that ever went through Paul's mind. He just wanted to go down to the pub like any other guy and relax with people he regarded as his friends.'

The two women watched each other in silence. Alison could hear the ticking of the kitchen wall clock and the occasional drip of the tap that needed a new washer. The pan of home-made soup that she'd left on the Aga began to send out a comforting aroma. But there was to be no relief from Daphne's offensive.

Her sister-in-law placed both of her hands on the table

in front of her and leaned forward. 'Alison.' She spoke as if she was trying to placate someone who was being unreasonably angry.

Of course this made Alison even angrier, but she struggled to control her rage. She didn't want to give Daphne the satisfaction of seeing how easily she could rile her. 'Yes, Daphne,' she said sweetly.

'I didn't come here to antagonize you.'

'Goodness. You surprise me.'

'Don't be so bloody flippant!' Daphne snapped, and Alison did her best to hide a smile.

'Sorry, Daphne. You were saying?'

'I came here this morning because, quite apart from your choice of place to eat, I wanted to ask you whether you thought it wise to be seen in public with a man like that.'

Alison was tempted to ask Daphne to leave but she reminded herself that this woman was her sister-in-law. Paul's sister, Matthew's aunt; and whatever her own opinion of the woman might be, she had no right to cause a rift in the family.

'I'll deal with that in a moment,' she said. 'But first, tell me how you knew we went to The Plough.'

'My dear, you shouldn't even have to ask. This is a small community and there is bound to be gossip.'

'So who passed the gossip on to you?'

Daphne shrugged. 'Mrs Slater, my cleaning lady, as a matter of fact. She and her husband were drinking there that night. They saw you arrive and go through to the restaurant.'

'I see. Did she also tell you that we were there to discuss business?' Alison felt uneasy at her own words. Because, of course, they hadn't really discussed business, not seriously. In fact Greg had been more concerned to see that she relaxed and enjoyed herself.

'Oh, I thought it would be something like that. I can't

imagine any other reason why you would want to go out with him. And I hope you didn't allow him to take advantage of you.'

'Advantage of me?' Alison's eyes widened but luckily Daphne obviously had no idea of the *double entendre* of her words.

She hurried on, 'Yes, talk you into selling the land too cheaply while you were under the influence of drink, or anything?'

'Daphne, do you really have such a low opinion of me? Do you really think that I'm as stupid or susceptible as that?'

Daphne looked uncomfortable. 'Well, no, but, obviously I was worried.'

'You had no need to be. We were only talking generally about the sale. No deal has been struck.'

'That's a relief. Now, you said you would answer my question.'

'Oh, yes. You wanted to know whether it was wise to be seen in public with "a man like that". I'll try to answer you but, first, you'll have to explain exactly what you mean.'

'Alison, I sometimes wonder how on earth you ever got into university. The man is a property developer –'

'Goodness, I didn't know that was a crime. Some property developers have even been given titles.'

'Let me finish. A property developer who may not always have followed the rules –'

'That may be slanderous –'

'Don't interrupt. I'm quite sure that Mr Leighton will have covered his tracks very well – after all he can afford the best lawyers. However, given his background, I'd be most surprised if his riches – his quite substantial riches, I understand – have all been honestly come by.'

'His background?'

'Do you mean to say that you really don't know?'

'I – there was an article about him in the press lately –'

'Have you read it?'

'No – but I understand it hinted at a difficult start in life.'

Daphne snorted. 'That's one way of putting it! And that article could only hint at the truth. Alison, the man came from the gutter. His mother was probably on the streets and his father could have been any one of a dozen or so of the petty gangsters she consorted with. Don't tell me that a man like that is going to be a model of probity.'

'How – how do you know all this? It can't have been in the papers.'

'Nigel works in the city, remember. It's his business to know the backgrounds of all the major players. And in this case, seeing that my nephew's inheritance was involved, he made it his business to delve into Mr Leighton's background thoroughly.'

'I see.'

Nigel Remington, Daphne's husband, was a stock-broker and, in spite of his ineffectual looks and his drawling upper-class voice, he was extremely astute. But, surely, Alison thought, even if everything about Greg's background is true, it doesn't mean that the man himself is a crook . . .

'Oh, dear. Now I feel guilty.' Daphne was staring at her with what passed for concern. 'I just wanted to warn you about the man's character – you mustn't think that you can't go ahead with the sale of the Orchard.'

'Really?' Alison was startled. She had imagined that Daphne, like her mother, was totally opposed to the sale.

'No, my dear –'

Alison flinched. Daphne trying to be kind and reasonable was infinitely worse that Daphne being unpleasant.

Her sister-in-law hadn't noticed anything and she hurried on. 'Nigel thinks that, so long as you allow him to advise you, you probably ought to go ahead.'

'But your mother –'

'Mother respects Nigel and values his opinions. She'll come round to the idea. Leave her to me.'

For the first time that morning, Alison warmed towards Daphne. It really would make life easier for her if she could go ahead with her plans without having to worry about her mother-in-law.

'Oh, Daphne – I'd be so grateful. I mean, I've been really worried about the way your mother's taking this –'

'Well, stop worrying. And, Alison, my dear, I hope you're not too upset by what I've told you about Mr Leighton. I mean, you're much too sensible to be attracted to him on a personal level, aren't you?'

The front door bell rang and Alison was saved from answering. 'I'll go,' she said and hurried from the kitchen. She had no idea who it could be but she was so grateful to escape from Daphne that she was smiling as she answered the door.

A cheerful youth stood there holding an enormous bouquet of flowers. Behind him she glimpsed a small delivery van. On the side was painted the name of a florist's in Norwich.

'Mrs Cavendish?' the youth asked.

'Yes, but who –?'

'Here you are, then.' He handed the flowers over carefully. 'There's a card.'

Alison cradled the bouquet as if it were a baby and watched as the youth retreated down the steps, got into his van and drove away down the drive. When it was no longer in sight she looked down and saw a small envelope attached to the cellophane.

'My goodness, Alison, what lovely flowers! But who are they for?'

She flinched as she heard Daphne coming up behind her. 'I – I don't know. Your mother, I suppose . . .'

'There's a card – let me see –'

Before she could stop her, Daphne had taken the envelope and opened it. 'No, the flowers are not for Mother, they're for you, look.'

Alison could hear the chill in Daphne's voice and she took the card hesitantly. She read it.

Alison.

> *See you soon.*

>> *Greg.*

She felt herself flushing and was most reluctant to look up again and meet her sister-in-law's eyes. When she did, Daphne was regarding her with a mixture of prurience and scorn.

'Well,' she said. 'Perhaps my little warning has come too late.'

'Carol – wait a moment!'

Carol paused just as she was going to get into her car and turned round. Luke was hurrying across the car park towards her. He was carrying some papers. It looked like work. Did he want her to stay after all? She would stay gladly. She didn't really want to go home and spend the afternoon alone.

'Yes?'

But he didn't want her to stay. He said, 'Take this lot home with you and have a look at it, will you? I'd value your opinion.'

'Sure, but what is it?' Carol dumped her briefcase inside the car and took the papers.

'Some information about a new computer software package – specially designed for firms like this,' he said. 'It looks good but it's expensive. You're my expert – tell me what you think.'

'Of course, but I'd have to see it in action . . .'

'There's a demonstration disk – there – in that envelope.'

'I – I haven't got a computer at home.'

'Oh, well, then –'

'I could stay and look over it now – I didn't really want the afternoon off, you know.'

'No. Forget it. Read through the paperwork if you have time and then have a look at it on the computer here tomorrow.'

'OK.'

'We-ell – I'd better –'

He didn't turn to go and Carol didn't make any further attempt to get into her car. They just looked at each other hesitantly. Then there was a moment when everything seemed to change. An unspoken, unformulated signal passed between them. But they didn't need words. Carol sensed that they had reached a different level of understanding. More intimate – and yet not intimate in the physical sense.

Luke had felt it too. He smiled in acknowledgement of their new rapport. 'I can't let you go without your lunch. Wait a moment, will you?'

Carol made no protest as he hurried back into the temporary office building. She stood there smiling foolishly until he returned.

'We'll take both cars, then you can go straight home after we've eaten. Just follow me. OK?'

'Fine.'

The state of euphoria that Carol had experienced in the car park stayed with her as she followed Luke along the familiar route to the White Swan. It was only when he drove on past the old tavern where they usually had lunch that she experienced a moment of confusion.

What am I doing, she thought, what am I *really* doing? Am I going for lunch with my boss and are we going to talk business as usual, or am I going for a meal with a man that I'm attracted to?

Perhaps I should just fall back and get lost in the traffic. I could phone Luke at work later and tell him that

142

I lost him so I thought it would be better just to go home . . .

But while she was still thinking this over, Luke signalled and turned into a service station. She could hardly drive on now. She pulled in and parked behind him outside the garage shop. He got out of his car and waved and grinned. He gestured for her to wait. When he came out of the shop he was carrying a couple of carrier bags. He walked over and she wound down her window.

'I thought we'd eat alfresco,' he said. He raised the carrier bags. 'Sandwiches, milk and fruit. I think I've covered everything.'

Not much later they were sitting at one of those wooden tables with fixed benches that you could find in designated picnic areas in countryside parks. The benches were splintered and a little damp, so Luke had spread a travelling rug out along one of them and they sat side by side.

The way the table was constructed forced them to sit closer than they might have done. Carol was overwhelmed by his nearness – his physical presence. She kept her eyes on the table as he took the food out of the bags.

'I've never seen you eat red meat so I got chicken, tuna, cheese, egg mayonnaise, salad –'

Carol laughed as he placed the cellophane and cardboard packages on the table. 'Oh, Luke, so many sandwiches – we'll never be able to eat all those!'

'Just choose what you want. Then I thought we'd better stay with the healthy eating theme and have these apples –'

'Two each!'

'I didn't know whether you liked red or green. Now, to complete the meal, a carton of milk and –'

'A giant bar of chocolate! Luke, I don't think chocolate qualifies as healthy eating.'

'But no picnic is complete without it, don't you think? Now, let's begin. All this fresh air has made me hungry.'

Luke produced a pack of paper plates and some polystyrene cups from one of the bags along with some paper napkins. Carol watched him spread four of the napkins out on the table and arrange the food on them in a more orderly fashion.

He's neat and painstaking, she thought, and she had a fleeting mind's eye glimpse of his office. It wasn't very much bigger than hers and it was a working office – not just for show. But his desk was always tidy and his filing cabinets orderly. The tops of the filing cabinets were always free from loose files or papers.

She wondered what his home was like and realized in that same instant that hers would probably horrify him.

'What are you thinking?' he asked.

'Nothing in particular.' She couldn't meet his eyes. 'It's lovely here.'

'Yes, isn't it?'

For a moment they both glanced round at the woodland behind them. The April showers had left the countryside fresh with the special greenness of spring. Carol breathed in slowly. The air was sweet and yet invigorating. Smiling, she turned towards Luke – and met his eyes.

As they held each other's gaze, his smile faded and he moved his head towards her. Carol felt as though she were suffocating. There was a steel band tightening round her chest. She opened her mouth to gulp in air and at that moment his lips touched hers, brushing them softly for just an instant. But it was long enough for her to feel how sweet his mouth could be.

And then he drew back. He looked at her solemnly. They stared at each other as they acknowledged the fact that they were on the brink of changing things forever. Without a word being spoken they had reached a doorway that would lead into a different kind of life for both of them. But they weren't going to cross the threshold. Not today.

Luke's smile returned but it was different; sad somehow. 'We'd better eat,' he said.

Carol sighed and turned her head away.

Later, at home, she dumped her briefcase in the hall, picked up the letters that she had pushed through the letterbox that morning and dropped them on to the hall table on the way upstairs.

After a swift shower, she pulled on a pair of dark trousers and a long-line, red cotton-knit sweater. She looked at herself in the bedroom mirror. Well, the outfit's cheerful enough, she thought. Now all I have to do is smile.

She headed for the kitchen, unloaded the washing machine and loaded the tumble dryer. She did this without even having to think about it; such chores had become an unwelcome routine. Then she put the kettle on. She would allow herself a mug of coffee – with cold milk so that she could drink it quickly – and then tackle the housework.

When Alan came home tonight the house would be clean and tidy and there would be a meal waiting for him. She wouldn't go to bed; no matter how late he arrived she would be downstairs waiting for him. And after he had eaten they would talk.

Should I phone him at work? she wondered. If I know what time to expect him I can't make a mess of things. No, I'd better not, he doesn't like me to phone work unless there's an emergency and, besides, he made a big point of reminding me that he'd gone over his new work schedule with me. If I phone to ask what time he's coming home, he'll be angry and say that I never listen to him. He'll say that I've lost interest in his job and what he does.

145

Have I lost interest?

No, of course not, it's just that we're both so tired when we get home that we never seem to be able to give each other the attention we deserve.

Carol sat down at the kitchen table with her coffee and brooded that the difference between them was – and always had been – that she could acknowledge that fact but Alan couldn't. *I wonder if he ever thinks that I might like it if he asked me how my day had gone?*

After she finished her coffee she inspected the freezer and decided to settle for a couple of frozen ready meals. She could get them out as soon as Alan arrived home and cook them in the microwave. It wouldn't be *haute cuisine* but fish pie and peas would look very welcoming.

I might even walk down to the Asian corner shop in the village and treat us to another bottle of wine, she thought. And she tried to suppress the notion that she was trying to compensate for her feelings of guilt.

When she'd finished tidying up she glanced out of the window. The sky was growing dark and there was a fine drizzle misting the glass with tiny beads of moisture. She pulled on a jacket, grabbed her umbrella and set off for the village.

It was when she was walking back from the shop with the wine and a box of the chocolate peppermint creams that Alan liked so much that she remembered the other phone calls she had intended to make.

Again she felt a surge of guilt accompanied by bewilderment. Only that morning she had been worried that her parents hadn't been in touch, and then the events of the day had driven that worry from her mind. She felt ashamed, and quickened her step, opening the door, shutting it behind her and picking up the receiver.

The line was dead. Carol sat down on the bottom stair and stared at the receiver in despair. She tried again but nothing happened. *How long has it been out of order?*

she wondered. She tried to remember the last time she'd made a call and couldn't. A few days ago, perhaps?

Which morning was it that she'd phoned in to work to tell Stacey that she'd had trouble getting the car started and she was going to be a little late? Was it last week? She realized that there hadn't been any incoming calls for ages. Not surprising if the phone was out of order.

Her parents had called her before they went on holiday – but that was weeks ago. Alan's parents hardly ever phoned. They regarded the phone as an instrument to be used only in emergencies and thought that people who called each other up just for a chat were extravagant beyond imagining.

Alan shared their opinion. He never phoned her from work if he was going to be late home; she'd never been able to convince him that she might worry. And he'd never, as far as she could remember, had to phone his firm to say that he was going to be late. He never was late. Just as he was never sick. Even when he felt off-colour, he believed in soldiering on – just as his parents had taught him.

She sighed. Alan was so hard-working, so dutiful, so right-minded that it made it very hard for her to disagree with him about anything. She remembered the occasions, earlier in their marriage, when he had complained about all the times she phoned her friends and he had lectured her about the phone bill –

The phone bill!

Carol got up and replaced the telephone on the hall table and picked up the two letters lying there. She opened them, scanned them hastily and let them fall. Then she remembered the unopened correspondence that she had stuffed under the sofa cushions two nights ago.

She sank down on her knees on the living-room floor and, lifting the cushions, she pulled all the papers and letters towards her. There it was – or rather there they were. The original telephone bill and the reminder. And the reminder was dated a few weeks ago. The telephone wasn't out of order. They must have been cut off for not paying the bill.

But when had they disconnected? A few days ago? A week ago? Carol realized that her parents might have been trying to phone her to let her know they were back from their holiday and would be worried not to get an answer.

She grabbed her bag, emptied her purse of all the loose change and dropped it in her jacket pocket along with the unpaid telephone bill. Then, oblivious to the rain, she left the house without the umbrella and hurried to the phone box in the village.

CHAPTER 9

Thursday afternoon – Yorkshire

Francine sat near the large, plate glass window of the café near York Minster and watched the busy scene on the streets outside. The journey from London had been easy; she'd made good time and now she needed a break while she thought out the next part of her plan.

Plan! she thought. Who am I kidding? I have no idea how I'm going to persuade the guy to talk to me. I'll be lucky if he doesn't just slam the door in my face. Even if I can find the right door in the first place!

None of the publicity sparingly revealed by his publishers about Marcus Holbrook ever mentioned *exactly* where he lived. Only that it was in an isolated cottage on the North York Moors. Francine guessed that, as the publicists were unable to persuade him to give interviews, they were making the best of a bad job by creating an aura of mystery around him.

Ever since reading his latest novel, she had been convinced that if she were going to present a serious arts programme he would be a wonderful subject to kick off with. Not only was she certain that, once he had been persuaded to talk, he would be fascinating, but also she couldn't help acknowledging that getting an interview with him would be a feather in her cap. No one else had managed it.

A little later she was surprised to discover that she had managed to eat all of the giant-sized baked potato and the accompanying salad. As she drank her coffee, she allowed her mind to tick over idly.

Two young people with haversacks stopped on the pavement just outside the café. Their jeans, anoraks and bobble hats were so cheerfully neutral that it was hard to tell whether they were male or female. Her glance travelled down and she saw the size of their boots. Male, she hoped. They had taken an ordnance survey map from a waterproof envelope and were inspecting it.

That's what I need next, Francine realized. A more detailed map. She paid for her meal and left the restaurant. The sun was bright but the air was cool; much cooler than in London. She wasn't surprised that the tourists thronging the narrow medieval streets that crowded around the Minster were warmly dressed.

There were plenty of bookshops to choose from, but she chose one that had a window display of *Still Breathing*, Marcus Holbrook's recently published novel. She chose a large, quite detailed map, which also included places to visit and lists of accommodation. After all, she thought, once I've located the elusive Mr Holbrook, I'll have to find a hotel or guest house to stay in for the next night or so.

While she paid for the map she nodded towards an in-shop display of the new novel and said, 'Great book. He lives in Yorkshire, doesn't he?'

The young woman assistant drew her brows together as if this required great thought. 'Yes, actually,' she managed eventually.

Oh, dear, Francine thought. I've chosen the wrong one. She watched as the girl took her proffered credit card and very carefully began to process it. She was dressed all in black, her complexion was pale and she wore tiny wire-framed spectacles that perched precariously on her sharp little nose.

150

Francine tried again. 'Have you read it?'

'Sorry?' The girl looked startled.

'The book, *Still Breathing*. Have you read it?'

'Oh – yes!'

The response was definitely enthusiastic. Francine decided to push her luck. 'Have you ever met him?'

'Who?'

Francine felt like taking hold of her bony shoulders and shaking her until her teeth rattled but she pinned on a gushing smile instead. 'The author – Marcus Holbrook – I mean, he's local, isn't he?'

'Oh, not exactly local. He lives up beyond Pickering. And besides, everybody knows he keeps himself to himself.'

She said that with her Yorkshire accent showing and also as if it were a thoroughly commendable way to live. Francine gave a small smile as she acknowledged defeat. That's it, then, she thought. Apart from the 'beyond Pickering' bit, I knew the rest already.

She signed the credit slip, put her card away and waited while the girl put the map in a bag. Just before handing it over, the young woman frowned again. Francine waited for the thoughts to be translated into words.

'It must be very lonely up there –'

Great, Francine thought, we're getting somewhere. 'Yes. But up where exactly?'

'On the moors.'

'Ah, well.' Francine took the bag and turned to go.

'I mean, I heard that interview he did on local radio with Gemma Parkin.'

Francine stopped and turned round again. 'Interview? But I thought –'

'Oh, it wasn't about his books; it was about conservation and keeping tourists' cars out of areas of outstanding natural beauty.'

'Really?' Francine stared at the girl in amazement. So

she could put a sentence together if she tried. And, furthermore, once she'd started, it seemed as if the whole process became easier.

The young assistant went on, 'Yes, he was very good. You could tell he felt very strongly about it – keeping cars away, I mean. And all the time he was talking, you could hear the sheep.'

That seemed to have exhausted her but Francine exclaimed, 'Oh, but that's marvellous!'

'Marvellous?'

'Yes. Thank you very much. You've been very helpful.'

'Have I?' She looked affronted.

Francine hurried out into the sunlight again. This time she knew exactly where she was going: to the local radio station on Bootham Row.

When she'd been based in Leeds, Francine had visited these studios regularly, but there was no one here who remembered her now. They recognized her, of course. Gemma Parkin, summoned from an editing suite, was trying not to show how excited she was that Francine Rowe had come to see her.

Gemma was large, untidy and very young. 'Of course, I'll help you in any way I can, Miss Rowe! Are you doing a programme up here?'

'We-ell –'

'How do you like your coffee? Black or white?' Gemma turned from the drinks machine and smiled.

Francine felt guilty. 'Black. But let me pay, I insist.'

'OK, then. But I'll have hot chocolate – it's a weakness of mine. Well, chocolate in any form actually, not just drinks.'

'Me too. But, now, where can we sit?'

'Follow me. If we go the staff restroom we shouldn't be disturbed.'

A few moments later, facing each other across a small

152

table, Francine made her request. She hated herself for the way Gemma's smile vanished.

'Oh, but, Miss Rowe, I couldn't – he trusts me. I mean, he's a friend of my father's. Dad farms up there, you know.'

'Up where?'

Gemma looked wounded. 'You know I won't tell you that.'

'OK. Sorry I asked. But, as a fellow reporter, you have to admit, it was worth a try.' Francine sighed as if she acknowledged defeat and smiled as if, nevertheless, she understood. She sat back in her chair.

Poor Gemma thought that the pressure was off. 'But how did you know about my interview with Marcus?' she asked. 'I mean, it was only on local radio . . .'

'Oh, word gets round . . . if a piece is good . . . you know . . .' Francine was deliberately vague but the girl was delighted.

'Really? Well, he made it very easy for me. I mean I hardly had to prompt him – he feels so passionately about the subject!'

'I suppose everybody feels the same – up there?'

'Oh, yes! We-ell, nearly everybody . . .'

'You mean some people actually welcome the extra traffic?'

'Of course; the people who profit from it. Shops, hotels, small businesses – and I suppose you can't blame them. The season is so short. But there are some, like Jack Surtees at Moor Foot, who would welcome twice as many tourists and all year round!'

'Moor Foot?'

'Moor Foot Caravan Park –' Gemma broke off as if she realized that she might have said something she shouldn't. She glanced at Francine uneasily.

But Francine tried to look as though she had hardly noticed. She covered a slight yawn as if she were bored and said, 'Oh, well, Gemma, it's been lovely chatting to you but I'll have to be going along now.'

They both stood up. 'I hope you're not angry with me, Miss Rowe?'

'Why should I be?'

'Well, you know, for not telling you where Marcus Holbrook lives . . .'

'No, you've got to protect your sources, I suppose.'

Gemma looked far from happy as they walked through Reception towards the door. 'But what would you have done? Tell me honestly.'

'Honestly? If I were just starting out, the way you are, and someone like me – someone who'd made big it in broadcasting – and who would never forget a favour – asked for help? I would have given it.'

'Would you? Would you, really?'

'Yes, but at your age I was more ambitious than you are.'

And that was true, Francine thought as she left the unhappy girl standing in the faltering sunshine outside the studios.

Was I cruel, just now? Probably. The poor kid has principles – but she's got to learn that, in this business, loyalty to your colleagues might be more important.

Francine wondered whether Gemma realized that, in any case, she had probably given sufficient clues. She hadn't been wearing a wedding ring so that probably meant that her father was also called Parkin – and he had a farm somewhere near to where Marcus Holbrook lived.

It would be no good knocking on Farmer Parkin's door, however, and asking for the address. He would probably be as loyal to his friend as Gemma was and tell her to get lost. And maybe not so politely.

But not too far away from the farm and the cottage there was a caravan park owned by a Mr Jack Surtees who was probably very peeved by Marcus Holbrook's efforts on behalf of the conservation lobby. He would have no reason to be loyal to the reclusive author. In fact he might be pleased if he could cause him some grief.

Back in the car park, Francine sat for a moment and studied the map. It was easy. There, in the right area, the caravan park and campsite was clearly shown – and named. Francine guessed it should take about forty minutes to get to Pickering and then she would have to leave the main road behind. From then on, using narrow local roads it was anybody's guess.

She glanced up at the sky. It had clouded over. In fact it was distinctly gloomy. She switched on the car radio before she set off; the weather forecast promised scattered showers. But nothing could dampen Francine's spirits as she left York behind and headed for the moors.

A couple of hours later, Francine gripped the steering wheel and wondered how on earth the weatherman could have got it so wrong!

Scattered showers! she thought. This was no shower; it was a tropical monsoon – without the heat. And there had been no mention on the radio of the howling gale that had come sweeping down off the moors to shake her car as if it were a toy.

She hunched forward and peered through the windscreen. The road ahead climbed at a dizzying gradient and the wind and the rain seemed to be uniting to force her back down again. Furthermore, she wasn't too sure whether she was going in the right direction any more.

Jack Surtees had been happy to help, just as she'd thought he would be. He had even drawn a map pinpointing the cottage for her. But not until she had promised him that her wanting to see Mr Marcus bloody Holbrook had nothing to do with – unmentionable word – conservation.

Easy, easy, easy, she'd thought as she pulled out of

Moor Foot Caravan Park and headed northwards yet again. And so it had been, until the rain started. She had watched in growing dismay as the black clouds approached. Negotiating these moorland roads in the gloom of a storm had not been part of the plan.

The plan!

Now, as she stopped the car at the side of a road that was hardly more than a rutted track, her wonderful plan – which involved turning up unannounced on the doorstep of a reclusive writer who lived in isolation on the moors – seemed more than harebrained.

She put on the car's interior light and looked once more at Jack Surtees's pencilled map. According to his instructions she was nearly there. There should be a road on the left any minute now – with an obliging signpost pointing the way to Moor Top.

Francine had learned that all that was left of the small settlement at Moor Top was a ruined farm and a couple of cottages. One of the cottages was empty and the other one was occupied by Marcus Holbrook. She folded the map and stuffed it back into her holdall, then switched off the light. She waited a few moments to let her eyes adjust and then peered forward again.

It had been murky before, but in those few minutes that she had been looking at the map, it seemed as though the rain might have stopped but the clouds had come down to envelop her. The cloud or the mist, or whatever it was, was patchy, so that one minute she could see the road ahead quite clearly and the next she could barely see beyond the bonnet of the car. She started up and began to move ahead slowly, all the time leaning forward and straining her eyes as she looked for the signpost.

There it was! Tall and ghostly, a whiter shape against the mist. When she reached it she started to turn left and realized that the incline was now even steeper – and the track was even more pitted. She wondered fleetingly what kind of vehicle Marcus Holbrook had. Probably a Land Rover or some other expensive four-wheel-drive. He would be able to afford it, considering the worldwide sales of his novels.

The track ahead of her had great gaps in the surface every now and then and, rather than risk the suspension of her brand new car, she did her best to avoid them. While she was swerving around a particularly nasty-looking pothole she felt the car slipping out of her control.

She tightened her grip on the steering wheel and tried to wrench the car back on to the track, but it was hopeless. The next moment she realized that the world had tilted sideways. Dripping wet vegetation screened the windows on the passenger side. She was in a ditch.

By the time Carol finally replaced the receiver, she was ready to weep tears of frustration. Not because of the phone call to her parents. They were relieved to hear from her. They told her that they had indeed been calling her and all they'd heard was a recorded message telling them that the line was temporarily out of service.

They'd assumed her phone was out of order and had already written to ask her if she knew. She didn't want to worry them so she went along with that idea and said that she would call them the minute it was fixed.

They told her that they'd had a wonderful time in Italy and that they were both very well. They sounded so normal and contented that Carol's throat ached with misery. She missed them – and she knew her feelings were more acute because of the situation between herself and Alan. It was painful to accept that her marriage was in no way like that of her parents.

But the phone call that nearly had her weeping was the one to the telephone company. She knew it was her own fault, of course, for not paying the bill on time, but the woman on the other end of the line was as unhelpful and rude as she could be. Getting the simplest information out of her was like getting blood out of a stone. Each simple question was greeted with an audible sigh and then a burst of recorded music while the woman seemed to consult with someone else. Carol was made to feel as if she were a thoroughgoing nuisance because she wanted to know how to get her line re-connected as quickly as possible. Finally, when she had all the facts that she needed, she felt as though she'd won a battle.

'Thank you so-oo much for all your help,' Carol said with thinly disguised sarcasm before replacing the receiver.

She realized that she felt hot and stuffy. I'm hot under the collar, she thought, and she giggled weakly. She pushed open the door of the phone box and stood for a moment in the rain.

She was generous enough to spare a thought for the phone company employee that she'd just done battle with. Perhaps I wasn't making myself clear, she thought. No, I'm sure I was. Well, perhaps it's that time of the month for her – or her lover has just left her – or her kids are making impossible demands –

For a moment Carol was intrigued with imagining all the circumstances that could have made the woman so hostile and then decided that, no matter what, it was her job to give information as efficiently as possible to customers – even customers who forgot to pay their bills.

Alan's car was parked in the street behind her own. Carol stopped and looked at it. Usually he used the garage because his car was newer than hers was and worth looking after. What was the matter? she wondered. Had he lost the garage key?

Then she noticed that the front door was ajar; a thin sliver of light spilled out on to the tiny garden. The leaves of the shrubs gleamed wetly and fresh earthy smells rose from the narrow borders. She walked up the path and pushed the door open. Alan was sitting on the stairs, his elbows resting on his knees and his head in his hands. He raised his head, slowly.

'Where have you been?'

He looked tired, weary. Carol thought with regret of the meal she had planned to have ready for him. She began to explain. 'I – the phone – the phone's been disconnected –'

'I know.'

'I've been to the call box in the village. It's all right – I can go to the Post Office – any Post Office – in the morning and pay the bill – then I phone them and tell them. With luck, we'll be connected again within twenty-four hours.'

'It's not all right.'

'What do you mean?'

'You shouldn't have forgotten to pay the bill.'

She pushed the door shut behind her. She took off her wet jacket and stood holding it uncertainly. Why did he look so grim? It was only the phone bill – it was inconvenient to be cut off but it was hardly the end of the world.

'I rely on you to pay the bills,' he said, and his voice was curiously flat. He looked pointedly at the two statements she'd opened earlier – they were still lying on the floor. 'Well, at least these two aren't due yet, otherwise we might have found ourselves without light or heat.'

'Alan, I'm sorry, but –'

'Are there any more lying round the house that I should know about?'

Carol flushed. She knew that the way she left things lying around infuriated him, but she always dealt with them eventually. He worked such long hours that he had been pleased to leave household matters to her – and this had never happened before. It was just that she'd been so tired lately. No, that wasn't it – she wasn't really tired,

159

she was unhappy – and her unhappiness had taken the form of an ever-present weariness . . .

She stared at her husband. 'Alan – this is ridiculous – we shouldn't be arguing over something like this – we should be laughing –'

'I'm sorry – I don't feel much like laughing just now.'

Suddenly she felt angry. *He* didn't feel like laughing? Well, in truth, neither did *she*! But she would have had a darned good try – and, furthermore, she would never dream of giving him the third degree like this about a piffling telephone bill.

She stared at him mutinously. 'For goodness' sake, Alan, lighten up!'

'Lighten up?'

'If you could see yourself! Sitting there moaning on at me as if I'd committed some heinous crime instead of just forgetting to pay a bill. I've never forgotten before, have I? I know you work long hours but I go out to work too, you know – and I do the shopping and the housework and I cook the meals – and –'

Carol stopped when she saw the way Alan was looking at her. His mouth was set in a straight line and his eyes – oh, God, his eyes were so cold. It suddenly hit her how far short of his ideal she must be.

She thought of his parents' home, how well run it was, how his father never had to look for a clean shirt, step over an untidy pile of magazines and papers on the sitting-room floor, or come home to a messy kitchen and a meal not ready yet – or burnt.

But, then Alan's mother had devoted her life to her home, her husband and her son. Even when she'd been working part-time, she'd done everything, including the household expenses; she even did the gardening and won prizes with her blessed chrysanthemums!

And yet . . . and yet Carol had always felt uneasy in the Kennedys' home. It was as if the comfort and the love, which should have been there, had been dusted and polished and tidied away. All unmanageable and potentially messy emotions to be kept out of sight.

When she'd met Alan she'd believed that that was why he was drawn to her. Apart from the obvious and overpowering physical attraction, he'd told her once that he loved the warmth and comfort of her. All this time she had imagined that a little mess and clutter didn't matter. That what they had between them – the joy and the laughter – was far more important than a home that looked like a show home on a new housing development.

But she couldn't remember when they had both laughed helplessly together and, now, there he was, sitting looking at her as if she had let him down and, what was worse, as if he hadn't expected anything different.

She realized that she was still holding her jacket. Suddenly, with a burst of anguished fury, she bunched it up and hurled it at him. Without waiting to witness his reaction she stormed down the corridor into the kitchen and slammed the door shut behind her.

She was too angry to sit down. Sheer frustration sent her slamming around opening and closing the unit doors for no reason apart from making as much noise as possible. She caught sight of the wine and the chocolate peppermint creams she'd bought earlier. Alan's favourites!

She tore the cellophane wrapper from the box of chocolates, opened it and took one. No – I bought them for Alan, she thought. Closing the box roughly, she snatched it up off the counter-top, whirled round and lurched across the room. She opened the door that led into the hall and screamed, 'These are for you!' as she hurled it with as much force as she could muster.

She saw it hit the doormat but she didn't wait to see whether Alan picked it up before she slammed the door shut again.

161

She realized she was shaking – and that the funny sound she was making was a mixture of sobs and laughter. Laughter because she still had the wit to realize how funny she must have looked and sobs because she'd been driven to behave like that in the first place.

She picked up the bottle of wine and looked at it. Good wine . . . it had cost much more than she usually spent. Far too good to throw at Alan and besides, if she smashed it, it would make a terrible mess.

'Mustn't make a mess,' she muttered aloud as she found the corkscrew and opened the wine.

Out of habit she took two wineglasses down from the cupboard and then deliberately put one of them back. She took the wine and the other glass over to the table – along with a packet of shortbread biscuits.

Halfway through her glass of wine she remembered the fish pies. She got them out of the freezer and discarded the temptingly illustrated cardboard sleeves. Then she stabbed the film that covered the meals in several places with a sharp knife as instructed. She enjoyed that bit.

Once the meals were cooking in the microwave, she topped up her glass of wine and opened a tin of peas. Mushy peas. Alan's favourite. Although she had lost track of why she was bothering.

When both meals were set out on the kitchen table and the second glass had been taken out of the cupboard again and set at Alan's place, she opened the door again and called for him. He didn't reply.

Of course he won't still be sitting on the stairs, she reasoned. Not all this time. But he wasn't in the tiny dining-room or the sitting room either. Carol stood at the bottom of the stairs. The box of chocolates that she had thrown earlier had burst open as they hit the floor and spilled some of its contents. There they lay, tempting little squares of dark chocolate, some of them half out of the little brown paper packets.

Carol knelt to tidy them up. Still kneeling, she tilted her head as she looked upstairs. 'Alan,' she called.

There was no answer.

He wasn't in their bedroom or the bathroom.

He looked exhausted – he's just gone to the spare room and gone straight to sleep, she told herself. But she knew she wouldn't find him there. She even looked in the tiny room that was supposed to be a third bedroom but which served as a box-room. He wasn't there, either.

She hurried downstairs again. Had she missed him somehow? Had he been upstairs when she first called him and then come down as she was looking in the dining-room and sitting-room? And then had he gone in through the other door when she went back through the kitchen? She knew that was crazy but she looked anyway.

Then she remembered the car.

Alan's car was no longer parked outside in the street. He must have put it away. She ran back into the house, got her keys from her bag and went to open the garage. It was empty.

He's hungry – he driven along to the next village to the pizzeria. He'll be back soon and then we'll have to decide whether we're going to eat the pizza or the fish pies . . . I'll leave the garage door open so that he can drive straight in . . .

But then she remembered something that she'd seen when she looked in the box-room. Or rather something that she hadn't seen.

She hurried back into the house and up the stairs. They were gone. Not just Alan's overnight bag but one of their cases as well. Carol sank to her knees in the cold, little room and, surrounded by boxes of unpacked books, photograph albums, souvenirs, and all the memories of happier times, she began to cry.

CHAPTER 10

Francine hung on to the steering wheel; only her seat belt stopped her from sliding over into the passenger seat. She was unhurt – but shaken. Blast it! she thought. Just when things were going so well.

When she realized that the belt held her securely she let go of the wheel and groped for her car phone. Only Peter, Rob Baines and her PA had this number. Francine used it only in emergencies. This was an emergency.

She fumbled in her bag for her membership card and, glancing at the number, she dialled the AA. At least she tried to. There was no welcome, reassuring voice telling her to stay calm, asking for her location and giving her an estimated time for the arrival of the emergency service; only a fog-like crackling.

She knew at once what the trouble was. She was obviously in one of those black spots – an area where the signals just couldn't get through. She knew about such an area in the mountainous Lake District. Well, there was another one right here.

What could she do? She knew the answer before she had formulated the question. There was no other option other than to abandon the car, go to the nearest habitation and ask to use the phone. And the nearest habitation was Marcus Holbrook's cottage.

The car was not quite on its side but it was lying at an uncomfortable angle. Clutching her handbag and hold-all, she scrambled up and out inelegantly – and almost fell back in when she lost her footing on the wet, slippery grass at the side of the road.

'Aagh!' She called out in shock and pain as she caught the right side of her forehead on the open car door. She slammed it shut viciously.

The central locking wouldn't work. She stood there in the swirling mist, jabbing at the key-ring control, but there was no familiar clunk of locks sliding into place. She leaned forward precariously and tried to lock the car the old-fashioned way. For some reason the key just wouldn't turn. She would have to leave the car open.

Francine rested her weight on the car. Her calf muscles were protesting at the way they were being stretched so cruelly. She was conscious of wet grass and something altogether pricklier brushing against her ankles, tearing at her tights.

After a moment, she opened the door again and launched herself forward. She eased herself in until she was kneeling on the front seat. She reached over to grab her overnight bag and swung it over and out of the car to join her other bags on the road. Then she scrambled out again.

It's just as well I didn't stow it in the boot, she thought; there's no way I could've opened that.

The sound as she slammed the car door seemed very loud. She glanced round apprehensively. It was definitely spooky. Swirling mists over a darkening moor – with not even the usual sheep to keep her company. At least, if they were out there, they were keeping very quiet about it.

She wasn't sure whether it had started to rain again. She felt a certain wetness on her face but it could have been the dampness of the mist – or perspiration. It trickled down her cheek on to her neck and she dabbed at it with the back of her hand.

Well, at least she couldn't get lost, she thought as she set out along the track. Jack Surtees' map had shown no other roads branching off this one. The way ahead led straight to Moor Top.

Sophie sat at the dining-room table with piles of exercise books spread out around her. Her mother had accepted an invitation to the home of one of her friends from evening classes. A girls' only night, she had been promised. Sophie smiled as she imagined those girls – most of them grandmothers – gossiping about their families, or their second careers now that their various offspring had left home. Laura had accepted a lift along to her friend's house but she'd told Sophie that she would get a taxi home. Sophie wasn't to wait up for her.

What has the world come to, Sophie thought, when I'm the one sitting home alone and my mother is out gallivanting until all hours? But she was pleased that Laura had good friends. It was going to be such a wrench for her when Sophie married and moved to Scotland.

She found herself wondering if her mother had ever wanted to remarry after her father died. She tried hard, but she couldn't ever remember any man who had come close to Laura in what must have been long, lonely years. They'd never talked about it, even when Sophie was a grown woman. Perhaps we should have done, she thought. She realized how much she'd taken Laura's love for granted.

She closed the last book and placed it on the appropriate pile. She stretched to ease her aching shoulders and frowned. She didn't want to be sitting here alone – she wanted to be with Alistair.

She knew that as the wife of a doctor who worked in Accident and Emergency at a busy hospital she would have to face long hours on her own. At the moment, as a senior house officer, it was part of Alistair's job to work awkward shifts, including night shifts. His new position in Scotland, as a senior registrar, might mean that they would share a few more evenings together, but he would often be on second call. She accepted that and she loved him all the more for his dedication to his work.

But he never talked about it. Sophie had come to believe that it was a way of dealing with the horror that he dealt with daily. As soon as they were together, he seemed to be able to leave work behind him and throw himself into the pleasures of the moment. Whether it was walking in the country, going to the cinema – which he loved – or simply enjoying a good meal out together, he extracted every moment of enjoyment from the experience.

And it was the same in their most intimate moments. Alistair never left her in any doubt as to how much he enjoyed making love to her. As for Sophie, she found it a totally fulfilling experience.

She wondered if her mother had ever guessed how easy it had been for her to embark on her first proper love affair. She wondered what her old friends would have said if they'd realized that, until she'd met Alistair, Sophie had remained a virgin. Perhaps Alison and Carol wouldn't have been surprised, but Francine would surely have made some wisecrack about 'good old Sophie, waiting for Mr Right!'

And Alistair was Mr Right in every way. So why was she being tormented by these niggling doubts?

Suddenly she pushed the chair back from the table and got up. It was so frustrating not being able to get in touch with her friends. Should she try again now? She glanced at her watch. No, it wasn't too late. She still didn't have a number for Francine but one of the others might know it.

She tried Carol first and frowned in disappointment at

the recorded message telling her that the line was temporarily out of service. What on earth can be the matter? she wondered. Perhaps I'll have to write a letter after all. I won't mention my wedding, I'll just say that I've been trying to phone her . . .

Next she tried Alison's number. She heard the phone ringing in the old house so many miles away; she tried to imagine the lofty rooms, the family portraits, the faded curtains and the Persian rugs. Alison looked so right there, Carol remembered. When had they first laughingly dubbed her 'the lady of the manor'? Was it when they'd all gone to Westbrook Hall for Matthew's christening?

That had been a wonderful day. Alison and Paul had been so happy and even Paul's snobby family had been pleasant to everyone. Francine had charmed everyone in sight and Carol and Alan couldn't bear to be parted even for a moment. She wondered if they were still so happy together?

Was Alison out for the evening? Would the phone be answered again by Mrs Cavendish senior or her pretentious daughter, Daphne? Sophie was almost sure that neither of them was passing on the messages. She was just about to replace the receiver when someone picked up the phone.

'Westbrook Hall.'

'Alison? Is that you?'

'Yes – Alison Cavendish here – *is that Sophie*?'

'Yes –'

'Sophie, I'm so sorry – I was supposed to call you but –'

'Never mind – you don't have to explain – oh, Alison – it's wonderful to hear your voice!'

The stone buildings loomed up out of the mist like something in the movie of a Stephen King novel. No – that was wrong – the movie would have to be much older and in black and white – a silent movie. Something viewed on television after midnight, when sensible people were asleep and only insomniacs surfed the channels looking for distraction.

The cottages were still some distance away. Francine thanked God for sensible shoes and hitched the straps of her bag and her holdall more securely over her shoulder. Her other arm was aching and she wished that she hadn't packed quite so much in her overnight bag. She was cold and her forehead was throbbing. She guessed that it would be bruised after hitting it on the door of the car.

I bet I'll have a massive bump there as well, she thought. The make-up girls will have quite a job disguising it when I get back to work.

From the place where she'd left her car the road had continued to climb and all the muscles in her legs were hurting. I must be out of condition, she thought. I can only have walked a mile at the most and yet my body feels as though I've run a marathon.

And then, miraculously, the incline began to level out as it approached a yard in front of the two buildings. Enclosing the yard was a stone wall with tall stone gateposts, but no gates hung between them. The mist had thinned out but the light was fading fast. One of the cottages was shuttered and dark, the other showed comforting lights at the windows.

There was a movement at one of those windows. Francine stopped and hung back in the shadow between the gateposts. The figure she had seen was out of sight now, but the room looked like a kitchen. She glimpsed the tops of taps just beyond the window glass; further into the room she could see a table and beyond that a fire glowing in the hearth.

She shrank back against one of the stone pillars when the figure came into view again. She shouldn't be watching like this. She shouldn't be looking into someone

169

else's home. The man had no idea that she was there and she felt like a peeping tom – a stalker. Tall and spare, the man bent over the sink. She saw the shock of white hair. It was Marcus Holbrook. But who else could it be?

Now that she had him in sight she found herself hesitant. She hadn't intended to arrive like this, a pathetic woman in distress, needing his help to get her car out of the ditch. She had never felt at such a disadvantage. If there had been anywhere else to go, she would have turned and run – perhaps abandoned the whole enterprise.

But she had no choice. It was dark now and the nearest village was miles away. So, unless she wanted to spend the night in her car, the only way was forward. Francine had only taken one step into the cottage yard when the world lit up around her like a film set coming into life.

'Wha – ?' she exclaimed. *Security lights!* Of course, she thought, living up on the moors like this . . .

She stood there blinking and, by the time she got her eyes back into focus, she saw that the cottage had been plunged into darkness. The floodlight surrounding her seemed to take on a life of its own; it was a physical force, holding her to the spot, forbidding her to even think of moving.

Someone was watching her.

Sheer fright jerked her back into life and made her turn and run back across the yard. She thought of her car, a mile or more back down the track, and knew that she didn't have a chance of getting there safely unless she abandoned her luggage. But she couldn't bring herself to drop everything – and that was her undoing.

She had only taken a few stumbling steps into the darkness beyond the wall when her overnight case swung against her legs and brought her down. The next moment her arms were gripped roughly and she was hauled to her feet again. An angry voice bellowed, 'Who the hell are you?'

'Don't shout!' Fright and outrage made her yell right back at him.

Silence. During that silence the grip on her arms slackened a little. She stared at her captor. He was all in black. The yard behind him was still flooded with light so she couldn't make out the expression on his face. He did not have the same disadvantage and she knew he was assessing her. She grew more uncomfortable as the silence lengthened.

Her hair had fallen over her face. She felt stupid – at a disadvantage. Her heart was pounding, but she kept her voice as cool as possible. 'Seen enough?'

'What?' He sounded startled.

'You can see I'm no threat to you. You can let go of me now.'

'OK.' He released her arms. 'Now tell me what you're doing here.'

This is not the moment for total honesty, she decided. Possible answers flashed across her brain and she settled for half the story. 'My car's broken down. Or rather it's in a ditch –'

'Where?'

'Er – back there . . .'

She kept her eyes on him and gestured, with a half turn of her head, towards the darkness of the moors behind her. She was tempted to turn and flee but she knew that was pointless. This man would be able to out-run her easily. He remained silent.

'I wondered if I could use your phone,' she said, 'and – er – call the AA. My car phone won't work – it just crackles –' She knew she was babbling but she couldn't help herself.

'Well, that's true at least,' he remarked finally.

'What is?'

'Mobile phones don't work round here. So where exactly is your car?'

On dangerous ground, Francine thought. *Not just my car . . . me too. If I tell him exactly where the car is he'll know I was heading here – there's nowhere else to go once you turn on to this track . . . and, right at this moment, it might be better to go on pretending that I'm a damsel in distress . . .*

'I'm not too sure,' she said. 'I – I think I've walked quite a long way . . .'

'Really?'

'Yes.'

'OK.' He seemed to have made up his mind about something. 'You'd better come in.'

He strode off towards his cottage, leaving Francine to scramble about in the semi-darkness picking up her bags. She was only halfway across the yard when he vanished inside; the next minute the floodlights went out. Francine stopped, momentarily disorientated. She closed her eyes and then opened them to see that the lights in the cottage had been switched on again and that Marcus Holbrook was nowhere in sight. But at least the door was open.

'He might be a literary genius but he's no gentleman,' she muttered as she covered the remaining distance.

She paused on the threshold, uncertainly. She was suddenly filled with the most unreasonable and terrifying fears.

Why does he live all by himself up here? she thought. *Why do his publishers go along with this 'I want to be alone' pose of his? Could it be because, no matter how talented he is as a writer, there's something lacking in him as a human being? Something dangerously lacking? After all, sex maniacs and even convicted murderers have written novels . . .*

'What is it?'

Francine jumped when he appeared right in front of her. 'Nothing . . . I . . .'

Suddenly his eyes widened and he stared at her. She

172

knew that something had changed.

Has he recognized me? Is he going to push me back out of the cottage and slam the door in my face?

He reached forward and she flinched. But he was reaching for her bags. He was trying to take them away from her. Francine tried to hang on to them.

'For goodness' sake give those to me,' he said. 'You can't stand there all night.'

He dumped everything on the floor behind him. She stared at him. He didn't look as though he intended violence. When he straightened up he was frowning with concern.

'What is it?' she asked.

He took her by the shoulders and propelled her gently into the room. 'I had no idea,' he murmured. 'Please forgive me.'

'No idea of what? Forgive you for what?'

He led her over to an armchair by the fire. 'Sit down.'

She did so and watched with wide eyes as he went back to the door and closed it. And turned the key in the lock. And bolted it.

'Forgive you for what?' she repeated. *Was he one of those serial killers who asked their victims' forgiveness in advance? How many victims were buried up here on the moors . . .*

'Your forehead – that's a nasty wound –'

'Is it?' Oh, yes, her head, she remembered. Francine raised a hand tentatively to her bruised forehead and flinched when her fingers made contact.

'I couldn't see it properly when we were outside,' he said. 'You should have told me.'

'I – I'd forgotten about it. Does it look awful?'

He smiled and the smile transformed his severe features. Until this moment he'd given no hint that he could look so human . . . and so attractive . . .

'Ah, vanity, vanity . . .' he said softly. 'Here.' He took

173

down a small mirror from the wall near the door. 'Look for yourself.'

Francine was appalled. So that was why he had looked at her so strangely just now. The bruise was much worse than she had imagined and the skin was broken. There was a trail of dried blood running down her face into the neckline of her roll-top cotton sweater. She pulled the neck of her sweater down and saw the blood as a darker stain against the red.

She realized that the wound must have been bleeding as she trudged across the moors and she hadn't realized because she'd thought it was rain – or perspiration. But it looked as though the bleeding had stopped.

'Slip off your jacket and come and sit here.' Her host indicated a chair near the table. He took a small first-aid box from one of the cupboards and placed it on the table beside her. Then he took a small glass bowl to the counter and switched on the kettle. While he was waiting for the water to heat up he poured some antiseptic into the bowl.

'Doctor – tell me if it will hurt?' She grinned raggedly up at him as he walked towards her and he responded with that wonderful smile again.

'I won't lie. It probably will. Here, put this round your shoulders.' He gave her a large, clean kitchen towel. 'Now keep still while I clean you up.'

And, even although he was gentle, it did hurt like crazy. When he was satisfied he said, 'Not as bad as I thought. But then even a superficial head wound can bleed a lot, can't it?'

'If you say so. But where did you learn your first aid? Were you a Scout?'

'Army.' His terse one-word answer barred the way to any further questioning. 'Close your eyes,' he said and his voice was gentle again.

She felt him touch her forehead near the wound and

take a fold of skin between his thumb and forefinger and lift it gently.

'What are you doing?' she asked.

'Checking to see how deep the cut is.'

'And?'

'You'll live. I'm going to stick a plaster on . . . there. You can open your eyes, now.'

'Thanks. But why did I have to close them?'

'Too disconcerting. I couldn't concentrate with you gazing up at me like a beautiful wounded fawn.'

Francine laughed. 'Why, Mr Holbrook,' she said, 'I think that's a cliché!'

The moment the words were out of her mouth, she knew what she'd done. She'd shown that she knew who he was and she would no longer be able to pretend that she'd stumbled across his cottage by accident. Would he ask her to leave?

He stepped back and looked down at her. The wan smile that pulled at the corners of his mouth was devoid of humour. 'So, tell me. Where exactly is your car?'

Francine sighed. 'In a ditch, at the bottom of this track, just past the signpost.'

What was he thinking? Why wasn't he furious with her? He'd been angry enough when she'd first arrived . . .

But all he said was, 'I'll have a look at it in the morning, but now, I think I'd better make you a hot drink.'

'The morning? But don't you want me to call the AA? I mean I'm trespassing – imposing on your hospitality.'

'You certainly are. But I'm not going to let you go wandering off into the night with a head wound – even although it's a minor one. You'll stay here and in the morning I'll see if Jed and I can get your car out of the ditch.'

'Jed?'

'Jed Parkin. His farm's only a couple of miles away.

The poor man will be safely tucked up in bed by now so I'll phone him first thing and ask him to bring a tractor over.'

He dropped a teabag into a pottery mug and filled it up with boiling water, then topped it up with milk and stirred in two spoons of sugar. He held it out towards her.

'Drink this.'

'I – er – I don't take sugar . . .'

'Take it, woman.'

'Er – thank you.'

Francine sipped the tea and watched as he moved around the kitchen, tidying up the bowl of disinfectant and the first-aid things from the table and wiping it down. She closed her eyes. The fire was warm and, in the silence contained by the old stone walls of the cottage, a deep feeling of peace crept over her. Her head was throbbing slightly . . . but it wasn't too bad . . . it was so comfortable here . . . she felt herself drifting towards sleep . . .

Then the throbbing in her head began to form itself into a nasty, little core of anxiety. The anxiety grew and began to worm itself into her conscious mind . . . Surely I shouldn't be feeling as tired as this, she thought . . .

Did he slip something into my tea?

She'd hardly had time to consider that alarming premise when a shadow fell over her. The shadow was moving nearer. She gave a moan of fright and opened her eyes.

'Be careful, you'll spill your tea.' Marcus Holbrook leaned over her and steadied the mug in her hand.

She stared up at him. 'Sorry – I feel so tired . . .'

'I'm not surprised. You crash your car into a ditch, you bump your head, badly, and you walk all this way across the moor. What you need is a hot bath, a bite of supper and a good night's sleep.'

'Do I?'

176

'No question. I'll take your things up to the spare room and run a bath for you.'

'Shall I –?'

She started to get up but he motioned for her to stay. 'No, just wait there by the fire until I call you, Francine.'

She was out of the chair and halfway across the room before he was out of the door.

CHAPTER 11

'What did you say?' Francine yelled up the stairs at the rapidly retreating figure.

He didn't look back. 'I told you to wait by the fire. In vain, it seems.'

'Don't try to be clever – you know what I mean!'

To her frustration, he was no longer in sight. She found that she was trembling and she cursed herself for her weakness. He had put on a light somewhere upstairs but it was dark in the hall. Francine gripped the stair rail and pulled herself upwards. Her heart was pounding.

I must have got up too quickly . . .

She heard doors opening and closing, and now she identified the sound of water running into a bath. Delicately curling, pine-scented steam began to drift down towards her. She stopped halfway up.

'Come ba-ack h-ere!' she yelled, and cursed inwardly when her voice cracked.

'What is it?' Marcus Holbrook loomed above her. The sound of running water had stopped.

'You *know* what it is. You called me Francine.'

'So? You called me Mr Holbrook.'

'That's your name.'

'I don't deny it. And Francine is your name. For Pete's sake, woman, you're shaking like a jelly.'

178

'Another cliché – I think I preferred the beautiful fawn.'

'Be quiet.'

'So-oo masterful!'

He glared at her quip as he came down towards her. She made no attempt to resist when he put an arm around her and helped her up the rest of the way. His nearness was shocking. Francine couldn't remember when she had last felt such a charge at being so close to a man – if ever. She held her breath until they reached the top landing and then, gently, moved herself out of his embrace.

'Did you think I wouldn't recognize you?' he asked her softly.

'Well, I wasn't sure – I mean, I am in a bit of a state and –'

'You certainly are.' He was laughing at her but he wasn't scornful. 'And I didn't recognize you at first; it wasn't until you came into the cottage.'

'You didn't let on – you didn't say anything –'

'Neither did you. You carried on with the rigmarole of your car being in a ditch – and you turn up here with all your bags and baggage –'

'It is! And I had to bring everything – the locks wouldn't work –'

'All right – I accept that – but you made no mention of the fact that you were on your way to see me when the accident happened.'

'How do you know that I was?'

'Well – I assume that you had some idea of getting me to do an interview –'

'Vanity, vanity!' Francine exclaimed, echoing his own words from earlier. He laughed.

'Touché. But what other reason would there be for the celebrated Francine Rowe to appear on my doorstep? And let's not argue about the fact that you were on your way here when the accident occurred.'

Francine slumped against the rough-plastered wall behind her and immediately wished she hadn't. It gave him the excuse to put his arm round her again. 'Come on – your bath is ready.'

He led her into a small, white-tiled bathroom. The floor, window blind and towels were dark blue. The room was very clean and completely bare of clutter. A functional room, Francine thought, no little touches of luxury. This man didn't indulge himself. Apart from the pine-scented bath oil.

'I wouldn't bother to get dressed after your bath.'

'Really!'

'Don't look so alarmed. I mean, you might as well put your nightdress on – whatever you wear. I'll put one of my robes on the bed; it should cover you up nicely.'

'Right. Thanks.' Francine was gratified to see that, just for a moment, he couldn't meet her eyes. 'And thanks for offering me a bed for the night.'

'I can hardly throw you out on to the moor.' When he spoke his tone was brusque. 'I'll leave you now. Your bags are in the room next door. Don't be long.'

'Officer, were you? Or drill sergeant?'

'I beg your pardon?'

'Giving orders seems to come so easily to you – and you did mention that you'd been in the Army.'

She had thought she might anger him but, instead, his smile widened. He took her chin very gently in one hand and raised her face towards his. 'Just watch it, Miss Rowe. Try to remember you're my guest before I forget my manners as a host.'

How could blue eyes seem so warm? she thought, as she gazed up at him. She saw his eyes widen in reaction to something he must have seen reflected in her own. He dropped his hand and moved away from her. Was it reluctantly?

'I haven't put a lot of water in the bath – not because

I'm mean – it's just because I don't want you sliding down and drowning yourself, OK?'

'Fine.'

'And when you're finished, pull the plug out before you stand up. Same reason – if you slipped and hit your head you could fall in the water and drown. It only takes an inch or two.'

'My, my . . .' Francine gazed at him wonderingly.

'What is it?' He looked at her suspiciously, no doubt because he'd caught the undertone of gentle mockery.

'So thoughtful,' she said. 'I'm impressed. Especially as I must be such an unwelcome guest.'

'Glad you know your place.' But his smile took the sting out of the words. 'I'm going down now – don't lock the door –'

'What?'

'Just in case I have to come up and give you mouth-to-mouth resuscitation. Otherwise, if you're downstairs in no more than fifteen minutes, I'll wait for you in the kitchen.

Francine sponged herself with the pine-scented water and regretted that she had not been allowed a deep bath to wallow in. But she supposed he was right – she did feel pretty groggy – and so tired . . . Not that she couldn't be revived immediately by Marcus Holbrook administering mouth-to-mouth resuscitation . . .

What am I thinking? She began to rub at her face vigorously and winced when she touched the swelling above her right eye.

She could hear him moving about downstairs; distant, reassuring sounds. It was like being a child, she thought; me in the bath and the grown-up downstairs making supper. She was surprised how readily she had handed over responsibility for her own wellbeing. She had never in her adult life had someone offering to take care of her like this.

181

No, that wasn't quite true . . . her friends at university . . . Carol, Alison, Sophie . . . They had all looked after each other. If any one of them had man trouble or money troubles or ill health, the other three would rally round and help in any way that they could.

Francine remembered one time when she'd had a feverish cold, her eyes running, her temperature sky high and her throat feeling as though it were full of needles. Sophie had phoned the doctor at Student Health and insisted on a house call, and then she had sat with her all night, bringing her cooling drinks and soothing her as if she were a baby. Not even her own mother had even taken care of her like that . . .

Especially not my mother, Francine thought. My mother believed in gritting your teeth and getting on with things. Any sign of sickness in the Rowe household was regarded as a serious character flaw. *For goodness' sake don't whinge, child*, was her usual response to any call for help.

So Francine had grown up quickly and learned not to ask. After leaving university and moving on from the cosy sisterhood of student friendships she had lived as independently as she could. It was true that Peter had helped to get her started in television but he was honest enough to have sent her packing if he had not believed in her talent. And she had fulfilled her part of the bargain – although she didn't like to call it that.

'Bargain' was too mercenary a word to describe a relationship that had given them both so much pleasure. It wasn't just sex – although that had been good. They were both intensely interested in the medium in which they worked and all the aspects of living that it covered. They could talk about work for hours.

Sometimes, when Peter came to her apartment, they didn't even make love. They would eat together, watch a programme on television or the latest video release and discuss it happily like a long-married couple.

Except that, unlike a married couple, they had spent very few whole nights together. Peter had to go home to his wife and family. And on those rare occasions, in the past, when Francine had been ill, he had never run a bath for her or told her to get into her nightdress while he made the supper . . .

'Sit down, it's nearly ready.'

Marcus Holbrook was standing at the cooker with his back to her. Francine did as she was told. He had built up the fire and closed the curtains. More than ever the cottage had the feeling of being not only isolated, but almost in another time – another world. And it's not just the place, Francine thought, it's the man. Then, immediately the paradox presented itself: how could a man who held himself so aloof, so apart from the world, write about his fellow human beings so accurately?

'What are you thinking?' He had turned to look at her.

She returned his gaze. 'I – nothing – just enjoying the moment . . .'

'You looked so far away.'

'No – I was right here. And actually, I'm quite interested in what you're cooking.'

'Hungry?' he asked, and Francine nodded. 'Good, Butter this toast, will you?'

He placed two plates on the table and then put two slices of toast on each. When Francine had finished buttering them he came over to the table carrying a pan and piled each plate high with deliciously fluffy-looking scrambled egg.

'That looks marvellous!'

They chatted easily about nothing in particular while they ate their meal. For a second course they had huge slabs of fruitcake – baked by Jed's wife, Rosemary, he told her – and then he made a pot of tea.

'Come on, we'll sit by the fire. And call me Marcus, by

the way. "Mr Holbrook" makes me seem old by comparison to a young thing like you.'

'I'm not that young; thirty-one, actually.'

'Absolutely ancient, then.'

'Don't laugh. Are you much older than I am? The details on your book jackets don't give any personal details – come to that, they don't give away very much at all, do they?'

'Feeling better, are you?'

'What do you mean?'

'I tend to your wounds, clean you up and feed you and then, like an ungrateful little wild creature in an animal sanctuary, you're on the attack and asking me questions.'

Francine saw that he wasn't really angry and she countered, 'Questions that you are very good at dodging. Do you always answer a question with a question of your own?'

Marcus took a sip of his tea and settled back in his armchair. The only sound in the cottage was the crackling of the fire and the measured tick of an old-fashioned clock on the mantelpiece.

She'd just decided that the conversation was over when he said, 'I'm forty; that's no big secret. I don't care who knows it; I don't have that kind of vanity. If I did I would probably have started dyeing my hair when I began to go grey –'

'White –'

'OK, white, then.'

'When was that?'

'If you're hoping for a dramatic revelation, something to do with my troubled past, then you'll be disappointed. The reason isn't even interesting. All the men in my family go grey – white – at an early age. In my case it started in my early thirties – it's genetic, I suppose.'

And in your case, very attractive, Francine wanted to add but, instead, she asked, 'And was your past troubled, then?'

'Very sharp. I asked for that. But in this case you can take it as a figure of speech – dramatic licence – I'm a novelist after all.'

The chair she was sitting in was large and comfortable. Francine pulled her legs up under her and cradled her mug of tea with both hands. She turned her head towards the hearth and stared into the glowing coals. In her wildest dreams she had never imagined that she would find herself in exactly these circumstances.

It was like a wonderful old movie, she thought; intrepid girl reporter gets lost in the fog on the moor; handsome, mysterious hero rescues her and takes her to his lonely cottage. Later, dressed in his amazingly romantic old-fashioned dressing gown, she curls up by the fire with him . . .

The camera pulls back from the couple, back through the window of the cottage and zooms away from it showing the smoke curling from the chimney up towards the wind-tossed moon in the cloudy sky . . .

What's the matter with me? she thought. *This is no time to get fanciful!*

When she'd first conceived the idea of interviewing Marcus Holbrook, she'd had enough confidence in herself to believe that she would be able to talk her way into his home. However, she had imagined that they would sit in somewhere like his study, surrounded by businesslike-looking manuscripts, while she tried to persuade him in very professional manner to appear in the new programme she planned.

Professional! If Rob Baines could see her now, or Peter – she shifted in the chair uneasily, not wanting to speculate about what her lover would think about her present situation.

In all the years they had been a couple, she had never allowed herself to dwell on any jealous feelings about his wife. After all, he had married Nancy long before

Francine had come on the scene; what right had she to be jealous?

But Peter? Had he ever suffered any jealous pangs about Francine? No, because she had never given him any cause. No matter where in the world she had been working, no matter how attractive the man she was interviewing, Peter had had no cause to worry.

Oh, there had been offers, that was inevitable; after all, as far as the world in general was concerned she was a single woman, a free agent. It had been easy to decline them, for, in her heart, ever since starting the love affair with Peter, she hadn't regarded herself as free.

Her parents had found out in the early days. She still couldn't bear to think about the time they had arrived at her flat and found them in bed together. Her father had told her, and her mother had backed him up, that she was no longer welcome at home. Not until she mended her ways and abandoned her loose, abandoned, adulterous way of life.

She was neither loose nor abandoned, but she couldn't deny that she was an adulterer – or to put it slightly more acceptably – a mistress. And, of course, in her parents' eyes, that still made her a scarlet woman.

'Asleep, Francine?' Marcus's voice was gentle and she opened her eyes.

'No – just thinking.'

'Not very pleasant thoughts judging by the frown.'

'Really?

'Look, I'm sorry that you've trailed all the way up here for nothing but, no matter how beautiful you are, I'm not going to change my habits.'

'Beautiful?'

Wrong response, Francine – you shouldn't care whether he thinks you're beautiful or not . . . oh, God, he's smiling that smile again . . .

'You must know that you're beautiful. Ever since I

first saw you on television I've lusted after you – *no*! – let me put that another way!'

Francine smiled at his confusion. 'Please do.'

'I – you – I mean I thought that you were one of the most attractive women I'd ever seen –'

'Should I be jealous?'

'What are you talking about?'

'Of the others?'

He grinned. 'Stop fishing. Oh, all right, then. I thought you were *the* most attractive woman I'd ever seen, and now that I've met you –'

'Yes?'

'Even with your hair hanging over your face like rats' tails –'

'It wasn't!'

'And a lump the size of an egg on your forehead –'

Francine's hand flew to her forehead and when it came into contact with the plaster she winced. 'Not that big, surely?'

'Don't worry, it's gone down a little already.'

'Good. But you were saying?'

'Francine, you're flirting. You don't deserve it, but I'll tell you anyway. Now that I've met you in the flesh, I think that you're even more gorgeous. Which makes what I'm going to say all the more regrettable.'

Francine sighed. 'You're not even going to let me explain what I want to do, are you?'

'There wouldn't be any point. I wouldn't change my mind.'

'Why?'

Marcus got up and walked out of the room. For a moment Francine thought that he was so exasperated with her that he had gone to bed. She was just wondering whether she ought to put the guard round the fire and retire herself when he returned carrying a bottle of Johnny Walker Black Label.

'I'm going to have a nightcap. Is this to your taste? Don't worry, it's long enough after your accident – I'll allow you a small measure.'

'Thanks.'

When he was seated again and nursing his glass of whisky, Marcus explained why he refused to give interviews. 'There's nothing very sinister about it,' he said. 'It's not that my publishers are scared to let me out in public –'

Francine remembered the thoughts that had gone through her head earlier, when her fevered imagination had prompted her to consider whether Marcus Holbrook might be a sex-maniac or a serial killer. She averted her eyes as she took a sip of whisky and hoped that he couldn't read her mind.

But he was aware of the change in the atmosphere. 'What is it?' he asked.

'Nothing – really – do go on.'

He looked at her levelly for a moment and then continued, 'I became a writer because I like to be in control – you must understand – I decide what I'm going to write and I decide how I'm going to do it –'

I'll bet you do Francine thought, *and woe betide any editor who tries to change one word of your manuscript. But then you're talented enough to get away with it . . .*

'But then you write a book that does well,' Marcus continued, 'and you're thrown into crowds where everyone wants to meet you, question you, argue with you – everyone wants a piece of you.'

'Can't you handle that?'

'Of course I can! But that's not the point.'

'So what is?'

'I met a best-selling woman author once who told me that she'd just spent three months promoting her latest book –'

'That's not unusual. And think of the pleasure she was

giving her fans by giving them the opportunity to meet her.'

'Look, I did a book tour once – oh, nothing grand – it was modest stuff. I was sent on safari round all the little local radio stations in the UK. I appeared on programmes you've never heard of, being interviewed by people who'd never read my book, nor even pretended that they had. They only wanted to talk about anything that happened to fit in with their own agenda.'

'That's par for the course,' Francine said. 'The book would have to have a tie-in with some local topic or some up-to-the minute media interest, but surely just getting it mentioned is enough?'

'I accept that and I should have been grateful, but I just couldn't do it. Halfway through the tour I realized that what I really wanted to be doing was getting on with the next book. I cancelled and came home.'

'And ever since then, you've never given another interview?'

'That's about right. In fact I have a clause written into my contract expressly freeing me from obligations like that.'

'And aren't you worried that people might find that attitude just a little bit precious?'

The look he gave her might have frightened her had she not been sure by now that his severe manner was tempered by a quirky sense of humour. She was right; the glare was replaced by a smile.

'You don't pull any punches, do you? You know, that's why I enjoy watching you on television. No matter how important or famous your guests perceive themselves to be, you seem to know just how to puncture their conceit. And the even cleverer thing is that you never seem to offend them.'

'So you watch my programmes?' Francine didn't like to admit to herself how pleased this prospect made her.

'Wouldn't miss them – I'm a fan!'

'So why not –?'

'You don't give up, do you? Listen Francine, I may be a fan, but I have to say that I don't see how I would fit in to the type of programme you do – all gloss and glamour – entertainment rather than information.'

Francine could have asked him what was wrong with entertainment, and she could also have pointed out that her programmes were not devoid of information. People were always interesting and that she might actually be doing the public a service by exposing different lifestyles. But she didn't. Because it was her very dissatisfaction with what she had been doing so long that had brought her here. She slumped back among the cushions and wondered whether she ought to admit defeat.

'No, Francine, if your public is used to seeing you interviewing the likes of Matt McConnell, they're not going to be interested in someone like me.'

That sounded final and Francine roused herself. This was the very point that Peter or Rob would have made. 'Perhaps I want to do a different type of programme,' she began. 'Something more serious . . . an arts programme . . .'

But Marcus wasn't listening. He drained his glass and then leaned forward to tidy the hearth and settle the fire. He put the cinder guard in place. 'It's late. I think you should go to bed. I put the electric blanket on earlier so I'll just come up and switch it off for you.'

It was on the tip of her tongue to say, don't bother, I'm quite capable of doing that myself, but she held her peace and followed him upstairs. There were three doors on the upstairs landing. One led to the bathroom and the one next to it was the room she'd been given. Marcus went in, switched off the blanket and came out again. He pointed to the door opposite.

'That's my room. If you need me just knock, but I'm

190

going down for a while so shout out if you have to.'

'Oh, the dishes – I should have washed them –'

'Forget it. I'll probably leave them until the morning.'

'Then why –?'

'I want to catch up with some work. Goodnight, Francine.'

She watched him go downstairs and push open a door at the other side of the hall, opposite to the door that led into the kitchen. His work. She hadn't even considered that she might be interrupting him. And he'd never mentioned it. She knew that her work was by its very nature intrusive – shining the spotlight on to people's lives. And yet the majority of the people she interviewed welcomed the publicity, or at least the novelty.

Marcus Holbrook was someone who genuinely didn't welcome intrusion and she had blundered into his life and interrupted his work just because she wanted to change the course of her own career. She felt, not exactly ashamed, but certainly discomfited. But she wasn't quite ready to give up on the idea.

Now that she had met the man, she was more convinced than ever that he would make a marvellous subject for a television interview. She had enjoyed his writing so much herself that she almost wanted to become a disciple – spreading the word, informing an even larger audience of the enjoyment that was waiting for them once they opened one of his books.

She would talk to him again tomorrow. Explain that the programme she had in mind would be nothing like anything she had ever done before. He'd already admitted that he respected her interviewing skills . . . surely he would see that she could handle something with much more gravitas.

And yet, as she began to surrender to the warmth and comfort of the bed in the old cottage on the moor, she knew in her heart that she might not win this battle.

CHAPTER 12

Friday morning

*I*s there such a thing as dreamless sleep? They say that everybody dreams . . . that you have to dream in order to hang on to your sanity, although nobody seems to know exactly why . . .

She knew it was morning because of the thin grey light showing through the gap in the blue and yellow print curtains, but the quality of the silence told her that no one else was awake. That Marcus wasn't awake. Francine pulled the duvet up and tucked it under her chin. She felt relaxed, refreshed, at peace and, if there had been any dreams to disturb her rest, she couldn't remember them. She drifted off to sleep again . . .

Perhaps she did dream this time, because she heard someone calling her name. No, not calling – 'Francine,' someone said quite gently.

'Mm?' she said. There was a faint movement of the air above her but there was no reply.

She opened her eyes. She knew even without looking at her watch that it was much later. She must have slept for an hour or more. It wasn't much lighter outside, but it was no longer silent. Out on the moors she could hear the bleating of sheep – where had they been last night? she wondered – and in the cottage someone was moving around.

She sat up and winced as her head throbbed, reminding her of the accident the night before. She closed her eyes and dropped her head into her hands for a moment, waiting for the pain to ease off. My car, she thought. Marcus promised that he would get his friend to help get it out of the ditch.

And then what shall I do . . . ?

She opened her eyes and turned to take her watch from the bedside table – and stopped with her hand outstretched. There was a cup of tea there. So she hadn't been dreaming. Marcus had come in to the room to awaken her and left before she was fully conscious.

The feeling of disappointment startled her. Why should she feel so upset not to have seen his face – to have wished him good morning . . . ?

The tea was still hot but she sipped it quickly and hurried to the bathroom. She dressed in a clean pair of grey slacks and a chunky, long-line oatmeal-coloured sweater. The cottage had central heating but it was still several degrees cooler than Francine kept her apartment. She went downstairs.

He wasn't in the kitchen. The fire glowed in the hearth, the clock on the mantelpiece ticked steadily, and a pale, wavering sunlight slanted through the window on to the table. The table was set for one. There was a jug of orange juice, a couple of packets of different cereals, a loaf of sliced bread still in its packet, butter and marmalade. There was also a note.

Help yourself. You'll find milk in the fridge and the toaster on the bench. Back soon.

So he must have gone out.

Francine ignored the cereals and made herself a couple of slices of toast. She also made herself a mug of tea. By the time she had eaten her breakfast it was eight o'clock and he had not returned. While she washed her few dishes at the sink she peered out across the yard and through the old gateway on to the moor.

It was no longer misty but the countryside looked bleak. The moor rose starkly against the skyline and everything looked colourless with cold. There was no sign of Marcus. Where could he be? Had he gone to Jed Parkin's farm to organize the tractor?

She wondered what time he must have got up this morning, and then she remembered guiltily that, after seeing her up to bed last night, he had gone back downstairs to work. Francine left the room and stared at the two doors on the other side of the hall. That was the one he had entered . . . that must be his study . . . she opened the door.

It was everything she expected it to be: book-lined, workmanlike and exceptionally tidy. The floor-to-ceiling shelves were full of both reference books and works of fiction. There was a computer on the large desk set side-on to the window, and notebooks and papers arranged in tidy piles. He had everything in order – everything under control.

I'll bet he works to a strict timetable, she thought, and how aggravating it must be for him to have me turn up on his doorstep.

She was aware that she ought not to have come in here. His work was private; he would be justified in being angry with her but, even so, her curiosity got the better of her and, when she closed the study door behind her, she couldn't resist peeping into the next room.

It was a large sitting-room furnished with all the paraphernalia of modern living. It was comfortable, even luxurious. Why should I be surprised? she thought. Just because he chooses to dwell in splendid isolation, it doesn't mean that the man has to live like a monk.

Before she left the room she noticed that there was a log fire laid in the hearth. It was ready for lighting. In front of a large, deep sofa there was a low table covered in books and magazines. How peaceful it must be to sit here at night with the fire blazing, safe from the wind howling down from the moors. Was he content always to sit here alone?

'Mr Travers just phoned – he isn't coming in today.' Stacey said as she came into Carol's office with a mug of coffee. She placed it on the desk.

'Oh?'

'No – he's off to have a look at a new artic; it'll cost us about £80,000, I should think.'

Carol knew that a good articulated vehicle would cost all of that and more but she also knew that Travers' Transport could afford it. At the moment she couldn't muster any enthusiasm. 'Right. I'd better start work.'

'Well, I can see how excited you are by the news!'

'Stacey – I –'

'You look dreadful, by the way.'

'Thanks.'

'Seriously, you look as though you haven't slept a wink.'

I haven't, Carol thought, but I don't really want to tell Stacey that. Or why. I don't want her – or anyone else – to know that Alan has walked out on me.

'Look –' the girl sounded genuinely worried ' – are you sure you ought to be here? I mean, I thought going home early yesterday would do the trick but it obviously hasn't.'

'No – I'm OK – really.'

'When Mr Travers came back after taking you to lunch yesterday, he said that you looked a bit better. He said that you might just have been overdoing things – but I'm beginning to think it's more than that.'

'For goodness' sake leave it alone, Stacey!' Carol suddenly snapped.

'What is it? What have I said?'

'I know you mean to be kind, but you're a proper Job's comforter. If you go on telling me how dreadful I look it's not going to make me feel any better, is it?'

'Sorry I spoke.'

'Look – thanks for the coffee – I –'

But the girl had already flounced out of the office, obviously miffed, and Carol couldn't blame her for taking umbrage. She shouldn't have been so sharp with her but she hadn't been able to help herself.

She had lain awake for most of the night listening for Alan to come back. But he hadn't. He had never walked out on her like that before – but then things had never got to quite such a pitch before. It seemed to Carol that the trouble – whatever it was – had been growing for some time. She should have had it out with him long ago – instead she had allowed it to get worse and worse.

But then so had he!

Even in her misery, last night, she had been unwilling to accept all the blame. How could you sort things out if you never talked to each other?

Why would Alan never talk?

And then she had remembered something that had finally destroyed any chance of sleeping. When she'd come back from the phone box Alan's car had been parked in the street in front of the house. She'd thought that he must have mislaid the key to the garage. Then, after she'd entered the house, the car had been forgotten about during the swiftly developing argument about the phone bill.

Why hadn't he put the car away?

Carol had suddenly realized that it wasn't just their argument that had driven him out of the house. He must have already decided that he was leaving.

That thought had tormented her for the rest of the night. And now, the next morning, she couldn't think of any other explanation. She had to face the possibility that their marriage might be over. And she didn't really know why.

Francine stood at the kitchen window as Marcus and his friend brought her car to the cottage. She had heard the tractor approaching long before she could see it, and now she watched as it manoeuvred its way between the stone gateposts into the yard. Her new car, her pride and joy, was attached to a tow bar and was following on with its front wheels raised off the ground in a most undignified manner.

When they came to a stop, a large man, so like Gemma Parkin that it could only be her father, jumped down from the tractor and Marcus got out of the car. They stood talking for a while, then both men unhitched the tow bar and lowered the Puma safely to the ground. Soon afterwards, Jed Parkin drove off again.

'Why didn't you wait for me?' she asked as Marcus came into the kitchen.

'I thought of hauling you out of bed but you looked so peaceful there.'

'But how did you manage?'

'It was easy – I called an expert. Jed has to pull farm vehicles out of ditches all the time – especially in the winter.' Marcus smiled.

'But you didn't have the keys –'.

'I didn't need them. You told me last night that you'd had to leave the car open and I knew that Jed and his tractor would be able to manoeuvre the car up the track. Do you want to come out and see if everything's in order?'

'Thank you, just a moment –' She scrabbled in her bag for her keys.

'I'd put a coat on if I were you. It's cold out there.'

Francine looked at him. He was wearing a shower-proof, dark blue padded jacket, the kind you saw in mountain shops, over an Aran sweater and navy cords. *Rugged*, she realized. He might be an intellectual but, right at this moment, he looks very much the hardy, outdoor type. *I wonder exactly what he did in the Army . . . ?*

Francine slipped on her jacket and followed him out into the yard.

The car was unscathed. She walked all round it, wonderingly, but there wasn't a scrape or a scratch on its beautiful silver body. 'Oh, that's wonderful!' she exclaimed.

'Hadn't you better give it a test run? Around the yard, at least.'

And everything was fine. Her pride and joy didn't seem to have suffered for its night in a ditch. To her puzzlement, even the central locking was working again.

'I don't understand,' she murmured.

'I can't help you there,' he said. 'I'm no mechanic but either the system didn't like being tilted on its side, or you weren't concentrating properly when you tried to lock it. After all, you'd just been shaken up quite badly; shock can do strange things to your perceptions.'

'I suppose so . . .'

'In any case you can easily have it checked out when you get home.'

'Yes.' Francine's happy mood evaporated.

He wants me to go.

He turned away from her and walked back into the cottage. She followed him dejectedly. She didn't want to go. And it wasn't just because she still hoped to persuade Marcus to appear in her new television programme. She just didn't want to leave him . . .

'Have you had breakfast?'

'Mm, thank you.'

'Fancy a walk?'

'Really?' She couldn't hide her surprise.

'Why not? I like to get out every day for about an hour

and, judging by those skies, it had better be sooner rather than later.'

'Skies?' Francine looked out of the kitchen window.

'Could snow later.'

'Could it?'

'Why so surprised? It's only April – last year we had snow as late as May.'

'I don't mean that – I mean can you really tell that by looking at the skies?' She leaned on the bench top and peered out uncertainly.

'I have to admit that I listened to the weather forecast on the radio,' he said.

'Cheat.' She turned, laughingly, to see that he was smiling that wonderful smile again.

'I'll lend you a scarf and some gloves, and what about your feet – oh!' He stared down at her desert boots bemusedly.

'What's the matter?'

'I'm not sure if they fit the image . . . I mean when I've seen you on television you're always so sophisticated – so fashionable.'

'I'll have you know that some young women think that boots like these are the height of fashion! But you're right, you won't have seen me wearing them on television – even though I do.'

'I don't understand.'

'It's different when I'm in the studios but if I'm out on location – as I am for a lot of my interviews – comfort is the main consideration. But I always have something more glamorous to slip into for the long shots.'

'You realize that you've spoilt everything for me? The next time I see you on television – no matter how gorgeous you're looking – I'll only be able to think about your feet. Oh, dear!'

'What is it?'

'That sounds kinky, doesn't it?'

They were still smiling as they climbed the track beyond the cottage that led to the top of the rise. The gradient was deceptive so that, when they stopped and turned to look back, Francine was surprised to see how small the cottages looked. There was a comforting curl of smoke coming from the chimney of Marcus's cottage and the other one looked cold and dead.

He must have read her mind. 'Sad, isn't it, when a house is unlived in?'

'Has it been empty for very long?'

'There was an elderly woman there when I first came, Mrs Fairchild, a widow. Her husband had been a shepherd. She was already quite frail and her family was worried about her. She stayed on as long as possible; I helped out with the shopping and whatever else I could do but, eventually, she gave in and went to live with her son in Harrogate.'

'And the cottage?'

'I've offered to buy it. I like living here but my cottage isn't really big enough. If I owned both cottages I could make one into my workplace and the other one for living in.'

'So what's the problem?'

'Well, her son and daughter are willing – they're both married and settled and they don't want to come back here. But she's reluctant to make the move final and I don't want to put any pressure on her. You see she lived here all her married life and I imagine she likes to think that her move to her son's house is temporary and that she might be coming back to the cottage one day.'

'I see. That's sad.'

'Yes, isn't it?'

Francine tried to imagine Mrs Fairchild coming to the cottage as a young bride, laughing, loving, and giving birth to her children. Then seeing them grow up and leave home – but she and her husband would still have

200

each other – until the day he died. The cottage would be full of memories. It must have broken her heart to leave it. And Marcus understood that.

The sky was an unremitting grey and the wind was biting. The sheep huddled for shelter against the ancient drystone walls. Francine shivered. Marcus put his arm around her shoulders and drew her close to his body. She turned to look up into his face and, as she did so, he slipped the other arm around her so that she was standing within the circle of his arms.

The sky grew darker and the wind even stronger. She felt buffeted by it. Marcus gathered her even closer. She rested her cheek against his jacket and closed her eyes.

What are we doing, she thought, what's happening here?

'We'd better go,' he murmured and she felt his breath lift her hair. 'We don't want to be up here if it starts snowing.'

Marcus took hold of her hand and held her steady as they ran back down the rough, moorland track. The cottage was warm and there was a delicious smell of something cooking. Francine was puzzled. 'Is somebody here?'

'I put it in the oven earlier and switched on just before we went out.'

'But what is it?'

'Chicken casserole. When I phoned Jed this morning and told him what the trouble was, Rosemary insisted on sending emergency rations over. What is it? Why are you looking like that?'

'Are you inviting me to stay?'

'I don't intend to eat it all by myself.'

'But . . . I thought that, as my car is OK, you would want me to leave as soon as possible. And first you take me out walking and now you want me to stay for lunch. I don't understand. Unless . . . unless . . .'

Marcus turned quickly from hanging up his coat on the back of the door. 'No, Francine, don't get any idea that I'm going to change my mind about being interviewed. That will never happen.'

'Then why do you want me to stay?'

'I'd like to keep an eye on you after that bump you had.'

Francine raised her hand towards her forehead and remembered in time not to touch it. 'But you said last night that you didn't think it was serious.'

'Don't be alarmed. I don't think it's serious, but it might not be a good idea to undertake a long journey.'

'Really?'

'Check the first-aid manual.' He smiled. 'But if what you're really asking is whether that's my only reason for advising you not to go, I'll come clean and admit that it's a marvellous excuse to keep you here just a little longer. Just for the pleasure of your company.'

'Oh.'

'Here, let me help you off with that.'

Francine allowed him to help her shrug off her jacket. He hung it next to his own. As she handed him the scarf and gloves he had lent her, she realized how natural it seemed to let him take charge in small ways like this.

'How . . . how long do you think I should stay here, then?'

'Until tomorrow morning, at least. And by then we might be safely snowed in here together.'

'You're joking!'

'I'm joking. I don't think the weather will get as bad as that; after all, the snow that was forecast has held off until now. But if the road conditions are going to be in the least uncertain, it might be better for you to have another good night's sleep and set off early in the morning.' Suddenly he frowned. 'Unless – I've just thought – you don't have to get back to work, do you?'

'No – no – it's OK. I'm free until Monday.'

As soon as she'd said that she wished she hadn't. She hoped that he didn't think that she was angling to stay here for the whole weekend. And yet the longer she stayed, the more chance there was of winning him round . . .

He didn't seem to notice her momentary confusion. 'Come over here, sit by the fire,' he said. And, as naturally as though he had been doing it for years, he put an arm around her shoulder and guided her across the room.

Francine wondered anew. They had only just met – and not in the best of circumstances – and yet they were behaving as if they'd known each other for years.

'You know, I feel as if I've known you for years,' he said.

She looked at him in awe. *Had he just read her mind?*

'Why's that?' she asked.

Marcus hunkered down in front of the hearth. He removed the cinder guard and shovelled some coal on the fire. Francine watched as he arranged it methodically. When he was satisfied with his efforts he sat back on his heels and resting his forearms along his legs he clasped his hands. He looked up at her.

'I suppose it's because I've seen you on television so often. I've heard that happens to a lot of performers. People meet them in the street and greet them like old friends, even although they've never actually met before.'

'That's true. It's happened to me.'

'And do you mind?'

'Not at all – so long as they say nice things!'

'You'll not hear a word of criticism from me. Now, I hope you like broccoli.'

'Love it.'

'Well, just sit there and relax while I prepare the vegetables; by the time they're cooked the casserole should be just about ready.'

* * *

After they had eaten they took a tray through to the sitting-room. Marcus set a match to the fire and, by the time he had pulled the large old sofa in closer and poured the coffee, there was already a satisfactory crackling coming from the hearth.

Francine glanced out of the window. The sky was gloomy but there was still no sign of snow. She was taken unawares when he suddenly reached across and took hold of her hand.

'What is it?' She looked at him with wide eyes.

'Do I have to have a reason?'

'Yes – I mean no – I mean – I don't know what I mean . . .'

He laughed. 'I never thought I'd see the day when Francine Rowe was lost for words. But, if that's the effect I have on you, I'll release your hand . . . reluctantly.'

Marcus withdrew his hand and Francine stared down at her own. His action had made her very conscious of the space between them . . . the small space . . . just one cushion-width . . . It was a while before she was composed enough to speak. Then she forced herself to look up.

He was still watching her and she had to nerve herself to ask, 'Marcus, why do you live here on your own?'

'What brought that on? You're not practising for an interview, are you?'

'No – I really want to know – I mean I'm surprised –'

'Why should you be surprised? I need peace and quiet for the kind of work I do but, even if I wasn't a writer, I'd still prefer the country to the city.'

'That's understandable – but it's not quite what I meant.' Francine frowned. 'Look, before I came here, I knew all about your reputation for being difficult –'

'My reputation for what?' He looked offended.

'Yes. You may not realize it but what to you seems a perfectly reasonable desire to get on with your writing has somehow become translated into "Marcus Holbrook is a difficult man – a loner – a misanthropist"–'

'Misanthropist! I don't hate anybody!'

'I know that. I knew that even before I met you. You couldn't write the way you do if you hated mankind, but the fact remains that you have the reputation for being – oh, I don't know – aloof, uncommunicative, taciturn –'

'All those things?' He looked deeply wounded and Francine thought she had gone too far until she saw that he was controlling a smile.

'Yes, all those things, damn you! You know what I mean. A man as clever as you are can't be unaware that the world would interpret your behaviour that way!'

'The world? I think you mean the press.'

'OK, the press. But I believed it. And then – and then I come here and you're not like that at all.'

'Flattery will get you nowhere.'

'I know, you've made it quite plain, you're not doing the interview. What I'm saying is that you're not the ogre I was expecting. You've been kind to me – you – you're quite civilized –'

'Thanks!'

'And I just don't understand why you live here all alone.'

'Are you asking me whether I'm married?'

'I suppose I am – or at least why there's no one in your life –'

'Perhaps there is.'

'Is there?'

'No.'

'There, you see.'

Marcus poured them each some more coffee and, as he put the cafetière back on to the coffee table, he said, 'Francine, I'm not sure why you're asking this, but I suspect that like all females –'

'You're not going to be patronizing, are you?'

205

'Probably. Even intelligent females, as I've no doubt you are, seem to be curious if a man gets to my age without being married or, at least doesn't have a lover – of either sex. So admit that you're being old-fashioned nosy and I'll tell you all you need to know.'

Francine laughed in spite of herself. 'OK, I'm being nosy.'

'I was married, once. I was in the Army, as I think you've guessed, and my wife was a nurse. She had a difficult job and life was hard for her. I was away a lot and I couldn't always tell her exactly where I was going.

'Each time I came home from a tour of duty all I wanted to do was have a good time. I never gave a thought to what she'd been through, coping both with her job and fears for my safety.

'Then one time when I came home, I found that she'd left me. I couldn't persuade her to return.'

'So what are you saying? That that experience put you off marriage?'

'On the contrary. It made me realize exactly what I'd lost. She was always there for me but I let her down. Marriage should be two people loving and supporting each other, not simply two people having a good time.'

He leaned forward to put another log on the fire. When he sat back again, Francine was completely unprepared for his question. 'And you? Is there anybody in your life?'

'I – oh – that doesn't matter –'

'Am I not allowed to be nosy, too?' He leaned over and picked up her hand again – her left hand. 'You're not wearing any rings –'

'No – but –'

Suddenly he groaned and his fingers moved to her wrist. He grasped it tightly pulling her towards him. She found herself nestling in the crook of one arm while the other moved round to cradle her head. She could feel his fingers caressing the soft skin at the nape of her neck.

She was trembling, not just with the shock of finding herself in his arms, but also with the shock of realizing how much she wanted to be there. He wouldn't let her turn her head away and, when she moved back, she found herself being pressed into the cushions of the sofa.

His head was moving nearer and she held her breath. She held it until she began to feel faint. Only seconds could have passed and yet she felt as though time had forgotten the rules. Everything was moving in slow motion. When, at last, his lips came down on hers, she welcomed them, kissing him hungrily, clinging to him even closer.

But it couldn't last. From somewhere she found the strength to tear her mouth away. 'No, Marcus, no –'

He released her immediately. 'What is it?'

'I'm – not –' *Oh, God, what was she exactly?* 'I'm not . . .'

While she struggled for the right words he drew back from her. 'It doesn't matter. I'm sorry.'

'Look, I'll go into my study and get on with some work for a couple of hours, if you don't mind. Later, if the snow holds off, I'll drive you down the village for a pub meal. Otherwise you'll have to put up with my cooking again.'

After he had gone Francine sat and stared into the flames. She couldn't find any pictures there. At least not any comforting ones. She couldn't remember ever feeling such anguish – such torment.

It wasn't just the frustration of unfulfilled physical desire. She knew that her emotions had become engaged in a way they never had been before . . .

But that's not possible, she thought. *I'm thirty-one years old and I don't believe in love at first sight . . . Love! What am I thinking? What's happened to me?*

And then, like a dash of cold water, *What about Peter . . .?*

CHAPTER 13

Francine brought her maps in from the car and glanced at them quickly as she sat and drank coffee at the kitchen table. She worked out the best route and was pleased to see that it wouldn't take as long as she had thought. That was important because, if it really was going to snow, she wanted to be well away before it started. It would be just too humiliating to have to abandon her car once again and trudge back to the cottage!

It's like planning an escape, she thought, as she rinsed out her mug and placed it on the bench. And, from somewhere deep inside where she was still quite sane, she summoned up enough humour to laugh at herself.

Sophie would just love this, she thought. Francine hadn't had many emotional crises in her life but it was funny how she always thought of Sophie when life's problems became too puzzling for her to work out on her own. She remembered the days when she had first gone to London to work and had to cope with a new, high-profile job and life in the capital city.

Sometimes she would phone Sophie and they would talk for hours. Or Sophie would come up for a weekend and they would eat takeaway meals, drink cheap wine and generally slob around like the students they had been when they met. She had never actually asked Sophie for advice, her pride would never have allowed her to do that. But, somehow, just talking to her old friend, testing her own ideas against Sophie's unwavering integrity, had always helped her to come to some kind of decision. And if Sophie didn't agree with her, she never said so.

Not like her mother. Ever since Francine had been old enough to express an opinion, her mother had seemed to take a delight in contradicting her. It was almost as if she didn't want her daughter to grow up into an independent human being with a mind of her own. And yet, Francine knew that she could never claim that she had been unloved. Her mother might not have known how to be the warm, soft parent that she craved, but she had always been fiercely protective.

As a child, if Francine had fallen down while she was out playing and run in crying, her mother would tell her not to be soft and get back out and get on with it. But if any other child had pushed her down, that was an entirely different matter. She remembered occasions when her mother had marched along their street with a delighted group of children in tow, to berate anyone who had dared lay a finger on 'our Francine'. And if the child wasn't suitably chastened, Mrs Rowe would have a go at the mother, as well.

Francine had always regretted that her love for Peter had meant severing links with her parents. But as her mother would have pointed out, she had made her own bed and, until now, she had been content to lie in it . . .

Apart from the crackle of the fire and the ticking of the clock, the cottage was quiet. It was about an hour since Marcus had gone into his study and he hadn't emerged once. Francine wondered if he would have a break, make himself a cup of coffee, perhaps? She thought it quite likely and she decided that she had better be gone before that happened. She didn't think that she could face seeing him again.

She slipped on her jacket and picked up the bags that she had already packed, then, with one last regretful look around, she opened the door. She was shocked to find how cold it had become and, after pulling the door shut quietly, she hurried across to her car.

Since they had gone for a walk that morning, the wind had become even stronger and that was probably why she didn't hear the sound of the other car approaching until it swung into the yard at breakneck speed.

She had just lifted her bags over into the back seat when she paused to watch in surprise as a mud-spattered white Metro drew up beside her. No sooner had it screeched to a stop when the door at the driver's side burst open and Gemma Parkin got out. She stared angrily across the roof of her car.

'I thought it would be you. I hoped it wasn't – but I couldn't think of anyone else!'

Gemma's long, brown hair was caught by the wind and whipped up into the air like angry snakes. They coiled around her head, making her look like Medusa, and her furious expression was enough to turn anyone to stone.

'You'll have to explain that rather confused statement,' Francine said.

Gemma's fury grew. 'Oh, aren't we *clever*! The famous television personality, Francine Rowe, getting the better of Gemma Parkin, the insignificant little local radio reporter!'

Not very little, Francine thought unkindly, but she could see that the girl was genuinely upset – and she thought she knew why. She felt sorry for her and she would have liked to approach her, tell her to calm down, but the sheer size of the girl made her cautious.

'How did you know I was here?' she asked quietly.

Gemma stared at her truculently. 'I was worried after you left yesterday. I – I thought I may have slipped up and given you a clue – and I was right, wasn't I?'

And that was partly the reason for her rage, Francine thought. No one, especially young women just beginning to make their way in their chosen career, liked to be made a fool of – and that was how Gemma saw it.

'But that doesn't explain why you came rushing up here.'

'I was on early shift this morning; as soon as I had a spare moment I phoned home – I hadn't worked out what I was going to say – but I didn't have to say anything. Mum told me that Dad was out helping Marcus get some woman's car out of a ditch – some woman who had turned up at the cottage – and I just knew it would be you!'

'So as soon as you finished work you leapt into your car and drove here. But, why, Gemma? What did you hope to gain?'

'Gain? What do you mean?'

'I'm here – it's too late to do anything about it. Unless you had some crazy idea that you could frighten me away?'

'Humph!' The girl snorted, and Francine saw how close to tears she was. 'I just – I just wanted Marcus to know that I didn't tell you where to find him – that it wasn't my fault!'

'Gemma, your name has never been mentioned.'

'You tricked me!'

'All right – calm down. You'll be pleased to know that I'm leaving now.'

Gemma looked uncertain. 'And – and the interview?'

'He wouldn't agree. And, Gemma –'

'What?'

Francine suppressed a smile. The girl was behaving like a sulky teenager. 'Marcus is working right now. You wouldn't want to interrupt him, would you?'

She wanted to get away – miles away before Marcus realized she had gone. She had the crazy idea – hope? –

that he might try and stop her . . . although she didn't know why . . .

'No, I suppose not –'

'Good, then I'll say goodbye.'

'I'll just let myself in quietly and get a meal ready for him.'

Francine had been about to get in her car but she paused and glanced back in surprise. Gemma had drawn herself up and was smirking – that was the only word for it – triumphantly.

'You do that.'

As she drove out of the yard she glanced in the mirror and saw the girl with her chin raised, watching her. She's seeing me off, Francine thought. Poor kid, she would probably never admit it, but she's in love with him.

So what's the difference . . . ?

The sky was heavy, threatening, and as she took the road that crossed the Pennines a few flakes of snow began to blow across the windscreen. Francine knew how bad conditions could be on this exposed route that crossed from one side of England to the other but after more than an hour's driving she was well on her way.

She should reach the small town just north of Manchester about five o'clock. Should she phone ahead, she wondered and warn them that she was coming? No, she decided, she would make it a surprise . . .

The digital clock in the bottom right-hand corner of Marcus's computer screen told him that he had been working for over two hours. He could allow himself to take a break – even although he had not written as much as he should have done.

It had taken most of his considerable self-discipline to leave Francine and go to his study. He was sure that she was as attracted to him as he was to her. And yet she had pulled back. He remembered her hesitation – her confusion – and he frowned. As far as he knew she wasn't married and neither did she appear to have a permanent man friend.

Of course there had been the occasional item in the gossip columns hinting that Francine Rowe owed her initial breakthrough in television to someone powerful behind the scenes. A married man, it was implied, who continued to control her. But Marcus had read between the lines and glimpsed the envy that inspired these pieces. He had always dismissed them as muckraking.

Could the stories be true? If there was such a man, could Francine be in love with him? He didn't think so, not from the way she had instinctively responded to his kiss. Didn't she realize what kind of signals she'd been sending him?

Suddenly he experienced a surge of exhilaration. He couldn't remember feeling as alive as this for years. She was here, wasn't she? In his cottage? And she'd told him herself that she didn't have to be back at work until Monday. He had a whole weekend to convince her that her instincts were right.

Marcus saved his work and switched off his computer. He knew that he wouldn't get any more work done today, but for once he didn't care. As he crossed the tiny hall he could hear her moving about in the kitchen, the rattle of pans. What on earth was she doing? Preparing a meal?

She didn't have to – he would take her out tonight. Show her that the village pub could provide as good a meal as any fancy restaurant in London. He had a joke half-formed on his lips – something really puerile about taking Cinderella to the ball – but when he opened the door he stopped in confusion.

'Gemma?'

'Hi, Marcus.' The girl was standing at the sink peeling potatoes. She turned round and grinned at him.

'When did you get here?'

'Oh, not very long ago. But I didn't want to interrupt you. I thought I'd make us a nice meal – a treat.'

She blushed. Her hair was hanging down untidily, as usual, and her clothes were crumpled. She looks like an unmade bed, he thought, and was ashamed of himself for being so uncharitable.

'But where's Francine? Is she all right? I mean, is she lying down upstairs, is her head hurting?'

'No.'

Why as the girl looking so upset? 'What's the matter, Gemma?'

'Look, Marcus, I'm sorry about that.'

'Sorry about what?' Marcus was getting alarmed. Had something happened to Francine?

'About her coming here. She tricked me into telling her where you lived. I wasn't going to tell you that, but it's better to be truthful, isn't it?'

So that was what was upsetting her. 'Gemma, I didn't know anything about that, believe me. And you don't have to worry, there's no harm done.'

'Aren't you angry with me?'

'Not in the slightest.'

'That's that, then. Now, I've been scrounging around in your fridge and I've decided on sausage and mash with onion gravy, OK?' She turned back to the bench and began slicing the onions.

'Gemma! You haven't answered my question. Where's Francine?'

'Oh, she's gone.'

'Gone! When?'

'Over an hour ago, just as I arrived as a matter of fact.'

'But why? Did she tell you why?'

'She said that as you wouldn't do the interview she had no further interest in you and she certainly didn't want to hang around.'

'I see.'

Sheer bad temper had carried Carol through the morning. At first she had been in a state of shock, almost numb with a feeling of helplessness. But slowly her anger grew and, although it was entirely focused on Alan – wherever he was – she couldn't altogether disguise her feelings from Stacey.

At lunchtime the girl had popped her head around the door of Carol's office and waved to attract her attention. 'Hey there!' she said.

'Yes?' Carol knew that she sounded terse.

'I just want you to know that I've forgiven you.'

'Forgiven me?'

'Yes, for snapping my head off when you arrived this morning.'

'Oh . . . Stacey . . . I'm sorry, truly I am, but –'

Stacey held up a hand. 'No, you don't have to explain. Let's just forget it. The sandwich man's here; shall I get you something?'

'No, thank you, I'm not very hungry.'

'Cheese savoury, did you say? Back in a tick, you can settle up with me later.'

After that Carol could hardly turn down Stacey's suggestion that they should sit together in the tiny staff kitchen and have a little chat over their coffee and sandwiches – for once the younger girl wasn't going home for lunch. Once the men had been given their assignments for the day they usually had the temporary building to themselves and the place was quite cosy.

'It's not a very cheerful place to have lunch, is it?' Carol noticed.

'That's right. Just as well I usually go home and you go off gallivanting with the boss.'

Carol flushed. 'We don't gallivant – whatever that means.'

'So you've told me. And I believe you. But, Carol, I

215

hope that whatever has been upsetting you for the past couple of days is nothing to do with Mr Travers?'

'No, it isn't.'

Stacey looked at her levelly and then gave a small smile. 'That's all right, then. But you haven't denied that you are upset and, if you do need a shoulder to cry on, mine's on offer.'

'Thanks, I'll remember that.'

As usual Stacey had managed to cheer her up. She realized that, in spite of the differences in their age and their backgrounds, they had the basis for a real friendship. But she didn't want to burden the girl with her marital problems. It might put her off the whole idea of marriage.

She felt vaguely guilty that she had denied that Luke had anything to do with her state of turmoil. Alan couldn't possibly know about the attraction she felt for her boss but if she hadn't been so bemused by Luke she might have concentrated more on what was bothering her husband . . .

After lunch she fed the presentation disk into the computer and had a look at the new software program that Luke was thinking of buying. She soon realized that it might be just what they needed and she became totally absorbed. Apart from bringing her a mug of tea mid-afternoon, Stacey left her to work in peace. And then, just after Carol had printed up some of the more interesting files, the young receptionist came into her office again. She looked grave.

'What is it?' Carol asked.

'It's your husband on the phone – shall I put him through?'

'Alan! Yes – but has he said something? Why are you looking at me like that?'

'I don't know – it's just that he's never phoned you here before – and you've been acting so strangely . . . I just thought I'd better warn you – better ask if you wanted to speak to him.'

'I see. Thank you but it's all right, Stacey. I'll take the call.'

Stacey shut the door as she went out. Carol let the phone ring twice before she answered it. She felt quite calm. 'Hello, Alan.'

'Carol.' There was a pause. 'I'm at home.'

'Home?' Her anger evaporated and she couldn't keep the relief out of her voice.

'No,' he sounded embarrassed, 'you don't understand, I mean I'm at my parents' house.'

'Oh, of course, *home*.' She was stung. After all these years of marriage he could still call his parents' house 'home'.

He sensed her displeasure and he hurried on, 'Listen, Carol, I don't want to argue, I just wanted to explain about last night. I was annoyed about the phone because –'

'Annoyed? You were paranoid!' She wasn't sure if that was the right word but he certainly hadn't been acting like a reasonable man.

'Carol – do you want me to explain or don't you?'

'Yes – go on.'

'My father phoned me at work to say that my mother was in hospital –'

'Oh, Alan!'

'She had a fall when she was cleaning out the kitchen cupboards. They don't think it's serious but she's badly bruised and they wanted to keep her in under observation for a while. Anyway, she was a bit weepy and she wanted to see me.'

'Of course!'

'I offered to drive down straight away but Dad said they might sedate her. He told me to go home and he'd phone when he knew a little more.'

'What can I say?'

217

'On the way home I thought that you might already have a message. But you weren't there. I sat and waited for the phone to ring and then, eventually, I thought I'd try the hospital –'

'And you discovered that we were disconnected. But why didn't you tell me straight away?'

'Do you know, Carol, I can't explain it. There've been so many things lately – I don't know – it just felt like the last straw. I sat there on the stairs and I listened to you and I watched you and I just didn't recognize you –'

'*You* didn't recognize *me!*'

'Carol – you came in as if there was nothing the matter –'

'But there wasn't – I mean not really – I mean I didn't know –'

'Will you listen to me? You behaved as if it were all a joke about the phone being cut off and you thought I should find it funny. When I told you that I didn't feel like laughing, you actually told me to lighten up.'

'Oh, no! But, Alan, I didn't know – about your mother –'

'And you didn't spare the time to find out why I was upset, did you? You just went on attacking me.'

'Yes, but –' What could she say? How could she tell him that she hadn't noticed that he was upset because she thought he was just being his usual crabby self? It had been so long since he had been anything but preoccupied and even downright morose that he had looked no different from usual.

Alan seemed to be getting angrier. 'You just kept going on about all the housework you have to do and about how much work you have to do. Incidentally, I don't suppose you've ever spared a thought about all the extra hours I work since I was given the responsibility for launching a new product.'

'Oh, but I have, I know how hard you work – I know

218

what effort you put in!'

'But you don't appreciate it enough to give me the right kind of support, it seems. And then, just when I was about to tell you what the matter was, you suddenly slammed off into the kitchen and started acting like a madwoman –'

'Alan – stop! I'm so, so sorry – but please, we shouldn't be quarrelling now – your mother's in hospital – you haven't told me how your she is –'

There was a small pause and then he said, 'She's all right. In fact she'll probably come home tomorrow, but she'll have to rest.'

'Of course. Look, shall I come down to Bournemouth? I can go home, pack a bag and be with you in just over two hours.'

'No, I don't think that's necessary.'

'But I could help – with the housework – with the cooking . . .'

'No, don't bother. You made a point of telling me how overworked you are. Dad and I will manage.'

'But –'

'No, Carol. What my mother needs is peace and quiet and a well-run home. She doesn't need your kind of housekeeping.'

'Oh.'

'Are you still there?'

'Yes.'

'Well, goodbye, then. I – I just wanted to tell you where I was, OK?'

'Sure. Goodbye, Alan.'

After she had replaced the receiver, she realized that she hadn't sent any kind of message to his mother. Another black mark, no doubt. She stared at the phone for a moment, wondering whether she should phone back and decided not to. She wasn't sure whether she would be able to sound convincingly sympathetic.

She looked up as there was a knock at the door and Stacey came in hesitantly. 'Everything OK?' she asked.

'Not really, but as there's nothing I can do about it, I'm going to go and collect a large portion of cod and chips with extra batter and take them home and make a pig of myself. Oh, and I might just buy a bottle of cherry pop to wash it all down with.'

'Ugh!' Stacey gave her what her mother would have called an old-fashioned look and then said, 'Well, try not to make yourself sick, will you, because if I know men, your husband will probably phone you later and you'd better talk sense?'

'Stacey, I know you're a very wise young woman, but I don't think he'll be phoning later.'

'Serious, is it?'

'Bad enough.'

'Well, even so, you'd better have all your wits about you because, while you were busy talking, Mr Travers came though on the other line –'

'And?'

'He wants to talk to you about this new computer software – something about a demonstration – he said he'd probably call you at home later. And talking about home, it's time we broke out of here and escaped for the night, right?'

'Right, Stacey, lead the way.'

As Carol drove home she wondered whether the phone had been reconnected. She'd paid the bill and done everything she'd been told to do and they'd said that by the time she got home, it should be working again.

But what if it wasn't and Luke phoned as Stacey said he might? Would he hear the recorded message and guess that she hadn't paid her bill? In spite of the mood he was in, would Alan try to get through? Should she phone him at his parents' home and ask how his mother was?

Sick of all the uncertainty, she resolved to postpone thinking about it all until later. The traffic was heavier than usual and she was glad to leave the motorway and head for the fish and chip shop in the next village. She dumped her parcel of cod and chips on the passenger seat and the smell wafted up to tempt her.

Funny, she thought, even when my life is falling apart, it doesn't spoil my appetite. Does that mean I'm not devastated by the way Alan is behaving or, quite the opposite, does it mean I'm suppressing my grief by eating for comfort?

When she reached home, she didn't use the garage, even although with Alan away she could have done. She just couldn't be bothered, so she left her car in the street as usual. As she walked up the front path she heard the phone begin to ring. She quickened her step. Her heart began to beat erratically.

Who would it be?

CHAPTER 14

Friday evening, Lancashire

The snow was too wet to lie and Francine's journey had been relatively trouble-free. By the time she left the motorway it had stopped altogether, but a fine drizzle had set in and the roads were wet and glistening. Just over two hours after leaving the cottage on Moor Top, she was negotiating the rush-hour traffic in the streets of a town just north of Manchester.

It was years since she had been here and she'd been shocked by how run-down and neglected parts of the old town centre were. But there was also evidence of attractive new developments and here, in the suburbs, the houses and the gardens were as neat as ever.

When she pulled up outside the house she intended to visit, she sat in the car for a moment and thought about what she should say. Should she pretend that she was 'just passing' – that she had an assignment nearby and had decided to call in? Or should she admit the truth, that she desperately needed to talk to someone? She was still undecided when she rang the front doorbell. She wondered who would answer.

'Francine!' Mrs Blake's kindly features registered surprise. 'But don't just stand there – come in out of the rain.'

Francine stepped in and Sophie's mother closed the door. The house was warm and smelled of recent baking.

'Come along, dear – give me your jacket – that's the sitting-room – go in and sit down and I'll put the kettle on.

'Tea or coffee?' she asked over her shoulder as she went along the small passage to the kitchen.

'Tea, please.'

Sophie mustn't be home yet, she thought and she went into the sitting-room as she was told. It was spotlessly clean and prettily decorated without being fussy. Francine sank gratefully into one of the comfortable armchairs. It was only now that her journey was over that she realized how tense she had been. There was a nagging ache between her shoulder-blades and the bump on her head was sending out its own signals of disquiet. Francine fingered the plaster that Marcus had put there; the skin near the edges was beginning to itch slightly. She wondered whether to take it off and decided to leave it a while longer.

Mrs Blake came in with a tray and placed it on the coffee table. She straightened up and looked at Francine, who smiled back wanly.

'You've had an accident?'

'Oh, that's all right, it happened yesterday.'

Was it only yesterday? Was it barely twenty-four hours since her life had been shaken up so thoroughly?

'Are you going to tell me how?'

'I skidded off the road – landed in a ditch – but I'm fine, really and, more important, so is my car!'

Laura Blake smiled at her and began to pour the tea. 'I seem to remember that you don't take sugar, but you look as though you need a hot sweet drink right now –'

Francine watched her stir the sugar into the cup and realized that it wasn't worth protesting. That's the second time in as many days, she thought; what's happening to me?

223

'Thank you,' she said as Mrs Blake handed her both a cup of tea and plate containing a generous slice of home-made chocolate cake.

'So,' she said as she settled on the opposite chair with her own drink, 'are you working up here at the moment?'

'No, I tried to set up a project but it didn't come to anything, so I thought – I thought . . .'

'That as you had nothing better to do, you would come and see Sophie.'

Laura Blake's tone was abrupt and Francine looked at her in astonishment. 'Well – it's not quite like that.'

Sophie's mother sighed. 'I'm sorry if I sounded sharp, but you haven't been in touch for quite some time, have you?'

'I know . . . I've been so busy . . . and . . .' Francine didn't know what to say. She knew that she'd been neglectful, but then, she hadn't been in touch with any of her old friends, it wasn't just Sophie.

'Sophie's been trying to get in touch with you, you know. I hadn't realized that she hadn't told you about –' She paused and started again, 'I mean, I didn't know that you'd been out of touch for so long. She only told me this morning that apparently you've moved and –'

'I didn't let her know! Oh, no – but I didn't let anyone know – I've had so much to do . . .' Francine knew it sounded feeble – and it was. What had she been thinking of? When had she become so careless about the people who mattered?

Laura was shaking her head gently. 'If it makes you feel any better, my dear, apparently she's been trying to contact Carol and Alison, too.'

Francine was alarmed. 'Why does she want to get in touch with all of us? She's not ill, is she!'

'No, dear, there's nothing to worry about, but I'm going to let Sophie tell you herself. When she catches up with you.'

'Catches up with me? What do you mean? Won't she be home soon?'

'Normally she would be home about now but, this morning, she told me she was going away for the weekend. She took her bags with her to school. By now she'll be on her way to Alison's.'

'Alison's? But . . . ?'

'Yes, she finally managed to get through to her last night. I'm not sure what was said, but Alison obviously asked her to stay and Sophie seemed to be quite pleased – relieved even . . .'

Mrs Blake frowned as if there were something she didn't quite understand, but, after a moment or two, she said, 'Now then, my dear, you look tired, let me make you a proper meal – and you're very welcome to stay the night, of course.'

'No – that's very kind of you but I'll be going now –' Francine got up and hurried towards the door.

Laura followed her; she looked distressed. 'Francine, please don't. I didn't mean to scold –'

'I know – it's not that –' Francine stopped and gave Sophie's mother a hug. 'But you did make me feel ashamed and I'd like to put things right.'

'Is this visit for business or pleasure?' Molly Harding welcomed Greg from behind the reception desk in The Plough.

'Business, Molly, but it's always a pleasure to see you again.'

'Now then, don't pretend it's my charms that's brought you down here again so soon.'

'I don't know what you're talking about. I – I needed to get away from the office – look at the site – work on – some details – you know . . .'

'Yes, I'm sure I do.'

225

He didn't like the look she gave him and he raised his eyebrows.

'Get on with you,' she said, 'Your usual room's all ready. Shall I get Alf to give you a hand with that lot?'

Molly meant the bundle of plans and files that Greg had dumped ostentatiously on the desk. If by doing so he had hoped to convince her that this trip really was all about business, he knew he had failed when he saw her knowing smile.

'No, that's OK, I can manage.' He lifted the carrying strap of his overnight bag over his shoulder and scooped all the paperwork into his arms. Clutching it to his body, he set off for the stairs.

He was halfway there when Molly called out, 'You've forgotten your briefcase – wait, I'll bring it.'

He turned to see that Alf had appeared behind the desk and was watching wide-eyed as Molly hurried after Greg and hooked the briefcase over the fingers of one hand.

'Thanks, Molly.'

'Don't mention it. Oh, Greg –' He paused on the bottom stair. 'You'll need the key.' She caught up with him and slipped the room key into his pocket. 'Now, if I were you, once you've dumped that lot I would come down to the bar and have a stiff drink. You look as though you need it.'

He could have sworn that he heard her giggle as she went back to join her husband at the desk.

Once he had negotiated the stairs and the narrow landing, he dumped everything on the floor while he opened the door. He realized that he had probably made a fool of himself. He hadn't needed quite so many props to convince his old friends that he had come down here to work. Or was it himself that he'd been trying to fool?

There was some paperwork he had to do, but he could have done that anywhere; his house in Chelsea had a large studio-cum-study, and as for the plans for the new development, they were complete, there was nothing else to do – except show Alison.

Alison . . .

Greg put everything on the other bed in the twin-bedded room and lay on his own with his hands locked behind his head gazing up at the ceiling. He closed his eyes and, with no difficulty at all, remembered her hesitant smile, her watchful eyes, her gentle way of talking.

He knew that he would do anything to make that smile more radiant, her look more confident and, as for the way she talked, it was perfect – he could listen to her forever. I've never felt this way about a woman, he marvelled. But I've always known that this is the way it should be.

He glanced at his watch. Could he ask her to come out to dinner again? He could pretend that he wanted to talk business – or he could be completely honest and admit that he just wanted – needed – to see her. He sat up, pulled the pillows up to support his back and reached for the phone that was next to the bed. He dialled her number.

'Westbrook Hall.'

It wasn't Alison who had answered, and Greg steeled himself for the ensuing battle of wits. He had a pretty good idea why the old lady never passed on his messages. She was probably opposed to the sale of the land, and he didn't really blame her. Someone of her age and her class would not relish having a modern housing development within view of the old family home – even if the old family home was acutely in need of the money it would bring in.

'Mrs Cavendish?' He was aware of the need to sound polite and businesslike.

'Yes?' The old voice was querulous.

'This is Greg Leighton. I wonder if I might speak to Mrs Alison Cavendish?'

'She's not here.'

Greg sensed that she was about to put the phone down and called out, 'Wait! When will she be home? I'd like to call back.'

He was furious. It wasn't Mrs Cavendish's actual words, it was her tone and her attitude. *She's not here*; as if that were enough – no offer to take a message and, come to that, no, *Oh, how are you, Mr Leighton?* Considering that his offer would just about save the family bacon, surely she owed him the basic niceties of polite conversational exchange!

Mrs Cavendish senior sounded both surprised and irritated. 'As a matter of fact, you've just missed her. She's only just left. I have no idea when she'll be home. Now, goodbye, Mr –'

But he was determined not to be brushed off, dispensed with like some lower form of life, and he intercepted quickly, 'Has she gone away?'

'I *beg* your pardon?'

The way she stressed the word 'beg' told him how incredulous she was and he smiled. 'You said that you had no idea when Mrs Cavendish was returning, so I asked if that means that she's gone away.'

There was an outraged silence at the other end of the line so Greg added, 'I need to see her to – er – discuss some details of the sale.'

The truth was that he needed to see her. Full stop. But he could hardly say that to Mrs Cavendish senior, of all people.

'My daughter-in-law will be back later. She's simply gone to the village to collect Matthew from his friend's house. Now, Mr Leighton, I really must say goodbye.'

The line was cut and Greg replaced his receiver and leaned back against the pillows. He felt drained. The skirmish he'd just had with old Mrs Cavendish reminded him of many an encounter with awkward business customers – only this time his emotions had been engaged.

He was used to people like Mrs Cavendish talking down to him. He hadn't been born into wealth and privilege. His rise to the position of powerful property developer had been due to his own efforts. He'd started off as a jobbing labourer, casually employed digging drains, mixing cement and driving dumper trucks. He'd soon realized that unless he acquired a skill, a trade, his future wasn't very bright.

So he'd signed up for a government training scheme and become a bricklayer. The money was better but the life was hard. Doing contract jobs, the more bricks you laid, the more you got paid but you were always subject to the vagaries of difficult employers and the weather. He started putting money away in a savings account.

He knew that big money could be made in Germany. A lot of British building workers were making small fortunes over there. So he joined them and worked even harder. Many of his friends drank and gambled their money away as soon as they earned it, but he just went on saving.

The first step towards a new way of life had been buying a small plot of land in Kent and building six houses. He paid a good young architect and employed tradesmen he'd worked with and knew were reliable. He'd worked out that, in theory, if you built three houses, one of them would be clear profit. Incredibly, it seemed to him at the time, it turned out to be true and, after that, the plots got bigger and his plans more ambitious – and his bank balance grew.

One of his schemes involved buying a run-down country mansion and converting it into eight prestigious apartments. It was then that he had realized just how many beautiful old houses were in a sad state of repair and needing huge injections of cash in one way or another. The result often was that an old house was saved and, as a bonus, some new homes were provided. Now he had a land agent whose sole job it was to find suitable projects for him. Westbrook Hall should have been just another project, merely a good business prospect. And it was – until he met Alison.

Alison . . .

She was in the village, her mother-in-law had grudgingly told him. It didn't take him long to shed his business suit and change into jeans and a navy blue roll neck sweater. He realized how ridiculous it was, a man of thirty-eight setting out to stroll around the village streets like some love-sick teenager in the hopes of catching a glimpse of the girl of his dreams, but he couldn't help himself.

To his relief, neither Alf nor Molly was at the reception desk. Alf would be in the bar serving the early regulars and Molly would be in the restaurant checking that everything was ready for the evening session.

Out in the street it was dusk. Lights glowed in cottage windows and street lamps illuminated the village green. He could hear children's voices echoing across the expanse of grass and his attention was caught by a small group standing under a tree. He stopped and peered across at them. There were two children – boys, he thought – talking excitedly and pointing up into the branches of the tree. Beside them stood two women. Or rather a woman and a girl. With a small intake of breath he saw that the woman was Alison.

She didn't turn as he walked across the green and long before he reached her he could hear what the problem was. One of the boys had kicked a ball and it had lodged firmly in the branches of the tree.

'Leave it, Oliver,' he heard the girl say. It was Ruth Morton. 'Dad will get it in the morning.'

'Why can't he get it tonight?'

'You know why – he's gone over to see our Gran.'

'But it's Matthew's football.'

'Matthew doesn't mind – do you?' Alison intercepted.

'No, I suppose not,' her son said, but he sounded doubtful.

'Can I help?'

They all turned to look at him and Greg felt foolish. Ruth grinned widely but Alison's smile was more uncertain. After a moment of surprise the boys looked up at him hopefully.

'I'm not sure,' Alison said at last. 'Look.'

The ball was stuck in a fork about twelve feet up and the lowest branch was probably eight feet from the ground. 'Oh, I think I can manage it,' he said. 'Get the lads to stand back, will you?'

As he watched Alison and Ruth marshal Matthew and Oliver out of the way he realized that he was probably just about to make a prize fool of himself. What the hell was he doing, showing off like a kid half his age? Still, he couldn't back down now.

Without giving himself any more time to think about it, Greg bent his knees then sprang up, reaching for the lowest branch. To his great relief, he made it. He hung there thankfully for a moment and then swung his long legs upwards to wrap around the branch and grip it monkey-fashion.

A small voice below said, 'Cool!' and Greg risked a glance down. In the fading light, two small faces were tip-tilted to gaze up at him admiringly and one older face, Ruth's, expressed amused admiration. He couldn't see Alison's face because she had withdrawn into the shadows of the overhanging branches of a neighbouring tree.

He realized that his arms were beginning to feel the strain, so hooked his left leg over the branch and began to lever himself up and round until he was sitting on it, legs astride. After that it was easy. He inched along until he could hang on to the upper branches and pull himself up to standing position; then he reached up for the ball.

'Here it comes!' he yelled as he tossed it down.

He watched the ball hit the ground, bounce up and then go rolling across the green. By the time he swung himself down to the ground the two lads had gone chasing after it.

'Huh! That's all the thanks I get. They might have hung around to see me get down safely!'

Alison laughed softly. 'I'll just go and round them up.'

Ruth came towards him. She was grinning. 'Well done, but you could have borrowed my dad's ladders, you know. We just live over there.' She pointed to one of the neat village houses facing the green.

'Thanks a bundle. Why didn't you tell me?'

'I didn't want to spoil your fun.'

'Does Alison – Mrs Cavendish – know about the ladders?'

'It's all right, I've no head for heights so I didn't tell her in case she suggested going up herself!' She winked at him conspiratorially and then averted her face. Greg had the strongest suspicion that she was suppressing laughter.

'Mr Leighton, Matthew has something to say.' Alison had brought the boys back to stand before him.

'Thank you very much, Mr Leighton.'

'Yeah – thank you,' Oliver echoed.

Greg smiled down at them. 'Why don't you call me Greg?' he said to Matthew.

The boy glanced at his mother and Alison nodded imperceptibly. 'OK. Thanks, Greg.'

'Thanks, Greg,' Oliver echoed again and his sister laughed.

'I think you've made a couple of friends for life, Mr Leighton,' Ruth said, 'or can I call you Greg, too?'

Alison shot her a reproving glance. 'It's time I took Matthew home,' she said.

'Oh, Mum!'

'Mrs Cavendish!'

'Do I have to go?'

'Of course you have to come home now. It's getting late.'

'But my mum said that Matthew could stay tonight,' Oliver said.

'That's right, Mrs Cavendish,' his sister affirmed, 'there's no school tomorrow and, as you're having your little party tonight, Mum thought you might want a bit of time to yourselves.'

'Well, it's hardly a party, but that would be nice. Are you sure, Matthew?' he nodded vigorously. 'Right, then.'

'Thanks, Mum.' Matthew darted forward and gave her a hug then the two boys raced towards Oliver's house.

'Don't worry about him, Mrs Cavendish,' Ruth said. 'He can borrow a pair of Olly's pyjamas and he can stay here for the whole weekend if you like. I only wish we could take in your ma-in-law as well and then you could have the house to yourselves.'

Alison laughed but Ruth suddenly frowned. 'You know, my mum was just wondering why old Mrs Cavendish doesn't go to stay with her daughter, Mrs Remington, now and then. It would give you a break, wouldn't it?'

'Yes . . . well . . .'

'Sorry! I shouldn't have said anything! I'd better be going. Just phone and tell Mum when you want Matthew to come home and I'll bring him back to the Hall. Bye for now.'

'Goodnight, Ruth – and thank you –'

All the time they had been talking Greg had remained

in the background, watching the scene with mixed feelings. Alison's love for her son was so transparent that it hurt. He wasn't hurting because the woman he now knew that he loved loved her son; he wasn't even remotely jealous. He was hurting because he had never experienced such love when he was a child. In fact, he probably hadn't even realized that it existed.

Just like Matthew, he had lost his father when he was very young but, unlike Matthew, he hadn't had a mother who had done her best to see that he didn't suffer because of it. To do her justice his own mother had been very young and she probably hadn't wanted to have a child in the first place. Once she was left to fend for herself, her only asset had been her stunning good looks. A succession of 'uncles' had come and gone from his life, and not all of them had been unkind to the fatherless boy.

Then, when Greg was about to leave school, one of them had actually married her. Greg hadn't fitted in with his mother's new lifestyle; one day she simply moved out, leaving him the keys and a couple of months' rent . . .

Greg had inherited his mother's good looks and there had been women; he was a normal man. But God forgive him, he had never expected more of them than pleasant company and a good time. Once he became wealthy, and even before that, he had been a generous lover, but only with his money, not with his emotions. His emotions simply hadn't been engaged. He had never allowed any of the women to become close; had never wanted anything beyond the present, never wanted a future with any one of them. He wanted that future now and he wasn't yet sure whether it was within his grasp.

'Well, then.' Alison turned to smile at him, 'I'd better go, I've quite a lot to do.'

'Of course. You're having a party.'

'Not exactly a party.'

He didn't like the way she was smiling. Whoever was

coming to Westbrook Hall tonight obviously had the power to cheer her up enormously. Who were they? People with the same kind of education as Alison? People from the same background? Would there be a man there? Someone special? Greg felt excluded. He realized that she was looking at him curiously.

'Is something the matter?' she asked.

'No – of course not. Look, would you like a lift home? My car's parked behind The Plough.'

'Are you sure? That's very kind of you, I do have rather a lot to do – rustle up some food, search out a good bottle of wine – or even two!'

'Come on, then.'

They walked together across the green and he hated the way her spirits had lifted at the very thought of whoever was coming to join her tonight. Why am I offering to take her home? Why am I making it easier for her to get herself ready for – whoever he is?

'Greg!' She had stopped walking and placed a hand on his arm. She was looking up at him and her eyes were troubled.

'What is it? What's the matter?'

'Nothing's the matter – yes, there is – it's me, I quite forgot – oh, what can you think of me?'

'Alison, I don't know what you're talking about.'

'The flowers – I haven't thanked you for the flowers. They were absolutely beautiful and so . . .'

'So what?' The light from the nearby street lamp shone down on her face. The way she was staring up at him made his heart contract.

'So . . . unexpected,' she breathed.

It took all his willpower not to take hold of her and pull her into his arms. He wanted to kiss her so much that it hurt.

'Thank you,' she whispered.

Suddenly, and totally unexpectedly, she reached up

and kissed him on the cheek. He moved his head so that his lips found hers and brushed over them softly. She gave a quick intake of breath and moved away.

'Alison – I –' His voice let him down.

'We'd better go,' she said. 'We don't want to be the subject of gossip, do we?' She was smiling.

'Gossip?'

'Perhaps you've forgotten, but we're standing on the village green in full view of anybody who happens to be passing by. And, as a matter of fact, I think you've already provided enough gossip for one day with your daring exploits up a tree, don't you?'

'You're laughing at me – you think I'm an idiot.'

'No, I'm not and no, I don't. I think you're "cool", as my son would say. Now, you did offer, so please would you take me home?'

Alison began to hurry across the road towards The Plough. The evening's customers for either the bar or the restaurant were arriving and he noticed heads turning in Alison's direction. He realized that in a small place like this, nothing she did would go unremarked.

It didn't take long to drive from the village to the Hall. At first, neither of them spoke and he was very conscious of her nearness. He could smell her perfume, a delicate, floral fragrance that nevertheless set his pulse racing.

It wasn't until they had swung into the drive and begun the approach to the Hall that he said, 'Will you be free some time tomorrow? I know I said that I'd phone you first, but I took a chance and brought the plans down. I'd like to show them to you – perhaps to involve you more. After all, Westbrook Hall is your home –'

'Matthew's home. Yes, I'd like to see the plans but I'm not sure about tomorrow.'

'Just for an hour?' He knew he was pleading but he didn't care. 'We could walk around the site.'

'I don't know – I'll try – I could phone you at The Plough.'

'Would you?'

'Yes – look – I'm grateful for the lift but I've really got to go.'

He sensed that he had lost her attention. Inexplicably the atmosphere had changed; cooled. As she unbuckled her seat belt, Greg leaned towards her, half expecting that she would turn and kiss him. But she didn't even seem to notice. Once the belt was undone, she got out hurriedly and almost ran across the gravel towards the entrance of the house.

Greg reached over and secured the door. He watched morosely as she hurried up the stone steps and vanished into the shadows underneath the classic portico. He was puzzled – perturbed. During the short drive from the village he'd had the distinct impression that an understanding was developing between them. Nothing had been said, but he was sure that they were beginning to relate to each other in the most elemental way – as a man and a woman. Then, suddenly, a barrier had come down between them. He had sensed her withdrawal and he couldn't explain it.

He could no longer see her but, as the massive front door opened and closed, light from the house spilled out momentarily. Greg noticed, for the first time, that another car was parked along at the end of the wide sweep of steps.

Was that why Alison's mood had changed so swiftly: because she had noticed the car waiting there? If so, who was the owner of the car? Reluctantly he turned and drove back towards the village.

CHAPTER 15

Her sister-in-law was standing by the telephone table. She turned and, keeping her eyes on Alison, she said into the receiver, 'I must go now.'

'Daphne,' Alison said. 'I wasn't expecting you.'

'No, we-ell . . .'

Why is Daphne looking at me so strangely? So – so disdainfully – as if I were something that had just crawled out from under a stone?

She watched as the other woman seemed to struggle with a desire to say something and then think better of it. When she did speak, Alison was sure that there was still something else uppermost in her mind, something else that she would rather be saying.

'Mother phoned me and told me about your plans for the weekend. I thought I'd better pop over and see if she was all right.'

'Why shouldn't she be?'

'You know she doesn't like her routine upset.'

'Yes, I do, only too well.'

'What do you mean by that?'

'Wait a moment, Daphne.'

Alison slipped off her jacket and walked into the cloakroom to hang it up. Should she tell her sister-in-law that she was sick and tired of arranging her days –

and more importantly, Matthew's days – to suit Lilian Cavendish? Should she tell her that, although she didn't mind that her own life was restricted – after all, she had nothing very much that she wanted to do – she did mind very much that Matthew couldn't even have his friends home to play, in case they disturbed his grandmother?

And, in fact, that was just an excuse; the house was big enough to lose a dozen small boys in. The truth was Mrs Cavendish didn't approve of Matthew's friends from the village. And that was intolerable.

She closed her eyes and breathed in slowly. No, she wouldn't say anything right now. She had a lot to do and she was determined that this weekend should go smoothly. It would be no good if she allowed herself to become a quivering mass of hostility. By the time she left the cloakroom she had controlled her anger.

'What did you mean by that?' Daphne hadn't forgotten and her tone was confrontational.

'I simply mean that I am perfectly aware of your mother's preferences – and her needs. I'll make sure that she isn't disturbed. Now, I have a lot to do so, if you want to talk to me, do you mind coming through to the kitchen?'

'Wait, Alison. Where's Matthew?'

'Why?'

'Mother said that you'd gone down to the village to collect him from that boy's house –'

'You mean Oliver's house and yes, I did, but he was invited to stay over.'

'Oh, really, is that wise?'

'Look, I can't stand here talking,' Alison set off for the kitchen, 'and I'm not going to argue with you about Matthew's choice of friends. The Mortons are a very nice family and –'

'Oh, I'm sure they're *nice* enough, but –'

'No "buts", Daphne. I'm not going to argue with you.

239

If I set your mother's supper tray, would you take it up to her?'

Daphne seemed thrown by Alison's new sense of purpose. She didn't pursue the subject of Matthew's choice of friends, but she was frowning as she sat down at the kitchen table. Alison poured milk into a pan and watched her sister-in-law warily.

'Alison – there's something else –'

Alison sighed. Here it comes, she thought, this is what she wanted to say when I first arrived home. 'What is it, Daphne?'

'Er – I don't know how to put this –'

'Just spit it out. You usually do.'

'There's no need to be unpleasant.' Daphne had recovered her confidence and Alison cursed herself for not being more circumspect. She shouldn't have tried to bait her.

'I'm sorry. What is it you wanted to say?'

The apology did nothing to soothe Daphne's feelings. She was back on form. 'In spite of everything I told you, you were seen in the village with that man. I could hardly believe what I was told. You were kissing him – in full view of anybody who might happen to walk by.'

Alison gripped the back of a chair and leaned on it for support. She stared at her sister-in-law's supercilious face. Daphne's bony features were animated with scandalized prurience.

'And who exactly was walking by, Daphne? Who was it that was able to report back to you so quickly? But let me guess. It was Mrs Slater, wasn't it, your faithful cleaning lady? Tell me, do you have to pay her extra for surveillance duties?'

'Surveillance?'

'Spying, Daphne, spying. Does she get a nice little bonus whenever she reports back to you about me?'

'Don't be absurd.'

'Absurd, am I? That was her you were speaking to on the telephone when I came home just now, wasn't it? As soon as I'd left the village she must have headed straight for the coinbox phone in The Plough, to tell you that I'd been seen in the arms of that dreadful man and that, furthermore, I'd got into his car with him! But one thing puzzles me, Daphne. How did she know that you were here?'

'Mrs Slater knew that I was coming to see my mother and it was perfectly natural for her to phone me. She knows how concerned I am about the situation.'

'Situation?'

Alison stared at her sister-in-law helplessly. Daphne didn't look the slightest bit abashed or ashamed of herself. On the contrary, she seemed to think that she'd done something clever.

'I'm surprised at you, Daphne,' Alison said finally. 'All that rubbish you and your mother hand out about *noblesse oblige* – noble people behaving nobly – and privilege entails responsibility! How noble do you think it is to gossip with your servants, and how responsible is it to bribe the poor woman to spy on your sister-in-law?'

'I don't bribe her! How dare you suggest that?'

'Really. I find it interesting that you didn't come out with this as soon as I walked through the door. The only reason that I can think of is that then you'd have had to admit that your spy had just reported in.'

Alison stared at Daphne for a moment and was willing to bet that the sudden rush of colour to her cheeks meant that she had scored, if not a bull's eye, then a very close hit. A sudden hiss behind her made her turn around. The milk had risen in the pan and was about to boil over. She lifted the pan off the heat with one hand and turned off the gas with the other.

Lilian Cavendish's evening routine never varied. She liked a milky drink, usually cocoa, and a couple of slices

241

of bread and butter. Alison made the drink quickly and set about buttering the bread.

'I don't know what's got into you lately.' Daphne was doing her best to sound wounded but Alison noticed that she couldn't meet her eye. 'Alison, did you hear me?'

'Yes, I heard you. Now, would you take this tray up to your mother? And, as you've already held me up considerably, I wonder if you would mind staying long enough to help her into bed? Not that she really needs help,' Alison couldn't help adding.

Daphne rose to her feet with an air of affronted dignity and picked up the tray. 'Don't think you can avoid the subject for ever, Alison.'

'And what subject is that?'

'You know very well what I mean – Greg Leighton. Have you given one moment's thought what it would do to your son if you began consorting with a man like that?'

'Like what?'

'A criminal –'

'He's not a criminal –'

'Oh, I know nothing's been proved but even if it never is, my brother wouldn't have wanted his widow to associate with a man whose background is so unsavory. Ask him; he won't deny, because he can't, that his mother was little better than a prostitute and that she probably even can't remember who his father is!'

'Is that all you have to say, Daphne?'

'I should have thought that it's enough – or have you no sense of shame whatsoever, contaminating your son by exposing him to a man like that?'

Alison was so angry that she took an involuntary step towards Daphne. Her sister-in-law's eyes widened in alarm and she began to walk towards the door. Alison thought how comical the other woman looked – trying to remain dignified and at the same time scuttling clumsily across the kitchen sideways like a large pink crab. Except that she wasn't pink – her face was blotched red with affronted anger.

She's surprised that I'm actually fighting back for once, Alison realized, and angry because she doesn't know what to do about it. Daphne had reached the doorway when she stopped suddenly and faced Alison.

'Do you know what I think?' she aid.

'I'm not sure if I care – and be careful, you'll spill your mother's cocoa.'

Daphne glared at her. 'My brother should never have married you. Oh, you might be well-educated, but the daughter of a couple of high school teachers is hardly from the same class as the Cavendish family. And, just remember, Alison, Nigel is co-executor to my brother's will; it's part of his duties to look after Matthew's inheritance.' She paused and raised her chin defiantly.

'So?' Alison was uneasy. Daphne had recovered enough poise to look smug.

'So that means you need his signature for any kind of deal you make with Mr Leighton. If you continue to consort with this man on a personal level, we may just withhold our approval.'

Alison could hear the thudding of her own heart, taste the rage rising in her throat. I was wrong, she thought. Daphne won't give in easily. She has no intention of giving up her ridiculous prejudices even if it means slandering a man who I'm sure is innocent of wrong-doing and, much worse, jeopardizing her own nephew's future in his family home.

As they stared at each other across the kitchen, Alison experienced a moment of truth. All pretensions fell away. All the hidden emotions at last rose to the surface Nothing was said but she could feel them as if they had a physical presence. Daphne's snobbish disapproval of her brother's bride, her resentment that Alison was living here in the family home – and that Alison, as

Matthew's mother, was in a position of influence . . .

And I'm not without blame, Alison thought. At first I was hurt by Paul's family's attitude but I had his love to sustain me . . . and after he died, I had Matthew . . . I've been prepared to do anything to keep life sweet for Matthew and yet, if I'm honest, I've allowed my hurt and my irritation to grow . . . But I can't let them spoil what is probably my best chance to save Matthew's inheritance . . . no matter what it costs . . .

'What have you to say?' Daphne, at last, demanded.

'Not much. Not right now, except your mother's cocoa must be getting cold. You'd better warm it up again before you take it up to her; you don't want to upset her, do you?'

Daphne's mouth twisted with fury and, for a moment, Alison was afraid. Her sister-in-law looked quite capable of striking her and if she hadn't been holding the tray, she might have done. Alison stared at her apprehensively, half wondering whether she was going to have to defend herself, and then the doorbell rang. The hostilities would have to be suspended.

Sophie stared at the tall, slim blonde woman who had just opened the door. Alison was as attractive as ever; even dressed in jeans and a sweater she looked elegant somehow. But her cool, classy looks had matured into something more austere and she looked distinctly strained.

'Sophie! Come in! Is that all the luggage you've got?'

'Yes – I've parked my car along there – is that all right or shall I take it round to the old stable yard?'

'Oh anywhere – there's plenty of room on the drive – so long as you don't block Daphne's exit, that is!'

'Oh no, I've left plenty of room. Daphne – that's your sister-in-law, isn't it? And where's Matthew?'

'Yes, Daphne's my sister-in-law, and Matthew's staying with his friend in the village – but you might see him tomorrow. Do come in, it's getting distinctly chilly with the door open!'

'Sorry.' Sophie stepped in and Alison closed the door behind her. 'This house must cost a fortune to heat. What do you do in the winter – go round lighting fires in every room?'

'Not every room, just the ones we're using. The house does have central heating, but it's very primitive. Paul's father had it installed sometime in the thirties. As soon as I can afford it I'm going to have the whole system overhauled and updated – along with a lot of other things.'

'Well, we'll have to see about that, won't we?' The acid tones came from behind them.

Sophie hadn't realized that they were no longer alone and she looked beyond Alison to see that Daphne Remington was standing at the foot of the staircase holding a tray. Alison had turned to face her sister-in-law and although Sophie could no longer see her friend's face she got the impression that there was some kind of battle of wills going on.

Alison didn't speak and eventually Daphne seemed to remember the formalities. 'Hello, it's Sophie, isn't it?'

'Yes, good evening. How are –?'

'Quite well,' she said unsmilingly. 'Now, if you'll forgive me, I'll just take this tray up to my mother.' She turned abruptly and hurried upstairs. Sophie stared after her bemusedly.

'Don't worry,' Alison whispered, 'it isn't you, she's like that with most people. Oh, Sophie – just dump those bags here for a moment and come into the kitchen. I planned to have a lovely meal ready for you but instead you'll have to settle for a cup of tea and a gossip while you watch me start the preparations.'

Sophie sat at the kitchen table while Alison moved

swiftly around the kitchen getting food from the freezer and plates and dishes from various cupboards. They talked about Sophie's journey and about the weather and the state of the roads. Sophie knew instinctively that Alison would want to save any serious talking there might be for later, when they were both more relaxed.

Just as the kettle began to boil, Alison turned round and grinned. 'You can still have tea if you want it, Sophie, or would you rather have a glass of wine? I know I would!'

'Wine it is, then.'

'That's my girl. Have you ever seen the wine cellar here?'

'No.'

'Come on, then!'

Alison opened a door that seemed to lead into a large pantry with a tiled floor and then another door that opened straight on to a flight of stone steps. She put the light on and the two of them went down into the cellars. When they reached the bottom, Sophie stared around at the wooden racks that stretched out on either side of either side of them towards the shadows.

'Wow! You know I've never been in any kind of wine cellar – let alone this one.'

'Well, this isn't really very grand compared to some of the great houses, but over the ages the Cavendish family certainly liked their wine. Some of this stuff is quite old – and Paul had been trained by his father to replenish the stock regularly Unfortunately I haven't got either the knowledge or the wherewithal to continue that tradition. I'm afraid when this lot is used up, that might be the end of it.'

Sophie stared at the dusty bottles. 'There's still an awful lot, Alison. And have you ever thought that some of it might be valuable?'

'Valuable? We-ell, Paul did mention once that it would

be worth having somebody down from a pukka wine merchant's, but he never got around to it. Paul did begin to educate me a little about it but, above certain civilized levels, the most I know about wine is that some I like and some I don't.

'Here' She took one of the bottles from a nearby rack. 'I've learned from experience that this is one I like.'

To Sophie's inexperienced eye, the bottle didn't look any different from many another wine bottle, but the label looked old. Sophie squinted at it in the dim light. She didn't know any more about wine than Alison did, but she felt uneasy.

'Alison – should we be doing this?'

Her friend paused and looked round at her. 'Why ever not? Oh, you mean because the house and everything in it belongs to Matthew? Don't worry, Matthew wouldn't begrudge his mother a bottle or two of plonk. Here, hang on to this, will you?'

Sophie looked critically at the bottle she was holding. 'But that's just it,' she said. 'I don't think it is plonk, I think it could be very expensive.'

Alison frowned. 'You're serious, aren't you?'

'Mm . . .'

'You know, if you're right, perhaps I should get somebody down to have a look at them. If I can make some money by selling them it would certainly help . . .

'But meanwhile –' she reached for another couple bottle with the same label '– Matthew wouldn't begrudge me – and the rest of the Cavendish family owes me! Come on – let's get back to the kitchen, I've got some cooking to do.'

'But do we need two bottles, Alison?'

'Don't worry, we're not going to drink it all ourselves.'

'What do you mean? Who's going to help us?'

'Wait and see.'

'Alison!'

Sophie's protest was in vain; her friend was already more than halfway up the stairs. When they reached the top, Alison reached out to flick the light switch with the same hand that was holding the bottle of wine. 'Be careful,' Sophie warned, and Alison turned to smile at her.

'You haven't changed, have you?'

'What do you mean?'

Sophie emerged from the stairway into the pantry and Alison nudged the cellar door shut with her bottom. 'When we all used to live together,' she said, 'you were always bossing us around – telling us what to do.'

'I wasn't! I didn't!'

'Oh, Sophie, it was in the nicest possible way. Sometimes I don't know what the rest of us would have done without you. I do love you – do you know that?'

Suddenly Alison looked serious. Sophie was embarrassed. 'Go on with you. Didn't you say you had some cooking to do?'

She followed Alison into the kitchen and they had just put the bottles of wine down on the large scrubbed table when Daphne walked in. 'I've got to go now. Mother says she'll get herself off to bed if she has to – oh!'

Daphne stared at the wine. Alison became very still and, once more, Sophie got the impression that there was something else going on here. 'I see you're going to enjoy yourselves,' Daphne said.

'Now why on earth shouldn't we?' Alison's voice was calm but there was an underlying hint of tension. There was definitely an unspoken challenge there.

Sophie watched Daphne, waiting for her reaction, and she was nonplussed when the older woman's stern features relaxed into what passed for a smile. 'No reason at all, my dear,' she said. 'In fact I'm very pleased that you're going to stay in and enjoy yourself with your friends. It's much, much better than going off and making a spectacle of yourself with that common little man.'

Daphne turned and swept out of the kitchen into the large entrance hall. Alison hurried after her. 'Daphne!' she shouted but her sister-in-law didn't pause on her way to the door. 'Daphne – Greg Leighton is neither common nor little and if you could bring yourself to meet him, you might see how ill-informed you've been!'

'*Meet* him?' She turned and stared at Alison as though she had suggested she should meet a mad axe-man. 'Meet him?' she repeated. 'No, I don't think so. Now, good-night. Oh – goodnight, Sophie.' She opened the door wide and swept out. A blast of cool damp air swept into the hall as she pulled it closed behind her.

Alison was standing with shoulders hunched and fists clenched. 'Goodnight, Daphne, dear,' she muttered. Then it seemed that she made a supreme effort to relax. She turned and smiled at her friend.

'Sorry you had to witness that. Sometimes I wonder how I've stayed sane. Oh, Sophie, I'm so glad that you're here, I need to talk to you so much. But first I'd better get those pizzas in the oven.'

'Alison –'

'Mm? Don't just stand there – would you mind giving me a hand? You could wash the salad . . .'

'Of course – anything – but first you must answer two questions.'

Alison paused in the kitchen doorway and grinned. 'That sounds like a test, or a task set in a fairytale – poor little Petronella must solve two riddles before the good fairy will grant her her heart's desire!'

'Be serious for a moment and don't try and bamboozle me.'

'Sorry. Your questions?'

'Who is Greg Leighton?'

'Ah. I was going to tell you, honestly, and I will later,

249

when we've had something to eat and we can relax with a glass of wine. I'm just sorry that you had to hear Daphne's vile opinion of him first. Next question?'

'Well, going on what your sister-in-law said, he can't be the person who you promised is going to help us drink that wine. She said she was pleased that you were going to stay here and enjoy yourself with your friends. So who –?'

'Hush!'

'What is it?'

'Look.'

Alison had turned towards the front door. A flash of light arced across the tall windows at each side of the door and Sophie could hear the crunch of wheels on gravel, a car engine and then silence. Alison took off across the hall with Sophie following. The doorbell rang just as they reached the door and Alison pulled it open.

'Carol!'

'You didn't tell me Carol was coming!' Sophie stared at Alison across the kitchen table.

'I wanted it to be a nice surprise.'

Carol was sitting at the table looking both pleased and tearful. 'She didn't tell me that you were coming either,' she said.

Sophie frowned. 'Alison, how did you manage this? When we spoke last night, I told you that I hadn't been able to contact Carol.'

'I know. I phoned her straight afterwards and got the same recorded message that you got. But I kept trying today and eventually I got through.'

'Listen, you two, I'm sorry about that.' Carol looked embarrassed. 'I – the phone – I forgot to pay the bill.'

'For goodness' sake – there's no need to look so tragic,' Sophie said. 'It's only a phone bill.' To her dismay, Carol's eyes filled up with tears.

'*Only a phone bill* – oh, Sophie, if only you knew!'

Alison had just placed three large pizzas in the oven and she turned round and looked at Carol sympathetically. 'Look, as soon as I've finished the salad, I'll take you two upstairs and show you where you're sleeping. We've got time to freshen up while the pizzas are cooking and then we can eat, drink and relax and pour out our hearts to each other.'

'Let me help,' Carol said.

'Me too.'

'OK. This is just like the old days in our student flat,' Alison said. 'Remember the fabulous meals we used to cook up out of next to nothing?'

'And remember all the pans and dishes that nobody ever wanted to wash up?' laughed Carol.

'I thought we had a rota for that – and for the other housework?'

'Yes, Alison, we did, but nobody ever took any notice of it – nobody except Sophie, that is!'

'Sophie . . .' Alison looked at her quizzically. 'You've gone very quiet. Are you all right.'

'Mm . . . I'm fine. Just a little tired perhaps.'

'Of course,' Alison said kindly. 'Teaching is a demanding job. When I spoke to you last night I thought you sounded totally drained.' Suddenly she stopped slicing the tomatoes and shot Sophie a keen look. 'Or was it strained? Sophie, why exactly did you want to talk to me?'

'And me,' Carol broke in, 'if you've been trying to phone me, you must have wanted to talk to me, too! Sophie – it's nothing serious, is it?'

Sophie smiled across at the two inquisitive faces. 'Don't worry, it isn't a matter of life or death, it's just something that I wanted to tell you about – and talk things over. But it can wait until after we've had our meal. As Alison said to me before, we can have a good old gossip when we're feeling more relaxed.'

'Good idea,' Alison said. 'You know, after I spoke to you last night, Sophie, I realized how much I've missed you and Carol and Francine. We've all been neglecting our friendship lately, haven't we?'

'I suppose so.'

Sophie could have said that the neglect was none of her doing. She'd probably made more effort that the others over the years. She wasn't bitter about it; she accepted that they had busy and sometimes difficult lives, whereas her life had been comparatively straightforward, with no real problems . . . until now . . .

'Well, anyway,' Alison continued, 'I tried to phone Francine, too; I thought it would be great to get the four of us together. I realized that I'm probably the only one who has a house big enough and that we should do this regularly.'

'Great idea,' Carol said. 'What did Francine say?'

'Nothing – she wasn't there. She's moved on somewhere and hasn't left her number.'

'I could have told you that,' Sophie said. 'I thought about phoning her at work but then I thought if she'd wanted to keep in touch she could have sent me her new address.'

'Well – she hasn't informed me either,' Alison said. 'Carol?'

'No. You don't think – I mean – do you think she just moves in different circles now – I mean she's famous, isn't she?'

'I know what you're suggesting and I don't think that's the explanation. Francine would never be too busy for her old friends. She just hasn't got around to telling us all yet. That'll be it. So it's her own fault if she's missing out on this weekend!'

'I wish she could be here,' said Carol.

Sophie didn't say anything but she wished so too. If

this wedding of hers went ahead she still wanted all her old friends to be there.

Alison placed the salad bowl on the table and stood back and surveyed it. She frowned. 'Now – the salad looks lovely but the table looks as if a bomb's hit it – or Carol's been left alone in the kitchen!'

'Please don't tease,' said Carol, and Sophie thought there was a hint of genuine anguish in her voice.

But Alison hadn't noticed. 'Let's tidy up the table and we'll eat in here. The kitchen isn't as grand as the dining-room but it's a darned sight warmer. Open these bags of crisps and nuts and things and empty them into these dishes, you two, and put these cheeses on to that cheese-board. Now what else have I got? Bread rolls, fruit – none of this is exactly *gourmet*, as Francine would say, but it'll be good and tasty!'

Alison and Carol were taken up with preparing the table for the meal and Sophie was relieved. She felt as though she had been reprieved for a while. She hadn't wanted to tell them about her wedding to Alistair and her secret doubts about it straight away. She wanted to ease her way into the subject.

Last night, when she'd eventually got through to Alison, she had sensed that Alison had something on her mind, too, and that was why she hadn't come out with it there and then. Alison had been pleased to hear from her but, almost immediately, it had become obvious that she needed to talk to someone just as much as Sophie did.

After a few minutes of trying to give each other a full update on the day-to-day trivia of their lives, Alison had said, 'Sophie – why don't you come down for the weekend? It would be marvelous to have a proper gossip like we used to!'

She'd agreed straight away. And, now it was even better to find that Alison had invited Carol, too. But from the look of Carol, and her tearful outburst earlier when she'd mentioned the phone bill, she looked as if she was as much in need of female advice and solace as any of them.

By now the appetizing combined odours of tomato and garlic and cheese were coming from the oven and Alison said, 'Come on – we've got time to take the bags upstairs and freshen up.' She paused and stared at the table. 'It looks good, doesn't it? When we come down I might light some candles.'

They were just about to leave the room when they were pulled up short by the sound of the front doorbell. They stared at each other and began to smile.

'It couldn't possibly be, could it?' Carol asked.

'Could wishing have brought her here?' Sophie murmured.

'Don't just stand there,' Alison shrieked. 'Let's go and see!'

CHAPTER 16

Francine stared along the dusty racks of bottles. 'What a collection! But why have *I* been elected to choose another bottle of wine?'

Sophie smiled. I'm so glad Francine's here, she thought. Now I can tell them all together. 'I guess Alison sent you because she thinks that you probably know more about this kind of thing than we do.'

'Why should she think that, for goodness' sake?'

'Oh, come on, Francine – you're a celebrity – a media person – you have a more sophisticated lifestyle than the rest of us.'

'You've been reading the wrong gossip columns – it's not like that at all.' The light was dim but Sophie was sure that Francine's grin wobbled for a moment.

'Maybe – but how do you explain the photographs? Francine Rowe at the premier of the latest film! Francine Rowe at the opening of a new play in London's West End! Francine Rowe at so and so's society party! And in those photographs, Francine Rowe is always escorted by a man who is either rich, clever, handsome or a combination of all three!'

'Most of those occasions are part and parcel of the work I do – and the papers never tell you that not one of those men ever comes home with me, do they?'

'What are you saying exactly? That they're all just

255

casual acquaintances? That you don't have a regular boyfriend? That you haven't been able to form a lasting relationship?'

'I think you know that last statement's not true, don't you?'

Francine's grin had vanished completely; her shoulders hunched up slightly as she crossed her arms and hugged them to her body as if she were cold. The two friends stared at each other in the circle of light cast by a low wattage bulb hanging high overhead. The plaster on Francine's brow looked touchingly out of place, Sophie thought; a child's wound on a perfect grown-up face. A drought had set the flex moving slightly, and the shadows of the wine racks moved in fantastic shapes, backwards and forwards over the walls and ceiling.

'I – I'm not sure –'

'Come on, Sophie – you used to visit me in the flat in Fulham when I first went up to London. I think you were perfectly aware that I lived alone because it was more convenient for the man in my life to visit me there – and, what's more, that he probably wasn't free to be seen in public with me.'

'We-ell . . .'

'Did the others know about him? Alison and Carol? Did the three of you ever talk about me?'

'Francine – don't do this –'

'Well? Did you?'

Sophie stared at her old friend miserably. 'Yes, I suppose we did – but none of us ever criticized you. I think we all agreed that it was a shame –'

'Shame!'

'Yes, a shame that you were wasting your life like that on a man who – who . . .'

'Go on – say it.'

'On a man who was probably never going to leave his wife and commit himself to you properly.'

'I see.' Francine turned her head so that Sophie could no longer see her expression. But, even in profile, her face looked pinched. 'Did it ever occur to you that I knew that all along – and perhaps that I even preferred it that way!'

'Of course it did – oh, Francine, please don't be angry – we know how intelligent you are –'

'What's intelligence got to do with it? I mean, we all know that Carol probably had the best brain in our entire year – and yet where did that get her? Married to Alan Kennedy!'

'Well – rational, then – sharp – you always have your wits about you. Every one of us knew that you wouldn't be involved with Peter Curtis if you didn't want to be.'

There was a sharp intake of breath and Francine said. 'So all along you knew exactly who he was. Just as well you didn't know what the tabloids would have paid for an interesting little snippet like that.'

'I hope you're kidding!' Sophie was angry. 'As if anyone of us would ever behave like that – ever betray a friend!'

Francine turned and took hold of Sophie's shoulders. 'Sorry, sorry, *sorry!* That was utterly crass. I don't mean it and I shouldn't have said it!'

'No, you shouldn't.'

'Forgive me?'

'I suppose so . . .'

'You know, the fact that I could say that is probably a sign of how paranoid I've become . . . how isolated I've been . . .'

'Well, don't ever say anything like that to the other two. They might not be so understanding as I am.'

'OK.' Francine's smile was back but Sophie sensed that she was having to make an effort. 'Now, come on, Alison's had plenty of time to get another pizza or two out of the freezer and into the oven.'

Francine took a bottle of wine down from the rack and showed it to Sophie. 'In spite of your lofty opinion of my lifestyle, I'm not an expert, but I do recognize this red – a full-bodied little number that's not too pricey, as they say!'

'Wait, a moment,' Sophie said. 'What exactly do you mean by "not too pricey"?'

Francine frowned. 'Oh . . . probably not much more than twenty quid a bottle.'

'Be serious.'

'I am being serious.'

'But, Francine – I've never spent that much on a bottle of wine in my entire life – and – oh, my goodness –'

'What is it?'

'I wonder how much those other two bottles were – the ones Alison chose before you arrived?'

'Does it matter?' Francine laughed. 'If you could see yourself, Sophie. You look just like you used to look when I would phone and order take-out Chinese meals for the four of us, instead of letting you slave over yet another pan of your favourite thrifty standby – spaghetti bolognese!'

'Thrifty or not, it was very good spaghetti bolognese – and easy to prepare – I even taught Carol how to make it!' Sophie began to laugh.

'Yes, darling, it was. And now, we'd better get back up to the kitchen or Alison will think the family ghost has got us.'

'Is there a family ghost?' In spite of her rational education, Sophie glanced around the cellar fearfully.

'In a house as old as this? Bound to be more than one, in fact. In fact if you look beyond that last wine rack, you'll probably find the spirits. Get it? Spirits!'

'Francine – that's a dreadful joke!'

'I know, but it's the first one I've heard here tonight. Now come on, I'm hungry.'

They were still giggling weakly when they joined the others in the kitchen. Alison glanced at them indulgently, but Carol seemed lost in thought. She sat at one end of the table, with them in body but not in spirit. She stared into the mid-distance as if she were content to let life wash all around and over her for a while.

'Here's a corkscrew,' Alison said to Francine. 'Do the honours, will you?'

The table looked good with the fruit, the cheeses, the salad and the first three pizzas already cut into slices and waiting. Alison had put out the overhead lights and lit some candles as promised; there were four of them in what looked like antique brass candlesticks, placed in amongst the dishes of food on the table. Light reflected from the smooth sides of the wine bottles and flickered and danced on the rosy skins of the apples in the bowl.

The room was warm and the atmosphere cosy, informal. Sophie glanced around the table. In the merciful candlelight her friends and, she hoped, herself, had shed the unforgiving years and they could easily be students again. Four young women with all their grown-up lives ahead of them.

'Now, let's enjoy this meal,' Alison said. 'We can talk later.'

Sophie glanced at her sharply. By saying that they could talk later, Alison had implied that the table was the place for idle chatter – amusing gossip – and this would give them time to relax and enjoy each other's company in a joyful uncomplicated way.

Had Alison sensed, as Sophie had, that once the meal was over, every one of them would have something more serious to say.

'It's like a stage set for an old play!' After the meal they had come into the library of Westbrook Hall and Francine was enraptured.

Sophie was trying to get the fire going and she glanced round and smiled. Francine was gazing at the floor-to-ceiling bookcases, the substantial furniture and the family portraits on whatever wall-space remained free. Alison pulled two sets of red velvet curtains closed and turned to smile at Francine.

'What kind of play, do you think?'

'Oh, it would have to be a murder mystery – you know –'

'Murder in the Library!' Alison laughed as she finished the sentence and Sophie thought how much less strained she looked.

'What do you think, Carol?' Francine asked. 'A murder mystery or a Victorian melodrama?'

But there was no reply.

Sophie sat back on her heels and looked at Carol, hunched up in the corner of a huge old sofa, and thought that, if Alison and Francine had relaxed a little over the meal, poor old Carol still had some way to go. She was staring towards the hearth where tongues of flame were beginning to lick around the logs; but she wasn't really focusing.

'Carol – did you hear me?' Francine asked and Sophie looked up at her and shook her head warningly.

Alison moved forward swiftly and knelt by a long, low table where she had placed a large jug of coffee, biscuits and sliced fruit cake. She poured four cups of coffee. 'Add your own cream and sugar,' she said. 'Francine – Sophie – you grab the chairs – pull them up nearer to the fire if you like – Carol and I will share the sofa.'

As Francine settled herself in one of the deep armchairs, she said, 'This is cosy. The wind's whistling round the old house, but we're safe in the library where the lights are low and the log fire's blazing in the hearth. Now what would be the next line of dialogue if we were characters in a detective story?

'I know!' She sat forward in her chair. 'If I were Hercule Poirot or Miss Marple, I'd look at you all and say, "You'll be wondering why I've gathered you all together!" '

Sophie noticed that this only raised a faint smile from Carol, whereas once she would have been laughing with the rest of them and probably vying with them to invent the next line.

'You know,' Francine said, 'I'm so very, very pleased that I came here tonight and, I have to say, I'm grateful that the rest of you will have anything to do with me.'

'What on earth do you mean by that?' Alison asked.

'Well, as I told you earlier in the kitchen, I was – erm – trying to set up an interview in Yorkshire and I decided to go and visit Sophie. And Laura told me that Sophie had come here. What I didn't mention before was that your dear little mother gave me an earful.'

'What! My mother?' I don't believe it!' Sophie exclaimed.

'''Fraid it's true. And I deserved it. She made it quite plain that, lately, I've been neglectful of my old friend, and that made me realize that it's not just Sophie – I hadn't bothered to keep in touch with Alison or Carol either.'

'Well, that's all right,' Alison murmured. 'You're here now.'

'Yes, but I have to be honest, even if it hurts. I only thought of going to see Sophie because I needed to talk to her about – well – all kinds of things. Funny, isn't it, whenever we needed advice or sympathy we all used to turn to Sophie . . .'

'That's right,' Alison said. 'And now, I have to admit that when Sophie phoned last night, the first thing I thought of was that I needed to have a heart-to-heart with an old friend.'

'Me too . . .' Carol roused herself. 'When I got home

from work today and the phone was ringing – and it was you, Alison – and you told me that you two were getting together for the weekend – I just wanted to come straight away.'

'So who's going to start?' Francine asked and they all looked at her.

'What do you mean?'

'Oh, come on, Alison. We can't help each other until we know what the problems are.'

'OK.' Alison leaned forward and cleared a space on the coffee table.

'What are you doing?' Francine asked. 'You're not going to produce a ouija board, are you? We're not going to ask the spirits to solve our problems?'

'First of all I'm going to get a bottle of very good brandy –'

She walked over to a cabinet set in a recess next to the fireplace and returned with the brandy and four glasses. She sat down on the sofa again and leaned forward to pour a generous amount into each glass. She handed the glasses round and smiled.

'Then,' she said, and she paused to take a sip from her own glass and savour it, 'as I would probably be the Lady of the Manor in this imaginary play of Francine's, I'd better make my confession first.'

They'd been talking for an hour or two and Sophie had gone to the kitchen with Alison to help her make a fresh supply of coffee. As Alison poured boiling water into the cafetière, Sophie dried the mugs she had just rinsed out and placed them on the tray again.

'Mm, that smells good,' she told Alison, 'but should we be drinking coffee as strong as that, as late at night as this?'

'I don't see why not; I don't think any of us is going to be able to sleep anyway – at least not until we've thrashed all these problems out.'

They crossed the draughty hall, shafts of moonlight slanted through the windows at each side of the door looking pale and insubstantial against the shadows. Sophie remembered Francine's joke about the Cavendish family ghosts. 'Do you like living in an old house like this?' she asked Alison.

Alison halted and turned to look at her. 'Why do you ask?'

'Well, it's lovely, of course, and there must be traditions – legends – ghosts . . .'

'Plenty of traditions and legends and there are supposed to be ghosts, but I've never met one.' Alison smiled.

'But there must be problems too – I mean the fabric of the house – there must be so much to do to keep it in good order – even to make it comfortable for modern-day people to live in.'

'And it all takes money.' Alison said. 'And that gets us back to the problem I've just been telling you all about. But, honestly, Sophie, I love this place. If Paul hadn't died I would have been perfectly happy for him to put all the money he made into maintaining and saving Westbrook Hall for our son. And now that he's gone, I'm not going to let him down.'

'I know you won't.'

While they had been absent from the room, Francine had built up the fire to such an extent that they had to push their chairs back from the hearth.

'I'm sorry, Alison,' she said, 'but Carol and I suddenly felt cold. Magnificent as this old pile is, it can't compare in sheer creature comfort to my new apartment in London.'

'That's OK,' Alison replied. 'The central heating is timed to go off at ten o'clock and, after that, if you're not in bed, you're supposed to suffer for your sins! You could say that's one of the old traditions that we've just been talking about, Sophie.'

'But that's dreadful,' Carol said. 'Why stick to a tradition as Spartan as that?'

'Does the system cost too much to run?' Sophie suggested.

'That's partly the reason,' Alison replied as she poured the coffee, 'but also it's old and noisy. When the house is quiet you can hear the boiler rumbling in the basement and the water gurgling along the old pipes. My mother-in-law complains that it keeps her awake.'

'Tough!' Carol suddenly exclaimed. 'Why don't you let the old bitch suffer?'

Alison spluttered into her coffee and they all stared at Carol in astonishment. 'Carol, that's not like you,' Sophie said at last.

'Well,' she said, and in the firelight her rounded, pretty face took on the look of a cross child, 'it's not just men that cause problems – at least not for Alison and me – it's mothers-in-law too!'

'Explain,' Francine said. She took her coffee from the table and sat back in her armchair. Her dark hair swung forward in two perfect wings as she sipped from her mug.

Carol leaned forward. She was frowning. 'I've told you how everything seems to be going wrong between me and Alan. Ever since they made him a new product manager he's been working longer and longer hours –'

'Almost as if he's using the job as an excuse to avoid coming home,' Francine suggested quietly.

'Francine, that's quite an assumption,' Sophie murmured; 'he may genuinely be trying to cope with an increased workload.'

'No, that's all right,' Carol said, 'Francine's right. Alan doesn't want to come home to the mess and the clutter. Most of the time I'm lucky if I even manage to get his meal on the table.'

'And does Alan ever have a meal waiting for you?' Francine asked. 'I mean, I thought that was what marriage was about these days. For goodness' sake, you both go out to work, so in my opinion you should share the housework.'

'I agree,' Alison said. 'I never had a job after Paul and I were married and he was away working a lot. But when he was home, he liked to help me – especially just after Matthew was born.'

'And what did his mother think of that?' Carol asked.

'Oh, she was outraged. She never said anything in front of Paul but when he went away again, she told me that his father had never been asked to do so much as flick a feather duster and hardly ever visited the kitchen. Mind you – neither does she!'

'But the principle's the same, isn't it?' Carol said. 'Mrs Cavendish thought that men should be waited on hand and foot and probably saw her duties as running the perfect home for him.'

'Where is this taking us?' Francine asked.

'Right back to my mother-in-law. She's never had servants like Mrs Cavendish, but she sees it as her duty to be the perfect wife and mother. Alan's father has never even washed or dried a teacup in all his married life and they brought Alan up to be the same.'

'Did she never work after she was married?' Alison asked.

'Yes, until Alan was born she continued working as a secretary and when he started school she sometimes had part time clerical jobs. But she always insisted that it was the woman's job to do everything in the home.'

'The more fool her,' Francine said. 'And, what's more, her out-of-date theories have completely ruined her son.'

'But Alan's an intelligent man; surely it was up to Carol to point out that life isn't like that any more,' Sophie ventured. 'I mean, he can't be totally unobservant. What about your friends?'

'Friends?' Carol asked.

'Other young couples – people you socialize with.'

'I don't think he was ever interested in what went on in other people's homes. The poor man was just concerned that his own home was an uncomfortable tip!'

Francine made an angry sound. 'Poor man, indeed! And, Carol, I have to say that a lot of this is your own fault. You've been far too soft with him.'

'Perhaps I have – but what can I do?'

'For a start, you need to talk,' Sophie said.

'Don't you think I know that? The trouble is we never seem to have the time – and now it may be too late . . .'

'Oh, Carol, why?' Alison moved closer to her on the sofa and put her arm around her.

'Well – I've told you – the mess I made of things – not paying the phone bill – and his mother being in hospital – and Alan not wanting me to go there . . .' She trailed off and stared into the fire miserably.

Alison turned her head to look first at Francine and then at Sophie, then she gave Carol a reassuring hug. 'Yes, it looks bad, but you still love each other, don't you?'

'Yes – I mean – yes . . .' Sophie saw that they had all noticed the hesitation.

'You're not sure, are you?' Francine asked.

Carol stared at her, her eyes widening with pain. 'Wh-what do you mean?'

'You think that there might be some other explanation for Alan coming home later and later, don't you?'

'Such as?'

'I think that you've considered the possibility that he's found someone else – another woman.'

'No – no, I don't think there's another woman . . .'

Alison had looked worried throughout this exchange and now she relaxed visibly. 'Well, if there's no one else, I don't think it sounds too serious.'

'Don't you?' Carol turned to her in surprise.

266

'No. I think you'll find that a lot of married couples have similar problems. My parents were both teachers, as you know, and from what my mother told me, they got into a similar situation in the early days of their marriage. They would both come home with a stack of books to mark and Dad would settle down and get on with his work, while Mum rushed around preparing the meal and afterwards trying to catch up with some of the housework. Often she was doing her school preparation late at night when Dad was already in bed.'

'Yes, but that was some time ago,' Francine said. 'Men were expected to be male chauvinist pigs in those dear old days!'

'Well, my mother didn't accept it. I think she came close to leaving him.'

'So, how did they sort things out?' Carol asked.

'Actually, they went to Marriage Guidance – it's called Relate now, I think.'

'And it worked?'

'Yes. They were both intelligent people – as you and Alan are – and most of all, they still loved each other.'

'I don't think Alan would go to Relate.' Carol looked wistful.

'You never know, he might,' Alison said. 'And, if he won't, it'll be up to you.'

'That's not fair,' Francine said.

'Who said life was fair?' Alison asked. 'If Carol loves him enough, she'll work hard to save the marriage. And she's always got us to talk to, hasn't she – we'll give her all the support we can, won't we? Sophie – you've been quiet – what do you think?'

'Oh, I agree with you.'

Carol sighed and leaned over to fill up her coffee mug. She didn't exactly look happier, Sophie thought, but she looked more at rest. As if talking about her problems – sharing them – had been a relief. And yet Sophie imagined that she hadn't told them everything – that she was keeping something back. That hesitation earlier when Alison had asked them if they still loved each other – and then, again, when Francine had asked if Alan might have found someone else . . .

Had Carol answered honestly? Did Carol and Alan still love each other? Did Carol imagine that he had found someone else? Or had she . . . no . . . surely not . . .? And yet something was the matter . . .

Sophie frowned as she watched Carol settle back into the cushions of the old sofa. Well, whatever it was, she wasn't going to confide in her friends . . .

'I'll tell you one thing,' Francine said. 'Whatever help and advice we give Carol in future, we mustn't forget that Alan's mother is part of the problem, just like in your case, Alison.'

'*Part* of the problem! It seems to me that if Paul's mother and sister would stop interfering, I could get this old house sorted out in next to no time!'

'That's easy,' Francine said. 'You're a grown-up girl and you've got to just tell them to get – I mean to take a running jump!'

'Easier said than done.' Alison looked rueful.

'On the contrary, it's very easy.'

'Oh yes? I imagine it would be for you, Francine, but I'm not used to asserting myself.'

'Then just think of your son.'

'Matthew? How would that help?'

'You want to save this place for him, don't you? And if you have to tread on a few toes in order to do so, there's no real contest, is there?'

'No . . . I suppose not . . .'

'So, no matter how much the Cavendishes might look down their snobbish noses at your friendly property developer, he's your best chance, and don't you forget it!'

'Don't worry, no matter what my in-laws say, I'll

probably go ahead with the deal. It's just that . . .' Alison trailed off uncomfortably and Sophie thought that the flush on her cheeks was caused by more than the heat from the fire.

'Greg Leighton is more than just a way to save Westbrook Hall, isn't he?' she said quietly.

There was a pause and then Alison avoided looking directly at anyone when she said, 'I can't deny it.'

'I thought so,' Sophie said. 'When you talk about him you can't help giving yourself away.'

Carol raised her eyebrows. 'Clever Sophie – I must say I didn't read the signs. And how does Greg feel, Alison? Is the attraction mutual?'

'I'm not sure . . . yes, of course I am . . . it is.'

'So why do you look so troubled?' Francine asked. 'I know who Greg Leighton is. I read an article about him recently; he's tall, handsome, clever, rich and single. What's the problem?'

'Is there a problem?' Carol asked.

'Paul's mother and sister – they don't like him.'

'Why not?' Francine asked. 'Oh – you don't have to tell me – it's all about social class, isn't it? They probably think he's too common for you!'

'Not for me, I'm only a Cavendish by marriage; it's Matthew they're worried about.

'What on earth for?' Carol asked. 'Do they think he'll contaminate him?'

Alison looked worried. 'My sister-in-law thinks that Greg may have criminal connections because of – well, because of his mother, I suppose.'

'Don't worry about that,' Francine said sharply. 'Whatever his family background may be, the man himself is clean.'

'How do you know that?' Alison asked.

'An investigative reporter I know once thought of doing an exposé of Greg Leighton –'

'Why Greg?' Carol asked.

'Because he was so amazingly successful, I suppose. Like the Cavendishes, my friend couldn't believe that a man could come from nothing so quickly unless he'd a bit of help from a few doubtful sources.

'Well, he spent months investigating him and came up with nothing. The man is successful because he's intelligent, astute and works hard. Your in-laws should be delighted that Matthew will be getting such a man for a stepfather.'

'Wait a minute!' Alison exclaimed. 'You're moving ahead far too quickly – *stepfather*! That implies that I'm going to marry him!'

Francine frowned. 'Sorry – but you certainly gave the impression that it could be heading that way.'

'Did I? We-ell . . . I suppose it could be . . . but . . .'

'What is it?' Carol asked. 'Is there another problem?'

'It's Paul, isn't it?' Sophie said suddenly. 'You feel disloyal, don't you?'

'Exactly.' Alison sighed. 'I knew Sophie would understand.'

'But, you must know that Paul wouldn't have wanted you to spend the rest of your life alone,' Sophie told her.

'I'm not alone – I have Matthew.'

'Not forever,' Francine said. 'Matthew will grow up and get married and bring his wife to live in Westbrook Hall and you'll be reduced to wandering about and complaining about her and her ways just like your mother-in-law does now.'

'Francine! You can't possibly imagine that I'd ever grow to resemble Lilian Cavendish!'

Francine frowned. 'I'm teasing – but only a little, you know. The danger is that if you could devote all your life to Matthew, you'll have nothing yourself when he doesn't need you any more.'

'I know that.'

'So why are you hesitating – as you obviously are?'

'Doesn't Matthew like Greg?' Sophie asked.

'I think he likes him very much – in fact there are signs that they could get on famously. But – but – oh, I don't know, perhaps I'm looking for excuses.'

'But why look for excuses?' Carol asked. 'I mean, if you're attracted to him and he's attracted to you . . .'

'Maybe it's because I'm out of practice,' Alison said. 'It's been so long since I've been wined and dined and kissed goodnight that I've forgotten what to do.'

'*Kissed goodnight!*' The others all yelled out together, and Alison burst out laughing.

'Yes – and before you ask – he hasn't done that yet . . .'

'But you obviously wish that he had!' Francine said.

Alison looked round at them all in friendly exasperation. 'Do you know, if you could see yourselves right now,' she told them, 'you wouldn't believe that you're all supposed to be responsible grown-up women!

'It reminds me of how we used to tell each other about our dates and analyse our responses. If the poor guys could have heard half what we said about them they wouldn't have come anywhere near us again!'

'Well, what about *this* poor guy?' Francine said. 'Has talking to us helped you to make your mind up?'

'Yes . . . I think so . . .'

'So what are you going to do about it?' Sophie asked.

Alison leaned back against the cushions and smiled at them. 'I think I'm going to try and stop even thinking about it and just see what happens.'

Francine raised her brandy glass in a mock salute. 'Good. And for goodness' sake don't feel guilty if you start to enjoy yourself again. I'm quite sure that Paul wouldn't have wanted you to mourn him for the rest of your life.'

'But I'll never forget him, you know.'

'Of course you won't,' Sophie assured her. 'And you'll

always love him, too – but that shouldn't stop you from beginning a new and entirely different relationship.'

For a moment they sat quietly. The fire had died down a little but a comfortable warmth radiated from the hearth and Sophie realized how tired she was. She glanced around at her friends. Alison seemed more at ease with herself and even Carol's face had lost some of its taut anxiety. She looked as though she had accepted the fact that she had problems and that it was up to her to sort them out. But Francine was frowning.

'So what about me, then?' she said suddenly. 'I've told you my problem. Am I going to go on doing what I do so well – interviewing celebrities and providing interesting but fairly mindless entertainment – or should I risk my reputation and go for something more demanding? A serious arts programme?'

'Mindless, or not, I like the things you do,' Alison said. 'But, of course, I know that you're capable of something more challenging.'

'Yes, you are,' Carol said. 'But I agree that it would be a risk. Your fans might not like it.'

'Francine, why are you asking us this?' Sophie said.

The others looked surprised. 'She's asking because we agreed to help each other sort out our problems,' Alison said.

'But that isn't a problem, is it?' Sophie persisted.

'What do you mean?' Carol asked. 'It sounds like a problem to me.'

'Not to Francine. She's perfectly capable of deciding which way her career should go. In fact I think she's probably already made up her mind. So what's the real problem?'

'Good old Sophie.' Francine laughed softly. 'I should have known I couldn't fool her. Of course it's not the real problem. Just like the rest of you, the root cause is a man.'

The others looked at her uneasily. Once she had met Peter Curtis, Francine had stopped confiding in them so openly and they had never pushed her. If Peter and she had ever had any problems she had never talked about them. So what were they to do now? Sophie guessed that something must have really unsettled her to bring her to this point.

'You all know about Peter – no, don't say anything – just let me talk. I've never regretted my involvement with him even although it's left me estranged from my parents. I've had a good life, I've worked hard and he's been very supportive –'

'Can you say that?' Alison asked. 'Can you say he's been supportive when you've had to keep your relationship secret? If you were ever ill or in trouble, was he able to be by your side?'

'Alison, don't –' Carol looked embarrassed.

'No, let her say it,' Francine said. 'In a way she's right. There's been a lot missing in our relationship, but then, I preferred it that way –'

'How could you?' Alison asked.

'I think I know why,' Sophie said. 'You preferred it that way because that kind of relationship left you free. With the kind of life you lead, you'd hardly want to be worried and harassed like poor old Carol about getting home in time to make some man's dinner – or cleaning up the house and ironing his shirts before you went to work, would you? In fact you must have been pleased to leave all that to his wife.'

'Sophie!' Carol was horrified. 'That's cruel!'

'But it's true,' Alison said softly.

'I suppose it is . . .' Carol said unhappily.

Francine grinned crookedly. 'Are you all ganging up on me? Well, don't worry, Carol. Sophie's right, of course. My work has been my life. I just can't imagine having to come home from the studios – or an exciting location – and having to switch roles from career woman to wife – and possibly mother. Peter has never expected that of me. He's happy if I want to talk about work all the time . . . we-ell . . .'

Sophie noticed a slight hesitation but Francine soon recovered herself. 'I really did love Peter and it was all the better for me because he wasn't prepared to commit – and neither does he expect that from me.'

'But now you've met someone who's thoroughly unsettled you, and your views on what a relationship should be, is that what's happened?' Sophie asked. 'And I can guess that that person is probably Marcus Holbrook.'

'Right again, Sophie, and until a very short while ago my emotions have been fairly chaotic. Can you believe I was even beginning to believe in love at first sight?'

'But you've changed your mind again, haven't you?'

'Clever Carol. Yes, I have.'

Francine kicked off her shoes and pulled her feet up on to the chair; she rested her chin on her knees and wrapped her arms around her legs. She stared straight ahead but she wasn't really seeing anything. Sophie guessed that she was thinking things through as she talked to them.

'You know . . .' she said '. . . I've always imagined that I was very lucky to live the way I do. I love my job – and Peter and I have had just the kind of relationship I wanted. I've never been remotely attracted to another man until now . . .'

'Marcus Holbrook,' Sophie said.

'Yes, Marcus Holbrook. I can't explain it and I don't want to even try; you'll just have to accept that the attraction is there and, suddenly, I had a glimpse of a different kind of relationship – one that would demand total commitment . . .'

'And?' Sophie hinted gently.

'And I panicked and headed straight for Sophie's

274

house and then here – thank goodness I did – it's helped me make my mind up.'

'How?' Alison asked. 'We haven't exactly advised you.'

'You don't have to. Sorry, Alison and Carol, but listening to your problems had made me realize how lucky I am after all. I'm going to enjoy the rest of my time here with you and then head back to London and tell Peter that nothing will persuade me to give up my idea for a new and different kind of programme. You know, the more I think about it, the more I think the whole weird episode with Marcus was probably brought on by frustration – frustration with my career, not my lifestyle – don't you agree?'

'It's feasible,' Alison said but Carol shook her head worriedly.

'I hope it's not my dreadful example that's put you off love and marriage,' she murmured.

'Of course not – I've just come to my senses.'

Francine smiled as if she was relieved to have made a decision but Sophie wasn't so sure. Perhaps it was Carol's chaotic marriage that had influenced Francine – perhaps Alison's crushing responsibilities had made her aware of what could happen when two people had committed fully – how promises had to be kept even beyond the grave. It certainly wasn't her feelings for Peter Curtis that were taking her back to her old life, Sophie was sure of that because of one little word, *did*. Sophie wondered whether Francine realized that she had described her love for Peter in the past tense.

'Well, that's it,' Francine said, and she stood up and stretched. 'We've discussed all our problems and, although we haven't solved absolutely everything, we all feel a little better about it, don't we?'

'I suppose so,' Carol said. 'Whatever happens now, I know I've got you lot to back me up.'

'And to spur me on,' Alison added. 'Now, perhaps we should go to bed.'

Francine began to collect the coffee mugs and put them on the tray and then suddenly she stopped and straightened up. 'Wait a moment,' she said, and she looked at Sophie. 'When I called at your house, your mother said that you had something to tell me – tell us all. I was worried that it might be something awful – that you might be ill – but she said it wasn't . . .'

'Oh, Sophie, forgive me,' Alison said. 'I knew that you wanted to talk but I didn't realize that it was about something special . . .'

'Is it something special?' Carol added.

Sophie looked round at their guilty faces and smiled ruefully. 'Depends what you mean by special. After listening to you all tonight I imagine you'll have mixed feelings about my announcement. You see, I wanted to tell you that I'm going to be married.'

You could have heard a pin drop. That was a cliché, Sophie thought, but at times like this, nothing but a cliché would do. Her friends stared at her and she watched their expressions change from surprise to joy. Yes, joy. She felt bemused.

It was understandable that Alison should feel that way; her marriage had been happy – so happy that she stood a very good chance of being happy again. But Carol? Francine? Carol, who had found that loving someone with all your heart might not be enough – and Francine, who only a moment ago had declared that she preferred a single life rather than take on the mundane responsibilities of commitment – they were both smiling as foolishly and as fondly as Alison.

It was Alison who spoke first. 'That's marvellous, Sophie, but why on earth didn't you tell us sooner?'

'We didn't give her a chance, did we?' Carol said. 'We were all too concerned about our own problems.'

'We're all ten years older but nothing's changed has it?' Francine asked and she smiled ruefully. 'Sophie, I'm surprised that you still want to maintain this friendship!'

'But, anyway, tell us who he is – what he's like – where you met him!' Alison said. 'This is the first really good piece of news tonight. Tell us *everything*, Sophie, and then we can all go to bed happy!'

Later, in the room she was sharing with Carol, Sophie found it difficult to sleep. The house was cold, so Alison had provided extra blankets, hot water bottles and bed-socks and Sophie had found herself burrowing down amongst the bedding like a small animal. But still she couldn't sleep.

At their insistence, she had told her friends about how she had met Alistair at an art gallery. She had stepped back to take a better look at a painting and bumped into him, literally. She told them about his stressful job at the hospital, about how good-looking he was, how clever, how cheerful; above all how practical.

It had not been difficult for them to press her into admitting how much she loved him. And they had been so happy for her.

'Sophie's found Mr Right at last!' Francine had exclaimed, predictably.

'And, knowing Sophie, he'll be right in every way,' Alison added.

Carol had had tears in her eyes when she had hugged Sophie and said, 'It's wonderful . . . just wonderful . . .'

So how could she have possibly admitted to them that it might not be so wonderful after all . . . ?

CHAPTER 17

'Alison – you should have waited – I would have helped you.'

When Sophie entered the kitchen the next morning, all evidence of their meal the night before had disappeared. The table had been cleared, the dishes washed and put away and Alison was just setting up a tray.

'No, that's all right, I wanted to spoil you – all of you – you're my guests, after all.'

'Well, now that I'm here, what can I do?'

'The kettle's boiling – make a large pot of tea – oh, and make this small pot, too; this tray is for my mother-in-law.'

'Do you always wait on her like this?'

'We-ell – she's old . . .'

'Is she frail?'

'Not particularly, but she never really got over Paul's sudden death, you know. He was her only son . . .'

'And he was your husband.'

'Yes.'

'Alison – things have got to change.'

'I know. Don't worry – they will, but I don't intend to be too cruel to Paul's mother.'

'Of course not. Now here's the small teapot – what else can I do?'

'Could you butter a couple of slices of bread – thanks – there – her eggs are ready – I'll take this up.'

Sophie poured herself a mug of tea and went to sit by the Aga. She wasn't alone in the kitchen for long. She heard Alison greeting someone as she went upstairs and, a moment later, Carol entered, yawning blearily. 'Hi, Sophie – I didn't hear you get up – you should have wakened me.'

'I didn't like to – you were sleeping so peacefully. Pour yourself some tea.'

'Mm – it took me ages to get to sleep, though. I just lay there wondering whether Alan tried phoning home last night and, if he did, whether he would care that I wasn't there.'

'Oh, Carol, I'm sorry, I don't know what to say . . .'

'No – I'm sorry. I shouldn't have mentioned it – especially not to you – our blushing bride and all!'

'Don't, Carol –'

'No, I mean it. I got myself into this mess and I'm going to sort it out one way or another. Any sign of Francine?'

'I heard signs of life in her room as I came down. I imagine she won't be long.'

'You've obviously forgotten! Francine can spend hours getting ready – she'll only emerge when she looks perfect as usual.'

Carol pulled one of the chairs out from the table and dragged it over towards the Aga. She sat still for a moment luxuriating in the warmth and sipping her tea. Then she asked, 'What do you think of what Francine told us last night, by the way? First she was hinting that she'd fallen in a big way for a guy she'd only just met and then she says that she's changed her mind and that she's quite happy with her life the way it is. What's going on?'

'I'm not sure, but there are a lot of women like

Francine today. They're thirty-something, they're successful, they have a certain amount of power; why should they widen the frame to include a husband and maybe risk giving up control?'

'I just know that you've been talking about me!' They both turned to see Francine in the doorway. She was grinning. 'At least I hope you were!'

'Oh, the conceit of it!' Carol exclaimed.

They were still smiling when Alison returned.

'Sorry I took so long,' she said. 'I had some phone calls to make and I thought it better to get them over with. Now, I suggest we have a fantastic fry-up!'

Alison's car had recently failed its MOT badly and, until she could afford to have the necessary work done, she had been walking everywhere. After breakfast all three of her friends offered to drive her into the village to collect Matthew from Oliver Morton's house, but she refused their offers.

'No, thank you. I might be a while. But you can wash the dishes, then clean the hearth and set the fire going in the library if you want to do something useful. And then, why don't you just sit around, read the morning papers, borrow a book – there are plenty – or listen to some relaxing music? Or do all three? Or walk in the grounds – it's a fabulous day.'

And it was. She pulled a duffel jacket on over her jeans and long-line sweater and set off for the village. The ever-present breeze lifted her hair, but the sky was cloudless and the sun was shining. It couldn't last, she thought; it was April, after all. But this morning, the air was fresh and sparkling. And her spirits were uplifted.

There were quite few people about. As well as the Plough, there was a general store, a greengrocers and a newsagent-cum-post office facing the village green, and they were all busy. Alison took the footpath that crossed the green and saw Miss Robertson working her way along the houses at the far side.

The vicar's sister was carrying a canvas bag over her shoulder and Alison guessed that she was delivering copies of the parish magazine. Miss Robertson's progress was slow as she stopped to chat now and then. When she saw Alison she waved cheerily.

'Mrs Cavendish,' she called as Alison approached her, 'good morning. Did you enjoy your little party last night?'

'My, my,' Alison said, 'word gets round.'

'Oh, dear, are you angry? That's village life, I'm afraid. But what could be nicer than having your old university friends to stay?'

'No, I'm not angry. I should be used to it by now. But can I help you with those? That bag looks heavy.'

'Let me.' Both women turned as Greg came striding towards them.

'Oh, Mr Leighton, isn't it? You look just like your photograph in the newspaper . . . although I must say you look even better in casual clothes . . . oh, dear, will I ever learn discretion!' Miss Robertson was flustered.

'Let me take that bag. I used to have a paper round as a boy – several, in fact. Just point me in the right direction.'

'Oh, I couldn't possibly impose on you – and besides, I enjoy delivering the magazine – it gives me a chance to – er – have a chat with people.'

And catch up on all the gossip, Alison thought, but she knew that, as far as Miss Robertson was concerned, gossip would never be malicious.

'There is one way you could help, my dear.' The old lady turned to smile at Alison.

'Anything – just tell me.'

'When I called at the Mortons', just now, I saw that Matthew was there with Oliver. Ruth told me that you'd phoned to say you'd be coming but, if I could borrow Matthew and Oliver for a while to help me with the magazines, it would keep them occupied.'

'Do they need occupation?'

'Well, I thought it might be pleasant for you and Mr Leighton to stroll along to Peg's Tearooms and – er – discuss business or whatever, over a nice cup of coffee.'

'Oh, definitely whatever.' Alison burst out laughing and she saw Greg looking at her strangely.

'Do I take it that's a "yes"?' Miss Robertson asked?

'That's a "yes",' Alison replied. 'Let's go and ask the boys if they agree.'

'Oh, they do, they're ready and waiting. Oh, dear . . .'

The old lady coloured a little, but she turned and waved towards the Mortons' house and immediately the door opened. Matthew and Oliver came racing out as if at a predetermined signal.

Alison watched her son running towards her and her heart filled with love. He was tall for his age and slim and rangy, just as his father had been. She knew, and it wasn't just a mother's bias, that he was going to grow up to be exceptionally good-looking. But, more importantly, he already showed signs of being sensitive and caring.

Poor Matthew, she thought. His father's dying so young may have made him a little too mature for his years . . .

She became aware that Greg was looking at her and she turned to meet his gaze. She was surprised at the understanding she saw in his eyes. And yet why should I be surprised? she wondered. Surely I was aware that first moment that he took me in his arms to comfort me that this man doesn't always need words to know what's going on . . .

It pleased her that, no matter how grown-up he was beginning to look, Matthew hurled himself into her arms. 'Thanks, Mum,' he said.

'That's OK, but I expect you to be a real help to Miss Robertson, not a hindrance.'

'Of course – and afterwards Miss Robertson says Oliver and I can go back to the vicarage for lunch. She's got her nephews' Formula One Scalextric set – they left it there.'

'Oh, but I wanted you to come home and see my friends – it's almost two years since they've seen you and –'

'I'll bring Matthew home after tea, Mrs Cavendish,' Miss Robertson said. 'Your friends are staying until tomorrow, aren't they?'

'Yes, but –'

'It would be such a pleasure for me. I've told you how much I enjoyed bringing up my brother's sons, and that motor racing game has been lying neglected for so long. . .'

'Please, Mum!'

'Please, Mrs Cavendish,' Oliver echoed.

'Oh, all right, then. But behave yourselves.'

'We will.'

Miss Robertson and her two eager helpers began to walk away when Matthew suddenly stopped and turned. 'Would you like to come to the vicarage, too, Greg? I'm sure Miss Robertson wouldn't mind!'

Greg looked questioningly at the vicar's sister. 'You're very welcome, Mr Leighton,' she said, 'although I'm only offering hamburgers and chips for lunch.'

'Well, I may come along after lunch,' he said. 'I think Molly's saving something special for me at The Plough.'

'Great! See you later!' Matthew and Oliver sang out in unison as they hurried off with Miss Robertson.

Alison and Greg watched them go and then they turned to smile at each other.

'He's a good kid,' Greg said.

'I know; he's special.'

'Well, then,' he said, 'I've met you on the village green

as you requested when you phoned earlier, so what's the plan?'

'I didn't really have a plan but I said that I'd phone you – and I did – and I hope you don't mind?'

'No, of course not, but you didn't say why you wanted to see me. Is it to discuss business?'

'Not right away. But I thought that, seeing as you've taken the trouble to make the trip down here, we could at least meet and arrange a proper time.'

'I see,' he said. But Alison could tell from his puzzled frown that he didn't really. Never mind, it might become clear to him later.

'Well, then,' he said, 'I think we were given our orders just now; whatever we are going to talk about, Miss Robertson has suggested we go to Peg's Tearooms. So, where exactly is this café?'

'Not far – if we walk along towards the church, there's an old barn set back from the road; it's been converted.'

'I thought that was an antique shop.'

'It is – but so many people started asking Harry where they could get a nice cup of tea that he started serving snacks as well. Now the café part of the business does better than the antiques.'

They had started walking along together and it seemed perfectly natural for her to slip her arm through his. She felt a slight tensing of his muscles but then he smiled down at her.

'Harry?' he asked.

'Sorry?'

'You said "Harry". What about Peg?'

'Oh, there never was a Peg. It's just that Harry and his partner, Gerald, thought that it sounded better than either of their names – more cosy – you know.'

'And do you go there often?'

She frowned. 'Well, I used to . . . but I can't remember the last time I was there . . . I don't seem to have had

284

much time to relax lately . . . to enjoy the ordinary little pleasures such as having coffee and cakes in the village teashop.'

Suddenly she turned her head and looked up at him. 'I'm so glad Miss Robertson suggested this, aren't you?'

Greg looked down at her and was immediately lost in her wide blue gaze. She was smiling but there was a hint of reticence, of uncertainty, and he had to fight the urge to tell her that, whatever was bothering her, it was all right. He wanted to take her in his arms – enfold her in his embrace – the expression came from nowhere – but it described exactly what he wanted to do. Wrap her up, take care of her, and do battle against all enemies for her, for now and forever.

The good Lord help me, he thought, I'm hopelessly in love.

'We'd better move on,' she whispered, and he realized that they had stopped walking and had been gazing into each other's eyes like moonstruck teenagers.

The café was quaint – deliberately so, he thought. The walls were rough-plastered and painted cream; the oak beams overhead looked original. Greg guessed that none of the jugs and the plates displayed on shelves around the wall were really valuable, but they all had price tags on them, as did the pictures. However, not one of the customers seemed to be remotely interested.

Alison had seen him looking around and she moved closer and whispered, 'They sell the occasional curiosity such as a Victorian shaving mug or a watercolour by a local artist to passing tourists, but Harry gave up keeping any really valuable antiques long ago.'

They threaded their way between the tables towards a table for two near the window and Greg couldn't help noticing heads turning as they went by. He ordered a slice of home-made carrot cake for himself but Alison, in spite of Harry's urging, confined herself to coffee.

'Do you know something I don't know?' he whispered across the table while they were waiting and she smiled.

'Don't worry, the cake will be delicious, it's just that I had a large meal last night and a large breakfast this morning.'

'Oh, yes, with your friends.' Unease returned as he remembered. 'Did I hear Miss Robertson saying that they were from university days?'

'You did – my three best girlfriends –'

Girlfriends, she'd said. Amazing how happy that made him. She was still talking – what had he missed?

'– and we teamed up almost on the first day there – soon we were sharing a student flat – oh, what times we had!'

'And you've kept in touch ever since?'

Her face clouded. 'At first we did – we used to phone and write all the time – and then – I don't remember when it started happening – but it eased off so that we only corresponded occasionally. Oh, we always remembered each other's birthdays and Christmas – but just lately I think our own lives began to get too complicated and we started neglecting the friendship.'

But then, her smile returned. 'And if it hadn't been for Sophie's wedding, I don't know how long it might have been before we saw each other again.'

'One of your friends has just been married?'

'No, she's going to be at the end of the month. And it's because she wanted to tell us about it that this weekend came about.'

'I see. Well, whatever the reason, your friends' visit has obviously been good for you.'

'Why do you say that?'

'You don't look as tense as you did before. You look more at ease with yourself.'

'Oh, I am – and, Greg –' She reached across the table

and took his hand. 'It isn't just because of my friends, you know . . .'

He leaned forward and captured her other hand and they sat, holding hands on the tabletop and staring into each other's eyes. Greg was aware that heads were turning to glance at them and also aware that not all of the looks they were getting were indulgent, but he was reluctant to let go.

Then, from the corner of his eye, he caught a movement on the pavement beyond the window. A small, bony woman with a face like a worried rodent had stopped and she was staring at them unashamedly. Without being too obvious, he exerted pressure on Alison's hands and signalled with his eyes and a slight tilt of his head, that she should glance in the same direction.

She did and then, to his surprise, she breathed, 'Oh, good!'

She pulled one of her hands free from his grasp and waved to the woman and smiled. Instead of smiling back, the woman actually looked offended. Greg saw her shrug and turn her head away in an attempt at disdain, then she scuttled away.

'Who on earth was that?' he asked.

Alison laughed. 'That was Daphne's secret weapon.'

'Are you going to explain that cryptic statement?'

To his surprise, Alison seemed to be embarrassed. She couldn't quite meet his eyes when she replied, 'Daphne is my sister-in-law –'

'Mrs Remington.'

'That's right, and Mrs Slater is her cleaning woman.'

'And that is supposed to be an explanation?'

'Oh, dear . . . well, you might as well know, she's been spying on me.'

'Mrs Remington or Mrs Slater?'

'Mrs Slater – but Daphne set her on.'

'You must know this sounds ridiculous.'

'I do and I'm sorry, but it's true. And now I have a confession to make.'

'Is your confession going to upset me?' Greg had a horrible feeling that it was.

'I do hope not . . . but Greg, before I say anything, there's a reason for what I did.'

'I see.' Greg withdrew his other hand and sat back in his chair. 'You don't have to tell me. I think I get the picture. Mrs Remington is spying on you for – for whatever crazy reason of her own; you are annoyed by this and decided to give Mrs Slater something to report back, right?'

'Right. But Greg –'

'So that's why you phoned this morning and asked me to meet you on the village green, in full view of whoever might be passing?'

'Yes, but –'

'And all this holding hands and gazing into my eyes has just been part of your little plan. I was just a convenient prop.'

'No – you're wrong!'

Greg knew that he was behaving like a wounded adolescent but he couldn't help himself. Male pride was a powerful emotion and he was entirely in its grip when he pushed his chair back, tossed some money on the table and stood up.

'That should take care of the bill,' he said and he headed for the door.

It didn't help that he saw heads dipping together as he went by, and he was sure that he heard suppressed laughter. As he shut the door he glanced back and saw that Alison was already on her feet and thrusting the money and the bill towards Harry, who was hurrying towards her.

I wonder how long it will take for the gossip to get back

to The Plough, he thought, and will I ever be able to face Molly and Alf again? I'll go straight back to London – I needn't come here again – even if the deal goes ahead, I can trust my site agent to oversee the work.

He had reached the village green before she caught up with him.

'Greg Leighton, will you please stop behaving like this!'

She sounded so angry that he turned in surprise. He was the one who should be angry, wasn't he?

'Now, will you listen to me?'

Her cheeks were flushed and her eyes were sparkling. The reserved, classy Englishwoman that Greg had fallen in love with had suddenly revealed that she had hidden depths of fire. He felt a surge of desire that almost made him dizzy. He had to control an overpowering urge to take hold of her, pull her into his arms and stop her mouth with kisses.

'What do you want to say?' he managed.

'First of all, I confess that it was quite deliberate. I asked you to meet me on the green because I wanted it to get back to Daphne. But you weren't just a prop – far from it. I wanted Daphne to know that no matter what she says I – I –'

'What? Tell me?'

Greg could feel his heart thudding painfully against his ribcage. He took a step closer and raised his arms involuntarily, but didn't quite make contact. He wanted, desperately, to hear what she was going to say next.

'I wanted her to know that, no matter what she says – no matter what kind of threats she makes – I am not going to stop seeing you.'

'Alison –' Greg's voice cracked, and then he did move forward. He swept her into his arms and, in total disregard to the comings and goings of the people passing by, he brought his mouth down on hers.

He would have to find out why her sister-in-law had been spying on her, and also the exact nature of the threats she had made. He knew that this was important but, right now, he couldn't concentrate. This moment was the sweetest moment in his entire life up until now.

As he tasted her lips and experienced the agonizing enchantment of having her body so closely moulded to his own, he knew that this woman was all that he would ever need or desire. And, wordlessly, mindlessly, she was signalling that she felt the same.

That was all he needed to know.

CHAPTER 18

Sunday afternoon

Amazingly the rain had held off and Alison felt as though the air was full of the promise of spring. Nature had taken a palette of pale gold, soft blues and the sharp green of new life.

As they walked through the old orchard, which was now no more than patches of rough grass between a tangle of ancient trees, she smiled at Greg. She thought about how easily he had fitted in today, and she savoured the moment when he had arrived at the Hall that morning – and the expression on her friends' faces – and the frantic eye signals!

'They liked you,' she said.

Sophie, Carol and Francine had left after lunch and Alison and Greg were out walking, with Matthew and Oliver leading the way at a run. 'Don't get too far ahead,' Alison called, and Matthew turned and waved.

'And I liked your friends,' Greg said. 'They weren't a bit – well – you know – snobbish. Normally, I couldn't care less what people think about me. I'm secure enough in my own achievements to know that that kind of behaviour doesn't matter. But, your friends – that's different – they must be important to you.'

'Of course they are. But why should they be snobbish? Like me, they come from quite ordinary backgrounds.'

'What you call an ordinary background is worlds away from the way I was brought up.'

'That was hardly your fault.'

'You can have no idea what it was like. The least damning thing I can say about my home was that it was far from respectable.'

'Greg,' Alison stopped and placed a hand on his arm, 'you don't have to tell me – not if it gives you pain. You see, I don't care. I can see the man that you've grown into and that's good enough for me. Perhaps too good . . .'

'Never.'

Alison looked up into his face searchingly. 'And, Greg, I wouldn't have friends who thought that kind of thing was important, would I?'

'No, of course you wouldn't.' He took her hand and they walked on together.

'But what about your sister-in-law?' he asked. 'You didn't really finish explaining yesterday, did you? I mean we – sort of got side-tracked.'

'We certainly did. By the time I came up for air I think I'd forgotten what day it was!' Alison laughed. 'But it's quite simple. Daphne told me that if I persisted in seeing you, she would get Nigel to scuttle the deal – the sale of the land. He could do that if he wished, because he's co-executor of Paul's will.'

'I see.' Greg looked grave. 'This deal is vital to you, isn't it? It would bring in the money needed to keep the house afloat – so to speak!'

'That's right – and you may have chosen the right metaphor! Sometimes, when the wind and the rain are driving hard against the house, I can hear the timbers creaking as if it were an old galleon about to be swept into dangerous waters!'

'And you want to save the house for Matthew – for Paul's son?'

'Of course. That's why I want to go ahead with your

plan – that's definite. And, as far as my personal life is concerned, I have no intention of bowing to Daphne's ridiculous class snobbery.'

They slowed down as the terrain became rougher. The boys were whooping and dodging in and out between the gnarled old trees as though their stores of energy were limitless. Greg caught at her other hand and turned her round to face him.

'You could go to court, you know. My offer is a very good one – and perfectly above board – I'm sure your decision would be upheld.'

'It's all right, we don't have to. When I phoned you yesterday morning and asked you to meet me, I also made a call to the Remingtons'. Daphne answered the phone herself, unfortunately, but when I asked to speak to Nigel, she could hardly refuse.'

'And?'

'I felt like the class sneak, but I told him exactly what had been going on. I was ready to be very angry, but he took the wind out of my sails completely when he said that I was to ignore Daphne's preoccupation with the superiority of the Cavendish family and do as I pleased.

'As far as he was concerned, he'd investigated you thoroughly and, not only was he enthusiastic about your plans but, if what Daphne was hinting at was true, "fresh blood" was always welcome. That's what he said.'

'Good old Nigel.'

'Good old Nigel, indeed. You know, I've always thought of him as something of a snob too, but he also told me yesterday that, in spite of coming from an old family himself, there was no money left and he's had to make his way in the real world – and that he respects you.'

'Really?'

'Yes, you're successful because of your own efforts and furthermore, you might actually be brilliant.'

'He said that? I think I like this man – if he ever needs a job, just let me know!'

'Then Daphne would never forgive me.'

'Why ever not?'

'You'd be her husband's boss. She'd never be able to act superior to me again.'

'In that case I'll definitely give him a job. So, be honest, was that charade on the village green really necessary? Couldn't you simply have ignored Daphne and got on with your life regardless?'

'Of course I could but – oh, I don't know – perhaps it was having my old friends here. Sophie told me that things had to change and they were all urging me to make a stand – so I did. I think the devil must have got into me, but I just wanted to show Daphne that the worm had turned. I thought I'd make a gesture. When I set out I had no idea that the gesture would be quite so spectacular!'

Greg laughed as he drew her into his arms and they stood for a moment simply savouring the feeling of contentment that finding each other had brought them. They pulled away when they heard the boys' voices coming nearer again along the old paths.

'I think we'd better go back to the house now,' Alison said. 'Miss Robertson and Ruth will have the tea ready.'

Matthew made no protest and he led the way back across land that had belonged to his family for generations. Land that his mother would soon be signing away. But she was easy in her mind about it; she knew that Paul would have approved.

'Thanks for inviting me today,' Greg said.

'Even if I hadn't wanted to, Matthew insisted. You've made quite a hit with the boys – and Miss Robertson and Ruth, too.'

'It was a great idea having us all for lunch – but all that work! Why did you do it?'

'My freezer is well-stocked and my friends all helped. I thought it wouldn't be much fun for Matthew, spending the day with all those females, so that's why I invited Oliver. And, as you three seem to have become inseparable over the model motor racing track, I couldn't leave you out.'

'Thanks!'

'And then, I thought, why not make a party of it and have Ruth and Miss Robertson and her brother, too? The vicar seemed to enjoy himself, didn't he?'

'Yes, he did. Pity he had to hurry away so soon, to prepare his sermon for evensong.'

'Miss Robertson said that wasn't the whole truth and that he'd probably be having a nice long snooze in an old armchair in his study. He does that every week but she goes along with the pretence that he's slaving over his sermon!'

'I like Miss Robertson, very much,' Greg said.

'Well, she's certainly a fan of yours. But our little party went well, didn't it? If only I could have persuaded my mother-in-law to join us in the dining-room instead of sitting all alone upstairs with her tray.'

They had reached the archway that led into the stable block at the back of the house; Matthew and Oliver were already running across the cobbled yard towards the back door.

'I feel sorry for Mrs Cavendish, you know,' Greg said.

'You do? After all the attempts she made to thwart you!'

'I've come across a lot of people like her during the course of my work. They can't accept that times have changed and they feel almost ashamed that they've got to make compromises in order to salvage what they can of their property. And, in her case, when you started showing signs of independence, she must have been worried that she was going to lose her home.'

'Oh, never! I would never turn the poor old thing out, whatever happens – I mean, Greg, you know that, don't you?'

'That's fine by me, Alison. Whatever happens.'

By the time they entered the kitchen, Matthew and Oliver were already being chivvied by Ruth into washing their hands before tea. The kitchen table was set up with salad, hardboiled eggs, cheeses, a bowl of fruit and two enormous cakes, one of them covered with chocolate frosting and the other with orange.

'Where did those cakes come from, Ruth?' Alison asked.

'My mum sent my dad up with them while you were out. She knows how the boys enjoy her home-baking.'

'Well, that's very kind of her, but where's Miss Robertson – and why is the table set for seven people?'

'Oh, your mother-in-law is coming down to join us. Miss Robertson persuaded her when she took her a cup of tea. She's just gone up to get her now.'

London – later

Francine was surprised to find how cold it was when she got back to London. The streets were wet from recent rain and pedestrians hurried by quickly, huddled up in warm clothes. The sun had shone for the whole weekend in Norfolk – perhaps that was an omen offering hope for all of them and the choices they had made, she thought. But now, the clouds lowering above her beloved city was a dismal, mottled grey. Ah, well, she thought, there's no accounting for the ever-changing British weather.

But nothing could spoil the view from her apartment – night or day, rain or shine, it was still fabulous. Francine dumped her bags, went into the kitchen to make herself a cup of coffee and then sat by the living-room window just gazing out and savouring the feeling of being home. In her own space.

All on my own.

But that's the way I want it, isn't it?

Impatiently she suppressed the doubts that had been waiting for this peaceful moment before pushing their way into her mind. She swivelled round and reached across to the coffee table for the TV remote control, then flicked through the channels until she found a twenty-four-hour news station. Normally she was intensely interested in news and current affairs, but this evening she found it boring.

Why? Why can't I concentrate?

She pressed the mute button and settled for a flickering screen in the background. Something interesting might come up, she thought, then I can turn the sound up again. She smiled when she realized how her behaviour had been influenced by Peter. He could never bring himself to turn the television off completely, even in the bedroom . . .

Peter . . .

Francine stared moodily at the talking heads on the screen without really seeing them. For the first time since she had started her affair with Peter, all those years ago, she had been seriously attracted to someone else. Thank goodness she had come to her senses in time and left the cottage on the moors without seeing Marcus again. Furthermore, thank goodness she had gone seeking Sophie and ended up being able to talk to all of her three old friends. That had probably saved her from going down a very dangerous path!

Just look where marriage and commitment had got Alison. It had all started out so wonderfully; Paul had been experienced, clever and handsome and had seemed to offer so much. It didn't matter that the historic family home was in a sorry state; the huge fees he had been earning as a world class photographer were all that was needed to keep things going. And then the fatal accident had changed everything overnight.

Paul was a lot older than Alison, but she had never expected to be widowed so soon. Poor Alison. Of course she had her son – and Matthew was just great. But she also had a decrepit estate to care for and her ghastly in-laws to cope with. And no matter that she seemed to have found someone else, someone who, in his own way, was just as exciting as Paul had been, Alison was stuck with a whole load of family responsibilities for the rest of her life. And Greg Leighton would want children of his own, wouldn't he?

Do I want children?

Carol did. She hadn't mentioned children this week-end but they had all known that Carol had wanted to start a family as soon as Alan was making enough money to allow her to give up work.

Why on earth did Carol want to give up working?

She had a first class brain and yet she'd settled for a series of temporary jobs – where they seemed to treat her like slave labour – in order to fit in with Alan's career. She was the one who ought to have been planning a career path, not that close cousin to the Neanderthals, Alan Kennedy!

I could never settle for a life like that!

But was Carol going to settle for it after all? She had let them all believe that she was going to go back and do her best to save her marriage to Alan, and yet Francine hadn't missed that moment of uncertainty when they were sitting by the fire in the library on the Friday. And she thought Sophie had tuned in to it too. Could their old friend Carol be about to surprise them all by doing something really reckless?

The sad thing was that she suspected that the some-thing reckless would involve another man . . .

No, Alison and Carol were not good advertisements for married life. I'm better off the way I am, Francine thought. Peter never makes impossible demands on me, whereas a man like Marcus Holbrook . . .

She sipped her coffee and stared moodily out of the window at the striking city skyline and, immediately, a different landscape rolled itself across her inner vision. Wild moors rising up towards immense, unpredictable skies . . . as unpredictable as the man living alone in his cottage at Moor Top . . .

Angrily Francine tried to blot out the unwelcome images, tried to forget the powerful physical attraction that had caught her unawares. *And it wasn't just physical attraction, was it? Right from the start there was no real feeling that we were strangers . . . we'd never met before and yet there, in that cottage, there were moments when we didn't seem to need words – we were as attuned to each other as a long-married couple . . .*

Stop it!

I'll work on my programme ideas, she thought. I'm determined to get an arts programme off the ground and I'd still like to involve Peter if possible. We've been a good team over the years. If I can get a good presentation together, I might be able to convince him.

She reckoned that she'd made enough preliminary notes so she picked up her briefcase and went through to the small bedroom that she'd converted into a study. The moment she switched on her computer she had a vision of another study, another computer screen, the neat piles of manuscript pages and the book-lined walls . . .

Go away! she howled.

Leave me in peace to get on with the life I love!

Love . . . what exactly is love . . . ?

Oh, for goodness' sake!

She was annoyed with herself. She didn't think anyone on earth could really answer that question – except, perhaps, Sophie. Francine smiled. Sophie was a centre of calm in a troubled world. We used to tease her about waiting for Mr Right – or at least I did. Was I really as smart-alecky as that? But she never seemed to mind . . .

And now, she has found Mr Right and, if anyone can make a success of marriage, Sophie can . . .

Thinking, with pleasure, that the next time they would all meet up again would be at Sophie's wedding, Francine managed, at last, to concentrate on her presentation and she worked long into the night.

The West Country – Sunday evening

Somewhere along the M5, after she had left Gloucester behind, a mist rolled in from the Bristol Channel and Carol had to slow down dramatically. Cocooned in her car by a moist grey blanket which deadened all sound from the world beyond, she imagined that she could have been the only person left alive after some strange alien invasion. Her eyes strained ahead towards the pinpoints of red which were the rear lights of the car in front. She realized that she needed a break.

She pulled into a service station, and so strong had been her sense of isolation that she was almost surprised to see other people strolling about, laughing and talking quite normally. She treated herself to a pot of coffee and a slice of Black Forest gateau and savoured the light, bright warmth and comfort of the place – and the total anonymity.

She looked around at the other tables in the restaurant and indulged her habit of speculating idly about the lives and the occupations of the people sitting there. There was such a variety of people, business travellers, holiday-makers, students both foreign and home-grown, and they had all been brought together by the basic human need for rest, food and comfort.

She was always surprised in these places to see how many small children seemed to travel the length and breadth of the motorways with youngish, tired-looking parents. And, quite separate from these family groups, there were more than a few elderly couples. Where could they all be going to or coming from? Did young couples live so far from their parents these days that weekends for one group or another had become a time to travel hundreds of miles in order to keep in touch?

She realized that she had sat there longer than she intended and pushed herself up from the table wearily. By the time she emerged into the outside world again, the mist had vanished as quickly and mysteriously as it had arrived. Driving was easier and yet she had no urge to pick up speed and make up for lost time. Why should she? What exactly did she have to hurry home to?

Not much later, Carol locked her car and then paused. She looked at the house, her eyes travelling to the upstairs windows, cold and empty-looking, and down to the light shining through the obscure glass panel set at the top of the front door. She had left that light on herself. The house looked empty. It didn't look as though anyone had been here, did it?

She smiled at her own foolishness as she walked up the garden path. How on earth could you tell simply by looking at a house whether anyone had visited it? She hadn't really expected Alan to come home, had she? Miserably she recalled that when Alan had phoned her at work on Friday, he had made no mention of when he might see her again.

And she hadn't asked him . . .

He had told her that his mother might need some help for a day or two and that his father and he would look after her. But what about his job? Was Alan actually going to take some time off? Unheard of! Or could he be intending to drive to Avonmouth from Bournemouth each day? That would take him more than two hours each way. He'd have to leave at the crack of dawn if not before, put in a long hard day slaving over the launch of his new product and then drive all the way back – poor Alan.

Wait a minute – why am I worrying about him? Why on earth should I care about him being overworked and tired when he's never stopped to consider what I have to do! She found herself brushing away tears of self-pity as she stepped into the hall and closed the door behind her.

She dropped her overnight case and stared at the phone on the hall table. Had Alan tried to call her while she'd been away? How she wished they had stretched their budget to include an answering machine. But there was one way of finding out if someone had called, she remembered, even if you could only discover who the last caller had been.

She punched 1471 on to the number pad and was excited to hear the recorded voice begin to relay a message. But it was a phone number that she didn't recognize at all, probably a wrong number, she thought; she replaced the receiver, ignoring the option to press 3 and return the call.

The kitchen was cold and unwelcoming. A lustreless skin had formed over the surface of the water in the pan she'd left soaking in the sink and it smelled stale and greasy. She thought of Alison's warm and welcoming kitchen, redolent of home baking, and before even making herself a hot drink she set to to scour the pan in a fury of self-loathing.

It didn't take long. The kitchen itself wasn't too bad; after all, she'd cleaned it up only the other day. The day she had wanted to prepare a special meal for Alan . . . Oh, why had everything gone so wrong?

Her friends had been sympathetic but they all seemed to think that it was up to her to put things right. Even Sophie. *Life's not fair*, Alison had said, and Sophie had agreed. She had expected more of her old friends than that. So she'd pretended to agree with them and made some kind of vague promise that she would come home and sort things out.

But did she really want to?

On the second night at Westbrook Hall, the Saturday, she had deliberately avoided talking about her own problems. She had listened with real sympathy when Alison had listed all the things that needed doing to the house and urged her to ignore the Cavendish family and use her own judgement. She had been genuinely interested in Francine's plans for a new series of programmes and she had joined with the others in making suggestions.

Sophie had been strangely shy when they asked her about Alistair but that was just Sophie, she supposed. Even when they were all a lot younger, she had never been quite so forthcoming as the rest of them. Or was it that we didn't allow her to be? Carol suddenly wondered. Perhaps we were all to taken up with our own lives – the young are unintentionally selfish – and we just took advantage of Sophie . . .

Anyway, last night, they had managed to win from her the information that her fiancé was about nine years older than she was, that he had not been married before, and that he was a doctor working in A&E. Also that he was tall and broad and handsome in a red-haired Scottish way.

His parents lived in Glasgow, his father being an eminent professor of medicine, and he had three older sisters, all doctors, whom Sophie hadn't met yet. In fact she wouldn't meet any of them until her wedding day. Poor girl! The prospect of meeting three clever Scotswomen, who no doubt adored their younger brother, was daunting. That was probably what was making Sophie just the slightest bit edgy.

Carol didn't think that anyone had noticed that she never mentioned her problems with Alan again and, in view of all the wedding talk, she'd had no intention of mentioning Luke Travers . . .

She made herself a cup of hot chocolate and carried it through to the sitting-room. She ignored the wine stain that she had been unable to remove from the carpet and sank on to the sofa.

So this is it, she thought. If Alan never comes home again, I'll be doing this every night. I'll come home, prepare a meal for one, and then read or watch television by myself for the rest of the evening until I go to bed.

But at least I'll be able to watch the kind of television programmes that I like instead of always giving in to Alan!

Where had that thought come from? Carol actually smiled. No – perhaps the single life would have its compensations! She fished the remote control out from its usual hiding place down the side of the sofa cushions and flicked through the channels. She found a film, just starting, that starred both David Duchovny *and* Brad Pitt and curled her feet up with a sigh of contentment.

It was only when she had to acknowledge that neither David nor Brad was making much impression on her that she realized that there was something wrong. That something had been niggling away at the back of her mind ever since she walked up the front path.

And then she remembered. She had wondered – hoped? – that Alan might be here waiting for her. But it had also crossed her mind that he might have been and gone again. She stood up and almost fell straight back down. Her heart was racing and a tight band had clamped around her forehead.

I got up too quickly, she thought, and she waited until her breathing steadied before she left the room and went upstairs. It didn't take long. The bedroom and the spare room looked exactly as they had the other night when Alan had first walked out. Nothing else had been removed. So the break – if it was a break – wasn't final yet.

But as she started to go downstairs again, she realized that she hadn't learned anything very significant after all. Alan's mother was ill. He might not want to leave her and drive all the way home to clear his things out right at this moment. She paused and gripped the stair-rail. Or he might even be coming home tonight . . .

There was no way of knowing she realized unless one of them got in touch with the other. Had he been expecting her to call over the weekend and ask how his mother was? He had made it clear enough that she wouldn't be welcome in person but he might have expected a call?

When she was halfway down the stairs the phone started ringing and she had to force to stay calm and not trip and fall the rest of the way. Nevertheless she was breathless when she picked up the receiver.

'Alan?' she said.

There was a pause.

'No – it's Luke here. I've been calling all weekend but you must have been away.'

'Yes . . . yes . . . I'm sorry . . .'

'There's no need to be sorry. Travers' Transport doesn't own you!' Luke laughed. 'But anyway, I'm glad I've caught you now. I've got something to tell you that can't wait until tomorrow.'

Lancashire

Laura was reading one of her library books when Sophie arrived home. She sat by the fire within the circle of light cast by the standard lamp and looked up and smiled. 'Are you hungry, dear?' she asked.

Her mother's kindly face was so reassuring that Sophie felt tears pricking at the back of her eyes. Tears of gratitude for the safe haven that Laura had always provided. 'I knew that would be the first question you asked,' she said, 'and, yes, as a matter of fact I am hungry.'

'Then, sit down and relax. I've got some home-made soup and it won't take long to heat up.'

Her mother placed her book and her reading spectacles on a small table and got up and went into the kitchen. Sophie had only broken her journey once on the drive north and now she gave herself up to the comfort of being fussed over and pampered by her mother.

She wouldn't be able to enjoy this luxury much longer – delicious meals ready and waiting whenever she arrived home. Very soon, she would be like Carol, juggling home and career. But Carol seemed to have opted for waiting hand and foot on her husband – mother's one-and-only darling, Alan Kennedy.

But thank goodness that Alistair had a very different attitude from Alan's. He was capable and competent and he loved experimenting in the kitchen. His three older sisters might be very fond of their baby brother but apparently they had never gone along with the idea that boys were in any way superior. He had not been fussed and indulged just because he was the only male child in the family.

Paul Cavendish had been the only son also but, thankfully for Alison, his character had obviously been strong enough to resist his mother's and his sister's valiant attempts to spoil him. Poor Paul . . . poor Alison . . . What huge responsibilities he'd left her with, Sophie thought. But at least having more money would ease the situation and it seemed that, if the relationship with Greg Leighton blossomed into marriage, money might never be a problem again.

And as for Francine – she'd had a shock, it seemed. The impact that Marcus Holbrook had made on her had been great enough to send her scurrying into the arms of her old friends. And, yet, almost at once she seemed to have made her mind up to turn her back on whatever challenge he might offer and continue with the present state of affairs. Earlier today she had seemed happy to be going back to the life she had made for herself in London. Sophie wondered whether it was the right decision . . .

'Did you enjoy your weekend with your old friends, dear?' Laura hovered over her with a tray.

'Mm, I did, but it wasn't quite what I expected.'

'What do you mean?' Laura settled the tray on Sophie's knee and resumed her place in the armchair at the opposite side of the hearth.

'I'm not sure.' Sophie paused while she took a sip of the soup. 'You know it's ages since we've all been together so I was expecting things to have changed –'

'Of course.'

'And yet they haven't really . . .' She looked up and caught her mother's puzzled look. 'I mean as soon as we all got together again it was as if the years fell away and we were talking and laughing and exchanging confidences just like the old days.'

'But that's good, isn't it?'

Sophie sighed. 'Yes, Mum, it's good and I suppose it's inevitable. I mean if we had all stayed close together – living near each other, I mean – we would have seen what was happening in each other's lives and accepted the changes that experience brings and had different perceptions of each other – that sounds jumbled. Do you know what I mean?'

'Yes, I think I do, dear. Because you only see each other occasionally, you all shed the changes the years have brought to your characters and revert to the kind of young women that you were when you first met.'

'Mum!' Sophie looked at her mother in awe. 'That was very well put. Are you sure it's flower arranging classes that you've been going to and not psychology!'

'But at least you were able to tell them about your wedding?'

'Of course – and they were all delighted.'

'So they should be. Now, if you've finished that soup, I'll go and make you a cup of tea and a slice of chocolate cake.'

'No cake – do you want me to have to order a larger size wedding dress!'

'Just a small bit, then.'

While Laura was in the kitchen Sophie lay back in her chair and closed her eyes. What had she really been expecting from this weekend? She had been able to tell her friends about the wedding but, if that had been her sole intention, she could simply have sent them invitations. No, she had wanted something more. She had wanted to be able to confide her doubts to them and ask for their advice.

But she hadn't been able to. It wasn't because they wouldn't have listened sympathetically and genuinely tried to come up with answers. It was just their assumption that she, Sophie, never had any doubts or problems of her own. They had greeted her announcement with such obvious joy that the moment she had been looking for had got lost in all their exuberant congratulations.

Even on that first night at Westbrook Hall she had realized that her old friends' view of her would never change. It seemed that, to them, Sophie Blake would always be practical, sensible and well-balanced. They would probably have been both startled and embarrassed if she had told them how worried she was. She'd decided to let them keep that picture of her. They had enough problems of their own.

CHAPTER 19

Monday morning

'Do you feel like making a run for it?'

Maggie Lomax's cheerful face appeared over the stack of exercise books she was carrying. The morning session was over and the corridor seethed with pupils and teachers making their way to the school dining-room.

Sophie laughed at Maggie's mock-frantic expression. 'You mean escape from this grim educational institution and never come back?'

'I wish! But no, I mean why don't we abandon our wholesome salad sandwiches and go round the corner to Joe's café and treat ourselves to double egg and chips?'

'Why not?' Sophie agreed. 'And why don't we go the whole way and finish off with steamed ginger pudding with treacle sauce and custard!'

'You're on! Let me just dump these books in my locker.'

'I'll get our coats.'

Sophie wasn't surprised that they got strange looks from some of the older pupils as they dashed across the school-yard, grinning like madwomen in a melodrama. Not all the high school students stayed for lunch, and many of them were making their way to the nearby high street to spend their dinner money on cans of pop, chips and various snacks.

'Watch out!' Sophie called suddenly, and a group of smaller girls dodged out of their way quickly, but Carl hadn't heard her warning cry. Carl Chadwick was a tall, sallow seventeen-year-old who, it was rumoured, spent most of his out-of-school life in his bedroom, sitting in front of his computer.

Just a moment ago he had been in some other world – in cyberspace, Sophie thought – and hadn't seen or heard them coming. He was nearly bowled over by Maggie but he recovered himself and stepped back, blinking.

'S-sorry, Carl,' Maggie gulped. Her face was flushed and her hair was hanging forward untidily.

Carl frowned, stared down into her face for a moment and then said, 'That's all right, Mrs Lomax, but if I were you, I'd try to chill out a little. I mean, I know teaching is a stressful job, but try to hang on to the fact that you're doing very well – yes,' he began to nod wisely, 'very well indeed.'

'Oh. Thank you, Carl.'

Maggie was staring at the boy bog-eyed, as her own daughters would have said, and Sophie saw a suspicious red creeping up her neck and about to invade her face.

'Thank you, Carl.' Sophie stepped forward. 'I'm sure Mrs Lomax appreciates your opinion of her teaching abilities. Now, I think I'll take her for a cup of tea or something . . .' She took hold of Maggie's arms and began to draw her away.

Carl turned his head and regarded Sophie gravely. 'Good thinking, Miss Blake,' he said, and then his eyes blanked over. He had retreated to the world he had been inhabiting before the incident occurred. He began to drift away in the direction of the science block.

'Walk slowly,' Sophie commanded Maggie. 'And hush!' she added when she heard a noise like a suppressed explosion coming from her friend's throat.

As soon as they were outside the school gates they took

310

to their heels and almost ran the rest of the way to Joe's.

'Don't you just *love* them?' Maggie asked breathlessly. 'It's pupils like Carl Chadwick who make teaching worthwhile!'

'Well, I'm glad there aren't too many exactly like Carl,' Sophie said. 'I mean, I sometimes think that there's not one teacher in the school who's even half as intelligent as he is. He's absorbed everything we have to teach him and is only marking time.'

'I know – but he's very understanding of us lesser mortals, isn't he?' Maggie grinned. 'Chill out indeed!'

The café was basic but clean, and if the menu consisted mainly of anything that could be fried, then that suited them today. They chose a table well away from the window – they didn't particularly want to be observed by passing pupils or other teachers, for that matter – and ordered a pot of tea while they waited.

Sophie watched Maggie pour the tea and she said thoughtfully, 'Of course it isn't pupils like Carl that we have to worry about, is it? Not in this school.'

Maggie handed Sophie one of the cups and spooned sugar into her own. 'No, and it's getting worse. Sometimes I wonder whether we're teachers or gaolers. Take my advice, Sophie, if you leave teaching to start a family, don't come back!'

'But I'd miss it.'

'Really? Can you honestly say that you'd miss working your socks off to try and stuff some education into the likes of Cheryl Jackson?'

'Maggie! That's not like you! And think of all the others – quite apart from natural geniuses like Carl, think of girls like Julie Hunter – don't they deserve as decent an education as we can give them?'

'Of course they do – and I'm sorry that I spoke like that. You can put it down to the approach of an interesting time of my life.'

'Oh, no, Maggie – not yet, surely?'

'Yes, hot flushes and all! But that's enough of my miseries – here comes the egg and chips – pass the ketchup, will you?'

For a while they were quiet as they enjoyed their meal and, when they'd finished, they decided to forgo the steamed ginger pudding and have a fresh pot of tea.

'So did you enjoy your weekend in Norfolk with your old friends?' Maggie said at last.

'You knew about that?'

'Mm.' Maggie sipped her tea. 'I phoned you on Saturday – my girl monsters wanted you to come and see the dress fittings – and Laura told me where you'd gone.'

Sophie couldn't meet her friend's eyes. 'I'm sorry, Maggie.'

'Whatever for?'

'Oh – I don't know – for not telling you.'

'But why should you? You didn't think I'd be jealous because you were going to spend a weekend with your university friends, did you? I mean, come on, Sophie we're not schoolkids!'

'No, it's not that . . .'

Sophie felt awkward; she didn't know quite what to say. She hadn't mentioned to Maggie that she was going away. She'd had every intention of confiding the fears that were haunting her to Alison, Carol and Francine rather than to Maggie – in spite of the fact that just last week Maggie had actually asked her what was worrying her. She had fobbed her off with only half of it – and the lesser half, at that.

Suddenly she made up her mind. 'How much time have we got?'

Maggie glanced at her watch. 'Another half-hour before the afternoon session starts. Now what's so serious?'

312

'I was going to tell my old friends this but – for various reasons – I found I couldn't. And now, I feel guilty about asking your advice when –'

'For goodness' sake stop agonizing and get on with it! What's worrying you?'

'This is going to sound silly, but I'm not sure what Alistair's feelings towards me are . . .'

'You must be joking! He asked you to marry him, didn't he?'

'Yes – but why did he ask me?'

'Because he loves you, presumably.' Sophie didn't answer immediately and she watched Maggie's indulgent smile waver. 'I mean . . . he does love you, doesn't he?'

'I don't know.'

She stared at Maggie helplessly. She felt black panic rising up inside her. She was aware that she was shaking slightly. Until now, she'd managed to keep her fears just about under control but, now that she'd voiced them to someone else, she knew that she would have to have some kind of answer. If she didn't have an answer, she couldn't . . . she wouldn't be able to . . . A small sob escaped her.

'Sophie –' Maggie reached across the table and took her hand '– what exactly are you telling me? Is it that you have some reason not to trust him? Not to believe what he tells you?'

'I would trust Alistair with my life. And I don't think he knows how to tell a lie.'

Maggie's eyes widened and at the same time her lips lifted in a faint smile. 'I think I get it,' she said. 'Alistair is the strong, silent type. He doesn't know how to put his feelings into words. The prize oaf has never actually said the words, "I love you," is that it?'

'That's it.'

'But Sophie, my sweet, a lot of men are like that – and – wait a moment – have you ever told him how you feel?'

313

'Yes, many times.'

Sophie blushed when she remembered the times she was talking about; when she and Alistair had made love and he had carried her into a world she had only previously dreamed of; a world beyond place . . . a world beyond time . . . She realized that her eyes were glittering with unshed tears.

'Here – you need this.'

Maggie took one of the folded paper napkins from the fluted glass sundae dish in the middle of the table and handed it to her. Sophie opened it out and dabbed at her eyes.

'Look, love,' Maggie said, 'I'm sure it's all right. And I can't understand why you haven't just come out with it and asked him.'

'I can't do that.'

'Why ever not? Oh, I know that you're a lot more modest and reserved than I am, but there must have been moments when you could have snuggled up to his manly chest, placed a hand over his strongly beating heart, looked up into his eyes and murmured something like, "Do you love me, darling?" '

Sophie found herself laughing, even though it hurt. 'Wonderful – you should be writing romantic novels. But, you're right, there have been times when I could have said something like that.'

'So?'

'So, I couldn't do it – I'm too scared.'

Maggie frowned. 'You've lost me. Why should you be scared to ask the man you love such an important question.'

'Because I do love him and because it is important. Maggie – what on earth would I do if he said no?'

Maggie sat back in her chair and looked at Sophie with wide, troubled eyes. Any other woman might have told her she was being silly, Sophie thought, or hysterical even. Or tried to assure her that she was suffering from pre-wedding nerves. But Maggie, bless her, took her seriously.

After a moment she asked, 'Is he likely to say no?'

'Maggie, I don't know.'

'So we're back to the question of why did he ask you to marry him. You must have some opinion about that.'

'I have. You know I told you the other night that it came as a bit of a surprise that – the subject hadn't even come up until he was appointed to this new post in Glasgow?'

'Yes, I did think that was a bit strange. But, then, I thought that he must suddenly have realized that he loved you and couldn't do without you.'

'That's what I thought – that the realization that we would be parted had jolted him into acknowledging his feelings. But if that's true, why didn't he say something like – like –?'

' "Sophie, ma' wee bonnie lass, the prospect of leaving you has made me realize how very much I love you and that I cannae live without you. Will you do me the honour of becoming Mrs Alistair McGregor?"!'

'Shut up, Maggie! But, leaving aside your pathetic attempt at a Scottish accent – yes – why didn't he say something like that?'

'Because he's a man – even worse, because he's a Scotsman! But what exactly did he say?'

'Nothing very memorable. He just went on about how well we get on together, about having the same sense of humour, enjoying the same kind of things. He thought it might be sensible to get married before he went away.'

'*Sensible*! He actually said *sensible*? For goodness' sake, why didn't you whack him with his stethoscope!'

'I should have done.' Sophie's laughter was very close to tears. 'But I was so surprised – and overcome – and happy – I just said yes.'

'Well, so long as you didn't actually add the word

315

please! Oh, Sophie, my friend, you're not very experienced in the ways of the world, are you?'

'You know I'm not.'

'So what would happen if you asked him now, and if he said something like, "What's love got to do with anything? Sophie, my dear, you are a nice, hardworking, practical little woman, and a doctor nearing forty needs a wife." '

Sophie stared at her. Maggie was playacting again but her words were very close to expressing her worst fears.

'So, what would you do?' Maggie prompted.

'I don't know.'

Her friend sighed. 'Well, I don't know what I can say to help, but I promise I'll think about it. And, meanwhile, I'm afraid it's time we got back to school.'

When they stepped out of the warm café, the cold air hit them and they linked arms and walked close to each other for comfort. They kept their heads down as they walked into the wind but they didn't hurry. Neither did they speak. Sophie was glad she had confided in Maggie, but she realized that she was no further forward. After all, how would even her closest friend be able to tell her whether Alistair really loved her?

'Is that all right, madam?'

The young hairdresser held the mirror behind Carol and angled it so that she could see what the back of her new hairstyle looked like.

'It's lovely – thank you.'

The salon was busy and, for a while, Carol had surrendered herself to the luxury of having someone else wash her hair, and cut and style it. All around other busy women were spending their lunch hour, it seemed in a ritual of relaxation, pampering and gossip. Carol, never having been here before – it was the salon that Stacey and her mother patronized – had preferred to

316

remain silent and let the girl, Lisa according to her name badge, get on with it.

Now, as Lisa replaced the hairdryer in its holder on the wall and tidied away the scissors and combs, Carol stared at her reflection in the large mirror ahead of her. It wasn't really a new style, of course. She had simply asked the girl to tidy up the existing one, but she had done a marvellous job. All the split ends and stray wisps had gone and the result was a shining fall of hair that fell to about shoulder-length and framed her face flatteringly.

She suddenly recalled something Francine had told her years ago. The cut is everything, she had said. All that most women need is to find a hairdresser who understands that. Well, this young woman, who had been the only person the salon could offer when Stacey had phoned from work earlier, had certainly understood that. Francine would approve. Carol smiled.

Lisa stood behind her and addressed her reflection. 'Going somewhere special tonight?'

Carol stood up and faced her. 'Why do you ask?'

'It was the way you smiled just now.' Lisa helped her out of the protective overall. 'You looked as though you were looking forward to something nice.'

'Oh, no –' Carol was flustered. 'I was just pleased with my hair. And tonight – well, that's just a business trip really –'

She stopped when she realized that she didn't have to explain anything. The girl was only being polite; she wouldn't be a bit interested in the fact that Carol was going away for a night with Luke Travers.

She followed the Lisa to the area where the coats were hanging. The girl found her jacket without comment and then helped her into it. Carol looked at her keenly; her young face was impassive. Her smooth features didn't betray whether she believed Carol or not. Or even if she cared.

317

Why should she? Carol thought. It's my own uneasy conscience that's making too much of this . . .

Lisa led the way to the reception desk where Carol paid the bill. She left a generous tip in the staff box provided, smiled her thanks once more and escaped into the cold April air. She kept her head down and tried to dodge a blustery breeze as she ran for the car park.

Once inside her car she glanced up anxiously into the rear-view mirror to see what damage the wind had done. Very little, she saw with relief. Her shining tresses had fallen naturally back into place around her face, which was now glowing with the effort of running in the wind. Or am I still blushing because of what the hairdresser girl might have been thinking? Abruptly, she pulled herself together and turned the key in the ignition.

Back at Travers' Transport, she went straight along the corridor to her own office and closed the door behind her. But she had just sat down at her desk when Stacey knocked and entered. 'My, you look nice,' she said.

'Thank you.'

'Sneaking along past my door like that, I thought it must have been a disaster – they'd given you a punk style or something and you were too embarrassed to show me.'

'Do you mean there was a chance that they might? Thanks for telling me now!'

Stacey smiled. 'No, I knew you'd be all right with Lisa, otherwise I wouldn't have made the appointment for you. Now, you've missed your lunch so I got you an egg mayonnaise sandwich and I'll make you a cup of tea. Or would you like coffee?'

'Tea, please, Stacey,' Carol said. She knew it was pointless to argue.

When Stacey left the room, Carol opened her briefcase and endeavoured to make sure that she had all the paperwork that she would need for later. But she found it hard to concentrate. She realized that she had riffled

318

through the papers at least twice without really seeing what they were, so she lifted them all out and dumped them on her desk.

She was sitting staring at them perplexedly when Stacey returned with a tray. The girl glanced at her and put the tray down on top of a filing cabinet. 'Here, let me,' she said. 'Have you got a checklist?'

Carol watched gratefully while Stacey sorted the papers into order and put them back in the briefcase. 'There,' she said, 'according to your list, that's all you need, including the demonstration computer disk, by the way.' She placed the briefcase next to Carol's overnight case on the floor at the side of the filing cabinet. 'Now forget about tonight and the trip for a while and have your lunch.'

She pulled the desk extension out from under Carol's desk and placed the tray on it. 'Mustn't put this stuff too near your precious computer,' she said and grinned. 'By the way, I hope you don't mind but I saved my sandwich to eat with you.'

For once in her life Carol found that she wasn't enjoying her food. She nibbled at her sandwich and sipped her tea alternately, until Stacey noticed her lack of enthusiasm and gave her a sharp glance. 'What's the matter? Don't you think you'll be able to handle it?'

Carol drew her breath in. 'What exactly do you mean?'

Stacey put down her own sandwich and looked as though she was thinking long and hard. Then she said, 'I know that you'll be on top of the business side of things. Mr Travers is taking you along to the seminar as the computer expert and –'

'But I'm not an expert –'

'You know what I mean. You did an Information Technology course as well as your degree, didn't you? And, anyway, you're the one who actually uses the computer here, every day. No, you won't let him down

319

on that aspect of things.'

'Stacey, if I give him the wrong advice, he could waste thousands of pounds on a system that's not suited to his needs – the firm's needs,' she added quickly and hoped that Stacey hadn't noticed her Freudian slip.

If she had, she let it pass without comment. 'That won't happen. You know exactly what's wanted. No, you can't be nervous about the business side of the conference so it must be the personal aspect.'

'Really.'

'Don't go all hoity-toity on me, Carol. I know I'm much younger than you are and that I'm a junior employee, but I like you too much not to worry about you. And just lately I couldn't help noticing – oh, drat, I can't actually say it!' The girl picked up her mug, cradled it with both hands and stared down into it worriedly.

'Now that you've started, I think you'd better go on,' Carol said. 'Unfinished business can ruin friendships.'

Stacey looked up and smiled. 'We are friends, aren't we? I mean, it doesn't matter that you've been to university and that I left school as soon as possible and then studied office skills at evening classes; you've never made me feel inferior. That's why I feel I can talk to you this way. Carol, please don't make a mess of your life just because your marriage is going through a bad patch!'

Carol stared at the girl at the girl gloomily. She realized that she didn't feel at all offended that this nineteen-year-old was presuming to offer her advice. Stacey was intelligent, sensitive and caring; it was difficult not to warm to her. There was something else about Stacey, Carol realized; nineteen or not, punk hairstyle regardless, she was also very wise. But, being young, she was perhaps still too idealistic; too optimistic that things would always turn out right.

She decided to meet candour with candour. 'Bad patch

might be an understatement. I think that whatever is wrong with my marriage might be terminal.'

Stacey's eyes widened. 'As bad as that?'

'As bad as that.'

Perhaps it was the set-up here in her office; a confined area where she had carved out her own little space around her work-station, but sitting here with Stacey in the warmth while outside the wind howled around the temporary building, buffeting it occasionally as its force grew, she felt secure enough to talk.

'You know I've been away for the weekend to visit my old friends,' she said.

'Yes – and I know that you and your husband had some kind of argument before you went. That was obvious after his phone call.'

'Well, I don't want to go into all the reasons but it was building up for some time – and then, because of something stupid that I did, it all came to a head.'

'Does he never do anything stupid?'

Carol smiled. 'If he does, he wouldn't see it that way.'

'Just like my Dad. He's never wrong and as long as Mum remembers that, they get along fine.'

'But that's not fair!'

'Who said life was fair?'

Stacey's words echoed Alison's. Alison had gone on to imply that it was up to Carol if she wanted to save her marriage, but if there was going to be any chance of success, Alan would have to want to save it too, wouldn't he? And it didn't seem as if he did.

'Of course she usually does what she wants whatever happens,' Stacey said.

'What are you talking about?'

'Not "what", "whom"! My mum. Life runs smoothly in our house because she does exactly what she wants most of the time but somehow she's persuaded Dad that it was all his idea in the first place.'

Carol laughed. She saw where Stacey got her old-fashioned worldly wisdom from. 'And I guess she knows how to keep those five brothers of yours in order, too!'

'Absolutely. They might act big and swagger a bit, but they know who's boss in our house – even if Dad doesn't. But let's get back to your problem.'

'Have I got a problem?'

Stacey gave her a reproving glance and continued, 'So your marriage is in trouble. You don't have to tell me why, it doesn't matter; what does matter is that you won't solve anything by starting something with – with someone else. There, I've said it.'

Stacey's cheeks were pink and she could barely meet Carol's eyes but she held her chin up defiantly. Carol had known this was coming and yet she still felt winded, as if she had been knocked sideways and didn't quite know how to regain her balance. They both knew who Stacey meant by 'someone else', but she realized that neither of them was going to mention his name. And, for that small mercy she was thankful.

'What if the problems can't be solved? It takes both partners to fight to save a marriage, you know. What if one of them doesn't want to fight?'

'You mean Alan?' Stacey asked and Carol nodded.

'Stacey – I think he's left me.'

'You think?'

'I'm almost sure.'

'Then I'm very sorry. But – oh, goodness, who am I to tell a grown-up woman what to do? Just think very hard about what you want – and do be careful, won't you?'

'I'm sorry, Miss Rowe, but Mr Curtis is still busy.' Peter's secretary, Gina Adamson, was apologetic but firm.

Francine tried to control her irritation. She was not accustomed to having to beg for an interview with Peter.

She was usually ushered straight into his presence. However, she remembered her own rule about not antagonizing the lesser mortals and smiled in what she hoped was a winning manner.

'But you said that if I came up again after lunch, you might be able to squeeze me in,' she said.

'I know and I'm sorry; that was my mistake. I had no idea that he – that his appointment book was full.' The woman had the grace to blush.

Francine was being forced to come to the conclusion that Peter was avoiding her – quite deliberately – and she wasn't quite sure how to deal with the situation. He had always found time for her in the past and, on her part, she had never abused the situation. He must know that she would never bother him with anything trivial.

Mrs Adamson was very uncomfortable. 'I will tell him that you were here again, I promise you.'

'All right, that's kind of you.'

I wonder if she's ever guessed about Peter and me, Francine wondered as she left the executive office suite and headed for the lift. We've always been discreet but personal secretaries, especially those as good as Gina Adamson, can usually sense these things . . .

She had the lift to herself and she glanced in the mirror. She was wearing a black silk blouse with a camel-coloured trouser suit. She hadn't actually been on camera today but she would never have dreamed of turning up for work at the television centre looking anything less than business-like. She was aware that some other female television personalities deliberately dressed down – a long way down – when they were not required to be glamorous, but that wasn't her way. She never wanted anyone to be able to say, 'You know, I saw that Francine Rowe in the supermarket the other day and wait till I tell you what she *really* looks like!'

So, her hair was smooth and shining, her make-up as

perfect as ever and only the new medi-plaster on her poor bruised forehead slightly dented the illusion of a perfectly groomed, successful woman.

The skin beneath the plaster was beginning to itch and Francine poked at the edges experimentally. She discovered that she no longer suffered an immediate stab of pain if she went near the area of the wound and decided to dispense with the plaster and resort to skilful make-up. She knew enough about the subject to do that herself.

The building was warm and, as she made her way along the circular, carpeted corridor back to her own office, she experienced an unfamiliar sense of claustrophobia. Suddenly she had a vision of herself walking round and round the corridors of Television Centre forever. Never opening any of the doors she passed, never seeing any other human being ahead of her, as she aimlessly went on trying to complete the circle, but never coming back to the point she had started from.

What on earth's the matter with me?

But she thought she knew. She was obviously feeling trapped right now and annoyed with Peter for wanting to push her into this *VIPs* series. She knew it was a good idea even although it was limited and, if she had time to do both, she would. But she wanted to tell Peter about her own idea for an arts programme – and Peter, for some reason, was refusing to see her. She had reached her own office and pushed open the door.

Something was wrong. As she walked in, Cameron and Susannah, the two young research assistants, looked up at her and back down again quickly. But she could tell that all their antennae were bristling. Marsha Parry, her PA, rose slowly and began walking towards her. By the time Francine had reached her desk and sat down, Marsha was standing over her. She was clutching a piece of paper.

Francine looked up at her; she had to drop her head back because Marsha was very tall. 'What is it, Marsha?'

'Someone rang about your new series.'

Francine was puzzled. Had Peter gone ahead with the VIPs idea without waiting for her decision? Had he started setting it up without telling her? Was that why he was avoiding her? She looked up at Marsha. The woman's expression was stony – that was the only possible way to describe it.

'What new programme, Marsha?'

'The one you didn't tell me about.'

So that was it. Francine sighed. She and Marsha were almost the same age and they had been working together long enough for Marsha to expect to be in on everything from the planning stage. Here at Television Centre, egos were extremely fragile, and there were all kinds of reasons why something like this would upset her. Marsha might think that her opinion was no longer valued or even that her job was in danger; that Francine was planning to appoint a new PA.

Francine rubbed the back of her neck with the fingers of one hand. 'For goodness' sake pull up a chair and sit down, will you? I'm getting a crick in my neck.'

Marsha did as she was told. She didn't speak and Francine wondered fleetingly whether her PA might be getting a little too possessive. She knew of other television personalities whose personal assistants behaved as if they owned them and wouldn't let anyone else come near them. That could be useful, of course, but it wouldn't suit Francine. She determined to watch the situation in future and reassert her authority – if that was what was needed.

'I didn't tell you because I haven't actually agreed to do it yet. Mr Curtis had no right to go ahead with the *VIPs* idea until we'd talked it over –' She broke off. Marsha was frowning and shaking her head. 'What is it?'

'I don't know what you're talking about. Nobody mentioned anything about *VIPs* – and I haven't heard anything from Mr Curtis. And if you haven't agreed to do it, why were you up in Yorkshire trying to persuade Marcus Holbrook to be your first guest?'

'What. . . ?'

'Rob Baines told me that you were exhausted and needed a few days off.'

Francine was perfectly aware that, in spite of appearing to absorbed in their work, Susannah and Cameron would be listening avidly. She made the effort to sound dignified. 'I don't know what to say,' she said, 'except that Rob wasn't lying to you. He really believed that.'

'So you didn't tell him about the new programme either?' Marsha was only slightly mollified.

'No, I didn't. Because there isn't a new programme – not yet.'

'He said that he wanted to talk to you about your new arts programme –'

'Wait a minute, Marsha. *Who* said that?'

But Marsha wasn't listening. She was in full flow. '– and I felt really foolish because I knew nothing about it. Francine – I'm your personal assistant – if people are going to phone and ask about your plans I'm supposed to know about them!'

'Didn't you hear what I said? There's nothing to know yet, believe me,' Francine said. 'I was just trying to set it up on paper – plan a pilot so that I could get some backing – I would have told you the moment I got the go-ahead, really. You know I would have.'

Marsha's expression softened a little. 'I see. I'm sorry if I jumped to conclusions – but he talked as if it was all settled.'

'*Who* did, Marsha? *Who* phoned just now?'

Francine's eyes suddenly focused on the scrap of paper that her assistant was still clutching.

Marsha pushed the paper across the desk. 'Marcus Holbrook – there's his number. He wants you to return his call.'

CHAPTER 20

Francine stared down at Marsha's large, untidy writing. A name and a telephone number and a message to return the call. Marcus Holbrook's name and telephone number and – why did he want to speak to her?

'Do you want me to get the number for you?'

Francine looked up and saw that her PA was still sitting at the other side of her desk and that she was regarding her curiously.

'No, that's all right, I'll get it. But . . .' Francine paused. How was she going to put this? Tell the truth, she decided. 'Marsha, this call won't be strictly business . . . Listen, I promise you that I won't keep you in the dark about how my plans are going but, right now . . .'

'The call is personal?'

'That's right.'

Francine was relieved that Marsha seemed to understand, but she was disturbed by the way her assistant was looking at her with eyebrows raised speculatively.

'OK, Susannah and Cameron –' Her PA got up and turned to look at the two researchers. Francine noticed that both of them put their heads down quickly. They had obviously been listening. She wondered what they would make of it all. 'It's time for a tea break,' Marsha told them.

'Shall I go and get the drinks from the machine?' Cameron asked.

'No, I'll treat you both to the cafeteria instead.'

The two young people looked surprised but they followed Marsha out of the office obediently. It wasn't long since either of them had left university and they considered themselves unbelievably fortunate to have landed jobs at Television Centre. Every day was still a wonderful experience for them – and they hadn't been here long enough to answer back, Francine thought.

When she was alone she sat for a moment just looking at the phone number on the piece of paper.

Why had Marcus called?

From the little Marsha had said, it could be that he had changed his mind about letting her interview him. But he had been so adamant . . . so set about personal appearances of any kind. What had his last words on the subject been?

'. . . *don't get any idea that I'm going to change my mind about being interviewed. That will never happen.*'

So why did he want to speak to her? There was only one way to find out. She reached for the phone on her desk.

'Marcus Holbrook here.'

Francine was glad that she was sitting down. She hadn't been prepared for the effect that hearing his voice would have on her. He sounded so strong and clear that it was hard to believe he was more than two hundred and fifty miles away.

'Marcus – it's Francine.'

'Ah.'

'You called – why did you call?' Suddenly she wasn't as articulate as she usually was. But then he didn't seem to want to speak at all. 'Marcus?'

'Why did you take off like that?' He sounded angry. 'I left you alone for two minutes –'

'Hours actually –'

'Francine! I left you alone to rest while I got on with some work and, without even having the good manners to tell me, you just packed up and took off!'

'I'm sorry – I thought it best . . .'

'You thought it best to sneak off and leave me to find out why from that overgrown schoolgirl, Gemma Parkin. There was I fondly envisaging finishing work and enjoying a romantic meal for two and I come into the kitchen to find Gemma steaming up my kitchen cooking sausages and mash!'

'Cooking what?' Francine couldn't help laughing.

'It's not funny, Francine. The Parkins are very good friends of mine otherwise I would have bundled her back into her coat and sent her packing.'

'Did you enjoy it?'

'What?'

'The sausage and mash?'

There was a strangled sound at the other end of the phone and then Marcus said, 'I'll treat that remark with the contempt it deserves.'

'I think you've just uttered another cliché, Mr Holbrook.'

She was relieved to hear him laugh. 'It must be the effect you have on me, Miss Rowe. After all, the situation I find myself isn't new – it's as old as time. And before you point it out to me – that's another cliché.'

Francine found herself gripping the receiver. 'Marcus – what do you mean by the situation you find yourself in?'

But he didn't answer her directly. 'You could have left a letter, you know – even a brief note – just to explain. You could have told me yourself instead of leaving it to Gemma to give me your message.'

'I didn't leave a message with Gemma! What did she tell you?'

'Didn't you? She seemed so certain – she said that as I wouldn't do the interview, you had no further interest in me and you didn't want to hang around.'

'Wow! She really was angry with me.'

'What are you saying?'

'I didn't leave a message like that – in fact I didn't leave any kind of message – I – I just thought it better to go . . .'

'Why?'

'I can't tell you.'

She heard him sigh. 'Marcus,' she said tentatively, 'what did you mean just now about the situation you find yourself in?'

'I'll tell you when I see you,' he said. She let that pass.

'My assistant, Marsha, said that you called about the new programme,' she said.

'I had to have some excuse to get through to you.'

'Don't you realize your name alone would have achieved that?'

And he probably didn't, she thought. That was one of his endearing features. Difficult he might be, but it was not out of a sense of false vanity.

'So – what did you want to say?'

'I'll do the interview.'

'What!'

'You don't deserve it, but you rattled me in more ways than one – telling me that I was considered to be difficult, a loner, a misanthropist – what else did you say? Oh, yes, aloof, uncommunicative, taciturn –'

'I'm sorry – I'm *sorry!*'

'So you should be. But, anyway, I had plenty of time to reflect after you took off so ungratefully, and I've decided that you might be right.'

'Oh, no! Now that I've met you, I know that you're not like that at all!'

'Be quiet. You're weakening your own case. Do you want me on your programme or don't you?'

330

'Yes, Marcus, I do.'

After she had replaced the receiver she leaned forward and, resting her elbows on the desk, she clasped her hands together to support her chin. She'd had to say yes, hadn't she? Marcus Holbrook would be exactly the right person to start the new series with. But she would have to be careful – have to be on her guard.

If she valued her career and wanted her exciting but uncomplicated life to stay on course, any future contact with Marcus Holbrook would have to be strictly business.

The gleaming new kitchen of her apartment seemed cold and impersonal compared to the kitchen in the cottage on Moor Top. The severe white and grey colour scheme, which she had loved until now, wasn't even half as attractive as the cosy, unassuming ordinariness of Marcus's kitchen. Francine made an effort and dismissed the images from her mind.

She had been shopping on the way home and she emptied the carrier bags on to the benchtop. She planned to cook fresh pasta with a basil sauce for starters, then scrambled eggs with smoked salmon and new potatoes for the main course, and strawberries and cream for desert. Nothing too heavy and all very simple and easy to prepare.

She wasn't going to give Peter the option of saying no. She would set the table for two and time everything so that when he arrived the meal would be almost ready. She hadn't bought wine because she guessed that he wouldn't be staying overnight. He would have to drive back to his home and to Nancy. And if she had another meal waiting for him, then tough!

Peter had called through to her office just as she was about to leave the television centre and he'd apologized for not being able to see her earlier. Then, before putting the phone down, he'd said, 'See you.' That was part of their code and it meant that he was coming to the apartment. He usually arrived an hour and a half to two hours after she did. Right from the start they had been careful never to be seen leaving work at approximately the same time.

When she had set the table and done all she was going to in the kitchen, Francine hurried to the bathroom and took a quick shower. Then, dressed in a long, black skirt and a red and black silk tunic top, she poured herself a glass of mineral water, added ice and a slice of lemon and waited. Not for long.

Peter rang the bell to warn her that he was on his way up. He had his own key. In the short time it took for the lift to ascend to the top floor, Francine arranged her programme notes on the coffee table in the sitting-room. They would eat first and then relax with coffee while she showed him her presentation.

Peter had often complained that he had hardly set foot in the door before she would want to talk about work, or, if she was honest with herself, more specifically, her own career. Well, not this time. She would try to play fair. She would let him relax after a busy day, listen to anything he wanted to say – just like a wife, she thought ruefully – and then try to lead the conversation on to her future project as naturally as she could.

What if he wants to make love to me?

The thought came from nowhere and caught her totally unawares. His visits to her apartment didn't always end in lovemaking – sometimes they would just want to talk and relax together depending on how the mood took them. She realized at that moment that their relationship might not have been so very different from a marriage in that respect. But she had never stopped to think about it before. And why was it bothering her now?

She hurried into the small, elegant dining-room and

332

hastily removed the candle-holders from the table. A candlelight dinner might give just the wrong impression . . .

She had just pushed the candles back into the drawer where she kept them when she heard the door of the apartment open. She pinned on a smile and hurried through to the hallway to greet Peter. There was no answering smile. He looks tired, she thought. No, not tired, harassed, perhaps even angry.

Is it my fault?

Francine knew that this was a typical feminine reaction. Something's wrong and it must be my fault! She was irritated with herself but, nevertheless, she couldn't help blurting out, 'Peter, you're not annoyed because I tried to see you today, are you?'

'No, of course not.' He produced a wan smile. 'Mm, something smells good?'

'Do you mean me or the dinner I'm cooking?'

'Both.' The smile grew a little wider.

Francine looked at him uncertainly. The 'something smells good' routine was an old joke between them and normally he would have taken her in his arms and nuzzled her neck and added something like, 'Which shall I devour first?' But this time he just stood there. He looked worried.

'Francine – I won't be staying tonight –' he began.

She realized that because she had taken extra care with her appearance he might have thought that she expected him to stay and she hurried to reassure him. 'That's OK, I didn't think you would be, but I hope that at least you've time to enjoy the meal I've prepared?'

'Of course.' He looked relieved. 'Nancy's out at some fund-raising do tonight, so I've got plenty of time.'

'Oh, good.' Francine turned away quickly, realizing that she had let the note of sarcasm show through. What's the matter with me? she thought. I've had years of having to fit into Nancy's timetable; I should be used to it by now.

'Why don't you wash your hands, or whatever you want to do, and then go through into the dining-room? Everything's just about ready.'

The meal went well and Peter seemed to enjoy it. He also seemed to be grateful that she kept the conversation light. They talked about people they knew, personalities in the news at the moment and even a little politics. She saw him relaxing before her eyes – but not completely.

While she was rinsing the plates and putting them in the dishwasher, Peter made the coffee. He put everything on a tray and asked, 'Where shall we have this?'

'I thought we'd go through to the sitting-room.'

By the time she had followed him through he had placed the tray on the coffee table, switched on the lamps and was sitting down leafing through her presentation. 'I take it that I was meant to see this?' he asked. His tone was light.

Francine searched his face for any kind of clue to how he was going to react. He was smiling. 'Yes,' she replied and set about pouring the coffee.

After placing his cup near to him, she sat back and tried to relax. She knew better than to interrupt. If he wanted to know anything he would ask her. He didn't take long.

'This is very good,' he said at last. 'You've done your homework and, personally, I think you have enough gravitas to handle that kind of programme. The problem will be convincing others of that fact.'

'Problem? But if you give the go-ahead – the controller has always trusted your judgement in the past –'

'I won't be in any position to convince anybody.'

She stared at him. He wasn't making any sense. 'Why?'

'I'm leaving the BBC – and, no, I haven't had a better

offer from commercial television. I'm taking early retirement.'

'But why? Peter, this is so unexpected –'

'Is it? It happens to a lot of men of my age and seniority. I'm expensive, Francine. A younger person won't cost the corporation so much –'

'They've *told* you to go? But that's –'

'No, don't worry, nothing so crude. They just made me a very good offer.'

'A golden handshake?'

'That kind of thing. Anyway, if I accept the offer now, I'll be in a better position financially than if I waited for my normal retirement pension. So I agreed to take the money and run!'

'In those circumstances I don't blame you. But you don't have to give up work, you know. There are all kinds of ways you can stay involved with broadcasting. Freelance work, for example –'

'Francine, would you make some more coffee? This has gone cold.'

'Of course.'

When she returned from the kitchen, Peter had the presentation open on his knee and he was making notes. He looked up and smiled. 'I think, rather than touting this round, you should form your own production company.'

'I've thought of that. Peter – would you like to be part of it?'

'I'll certainly put some money into it, but there's no way I could be involved actively. You see, Nancy and I have decided to retire to our house in Provence.'

'What?'

Francine was still holding the coffee pot. She put it down on the table and sat down slowly. He was staring at her and she recognized the same expression that had been on his face when he had arrived. He hadn't been either tired, harassed or angry. He had been deeply worried.

'Well, the children are grown-up now and more or less independent, so we thought we'd sell the house in Surrey and maybe buy a flat in town for them. But Nancy and I will base ourselves in France.'

Nancy and I . . .

He'd said it so naturally that, paradoxically, Francine realized that it was probably rehearsed. She knew what he was telling her but she wanted to hear the words.

'And you and I?' she asked.

'There won't be any you and I. There can't be. It's over.'

Francine waited for the grief and the rage to hit her but it didn't happen. Certainly there was a strange hollow feeling in the pit of her stomach but the hollowness began to fill up with a heavy feeling of regret. Regret that it was over? Yes, of course. Regret for what might have been? No, she didn't think so . . .

'Peter,' she found herself saying, 'did you ever think, over the years, I mean, did you ever think that when this moment came, you might be retiring somewhere with me?'

His eyes widened with alarm and, at that moment, she found herself disliking him – but forgiving him at the same time. 'No – that was never on the cards – it wasn't – I mean – we didn't have that kind of relationship, did we?'

'I suppose not.'

'So why did you ask such a question.'

'Oh, I don't know. Maybe I'm wondering exactly what kind of a relationship we did have.'

'Francine . . . I'm very grateful . . .'

'Don't, Peter! Don't you dare talk about gratitude!'

'Look – the *VIPs* series is still yours, if you want it. I made that perfectly clear. And, if you do start your own

336

production company, I'll be glad to invest in it. I'll use any influence I have –'

'That won't be necessary. I've never taken money from you and I never will.'

'But this is different. It wouldn't be a gift, it would be a sound business investment.'

'All the same, it would be better to make a clean break. I mean that. Now, if you'd like to finish your coffee . . .'

'I think it's gone cold again.' He gave a twisted smile and then reached into his pocket. 'Here are your keys.' He dropped them on the table. 'I expect you'll be changing the code in the security alarms.'

'Of course.'

'Well, then . . . ' He stood up and looked at her irresolutely. 'Goodbye . . . and –'

'Just go, Peter. If I find any of your belongings here – socks, underpants, you know – I'll post them.'

'No, don't do that!'

'I'm joking.'

She was glad that he didn't offer to kiss her goodbye. She couldn't have borne that. Not because it would break her heart – she was puzzled to find that it wouldn't. This had come as a tremendous shock and she couldn't figure out why her strongest feeling was of unease – of gears shifting – of being about to move into new territory. She was bewildered.

I'm a discarded mistress, she thought. After all these years, Nancy is calling him in. So why am I so calm?

Peter was frowning. 'Are you going to be OK?'

'Of course. Now, off you go.'

He gave her a strange look and then began to walk to the door. She followed him into the hall. 'Will it take you long to sell the house?' she asked. She was simply being polite.

'I don't know. But we'll probably just pack up and leave everything to the estate agent.'

'Very wise; it ought to be lovely in Provence right now. In fact summer will have started already.' She was aware that she was babbling but she just wanted to keep talking until he was out of the door. And then something occurred to her. She called him back.

'Peter – there is one thing I'd like to know.'

'What's that?'

'How long have you known that this was going to happen?'

Suddenly he couldn't meet her eyes. 'Not long.'

'How long?'

'They – they gave me a month to think about it – to decide.'

'Bastard.'

'Francine . . .'

'Goodbye, Peter.'

The door closed behind him and she stood for a while and listened as she heard the lift descending. Then she turned and went back to collect her cup of coffee from the sitting-room. Ugh! Peter was right, it was cold. She went into the kitchen and poured the coffee from the cup into a pottery mug, then she warmed it up in the microwave. She didn't usually take sugar but she added a spoonful to disguise the warmed-up taste.

She wandered into the sitting-room. Why hadn't the shock wave hit her yet? she wondered. She sat in her favourite place by the window and waited for the storm of rage and grief. It didn't come. Oh, she was angry enough. Angry that Peter hadn't told her about his offer of redundancy, hadn't let her share the decision-making process.

But how could he have done? she thought. He must have realized straight away that retirement would bring an end to their relationship. It had to – unless he had been planning to leave Nancy. And, as he said, that was never on the cards.

But what if he had decided not to go? she wondered. She would never have known and he would have worked on until he reached the official retirement age. And then what would have happened? No doubt he and Nancy would have departed for France just as they were doing now. And I would have been that much older . . .

She heard rain spatter suddenly against the window and she looked out to see clouds racing across the sky. It was wild out there, she thought. But I'm secure and warm in my own ivory tower . . . that was what Peter had jokingly dubbed her new apartment . . .

She was still sitting there when the lights in the buildings on the other side of the river began to wink out one by one . . .

CHAPTER 21

The West Country – Monday evening

'Carol, I didn't understand a word of that; I hope you'll be able to explain it all to me later.' Luke turned and spoke quietly to her as they rose from their seats and began to make their way along to the central aisle of the conference room.

She smiled at him. 'That was only the welcome speech and introduction. It's going to get much more complicated!'

'Then I'm glad that you agreed to come with me. I would have been totally lost without you.'

They had reached the end of their row of seats and they fell in behind the other business people who had taken up the software company's invitation to the sales promotion.

It was Monday evening and they had come here straight from work. She'd left her own little car locked up safely in the compound at Travers' Transport and travelled with Luke. Stacey had waved her off nervously, and Carol had tried to ignore the meaningful looks the younger girl was giving her.

But Carol knew that, no matter what Stacey might think, this was strictly business. She had already studied the demonstration software disk thoroughly, and she guessed that she might be better placed than Luke to make a judgement about whether he should buy the whole package or perhaps only part of it. It was only natural that he should ask her to accompany him.

'Seriously, Carol, I'm very grateful,' he told her now. 'Especially as I gave you such short notice. But I did phone you at home on Friday evening, you know, and a few times on Saturday. Eventually, I guessed that you must be away for the weekend and I left it until Sunday evening.'

'And caught me just as I arrived home.'

'Not "we"?'

'Excuse me?'

'You said, "*I* arrived home". Were you and your husband not away together?'

'No – er – Alan's staying with his parents at the moment. I spent the weekend with my old friends from university.'

'I see.'

What exactly did Luke see? Carol wondered, as they crossed the hotel foyer. Could he possibly have guessed what a terrible state her marriage was in and, if so, what would it mean to him? She risked a glance up at his profile but he was staring straight ahead. His expression, at least the sideways view of it, gave nothing away.

Carol wondered if he'd given any thought at all to the picnic they had had together last week – and to what had happened. Had anything happened, or was she fantasizing? The kiss and the moment of intimacy had been so brief that it had taken on a dreamlike quality in Carol's memory.

Did it really happen or did I just want it to happen because I was unhappy, lonely, neglected by my husband and – let's face it – attracted to my boss?

Many of the other delegates were heading for the bar and Luke stopped and took hold of her elbow. 'We have time for a drink before dinner, if you like. There won't be time afterwards because the lecture and demonstration starts straight away.'

'No, thanks, Luke. I'd like to go to my room and freshen up a little.'

On arrival they had only had time to book in and place their bags in their rooms, before everyone had been rounded up and herded along into the conference room. Carol was still wearing her business clothes and she wanted, at the very least, to have a wash and change into a blouse more suitable for dinner in the hotel dining-room.

'Good idea,' Luke agreed. 'Me too.'

They walked over to the lift and Carol prayed that they wouldn't be the only passengers. The last thing she wanted was to be alone and close to Luke in such a confined space. She was relieved to see two other people waiting there; two serious-looking businessmen who were deep in conversation.

Just as the lift doors were closing, a substantial-looking woman jostled her way in and Carol was propelled forward against Luke's body – and trapped there. Then she realized that being alone in the lift with Luke might have been a better option, after all. She was wedged up so close to him that she could hardly breathe. Her face was pressed sideways and she didn't dare try to look up in case she should discover that he was as embarrassed – and something more – as she was.

It was shocking to be body-to-body like this – and in a public place. Her breasts were pushed up against his ribcage and she was horrified to feel her senses responding.

Oh, no, she groaned, and she didn't realize she had spoken aloud.

'Are you all right?' She heard Luke's voice coming from above her head.

'Yes,' she croaked.

'You're trembling.' Luke's hand came round and found the small of her back, pressing her even closer. 'Hang on, we're nearly there.'

Oh, please, she thought, let the lift stop soon and let someone get out. I don't know if I can bear this much longer!

In response to her wish, it seemed, the lift stopped abruptly. When the doors swished open and the large lady got out, Carol almost fell backwards into the corridor. Luke grabbed her and steadied her. While she was trying to collect her scattered wits, they were momentarily distracted as the woman dived back into the lift, proclaiming loudly that she hadn't wanted to come to the top floor. She stared at them accusingly as if it were their fault.

The two businessmen were already walking away down the corridor still deep in conversation and, as the lift doors closed once more on the solitary angry passenger, Carol and Luke dissolved into helpless laughter. The laughter provided a blessed release of her pent-up emotions and she found that she was able to look at him with a little less embarrassment.

'Are you OK now?' he asked.

'Yes, it was just – just the confined space . . .'

'Yes . . . that was probably it . . .' He regarded her solemnly for a moment and then he smiled. 'You've got about twenty minutes,' he said. 'Shall we meet just here?'

She felt herself flushing. 'No, I think we'd better meet downstairs in the foyer, don't you?'

'OK.' He turned and walked away from her. She was glad that their rooms were at opposite ends of the corridor.

Carol was used to getting ready in a hurry and twenty minutes was quite enough time to strip off and shower. She didn't wash her hair, and when she pulled off the

343

shower cap she was relieved to see that her new style fell back into place. She slipped into fresh underwear and tights before donning her plum-coloured silk blouse, which made all the difference to her everyday grey skirt and jacket. Then, after she'd put on her make-up and flicked a comb through her hair, she was ready to go down for dinner.

The food was excellent but the meal was hardly a social occasion, as most of the conference delegates seemed to want to talk business with old and new acquaintances. She was grateful that an old friend of Luke's father had noticed him as they walked into the dining-room and insisted that they sit together. She wasn't ignored but neither was she expected to join in most of the conversation that followed, which was part business and part fond reminiscences of their rival businesses in the old days. She was grateful to be allowed the opportunity to enjoy the meal and try to get her mind on track for the lecture and demonstration to follow.

It wasn't so bad. The demonstration disk had prepared her for much of what was to come. The package covered everything you would expect, including routing, utilization of vehicles and storing efficiency, as well as the more usual wages and accounts. The graphics were superb and the graphs and diagrams projected on to the giant screen were so self-explanatory that she was sure even Luke, who pretended to be computer illiterate, would understand them. Nevertheless, she took notes and was prepared to explain everything in detail, if necessary.

The conference broke up in time for the delegates to head for the bar again, but Luke ordered a tray of coffee and biscuits and they found a corner of the lounge in order to discuss what they'd heard. After breakfast the next morning, the hard sales pitch would begin and Luke wanted to be sure of his facts.

'So, what do you think, Carol?' he said after the waiter

had poured their coffee and left them with the tray. 'Should I buy it?'

'I can't tell you that, Luke; I can only say that the program is probably the best that's available at the moment –'

'So why do you look doubtful?'

'Because it's also the most expensive.'

'Ah. And going by that worried frown, you think that Travers' Transport can't afford it, right?'

'No – actually I think you can. But you're already financially extended with the expansion scheme and –'

'Let me worry about that, Carol. Just take me through those copious notes I saw you making.'

Over the next hour, Carol realized that, just as she had suspected, Luke was much more *au fait* with computers than he pretended to be, and this eased her mind considerably. Any decision he made would be his alone, even though she might have had to explain some of the finer points.

Eventually, she closed her note file and gave a tired sigh. 'That's it, Luke. Now it's up to you.'

She glanced around the hotel lounge and was surprised to see that they were the only occupants.

'Yes, it's late,' he said, rightly interpreting her expression. 'Can I buy you a nightcap of some kind? It would help you to wind down.'

Carol smiled. 'No alcohol, not if I'm going to be on the ball for the sales talk in the morning.'

'You don't have to worry about that,' Luke said. 'Thanks to all your work and this list of questions you've prepared for me, I can handle that by myself. In fact you can sleep late and have your breakfast in bed if you want to. So what would you like to drink?'

'You know what I'd really like?'

'Tell me.'

'A cup of hot chocolate.' Carol found herself smothering a yawn. 'Mm . . . sorry . . .'

Luke laughed. 'No, I'm sorry for keeping you up so late. Just sit back and relax for a moment, I'll go and see if I can round up a night porter and order what madam requires.'

She watched him go, tall and purposeful, striding across the room just like Stacey's mum's Mr Masterful would have done, she thought, and found herself giggling. She was grateful that he, at least, still seemed to have enough energy to make the effort. She hadn't realized how tired she was until the moment they had stopped talking business. She closed her eyes and emptied her mind of the strains and stresses of the day.

She had welcomed the extra work, of course. First because she enjoyed the challenge and felt confident of her abilities, and secondly because the harder she was working, the less time she had to brood over her personal problems when she was secure in her small office at Travers' Transport, no one questioned her methods or accused her of failing in her duties. She was actually appreciated there. And that was not the situation at home . . .

But, no, she didn't want to think of home – that dismal, discordant place where she was constantly made to feel inadequate. She had enjoyed her brief escape to Norfolk to stay with Alison at the weekend but, she had to be honest with herself, she had been anxious to get back on Sunday evening to see whether Alan had returned. Well, he hadn't, and she never wanted to experience again that sudden feeling of blind panic when she had gone racing upstairs to see whether he had been back to remove any more of his clothes or belongings.

She remembered that moment when the phone had rung and she'd thought it might be Alan – she'd hurried down the stairs to answer it. She remembered the disappointment, tinged with shocked excitement, when she'd heard Luke's voice. He'd asked her if she could

346

come to this seminar with him. They would have to go straight after work the next day, he'd said, stay one night at the hotel and return on Tuesday.

She had sunk down on to the stairs, still clutching the receiver and stared through the bars of the stair-rail across the narrow hall and into the empty living-room. 'Yes,' she had said, 'yes, I think that would be possible.'

And now she was here and, whenever she returned home, she didn't really think that Alan would be waiting. So tonight she was in a kind of limbo. The hotel was comfortable – even luxurious – and all she had to do was order something – like hot chocolate – and it would appear. She wondered if she ought to have asked for some custard creams . . . no, perhaps not, the hot chocolate would do nicely . . .

In this wonderfully comfortable hotel, removed from her everyday world and all her worries, she might be able to get a good night's sleep for a change. She sighed with contentment. Luke had said he could handle the session tomorrow and she might just take up his suggestion and have breakfast in bed . . .

At some stage, without her noticing, the overhead lights must have been dimmed and the atmosphere in the room was discreetly warm and quiet. And so peaceful . . . She yawned openly this time as she sank back and gave way to the well-upholstered comfort . . .

'Wake up, Carol.'

'Mm?' She opened her eyes with difficulty, blinked and looked up. Luke was standing over her holding a cup and saucer. 'Oh . . . sorry . . . was I asleep?'

'It seems so.' He turned sideways and bent down to place the cup on the table . . . 'Here, give me your hands.'

She obeyed him and found herself being gently hauled up to her feet. He took hold of her arms and steadied her. 'Now don't fall over.'

'Don't be silly.' She grinned at him sheepishly. He took hold of her left hand and lifted her arm. 'Hey – what are you doing?'

'Just putting the strap of your handbag over your shoulder – there. Now, if I put your notes into my briefcase – like this – do you think you can manage to carry it?'

'Of course I can, but why?'

'Good, here you are.' She took the briefcase obediently. 'Because now –' he paused while he bent down to pick up her cup of hot chocolate '– I'm going to guide you up to your room –' he put his other arm around her waist and began to propel her gently towards the door of the lounge '– where you can enjoy this delicious confection in the privacy of your own bed.'

'Luke – it's all right – I can manage –'

'Be careful or you'll make me spill this.'

His arm remained where it was and she stopped protesting. How comforting it was to have someone guiding her like this, she thought. Someone to notice how tired she was, someone to look after her – to spoil her a little . . .

When they reached the lift a recent memory pierced the haze and Carol disentangled herself and retreated to the far wall. She leaned back against it gratefully. When the doors closed behind him, Luke turned to face her but remained where he was. And there they both stayed, three feet apart from one another, smiling foolishly, until the lift reached the top floor. Strangely, the very fact that they had both agreed, wordlessly, to keep this small distance between them brought them closer together . . .

But once they had stepped out of the intimate atmosphere of the lift, it seemed quite natural to let him put his arm round her again to support her as walked along the corridor towards her room. It crossed her mind that she could probably have managed the last short distance

348

on her own but, before she could say anything, he'd said, 'I might as well see you safely to the door.'

But of course he didn't stop there. Had she expected him to? Still holding her cup of chocolate, Luke waited while she fumbled for her key and then followed her into the room, closing the door behind him. He put the drink down on the bedside table and turned to face her. She was still clutching his briefcase.

'I'll take that,' he said. But instead of turning to go, he put it on the floor and reached out to slip the strap of her bag from her shoulder. She let it fall on to the bed behind her.

Luke took a step towards her and her eyes widened. 'Luke –' she began, but he took hold of her shoulders, pulled her into his body and his mouth came down on hers, stopping any further speech.

Carol's hands clenched and unclenched helplessly for a moment, before her mind began to blank out and she gave herself up to his kiss. She hardly noticed when he let go of her with one hand and began to undo the buttons of her jacket. Then he pushed it gently from her shoulders and it landed on the bed along with her handbag.

His hands came up again and caressed her shoulders through the thin silk of the blouse. And all the time the kiss went on and on, until Carol had to pull her mouth away from his and take in great gulps of air. Her head fell backwards and his mouth came down on the soft curve of her neck.

'Carol,' he groaned, 'I've tried so hard to stop thinking of you this way.'

This way . . . The urgency of his words at last began to break through the overwhelming tide of emotion that had taken hold of her. *This way*!

What was she doing? How had she allowed this to develop? This wasn't what she wanted – was it?

She brought her hands up between them and pushed

349

as hard as she could. 'No, Luke – no –'

He didn't resist, he stepped back immediately. 'Carol? What is it? What's the matter?'

'I can't – we mustn't – this is wrong. Oh, Luke, I'm so sorry!'

Luke's hands dropped to his sides and his eyes sought her face. She didn't know how long they stood there, just looking at each other, but just as it had happened once before, an unspoken communication passed between them. They were telling each other about desire – and about denial . . . She saw the moment when the hope drained from Luke's face to be replaced with regret.

'No, Carol,' he said at last, 'I'm the one who should be sorry. I misjudged the situation.'

She felt herself burn up with embarrassment and shame. He was prepared to take the blame and yet she knew that he had only reacted to the signals that she must have been sending. She was attracted to him, yes – but she was wise enough to know that if, her marriage hadn't been so miserable, if she and Alan had been happy together, she would never have allowed this situation to develop.

'Carol –' he had picked up his briefcase '– I want you to know that this would have meant much more to me than a brief affair.'

'Luke, don't –'

'No, listen to me. You owe me that much. I value you both as a person and as an employee and I would never do anything to endanger that relationship. No – to me, this would have been the beginning of something serious –'

'But, Luke, I'm married.'

He sighed. 'I know – and, believe me, I've never made a pass at a married woman before. And I wouldn't have done so now if I hadn't had reason to think that your marriage might be over.'

'You thought that? But how . . . ?'

'I've watched you change over the months since you first came to work for me. Change gradually from a cheerful, effervescent young woman into an unhappy, worried shadow of your former self.'

'But that could have been for other reasons –'

'I didn't think so. I recognized the signs. I watched my sister's marriage disintegrate and it was all sadly familiar. However, I told myself to keep away – that it would be very wrong of me to interfere, even though I could hardly bear to see how unhappy you were.'

'Please don't –'

'Don't worry, I'm going soon.' He managed a quirky smile. 'But I want you to know that you might have made the mistake of your life!'

She was grateful to him for lightening the mood and she responded in the same vein. 'How's that?

'We'd make a good couple you know – a good partnership. Your brains and my determination –'

'Your sense of order and my chronic untidiness!' she added.

He laughed. 'But your mind isn't untidy, is it, Carol? And I'm pretty tolerant. So long as we didn't have to share the same office, we'd get along just fine.'

But what about the same home? Carol thought. If Luke and she had ever shared a home, his tolerance might have been put to the test. He might have ended up being as irritated with her as Alan was . . . She sighed. That was all speculation because it wasn't going to happen . . .

Luke had reached the door of the room and he turned once more to face her before he opened it. 'I apologized just now for misjudging the situation, but if it turns out only to have been a matter of bad timing, I want you to know that I can be patient.'

'No – don't say that –'

'Don't worry, Carol. I won't put any pressure on you. In fact I'll be the model of discretion. But if ever you change your mind – I'll be there for you.'

She waited until the door had closed behind him and then she sank down on the bed and stared miserably ahead. It would have been so easy to give herself up to Luke's lovemaking. It wasn't just that she was neglected and frustrated, she was genuinely attracted to the man. He was good-looking, hardworking, decent – and she'd sensed even before he had told her that this would never have been a one-night stand or a cheap affair. As well as physical desire there was the chance that genuine emotion, even love, would have developed between them.

So why had she pulled back? She guessed that, in spite of everything, she had just been forced to realize that she hadn't given up on her marriage. Alison had told her that, if she still loved Alan, it was up to her to make a go of it – even if that seemed unfair. And, just a few moments ago, when she had been in Luke's arms and all her senses were telling her to go on and make love with him – she couldn't. Because, she realized ruefully, she did still love her husband.

Whether Alan still loved her or not was a different matter. She had to admit that things didn't look too good. But she had to be absolutely sure – because until then she would not be free.

Carol kicked off her shoes. She had been tired to begin with and now, emotionally drained as she was, she was downright exhausted. She was tempted simply to curl up on top of the bed and pull the coverlet over her. But she forced herself to take off her clothes and even hang them up before pulling on her nightdress and crawling into bed.

She reached over to switch off the bedside light and only then did she remember the cup of hot chocolate. She stared at it and frowned. It would be cold. Cold chocolate, she thought, not very comforting. Shall I order another cup? That would be easy enough; all she had to do was pick up the phone and ask for room service . . . they might even be able to bring her some sweet biscuits to go with it . . .

No . . . she couldn't be bothered . . . and, besides, no amount of hot chocolate or custard creams would be able to stave off the feeling of misery that was gnawing away at her tonight. There, in the warmth and comfort of the hotel room, Carol cried herself to sleep.

CHAPTER 22

Lancashire – Tuesday

It was mid-morning, but it was one of those days when it seemed as if it was never going to get light. Sophie, seated on the raised platform at one end of the school assembly hall, stared dispiritedly over the bent heads of the pupils taking the maths exam. Inside the hall, all the lights were on so that made the school yard outside look even darker. As black as night, in fact.

The neat rows of single desks and the young people sitting at them were reflected in the floor-to-ceiling windows that lined one side of the hall. By a trick of the light, the reflection of the scene seemed to extend outwards and forever into the black wetness beyond.

It had been raining steadily and unremittingly ever since she had awoken that morning. It was more like a tropical monsoon than normal April showers, she thought fancifully, except that in countries where the monsoon occurred it would be much warmer than it was here in a north of England industrial town!

Sophie tried to recall whether there had ever been an April when it had rained quite as much as this year, but she couldn't. But then in previous years she hadn't had a wedding to worry about. *Her* wedding, she thought, and sighed. Why, oh, why couldn't she feel more optimistic?

354

Of course Alistair loved her, didn't he?

She felt the familiar knot of pain begin to tighten in the pit of her stomach. Maggie had been right, any sensible woman would have simply come right out and asked him. But she wasn't sensible as far as Alistair was concerned. She loved him so deeply that the thought that he might not feel the same filled her with dread. Or did it . . . ?

Sophie contemplated what she would do if the answer to her question wasn't what she wanted to hear. Would she be able to break off the engagement? Tell him that what he was offering – a practical, *sensible* life together – wasn't good enough? Of course she wouldn't. She realized at that moment – and to her shame – that she would marry him anyway, and try to take joy from the fact that it was she, Sophie, that he had chosen.

Suddenly she remembered where she was and what she was supposed to be doing. She was invigilating this maths exam and she should have been keeping her eyes open for any possible attempt at cheating. She glanced around the hall quickly. There were upwards of fifty pupils taking the exam and three teachers supervising. Maggie Lomax was standing at the far end of the hall and Mr Scott, the deputy head, a bearded giant, was pacing silently between the aisles.

All pens and pencils and mathematical instruments had to be laid out on the desks before the exam began. Any pen or pencil case had to be made of transparent material, all calculators had been checked to see that their memories had been wiped free from mathematical formulae. But you still had to watch out for the older, more time-honoured methods of cheating – like important data inked on to the insides of a wrist or even the more blatant note-passing.

Sophie sighed. She was sure that today's young people were no worse than young people had ever been. There had always been bad apples, as her mother called them. It was just that these days young villains had more sophisticated means of wrongdoing.

Maggie and she had changed places at regular intervals to give each of them the chance to sit down, but Mr Scott never seemed to need to rest. She saw him glance at his watch; a moment later he gave the ten-minute warning. Some of the boys and girls had already finished and were getting their papers together, while others were still writing frantically. One of the latter was Cheryl Jackson, who had quite a good brain, even if her behaviour left much to be desired.

Sophie glanced thoughtfully at Julie Hunter. Cheryl and her cronies seemed to have left the girl alone since the incident last week, but it was a situation that would have to be monitored. Bullying in schools was a problem that never seemed to go away. Sophie didn't know what the solution was – she only knew that it needed constant vigilance.

'That's it!' Mr Scott called. 'Time's up, ladies and gentlemen. Put your pens down now, please.'

Sophie and Maggie moved swiftly between the desks collecting up the papers. Question papers on the left and answer papers on the right of the desks, and a whole mess of sweet wrappers in between, Sophie noticed. It was amazing how many sweets some of them managed to consume during the course of one examination – not to mention the gum that was chewed.

A few of them had to be reminded to take their litter away with them but Sophie saw that Cheryl, who had chewed throughout the examination, had already cleared her desk. Then, just as she was about to move on, Sophie noticed a chewing-gum wrapper on the floor at Cheryl's feet. There was something odd about it – odd enough to make Sophie pause.

Cheryl saw the direction of her glance and quickly bent to retrieve it. Sophie moved swiftly and covered the wrapper with one foot. The girl shot her a look full of panic, then her face was suffused with rage.

'Mr Scott,' Sophie called softly but quite clearly. 'I think you'd better come over here.'

Later, in the staff-room, Sophie and Maggie were enjoying a cup of coffee. They had taken their packed lunches to a cosy corner well away from the chattering throng.

'Fancy the cunning little devil having mathematical formulae written on the inside of the chewing-gum wrapper!' Maggie exclaimed. 'She must have carefully opened out the wrapper, written the information on it and then, just as carefully, stuck it up again!'

'Yes.' Sophie paused as she sipped her coffee. 'And not just the one. Mr Scott made her empty her pockets, and every one of the wrappers had something written on it. She'd covered all possible options.'

Maggie shook her head wonderingly. 'Well, I have to say it, but she probably gets full marks for initiative.'

'Surely you can't admire what she did!'

'Not at all. It does make me sad however, that a girl who obviously has a brain of some sort looks set to waste it by going off in the wrong direction.'

'Mm.' Sophie stared distractedly out of the window. The rain had stopped for the moment but the sky was still dark with the threat of more to come.

'What is it, Sophie? Are you worrying over what she said to you?'

'No – yes – I suppose I am.'

'Forget it. It wasn't a real threat – the girl was angry because you caught her cheating – she was just expressing her rage in the only way she knows how. A lot of those big girls are all bluster. Oh, they find it easy to pick on other kids, kids smaller than themselves, but she wouldn't dare lay into a teacher.'

Sophie hoped that Maggie was right. As Mr Scott was taking Cheryl to the principal's office, Cheryl had suddenly turned round and hurled a mouthful of venomous abuse at Sophie. Most of the language was unrepeatable but the meaning had been quite clear. She intended to get her own back.

'Well, anyway,' Maggie said, 'at least that was the last of the exams. This afternoon we can resume normal service.'

Sophie smiled. 'No matter what you sometimes say, you really like teaching, don't you, Maggie?'

Her friend leaned forward and assumed an exaggeratedly wary expression. She pretended to check all around for eavesdroppers, and then she whispered, 'You've guessed my secret – but don't let it get any further – you'll ruin my reputation!'

Sophie couldn't help laughing. 'You know that you've probably missed your vocation – you ought to be on the stage.'

For a while they chatted about anything other than work – and Sophie noticed that Maggie avoided mentioning the wedding too. Her friend had promised to think about Sophie's predicament but she obviously hadn't come up with an answer, otherwise she would have told her. But then, in her heart, Sophie knew that no one could solve this particular problem except herself.

'Doing anything exciting tonight?' Maggie asked as they rose to leave at the end of the lunch hour.

'Not a chance. Alistair's on late shift again.'

'Not again!' Maggie rolled her eyes sympathetically. 'It's amazing how you ever manage to see each other. You work all day and he works all night. Tell me – how do you manage to keep in touch?'

'Like most people, of course: we phone each other. But the new job will make it easier. At nights he would usually only be on second call – you know, called in as a last resort, or for something major.'

They had left the staff-room and were walking along the corridor. 'So, would you like to come along and have a meal with Ken and me tonight?' Maggie asked. 'Your mother's invited, too, of course.'

'I can't, Maggie. I've got a lot of paperwork to catch up with and, as Mother has a date, I thought I'd stay at school until it's finished and collect a pizza on the way home.'

'What!'

'I said I'll have to work late on my reports and get a pizza –'

'No – not that bit. The bit about your mother –'

'Oh.' They had reached an intersection and were about to walk in separate directions. 'There are no evening classes tonight so Vic is finishing early –'

'Vic?'

'The head caretaker at the City College. He and my mother have become quite friendly. They're going for a Mexican meal and then to the cinema.'

'Well!'

'Great, isn't it?'

For once, Maggie seemed to be speechless and Sophie smiled as she watched her friend walking away shaking her head in what could only be described as bemusement. She'd felt pretty bemused herself, she thought, when her mother had told her about her date with Vic that morning over breakfast. But pleased. Very pleased indeed.

Carol ordered breakfast in her room, as Luke had suggested, but her usual enthusiasm for food seemed to have deserted her. She managed about half of a croissant but was grateful for the full cafetière of strong coffee. By the time she appeared in the hotel lounge for the seminar's mid-morning break, she felt that she had pure caffeine running through her veins, and was all the better for it. Even though she knew that she might suffer later.

True to his word, Luke acted as though nothing out of the ordinary had happened between them the night before. He smiled when he saw her and told her that he'd concluded all business, and it was only the promise he had made to have lunch with his father's old friend that was keeping him.

At that point Carol really wished she had taken Stacey's advice and travelled in her own car. She spent the rest of the morning trying to read some newspapers and magazines that she bought in the hotel shop. And then only picked at her lunch.

They were both subdued on the journey back to the office, and Carol was glad when Luke slipped a tape into the cassette player. But the fact that it was Enya, and that Luke murmured that it was one of his favourites, brought tears to her eyes. It was one of her favourites too.

When they arrived back in the compound at Travers' Transport, Luke stopped the car and reached over to take her hand.

'Luke – no –'

'It's all right, Carol. I just wanted to assure you that you needn't worry about how I'll behave at work. But I think we'd better stop going for pub lunches together, don't you?'

'Luke – would you like me to leave – I mean do you want my resignation?'

'Good heavens no! Travers' Transport needs you, and I would never forgive myself if I thought I'd forced you leave a job you so obviously like! Look, Carol, it won't be much longer before the new office block is finished. There'll be more space – it won't be so intimate – you and I might even be on different floors!'

'Stop, Luke. I won't leave if you don't want me to.'

But Carol was pleased that he'd reminded her about the new premises. When they were complete, he planned to take on more staff. If necessary she could always train someone to take over her projects . . .

'So now, why don't you just take the rest of the day off? It's hardly worth coming in to work now, anyway, and you deserve a break.'

'Thanks, Luke. I'll do that.'

As she was unlocking her car, Carol saw Stacey looking out of the window of her office. The younger girl looked worried so Carol smiled broadly and tried to convey with a nod that she was fine. She realized that her acting abilities must have been better than she thought they were, when she saw Stacey's answering smile.

So what now? she wondered as she took the familiar route home. What exactly am I going to find there? An empty, lonely house or a house with someone in it who is so miserable – and has the power to make me even more miserable – that the empty house might be a better option?

She found herself slowing down as she drew nearer to her turn-off, and even contemplated just driving on down the motorway to Exeter . . . and then why not go on to Plymouth, she thought . . . and, having got that far, why not board the ferry and go to Roscoff . . . or even Santander . . . ?

Roscoff was in Brittany . . . northern France might be just as cold and wet as it was here . . . but she could always drive on down through France until she reached Provence . . . it would be almost summer there . . .

But why not opt for Santander and Spain? Mm . . . crossing the Bay of Biscay at this time of the year might be a little scary. Four hundred years ago the Spanish Armada had set out from Santander on an unsuccessful attempt to conquer England . . . she wondered how the Spanish fighting men had coped with the Bay of Biscay, and whether any of them had been seasick . . .

She didn't carry on down the motorway, of course, and she was still smiling at her own flights of fancy when she drew up in front of her own house – where no other car was parked.

She dragged herself up the path and inserted the key in the lock. But, even before she had the door open properly, she knew that the house was not empty. It wasn't just because the hall light was on; she had left it on as usual. The house felt different – warm – welcoming. What had changed?

She leant against the door to push it closed and dropped her overnight bag. She stood there savouring the warmth. The central heating was on – that was it – and yet she was sure that she had turned the system off before she left yesterday morning. She supposed she must have simply intended to and then forgotten – Alan would be furious if he thought she was being wasteful . . .

And then the door at the end of the narrow, little hall opened and Alan came out of the kitchen. 'Alan!' she gasped. 'But, your car –'

'In the garage, where I usually put it.' He was searching her face worriedly. Why was he worried? Did he have something to tell her? Something that she would not like?

'In the garage,' she found herself repeating. 'So, you're staying here? I mean you're not going away again tonight?'

'Why should I do that? I live here, don't I?'

And then something strange happened. Alan came towards her and took hold of her. He began to draw her slowly into his arms and she searched his face in wonderment. He was looking at her as if he was pleased to see her – no, more than that – as if he had been worried that he might not see her again and that as if her being here had brought him tremendous relief – and joy.

362

'Carol,' he said. 'I was so worried – you never phoned me at my parents' house – and when I came back last night and found the house empty, I thought you might have left me. Thank goodness you're home!'

Wait a minute, she wanted to say. I never phoned? What about *you* phoning *me*? What about all those hateful things you said to me last time we spoke? What about you leaving *me* to think that *you* were the one who'd left home? But she didn't say any of those things because Alan didn't give her the chance.

And by the time he'd finished kissing her, she had remembered her friends' advice about its being up to her. If Alan and she were going to make a go of this marriage – and it looked as if they were – she might have to be the one to make the greater effort. So be it. Right at this moment she knew it would be worth it.

Later, much later, when hunger had driven them downstairs again, they went to the kitchen and together they cooked a meal of French toast, bacon and mushrooms. They took it through to the sitting-room to eat by the fire. It was only a gas fire with a false coal effect, but Carol loved it and, with only one lamp lit, it looked real enough. Usually Alan complained that, as they had central heating, it was extravagant to put the fire on as well, but tonight he was the one who lit it.

Carol watched him wonderingly as he moved the coffee table out of the way and drew the sofa nearer to the hearth. 'Now,' he said, 'let's eat this before it gets cold, then I'll make you a cup of hot chocolate and we'll talk.'

There was no threat in his words.

And when they did talk, Carol didn't hear what she had expected to hear. She had been prepared for Alan to discuss her failings – her inability to run the house the way he wanted it run, the way his mother would have run the house and instead – could she really believe this? – he

363

was telling her that after a few days with his parents, in their perfect house, he was glad to be home.

'Wait a minute,' she interrupted him in the middle of a story about how his father had wasted a whole loaf before he achieved a piece of toast that his mother would eat, 'what exactly are you telling me?'

He smiled and put his arm round her, drawing her closer. 'Listen, Carol, I never questioned the way my parents lived, I thought everyone should live like that. I thought they had things worked out pretty neatly – the right division of labour and all that jazz. But I was wrong – they were wrong – and it took an accident to make me realize it.'

'What do you mean?'

'My mother wasn't seriously hurt but she had to have bed-rest. And Dad simply couldn't cope. He can't cook, he can't clean – he can't even make up a grocery list.'

'But, Alan, there must have been times in the past when your mother was poorly – too ill to manage the housework?'

'Not very often. But if she was, her sister used to come to stay. Woman's work you know – can't ask a man to make his own breakfast or iron his own shirts! Aunty Beattie never married, as you know, and I think she used to regard coming to us as a kind of holiday – another, larger house to organize!'

'Oh . . . and your Aunt Beattie died last year . . .'

'Exactly. And everything Dad and I did for Mother was wrong. You should have seen the way her face twisted up every time we presented her with a meal that was less than perfect, or a tray cloth that hadn't been ironed! Oh, my darling, am I glad to be home!'

'But, wait a minute – does that mean you've left your father to cope with your mother alone?'

'Why not? He's big enough. Carol, don't get me wrong – I love my parents very much, and I can't deny that I could see the funny side of it all, even though poor old dad couldn't – but they'll have to sort themselves out. I've got my own home and my own wife to look after!'

Carol closed her eyes and snuggled up to him happily. She knew that they might still have some sorting out to do – and she had a plan up her sleeve that might take him by surprise – but with goodwill, and love, especially love, she suspected that they were going to make it.

Lancashire

Dr Alistair McGregor sipped coffee from a plastic beaker and reached for the phone. There was a welcome lull in the activity in the casualty department and he thought he would seize the opportunity to call Sophie.

He let the phone ring for a full minute before he decided that she couldn't be home yet. He glanced at his watch and frowned. He knew that her mother had planned to go out that evening and that Sophie had decided to catch up on some paperwork at school – but surely she would have had enough of it by now?

What should he do? Phone the school? He realized that he didn't have the number. And then it occurred to him that Sophie might have gone to Maggie's house. He'd phoned Sophie there in the past. He dialled the number. The phone was answered after the first ring.

'Yes?' The voice was urgent – expectant.

'Ken? It's Alistair – is Sophie there by any chance?'

There was a slight pause – just long enough to trigger a niggle of anxiety. Then, 'Er – no – she's not here, Alistair – er –'

'What is it?' Alistair was alert. He knew Ken Lomax well enough to sense that the usually easygoing, father of three harum-scarum daughters was rattled about something.

There was another pause and Alistair found himself

gripping the receiver. 'Listen,' Ken said at last. 'It's probably nothing, but Maggie got a phone call about twenty minutes ago and went dashing back to school –'

'Why – what – who?' The anxiety grew.

'The call was anonymous – but Maggie thought she recognized the voice. She thought it was Julie Hunter, a sweet kid who –'

'Ken! What did the girl say?'

'Not very much, actually. She just said that Miss Blake might be in trouble, and then she rang off. She didn't give any more details than that, so Maggie phoned Sophie at home and there was no answer –'

'I know I've tried.'

'So then she decided to go back to school and see if Sophie was still there. She promised to phone home – I thought that was her when you called.'

'OK, Ken. Thanks. I'll get off the line. Will you call me at the hospital as soon as you hear anything?'

'I will – but it's probably nothing – I mean, perhaps the kid was just playing a trick.'

'But Maggie didn't think so, did she?'

'No. Maggie didn't think so.'

Alistair replaced the receiver but he didn't have time to sort out his thoughts. A nurse appeared in the doorway of the small office. 'Dr McGregor – there's a head injury – you'd better come –'

Alistair's professional training took over and he was on his feet immediately. The nurse stood aside to let him walk ahead and he set off at speed down the broad, well-lit corridor, his tall, broad-shouldered figure making hospital staff and patients alike melt out of the way. As the most senior doctor on duty it was his job to attend to any head injury that came in and he forced himself to put his own worries aside.

But then he saw something that halted his stride. Maggie Lomax was watching anxiously as a patient was taken into one of the curtained cubicles.

'Maggie?' he said, and the anxiety returned full force.

She looked up at him and her kindly face was grey with worry. 'Alistair – it's –'

He didn't wait. He knew what she was going to say but, even so, when he saw Sophie lying there, her face bruised and swollen, her baby-fine hair matted with blood, his heart almost stopped beating.

'Sophie!' he cried, and his anger and pain could be heard throughout the length and breadth of the casualty department. 'Oh, Sophie, my love, what have they done to you?'

CHAPTER 23

She was somewhere where the lights were bright . . . that was better. Better than that other place. She wondered how long had she lain there in that other place, in the dark and the wet? And why had she been lying there? She couldn't remember . . .

She could only remember that she had been lying on the ground . . . and that she had tried to get up, but she couldn't. She remembered thinking that it would help if she opened her eyes – but she couldn't do that either. And then . . . and then . . . what had happened next?

She had been lonely and afraid . . . afraid that no one would find her. How long had she been lying there? How much later was it that she had heard a voice . . . a voice that she thought she knew – and it had been shouting a name. Whose name?

She didn't know, but somehow that voice had made her feel safe and she had drifted off to sleep. No, she hadn't been sleeping . . . a kind of red darkness had closed in on her . . . it had been much deeper than sleep . . . and yet, strangely, not so deep that she didn't keep hearing things and sensing movement . . .

She must have moved, or been moved somehow, because she wasn't alone in the dark any more, she was here in this bright place and she could hear more voices . . . urgent voices . . . reassuring voices . . . but what were they talking about?

'– Sophie –' someone said.

They were discussing somebody . . . they were talking about someone called Sophie . . . that was the name she had heard before when she had been lying in the cold and the wet . . .

They were taking her wet clothes off . . . did they have to use scissors? She was sure that that snip, snip, snip sound was scissors . . . her clothes would be ruined and she felt tears pricking at the back of her eyes. Her eyes that she couldn't quite get open . . .

It was all too much. She was tempted to drift off into the red darkness again but she realized that someone must be washing her face . . .

Ouch!

'Sorry, my darling,' someone said. Why had he called her his darling?

But whoever that presumptuous person was, and whoever all the other people were, they seemed to know what they were doing. She gave herself up to their ministrations. Ministrations, she thought, what a comforting word . . .

She felt gentle hands, gentle movements but, no matter how gentle, there was a sense of urgency all around her. All these things they were doing to her were obviously important. If only she could open her eyes, if only she could speak to these people and ask them what was happening . . . but the red darkness pressed in on her and she felt herself drifting off again . . .

Next time she could hear anything, she sensed that some of the people had gone. There were only two voices and she could hear them quite distinctly.

'– and the wound's superficial.'

'Thank God. But there was so much blood!'

'Head wounds can bleed a lot – it must have been

dreadful for you finding her there.'

'And you when you realized who your patient was. If only you could have seen your face.'

'Have you phoned Laura yet?'

'She's on her way.'

That's good, she thought, my mother's on her way, and suddenly she was tremendously pleased with herself. Laura is my mother, she thought, and I am Sophie. I am the Sophie that they're talking about. Well, at least I've got that sorted out.

The two people were still talking.

'Perhaps you should go and wait for Laura, intercept her, tell her not to worry too much and that I'll explain everything that has been done.'

There was a movement, a shadow crossed the light and Sophie could smell perfume – a familiar flowery perfume – as someone came nearer to her. She felt one of her hands being lifted, just a little, and the shadowy someone kissed it gently. Then the shadow retreated, just as Sophie remembered who wore that flowery perfume. It was her friend, Maggie Lomax . . .

She could feel her own lips curling up into a smile and the other person, the one who hadn't gone with Maggie, gave a great sob. Sophie tried once more to open her eyes – still no success – but she felt her eyebrows lifting in surprise. The other person came nearer and took her hand in both of his own.

'Sophie, my heart's own darling,' he said, and there was such a lovely lilt to his voice. 'Sophie, I love you so much.'

She felt her lips opening and she heard a cracked voice that she supposed must be her own. 'That's good,' the cracked voice said. 'If you love me, I'd like you to tell me what on earth is going on.'

She couldn't understand why the other person seemed to be laughing and crying at the same time. She couldn't understand why he was covering both her hands with kisses. She only knew that, this time as she drifted off again, it wasn't the red darkness that had come to claim her . . . she knew that, when she awoke, everything would be all right . . .

'Dr McGregor,' a young nurse appeared in the doorway, 'is Miss Blake well enough to see this police officer?'

Sophie was lying in a small room, propped up amongst her pillows. She was still disorientated, and more than a little confused, but Alistair had assured her there was nothing to worry about. She had been given a blood transfusion because she had lost quite a lot of blood – and she thought he had told her that she had had a scan. And now she was being kept in hospital under observation.

The trouble was, that she had only the faintest memory of the incident that had brought her here in the first place.

Alistair took her hand. 'What do you think? Are you up to answering some questions?'

'I'll try.'

'Good girl. I have to go now, but I'll ask the nurse to stay with you.'

Then, and quite unprofessionally, he bent over, raised her hand and kissed her gently in the centre of her palm.

The young policewoman was very patient; she knew just when to prompt and when to wait, but all that Sophie could remember was crossing the school car park towards her car, bending to insert the key in the lock – then there had been a sudden flash of bright light – and that was it.

'I'm sorry,' she said and looked at the young woman helplessly.

'Don't worry. We know from your wound that you were attacked from behind. The flash of light was what you saw when you were hit – you've heard the expression seeing stars, haven't you? Anyway, from the angle of the blows, we can even make a pretty good guess at out how tall the assailant was – so just you try to rest and get better.'

'That's right,' the nurse said after the policewoman had gone. 'You know, you might never remember it all. But they'll catch the young villain, you'll see. Your friend Mrs Lomax has already helped them, I understand.'

Sophie frowned. Assailant . . . young villain . . . why would anybody attack her? She knew that a woman teacher from another school had been mugged and robbed a few months ago, but Alistair had told her that nothing had been stolen. Her bag had been lying on the ground next to her, unopened. He said that her mother had checked the contents and, as far as she knew, everything was still there.

But the nurse had said that Maggie had helped the police . . . what did Maggie know about it? Oh, it's all too confusing, Sophie thought. Perhaps I'll just go to sleep again . . .

Next time she opened her eyes, Laura was sitting by her bed. She was crying softly into a wad of paper tissues.

'Mum – don't cry.'

'Darling, you're awake again.' Laura raised her head and Sophie was shocked to see how drawn her mother looked.

'Mum . . . were you here last night?'

'Yes, love, I stayed with you as long as I could. In the end Alistair insisted that I go home and get some rest.'

'But why can't I remember that you were here?'

'You keep coming and going – your memory, I mean. But Alistair says not to worry – the tests show that everything's as it should be and everything will settle into place. And the bruises have a good chance to fade before the wedding day.'

Sophie stared at her mother. Bruises, she had said. Wedding day . . . oh, yes, she was going to be married. She was going to marry Alistair . . .

'Mum?' She focused on her mother again.

'Yes, love?'

'How did you get here last night? I mean, it was late, wasn't it?'

Did she imagine it or did her mother colour up a little? 'Vic brought me to the hospital. When he took me home from the cinema I was worried that you weren't there. We were just about to phone the school when Maggie rang – so he brought me here. And then he waited to take me home again.'

Sophie sank back into her pillows. 'That's good . . .'

For a while it seemed that every time she woke up, someone different was sitting by her bed. Alistair, her mother, Maggie and even Vic Watkins. She supposed that they were taking turns, and eventually she gave up being surprised.

Then – was it the next day? – she awoke to hear the door being pushed open and Maggie's voice saying, 'She's ever so much better but she's still a bit disorientated. But I know she'll be overjoyed to see you.'

She was already sitting up and looking expectantly towards the door as Alison walked in.

'Sophie – oh, Sophie!' Alison hurried over to the bed and stopped. She stood there helplessly. 'Am I allowed to kiss you or does everything hurt too much?'

'Hurt?' Sophie put her hands up and fingered the bandage that seemed to be covering most of her head; she considered Alison's question. 'No, I'm not hurting but I think they must be giving me painkillers.'

'I'm sure they are.' Alison leaned over and raised one of her hands, kissed the back of it, and then sat down in one of the two chairs provided.

'Alison,' Sophie said as soon as her friend was settled, 'would you tell me why everyone has been kissing my hand? I mean, have I suddenly acquired royal status?'

'Oh, dear – I think it's because, like me, they're afraid of hurting you.'

Sophie frowned as she puzzled over the full meaning of Alison's words. And then she realized their significance. 'Have you got a mirror in your bag?' she asked. 'Would you lend it to me?'

'You mean that you haven't seen yourself yet? Oh, my dear . . .' But Alison, sensible friend that she was, opened her bag immediately and took out a small mirror. As she handed it over she said, 'Don't be frightened. You know I wouldn't lie to you. You look much worse than you really are. Your friend Maggie Lomax assured me of that before she opened the door.'

Sophie stared into the mirror and a cruel, lopsided imitation of her features stared back at her. One side of her face was discoloured and swollen; it looked like a Hallowe'en mask. She turned her head towards the light to view the damage more closely.

'Apparently the bruising is already fading,' Alison assured her. 'You took the main blow on the side of your head, but you hit your face on your car as you fell forward. I don't suppose there was any chance that you saw who did it, was there? Do you remember anything at all?'

Sophie shook her head as she handed the mirror back. 'I can only tell you what I told the policewoman. I walked over to my car . . . wait a moment . . . there were footsteps . . .'

'Yes?' Alison prompted.

'But they could have been mine, couldn't they? I mean, am I just remembering my own footsteps echoing across the yard, or was someone following me . . . ?' She stared helplessly at Alison.

'OK. Forget it for the moment. If you get upset, I'll be in trouble with that teacher friend of yours. Incidentally, she super, isn't she? Do you know it was her idea to phone Francine, Carol and me and round us all up!'

'You're all here? But where . . . ?'

'Francine and Carol are sharing the spare bedroom at Maggie's house, if that's what you mean, and I – I mean Greg and I –'

'*Greg* and you?' Sophie's eyes widened. Alison was blushing.

'Yes. Greg and I are staying at your house with your mother. In separate rooms, of course.'

'Of course.' Sophie grinned. 'We wouldn't want to shock my sainted mother, would we?'

'Sophie, it hasn't quite come to that, if you know what I mean – but I'll admit that both of us are quite serious about this – we're not going to start anything lightly.'

'I'm very happy for you. But, tell me, where's Matthew?'

'Remember Miss Robertson – you met her on the Sunday?'

'Oh, yes, the vicar's sister.'

'She's moved into the Hall while we're away. She said her brother was quite capable of managing on his own for a day or two, and it might actually encourage him to sort his life out.'

'What on earth did she mean by that?'

'I'm not sure – but I suspect the poor man might suddenly find himself invited to eat at the houses of various eligible widows and spinsters.'

'Oh, dear – don't make me laugh – it hurts –'

'But, anyway, Miss Robertson is looking after Matthew and my mother-in-law, too. Actually, she's very good for Mrs Cavendish; she's kind but she won't spoil her. And she certainly won't be prepared to carry her meals up on a tray!'

375

'Marvellous. You should have got tough with her long before now.'

'I know that. Well, anyway, Greg left all kinds of central heating brochures for Mrs Cavendish to look at while I'm away, and Miss Robertson is going to help her make a decision.'

'Is that wise?'

'Don't worry, I've already decided which one is the best and I trust Kathleen Robertson to guide her in the right direction.'

'So the sale of the land is going ahead?'

'Yes, and the money raised will cover the new heating system, a new roof, and a lot more besides. I'm not going to have to sell off the contents of the wine cellar, after all.'

'I'm pleased,' Sophie said, 'so pleased for you . . . and for Matthew, too . . .' She found herself yawning.

'I've stayed too long,' Alison said. She got up quietly and crossed to the door. 'I'll go for the moment but remember I'm here . . . we're all here for you, Sophie . . .'

But her friends were only allowed to come and see her one at a time. Orders from the top – probably Alistair – Sophie thought, decreed that she must not be upset, must not be excited. Her mother, aided and abetted by Maggie, made sure that these orders were carried out.

Sophie was still a little hazy about time. Sometimes she wasn't sure what day it was but, on one of her visits, Francine, to the nurse's disgust, plonked herself on the neatly made bed. Sophie looked at her and sighed. 'Francine, what am I going to do? I can't get married looking like this – I'll ruin the wedding photographs apart from anything else!'

'Hush! Don't get excited or that Maggie Lomax won't let me visit you again. Honestly, Sophie, she's a bit of a dragon.'

'Maggie? A dragon? Never!'

'In the nicest possible way, of course. In fact I like her very much.' Francine smiled. 'Now, about that poor face of yours – you mustn't despair.'

'Mustn't I?' Sophie looked at her friend hopefully.

'Your gorgeous Dr McGregor has assured me that you'll look just about normal by the time of the wedding and I'm going to do your make-up for you – all my years in television haven't been wasted.'

'But you're not a make-up artist, Francine.'

'Goodness – you don't think I leave it to them, do you? I learned all I could from them and then went on to do my own. That way I can't complain if I look dreadful!'

'We-ell – thanks – that's wonderful. But what about my hair? They shaved some off, you know.'

'Yes, Maggie told me. But it's not so bad – and there's enough long hair on top to fall down and cover the shaved bit. And surely your headdress will have a lot of veil attached?'

'Yes, it has.'

'So stop worrying. You are going to look absolutely fabulous and Alison and Carol and I are all going to weep buckets at the sheer romance of it all!'

'*You* get romantic? That's not the Francine Rowe that I know.'

'I wouldn't be too sure of that.' Sophie noticed that Francine's smile faded a little.

'What is it? Have I spoken out of turn?'

Francine got up and wandered over to the window. She looked out across the hospital grounds unseeingly and then she turned and smiled a little sadly. 'You might as well to be the first to know that Peter and I are no longer an item.'

Sophie was aghast. 'Francine – I'm so sorry.'

'It's all right. There's no need to be.'

'But you were together for so long.'

'Yes. Look – I don't want to talk about it – not yet. I've

still got some sorting out to do in my mind.'

'That's all right – but if ever you need – oh, you know what I'm trying to say . . .'

'I do – and thank you. But the good news is that I'm going ahead with my new programme idea. I'm getting together my own production company, and Sophie – I'm really excited. I've not felt so enthusiastic about a work project for years!'

'That's wonderful. I know you can do it.'

Francine walked over and sat on the bed again. 'Now that you're looking so much better, I'm going to take leave of you – don't worry, I'll keep in touch and I'll get back in good time to plan your wedding day make-up and hairstyle. But, right now, there's somewhere I have to go.'

'Where's that?'

'To my parents' house. Don't look so worried – I'm quite prepared to have the door slammed in my face – and I'm big enough to take it. But, Sophie, I've decided that I can't go on being estranged from them. Their ways are not my ways, and I'm not going to apologize for the way I've lived my life up to now – but they're honest, God-fearing people – and if anyone has to swallow their pride and compromise a little, it should be me. Don't you agree?'

'Absolutely.'

'Bye for now, then.' Francine leaned forward and kissed her gently on her bruised cheek.

Sophie raised one hand and probed the place where Francine had kissed her with her fingertips. That didn't hurt, she thought. I really must be getting better . . .

Carol had to leave, too. 'Now that I'm not so worried about you, I'd better get back to work,' she said.

'I could be wrong, but I don't believe it's the prospect of getting back to work that's making you smile like that.'

'No, it isn't. The others have probably told you – Alan and I seem to be working things out.'

'That's wonderful, Carol. I have to admit I was worried about you. I don't know how to put this, but I suspected there was more of a problem than you were admitting to – something you weren't telling us.'

Her friend looked uneasy. 'Yes, well, there was – but that's all right now.'

Sophie knew that that was the end of the matter for the moment. In the future Carol might want to tell her more about what had caused her such turmoil but, for now, she was obviously coping.

'And when I've got the details worked out, I'll tell you all about my new life plan!' Carol said.

'Hey – wait a minute – you can't just leave it at that. Remember it's not good for me to be worried or excited!'

'I think that's called blackmail – but, OK. I've decided to leave work – not straight away, I'll have to train someone to take my place, but as soon as I can I'm going to work at home.'

'How? As a freelance?'

'Sort of – I'm going to set up my own modest little consultancy – information technology – advising businesses what kind of computers and computer software they need. I would never have thought I could do that until I was thrown in at the deep end in my present job.'

'That's wonderful, Carol. What does Alan think of the plan?'

'He's all for it. He says that he trusts my business acumen completely and he'll back me all the way. Why are you looking so surprised?'

'Am I? Forgive me – but is this Alan Kennedy we're talking about?'

'Yes – isn't it wonderful? Mind you, perhaps the poor man imagines that if I'm working at home, he might come home at night to a few more hot dinners!'

'And won't he?'

Carol had the grace to look shame-faced. 'Fair's fair – yes, he will. Sophie, I'm really going to make the effort. But so's he – he's promised not to be such an old-fashioned male chauvinist in future.'

Footsteps echoing across the yard . . . are they my own footsteps or, if I stop and listen and hold my breath, will the other footsteps keep on coming towards me?

Here's my car . . . safe now . . . just find the key . . . there . . . oh no! Who's that – Aargh! Hurting! Falling!

But just before the red darkness engulfed her she heard the footsteps gain – they were running away . . .

'Wake up, Sophie.' She opened her eyes to see Maggie Lomax staring down at her. Her friend looked concerned. 'You were moaning in your sleep. Bad dreams?'

'Yes, I've remembered more about what happened that night. But, Maggie, I still don't know who attacked me.'

Maggie sighed as pulled up one of the chairs and sat down. 'We know who it was, Sophie; it will just be a matter of proving it.'

'How do you know?'

'Think about it – she threatened you that very day – in front of witnesses.'

'Witnesses?'

'Mr Scott and quite a few of the kids – and Mr Scott has already told the police that after you caught her cheating, Cheryl threatened to get you. Sophie, it couldn't have been anyone else.'

'I suppose not, but as I didn't see her –'

'We think that someone else did. Someone phoned me at home that night to warn me that you might be in trouble, remember? That's why I dashed back to school.'

'Yes . . . you told me . . . and thank goodness you did. But you said the caller was anonymous.'

'She was trying to disguise her voice but I'm pretty sure it was Julie Hunter.'

'Poor kid – she won't want to get involved any further, will she? She'll be too scared of Cheryl and what she might do.'

'That's right. But, if Cheryl's guilty, she got to be caught before she does anything worse . . . you know what I mean . . .'

They stared at each other solemnly for a moment and then Maggie took her hand. 'Anyway, that's not your problem. The police are hoping that someone else was there – that someone else will come forward. You never know, even Cheryl's cronies might be sickened by what she's done to you. You're pretty popular with the kids at school, you know.'

Maggie got up to go. 'So, right now you've got to concentrate on getting completely better in time for your wedding,' she said.

'I will, Maggie, I will – and there's something that I've been wanting to tell you about that.'

'If it's about the church hall or the catering, forget it – everything's in hand, just you wait and see –'

'No, it's none of that. It's about the bridegroom. You know – what I told you about Alistair? My problem? You said you'd think about it.'

Maggie suddenly looked grave. 'I know I did, Sophie, but surely –'

'It's all right, I'm teasing you. Everything's fine. I don't remember much about the night they brought me in here, but there are some words of Alistair's that I remember quite distinctly – they're engraved on my heart. And do you know the best thing, Maggie? He hasn't stopped saying them.'

381

EPILOGUE

The wedding breakfast was over and the guests had divided into cheerful groups. Sophie saw her mother talking to Maggie and she turned and pulled at Alistair's sleeve. 'I'm leaving you for a moment. Can you cope?' She smiled up at him.

'OK, but don't be too long; this lot can talk the hind legs off the proverbial donkey!'

By 'this lot' he meant Maggie's three daughters, looking unbelievably feminine in their bridesmaids' dresses.

'Come here,' Sophie said quietly, and he leaned over so that she could whisper in his ear. 'When you've had enough, tell them that it's the bridesmaids' duty to mingle with the guests and try to talk to everyone. That should do the trick.'

'Clever Sophie.'

He squeezed her hand and they smiled at each other. Then Sophie left him and threaded her way towards Maggie and her mother.

'What can I say?' she said when she reached their side. 'I can never thank you enough. Mum, the food was just marvellous – and as for the flowers –!'

'Aren't they great?' Maggie agreed. 'The garlands, the table arrangements – all white and green. Just perfect.'

'And the church hall, Maggie – I'm overwhelmed. You told me I'd be surprised but stunned is more like it!' Sophie said.

'Well,' her friend replied, 'you can thank Alison and Greg for that. When I told them what the problem was, Greg just moved a team of men in to obey my orders.

'The walls and ceiling need painting? No bother. The floor is scuffed and dirty? Sanded and polished over-night! And that's not all. The windows were cleaned of the grime of ages and even the little garden at the back was weeded and planted up.

'And all at Greg's expense. Our minister thought that he'd died and gone to heaven!'

'Oh, Maggie, it's been perfect.' Sophie found that her eyes were smarting suspiciously.

'Hey – you're not allowed to cry on your wedding day – your mother's already cried enough for two!'

'Maggie, I'd like to speak to Mum alone for a moment –'

'Of course. I'll push off.'

'No, wait. I'd like you to do something for me.'

'Anything.'

'Would you round up Alison, Carol and Francine for me? Detach them from whoever they're speaking to and ask them to meet me in the little garden. I'd like a word with them before Alistair and I slip away.'

'Of course I will. But just take a look around the hall, will you? Can you see either Greg Leighton or Alan Kennedy? Wait a minute – my Ken's missing too – so they really meant it – no, they wouldn't, would they?'

Sophie was bemused. 'Maggie what on earth are you talking about?'

'I think those overgrown schoolboys have gone looking for Alistair's car – you know – to tie old boots and balloons and all the other wedding paraphernalia on it!'

'What makes you think they would do that?'

'My girl monsters told me that they'd overheard them joking about it – I didn't believe that they'd really do it. But, now they're missing and I'm not so sure.'

'Don't worry,' Laura said, 'Vic's got the car well hidden. 'They'll never be able to find it.'

'I wouldn't count on it!' Maggie said, but she was laughing as she left them.

'Well, Sophie,' her mother said, 'are you happy?'

'Very happy. And I wanted this moment to thank you not just for the wedding, but for everything. I know how difficult it's been for you all these years without Dad.'

'Darling,' suddenly her mother's eyes were full, 'he would have been so proud of you. And so happy if he could have been here today.'

Sophie reached out and took her mother's hands. She held on to them tightly. 'And there's something I want to say . . . about Dad . . . he wouldn't have wanted you to be lonely. You know what I mean.'

'Yes, dear. I know. Now go and talk to your friends. I want to go and see if the children have had enough to eat.'

The children she meant were Matthew Cavendish and Alistair's young nieces and nephews who had all been sitting together. Personally, Sophie thought that they had probably had quite sufficient, but she knew that her mother simply wanted an excuse to be with them.

The rain had held off all day and the small courtyard garden behind the church hall was fresh with the promise of spring. Her three friends, rounded up by Maggie, were waiting for her. She hurried out to them and hugged them each in turn.

'Alison,' she said, 'your Greg is an absolute gem – and I don't just mean because he helped Maggie redecorate the church hall. He's charmed my mother totally, and he had Alistair's three serious-minded sisters and their husbands hanging on to his every word!'

Alison smiled and Sophie could see how truly happy

she was. She turned to Carol. 'How's your business project going?'

'I'm working on it, but Alan's raised a point that may mean some extra planning.'

'What's that?'

'He was wondering if working from home meant that we could start a family.'

'And you said?'

'That it might take some extra effort on his part –'

'Carol!' the other three exclaimed laughingly, and she blushed.

'You know what I mean – that he would have to help with the baby and not leave it all to me. Anyway, I said I thought it was a marvellous idea.'

'Me too,' Sophie said. 'And you, Francine? Is everything going as planned?'

'Absolutely. In fact, when I leave here I'm going to stay with my parents for the night and tomorrow I'm going to have a meeting with my first subject.'

Sophie looked at her meaningfully. 'And is that subject Marcus Holbrook?'

'Yes. I didn't expect he would – but he agreed to be interviewed.'

'So do you think you can handle the situation?'

'What do you mean?' Carol interrupted. 'I should think Francine could interview just about anyone.'

'I think I know what Sophie is getting at,' Alison said. 'Marcus means more to you than just a subject for your television programme, doesn't he?'

'I admit, he does.'

'So?' Sophie prompted gently 'Are you going to answer my question?'

Suddenly Francine grinned. 'You know what? I don't really know myself what the outcome of this will be – you'll just have to wait and see.'

Then they said their goodbyes, and Sophie was just

about to slip away and change into her going-away clothes when her mother came out into the garden to join them. She was holding a camera.

'Not another photograph, Mum!' Sophie exclaimed. 'I think the photographer's already covered all the possible permutations.'

'All but one,' Laura said. 'I haven't got a shot of the four of you together. Now, will you arrange yourselves – Sophie and Carol, the two smaller ones in the centre and slightly to the front? Alison and Francine, will you move in slightly? That's it. Now look at the camera and smile.'

As Laura saw the four of them framed in the view-finder, she couldn't help remembering another photograph she'd taken ten years ago . . .

This time the picture was complete.

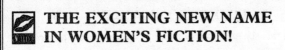# THE EXCITING NEW NAME IN WOMEN'S FICTION!

PLEASE HELP ME TO HELP YOU!

Dear *Scarlet* Reader,

I have some wonderful news for you this month – we are beginning a super Prize Draw, which means that you *could win an exclusive sassy Scarlet T-shirt!* Just fill in your questionnaire and return it to us (see addresses at the end of the questionnaire) before 31 November 1998, and we'll do the rest! If you are lucky enough to be one of the first four names out of the hat each month, we will send you this exclusive prize.

So don't delay – return your form straight away!*

Looking forward to hearing from you,

Sally Cooper

Editor-in-Chief, *Scarlet*

QUESTIONNAIRE

Please tick the appropriate boxes to indicate your answers

1 Where did you get this Scarlet title?
Bought in supermarket ☐
Bought at my local bookstore ☐ Bought at chain bookstore ☐
Bought at book exchange or used bookstore ☐
Borrowed from a friend ☐
Other (please indicate) _____

2 Did you enjoy reading it?
A lot ☐   A little ☐   Not at all ☐

3 What did you particularly like about this book?
Believable characters ☐   Easy to read ☐
Good value for money ☐   Enjoyable locations ☐
Interesting story ☐   Modern setting ☐
Other _____

4 What did you particularly dislike about this book?
_____

5 Would you buy another Scarlet book?
Yes ☐   No ☐

6 What other kinds of book do you enjoy reading?
Horror ☐   Puzzle books ☐   Historical fiction ☐
General fiction ☐   Crime/Detective ☐   Cookery ☐
Other (please indicate) _____

7 Which magazines do you enjoy reading?
1. _____
2. _____
3. _____

And now a little about you –
8 How old are you?
Under 25 ☐   25–34 ☐   35–44 ☐
45–54 ☐   55–64 ☐   over 65 ☐

cont.

9 What is your marital status?
   Single ☐   Married/living with partner ☐
   Widowed ☐   Separated/divorced ☐

10 What is your current occupation?
   Employed full-time ☐   Employed part-time ☐
   Student ☐   Housewife full-time ☐
   Unemployed ☐   Retired ☐

11 Do you have children? If so, how many and how old are they?

_____

_____

12 What is your annual household income?
   under $15,000 ☐   or £10,000 ☐
   $15–25,000 ☐   or £10–20,000 ☐
   $25–35,000 ☐   or £20–30,000 ☐
   $35–50,000 ☐   or £30–40,000 ☐
   over $50,000 ☐   or £40,000 ☐

Miss/Mrs/Ms _____

Address _____

_____

_____

Thank you for completing this questionnaire. Now tear it out – put it in an envelope and send it, before 31 December 1998, to:

Sally Cooper, Editor-in-Chief

USA/Can. address	*UK address/No stamp required*
SCARLET c/o London Bridge	SCARLET
85 River Rock Drive	FREEPOST LON 3335
Suite 202	LONDON W8 4BR
Buffalo	*Please use block capitals for*
NY 14207	*address*
USA	

SOWED/6/98

Scarlet titles coming next month:

A TEMPORARY ARRANGEMENT Margaret Callaghan
Businessman Alex Gifford is a fairly unusual parent. He
denies his young son James nothing – except affection.
When Stella starts her nannying job with him, he makes
it clear that this is part of her job! However, he is not
incapable of strong feelings – he wants her and he always
takes what he wants!

SECRETS RISING Sally Steward
When Rebecca Patterson's parents die in an accident, she
discovers she was adopted. She enlists the help of private
investigator Jake Thornton to help find her biological
parents but he is reluctant, knowing her quest may not
end happily. And soon it becomes clear that someone else
doesn't want Rebecca to find out the truth . . .

**WE ARE PROUD TO ANNOUNCE THE JULY
PUBLICATION OF OUR FIRST _SCARLET_ HARD-
BACK:**

DARK DESIRE Maxine Barry
Determined, angry, clever, sexy and power-packed Haldane
Fox is a man with a mission. Fox plays with fire, but always
wins. Electra is very beautiful but, due to a traumatic past,
has dedicated herself to her career as an orchid grower.
When these two ambitious people meet, something's gotta
give and Electra is determined it won't be her.

JOIN THE CLUB!

Why not join the *Scarlet* Readers' Club – you can have four exciting new reads delivered to your door every other month for only £9.99, plus TWO FREE BOOKS WITH YOUR FIRST MONTH'S ORDER!

Fill in the form below and tick your two first books from those listed:

1. *Never Say Never* by Tina Leonard ☐
2. *The Sins of Sarah* by Anne Styles ☐
3. *Wicked in Silk* by Andrea Young ☐
4. *Wild Lady* by Liz Fielding ☐
5. *Starstruck* by Lianne Conway ☐
6. *This Time Forever* by Vickie Moore ☐
7. *It Takes Two* by Tina Leonard ☐
8. *The Mistress* by Angela Drake ☐
9. *Come Home Forever* by Jan McDaniel ☐
10. *Deception* by Sophie Weston ☐
11. *Fire and Ice* by Maxine Barry ☐
12 *Caribbean Flame* by Maxine Barry ☐

ORDER FORM

SEND NO MONEY NOW. Just complete and send to **SCARLET READERS' CLUB, FREEPOST, LON 3335, Salisbury SP5 5YW**

Yes, I want to join the *SCARLET* **READERS' CLUB*** and have the convenience of 4 exciting new novels delivered directly to my door every other month! Please send me my first shipment now for the unbelievable price of £9.99, plus my TWO special offer books absolutely free. I understand that I will be invoiced for this shipment and FOUR further *Scarlet* titles at £9.99 (including postage and packing) every other month unless I cancel my order in writing. I am over 18.

Signed ....

Name (IN BLOCK CAPITALS)..

Address (IN BLOCK CAPITALS)...

....

Town.. **Post Code**...............................

Phone Number ....

As a result of this offer your name and address may be passed on to other carefully selected companies. If you do not wish this, please tick this box ☐.

*Please note this offer applies to UK only.